"I could help you search," Rosalind offered.

"Too dangerous." His voice was thick. The air was laden with her scent—the light, clean smell of soap and something uniquely hers. He would never have known it again if he'd been killed.

Nonsense. Any man who thought about being killed would be dead very soon. He'd seen that happen often enough during the war. No, what he had to focus on was saving Viola and William. Do something concrete, not dwell on what could be lost.

Still, his hands were shaking slightly when Hal cupped her face and his chest was tight. "Let's think about this instead." The one sure way to stop her talking and keep him from thinking.

He bent his head towards hers. She immediately tilted her head back, slanting it to meet his approach. He kissed her lightly, his lips teasing her.

THE RIVER DEVIL

DIANE WHITESIDE

BRAVA

KENSINGTON PUBLISHING CORP.
www.kensingtonbooks.com

BRAVA BOOKS are published by

Kensington Publishing Corp.
850 Third Avenue
New York, NY 10022

All Kensington titles, imprints, and distributed lines are available at special quantity discounts for bulk purchases for sales
promotions, premiums, fund-raising, educational, or institu-
tional use. Special book excerpts or customized printings can
also be created to fit specific needs. For details, write or phone
the office of the Kensington special sales manager: Kensington
Publishing Corp., 850 Third Avenue, New York, NY 10022,
attn: Special Sales Department; phone: 1-800-221-2647.

BRAVA and the B logo are Reg. U.S. Pat. & TM Off.

ISBN-13: 978-0-7582-0795-1
ISBN-10: 0-7582-0795-6

First Kensington trade paperback printing: July 2005
First Brava mass market paperback printing: December 2008

10 9 8 7 6 5 4 3 2 1

Printed in the United States of America

Prologue

New York, December 1871

Rosalind Schuyler limped off the dance floor on her fiancé's arm, her flounce trailing after them, half ripped from her Worth ball gown. Mercifully, David was somewhat more adept at carnal temptations than the Virginia reel.

The conductor glanced at the hostess, then led the string orchestra into a slow waltz. Three dances after the midnight supper, most of the early departures had already occurred. Voices rumbled from the card rooms, while other guests levered themselves out of their seats to step onto the dance floor.

"My dear," David purred into her ear, his dulcet tones well trained for his planned career as a politician and orator.

Rosalind came alert, wondering what he would do next. Try to seduce her? Heaven knows she enjoyed being cuddled and treated as a woman by someone taller than herself.

"I'm sorry, my dear, but I must take my leave now."

Hazy visions of rapture in David's arms vanished quickly.

"I've promised," he continued, "to go riding with Nick Lennox before breakfast at the Pericles Club."

"Really? Well, of course, you must be awake then, if you are to spend time with a banker," she teased gently. Something about Nicholas Lennox always made her skin crawl, possibly his never-ending pursuit of the right friends.

"You may see him solely as that, because he's a junior partner at your father's bank, but I know him as a friend. Will you see me to the door? I'm sure your father will take you home after the last dance."

"Of course."

David smiled down at her and gently tweaked one of her curls.

They strolled down the opulent brown and gold ballroom to bid farewell to their hosts, Juliet and Walter Townsend. Rosalind tried not to envy the society leader's self-confidence or her very low-cut velvet gown, that exactly matched a magnificent sapphire necklace. She herself was more at ease in a frock coat and trousers than an expensive Worth ball gown.

Townsend nodded absently at Rosalind before turning to David and launching into speech. "I understand you plan to run for the legislature next year. Will you take your wife with you to Albany or—"

Rosalind gritted her teeth, but her polite smile never faltered. She was far too accustomed to being treated like a piece of wood, just because she was a woman, to openly show irritation. But the thought of a lifetime of similar slights, thanks to becoming a politician's wife, was enough to make her skin crawl.

If David hadn't been so very good with children and the only man in New York uninterested in her father's money, she would have given him no more than the courtesy due to a wartime companion of her late brother. As it was, she sometimes had to remind herself that his advantages also included being polite and respectful to women in public, in order to stop herself from breaking their engagement.

After that irritation it was almost a relief to find the magnificent marble entrance hall on the ground floor nearly deserted. Tapestries hung on every wall between the heavily carved doorways and under an equally ornate ceiling, all designed to emulate a Renaissance king's chateau. Silver bowls and vases full of hothouse roses and matching candlesticks wreathed with evergreens adorned the tables scattered between uncomfortable sofas. Gas lighting hissed and glowed from an immense chandelier, turning the rich tones of the Brussels carpet into a shimmering ocean of color. Maroon-clad footmen stood by the front door and the cloakroom, ready to assist guests.

"My dear Portia, you must always remember what is expected of you as a lady and act accordingly." Across the room, Desdemona Lindsay, diamonds in her graying hair and her curves set off by a very snug ice blue gown, spoke earnestly to a ten-year-old girl. The child must be Juliet Townsend's eldest, given the strong similarities in coloring and cameo-pure features. "It is not seemly to leave the children's wing and spy upon your mother's ball."

"Yes, Grandmother Lindsay," Portia Townsend said politely, her eyes sliding toward the front door. She looked far more repentant, in her simple blue gown with her blond hair neatly braided into pigtails, than she sounded. Rosalind's mouth quirked as she remembered all the times she, too, had crept down to watch one of her parents' balls, while her mother was still alive.

Just then, a footman sprang forward and swung open the great door, admitting a new guest in a burst of cold air and swirling snow.

He seemed the embodiment of a barbarian leader, barely tolerating the trappings of civilization, as he entered the overdecorated room. His face had the hard-edged strength of a medieval sculpture, with those level dark blue eyes, slightly crooked nose, and narrow scar slicing his strong jaw. A naval commander's magnificent dark blue uniform, with gold buttons and braid and a gilded sword at his hip, showcased a body fit for one of Arthur's knights. His golden hair and goatee glinted in the lamplight, where he towered a head taller than either of Townsend's handpicked footmen.

Rosalind bit back a groan of pure feminine appreciation.

Desdemona and Portia glanced up, Portia's face blazing in undisguised hero worship. David stiffened to alertness beside Rosalind.

"Uncle Hal!" Portia exclaimed and raced across the room.

A smile broke out across the big man's countenance as he caught the child up in his arms. "Hello, princess! Did you wait up for me?"

"I promised I would, didn't I?" Portia retorted and the big man laughed.

"Look, it's Hal Lindsay," David hissed. "He must have just come from Admiral Porter's banquet at the Brooklyn Navy Yard."

Rosalind nodded, unable to say a word. Of course, the stranger had to be one of the famous Lindsays. Golden in coloring and wealth, the men always made very successful careers in the Navy or business.

"Have you met him? He's rarely in New York. Can you tolerate meeting another veteran?" David teased gently.

Rosalind chuckled at the familiar joke and shook her head. He patted her hand indulgently.

"Come along, I'll introduce you."

Lindsay's hooded gaze swept over Rosalind, then went to David, as they came up. He frowned slightly, then his face cleared. He set his niece down carefully. "Rutherford?"

"Indeed. Good to see you again, Lindsay." David pumped Lindsay's hand enthusiastically.

Rosalind wished, a bit wistfully, that Lindsay had looked longer at her. Or perhaps not. She could feel her heart pounding like a trip-hammer and strongly suspected her cheeks were flushed from excitement, a most unusual reaction to a man. She usually calculated every new acquaintance's degree of interest in her father's money, not a man's physical desire for her.

What would she have done if he'd stared at her? Have a fainting spell? Impossible and yet . . .

"Rosalind, my dear, this is Commander Hal Lindsay, late of the Mississippi Squadron. Lindsay, my fiancée, Rosalind Schuyler."

"Miss Schuyler." His voice was a deep bass that could melt a woman's bones. He bowed over her hand, his big, callused hand warm against her bare skin.

A most proper and precise movement, exactly what any other man of breeding would perform. Yet her throat tightened until she was barely able to murmur a polite response.

"He brought a gunboat to our relief at Shiloh," David enthused. "And he was one of the brave captains who led the squadron past the great Confederate forts at Vicksburg."

He gestured broadly, as if marking the size of those defeated forts, and smacked a tall, narrow Chinese vase. It tottered and started to fall. Lindsay took a step toward it, but she grabbed it first, just as water splashed her dress.

David didn't notice, of course, but simply carried on with his oration. "Then Lindsay—"

"Rutherford."

The single word cut David off like a knife.

Rosalind spun around. Nicholas Lennox crossed the entrance hall toward them, wearing the black armband of full mourning and carrying an elegant swordstick. He stood a few inches taller than Rosalind's unladylike height and was built along racehorse lines, with dark brown hair and luxuriant muttonchop whiskers. His dark brown eyes were as keen as those of a three-card monte player looking for a pigeon to pluck.

His family was old, if not a match for the Schuylers or Lindsays. They'd fallen on hard times in the last generation, and Lennox's older brother had died seeking his fortune out West.

But why would David obey Nicholas Lennox and fall silent?

Lindsay's voice filled the brief silence. "Lennox. My condolences on your brother's death." He extended his hand to Lennox.

Lennox sneered at Lindsay's gesture. He clasped his hands behind his back and straightened to his full height. "My brother's murder, you mean? After all, Lindsay, we have only your word and Donovan's for how he died."

Lindsay stiffened, and the footmen froze. Rosalind choked. Lennox had just given Lindsay a mortal insult. Years ago, the next step would have been a duel and one man left lying in a grave.

"How dare you say that about my uncle!" Portia Townsend demanded.

Lindsay's eyes narrowed. "Portia, honey, go sit with your grandmother."

Portia glared at Lennox before slowly, very slowly, walking away, all the while eyeing him like a mongoose facing a cobra.

Hal waited until the child reached safety before he spoke again, his voice coldly disciplined. "Your brother died in a flash flood. Or do you have some knowledge denied to those of us who were there?"

Lennox fairly vibrated with rage, surprising in a man famed for his polished manners.

Rosalind's blood ran cold. She'd visited many gambling hells with her father and her brothers before their deaths. But she'd rarely seen an atmosphere so edged with violence.

"Perhaps we should speak of your sister, the slut, instead?" Lennox gibed.

"Oh, dear," David muttered.

Lindsay's hand clenched on his sword hilt, then released it slowly. "Excuse me?"

Lennox smiled, not kindly. Rosalind's hand reached instinctively for her pocket Navy Colts before remembering she was wearing women's clothing.

"Tell me," Lennox went on, clearly enjoying the reaction he'd caused, "is she still sleeping with that grubby mick?"

Lindsay hit him with one massive fist. Lennox staggered but quickly freed the blade from his swordstick. Lindsay drew his sword and attacked. Their blades came together with a clear, bell-like ring—indicating very high-quality steel. Neither blade had the advantage, then, so the match would be decided by the swordsman's skill.

The two men slashed and parried and stabbed at each other, ignoring Desdemona Lindsay's impassioned pleas for them to stop. Lennox was much faster than Lindsay, an advantage limited by the other's strength and cunning.

Suddenly, Lennox thrust for Lindsay's chest. Lindsay's curved sword, probably a cavalry saber, barely managed to sweep up and block Lennox's narrow blade only inches from him. Steel rang with the collision's force.

Desdemona Lindsay shrieked.

"Remember our first fight?" Lennox hissed. "I notched your face and now I'll notch your heart."

Lindsay laughed. "If you can—after I've fed your lying tongue up your ass, along with your dick." He disengaged with a strong twist.

Lennox flushed angrily and charged. Their blades flashed and sang with the speed of their thrusts. Lennox was faster—with a vicious skill that spoke volumes about the dishonorable hells he must have learned it in. Several times, his blade came within an inch of Lindsay. But Lindsay was stronger and cannier; his heavy blade somehow always matching Lennox's thrusts.

"Now see here, men," David began, then tripped over a carpet edge and fell flat on his face, landing mere inches from a heavy table.

Rosalind looked around for something, anything to stop the fight, before Lindsay was hurt. A flash of blue shot past her as Portia ran up the stairs towards the ballroom.

"Henry Andronicus Lindsay," Desdemona cried out, "stop this nonsense at once!"

Both combatants ignored her. Blood dripped unheeded down Lindsay's arm as he fought, although it would probably slow him later. Lennox pushed a very ugly marble bust of Washington into Lindsay's path, but the big naval officer leaped over it.

The footmen, who'd been staring at the two men as if watching a boxing match, finally moved—and edged towards the door to the servants' quarters.

The struggle reached an even deadlier pitch. In a flurry of thrusts and parries, Lindsay's saber sliced Lennox's jaw barely an inch from his jugular. A very small hit, which could be easily hid by a fancy cravat.

"Nicky!" screamed Desdemona.

Nicky??? But Rosalind had no time to wonder why Mrs. Richard Lindsay was calling another man by his nickname; she'd finally spotted something useful.

Rosalind snatched up a particularly large silver vase and waited. Her dirk would have been much more helpful. Honors were now even between the two men, with Lindsay's wounded arm and Lennox's cut face. She wouldn't care to wager on who'd win the bout; Lindsay's strength and Lennox's speed made them an equal match.

"Damn you," Lennox snarled, clapping his hand to his jaw. Blood trickled between his fingers.

"Next time, I'll have your head, Lennox," Lindsay warned. "You went too far when you attacked my sister."

Lennox sprang at him, spouting curses. Lindsay brought his sword up.

"Gentlemen," an older man's voice boomed. Rosalind's jaw dropped as Captain Richard Lindsay, the famous Civil War naval hero and owner of the great Cincinnati-Louisville Packet Line, came down the stairs. His three brothers followed him with their sons, in a solid phalanx of golden masculinity, every one of them obviously ready to fight. Portia had brought the entire Lindsay clan to help Hal.

Hal Lindsay's face hardened. He released his hold on Lennox, who quickly stepped out of reach and glared at the newcomers.

Captain Lindsay considered Lennox from the vantage point of greater age and experience, emphasized by his formal evening wear. His clan filed into position behind him, all looking more than capable of dismembering any mortal single-handed.

Lennox's mouth tightened, and his eyes blazed with frustration. Hal Lindsay also lowered his sword, his expression carefully blank.

Desdemona Lindsay looked down for a moment, visibly fighting to compose herself. When she looked up again, she wore the serene countenance of a successful hostess contemplating a roomful of guests.

Cornelius Schuyler, Rosalind's father, quietly joined Rosalind, his gray eyes questioning. She smiled up at him reassuringly and carefully set the vase down on the nearest table, her hands only a little unsteady. David scrambled to his feet and began to brush marble chips from his coat. The ball's hostess, flanked by other satin-bedecked ladies, appeared on the stairs to gawk at the scene.

"Good evening, gentlemen," Hal Lindsay said as he calmly cleaned his sword with his handkerchief. His eyes were carefully hooded, but they still held a murderous gleam.

Captain Lindsay spoke again, his voice rolling into the silence like a courthouse bell at a public execution.

"Mr. Lennox, would you explain why you drew steel in my daughter's house upon my son?"

Lennox gritted his teeth. Rosalind shivered and her father patted her arm reassuringly.

"It was nothing of importance, sir," Lennox said harshly, his eyes darting around to judge his words' effect. "We were simply enjoying a moment's exercise. Please forgive us, Townsend, for disturbing you."

Captain Lindsay lifted his eyebrows at that bit of specious nonsense. "I believe you owe my son an apology," he observed.

Lennox started to say something hasty but stopped abruptly each time Lindsay took a half step forward, his hands clenching into fists. He bit his lip, then managed to speak. "My apologies, Lindsay. I am deeply sorry if I caused any distress to you or your family's honor. My words and behavior were unacceptable and disrespectful of the homage due to my host and hostess's families."

A very pretty speech indeed, one which made the ladies on the stairs relax. Rosalind, however, would have trusted a gambler with a mismatched deuce and trey farther than Lennox.

Hal Lindsay nodded, his eyes hooded as he watched Lennox. "Apology accepted. And my apologies, Juliet, if we distressed you." He bowed to his sister, who clucked at him.

"You big oaf!" She ran down and examined his wounded arm. "I asked you to liven things up. But this is absurd!"

The other ladies chuckled at the face-saving excuse, and the room's tension visibly lightened.

It was hardly the time to demand an apology from Lennox for insulting Hal Lindsay's younger sister. But Rosalind did wonder what would happen when Lindsay met him again.

A moment later, Lennox was gone, after one last fulminating glare around the hall. Portia bore her protesting uncle off to put a poultice on his incipient shiner, while Captain Lindsay gallantly escorted his wife back to the ballroom.

Rosalind refused to watch Hal Lindsay disappear. He was far too magnificent for her peace of mind.

Chapter One

Kansas City, April 1872

Hal Lindsay steered the Cherokee Belle with all the ease of long familiarity. One hand on the wheel and a straw between his teeth, he glanced out the window to his left, casually checking the landmarks. His Navy Colt shifted in his shoulder holster at the movement, but his Arkansas toothpick, with its eighteen-inch narrow steel blade, rested quietly against his back.

After weeks spent traveling upriver from St. Louis, he was almost home. Tonight he'd show off his beloved Kansas City to his little sister, Viola, and her new husband before they sailed with him tomorrow to Montana on the *Belle*.

Only a few clouds darkened his horizon, now that he was reconciled with his dearest friend from childhood. If the railroads would disappear, he'd be a happy man.

He scanned the railroad bridge upstream for signs of trouble. Impossible to guess what those piles of stone concealed—driftwood, debris, or an unexpected eddy, since railroads notoriously built their bridges to ruin the water patterns for riverboats.

Hal double-checked the current's speed, looking for unexpected bursts or eddies before the levee. Here, the Missouri was twice as fast as the Mississippi at New Orleans, almost double the speed of Sherman's march through Georgia—and entirely too similar to a waterfall's headlong rush toward oblivion. It was damned late in the spring rise for it to be running so fast.

He scanned the Hannibal Bridge one last time, found no signs of danger, and turned the *Cherokee Belle* for the levee.

A tree hurtled out from behind the bridge. Hal came to full alert with a vicious curse. He quickly rang down for three-quarters speed ahead and slammed the *Belle*'s wheel hard over.

The boat-killing missile raced east, heading directly for the *Belle*, its bare branches reaching for the big white riverboat. A brush from those sharp-edged lances would shred the *Belle*'s planking and send her straight to the bottom.

Hal's only chance was to tuck the *Belle* behind the wharf boat before the tree tore her apart, then rapidly back her away from the levee before she rammed it. But this April's unusually high water and faster currents made those maneuvers sound like a drunkard's dreams of glory.

The *Belle* answered the helm immediately and leaned into the turn like the racehorse she was, racing for the levee and safety. Norton set the bell dancing with the engine room's response as a cloud of smoke abruptly roared from the tall stacks.

Passengers shouted as they staggered on the slanting deck. Chickens screeched angrily from their coop aft of the pilothouse and the two milk cows bellowed their protests from the main deck. O'Brien, the mate, boomed a flurry of profanity, as he demanded poles and boat hooks to defend the *Belle*.

The raging brown waters caught the tree and bounced it, sending the waves into a froth of brown and white. The rootball dropped from sight, as if the tree wanted to plant itself in the river bottom then and there.

Hal held his breath and watched.

The tree spun like a top in the fast current and pitched it-self at the *Belle* yet again.

One of its brothers had sunk Morris's *Pretty Lady* that morning, according to gossip at the last woodyard. God will-ing, the *Cherokee Belle* wouldn't die the same way. Not today.

Hal cursed and rang for full-speed ahead. Norton's response from the engine room was even faster this time. Black smoke gushed from the stacks, tendrils brushing the pilothouse be-fore they raced away. Hal would rather face the Missouri's vagaries with Black Jack Norton than with any other engi-neer west of the Mississippi.

He sharpened the turn, praying the *Belle* wouldn't come in so fast she crumpled her bow against the levee. He had to bring her safely past that tree.

The drowned tree raced past the wharf boat, still heading straight for the *Belle,* its branches as menacing as any bayo-net charge.

Thundering feet along the main deck announced O'Brien's roustabouts arriving on the starboard. Curious passengers rushed to the same side, like sheep too stupid to flee from danger.

The first barren branch lunged toward the *Belle,* but a boat hook pushed it away. Another wicked limb reached to-ward her prey, and another. Boat hooks and poles defeated every attack.

The root-ball passed within a yard of the *Belle*'s paddle-wheel. Passengers applauded. Then a woman screamed from the bow.

Hal immediately spun the wheel, turning the *Belle* back toward the river, as he rang for all back full. Norton's answer set the bell jangling before Hal could remove his hand. The old devil must have been desperate for that order.

The *Belle*'s paddlewheel churned the water into a frenzy. Her bow bumped against the muddy bottom, sending a long shudder through the boat as she escaped into deeper water.

The deckhands raised a cheer. O'Brien cursed them, albeit with less heat than before, and sent them off once again to prepare to tie up at the wharf boat.

Hal straightened the wheel and rang for quarter-speed ahead. Norton's answer seemed a tad leisurely this time.

Five minutes later, the *Cherokee Belle* decorously docked beside the wharf boat. The gangplank dropped into position and passengers jostled to go ashore first. On the main deck, Hezekiah led the other Negro roustabouts in a rhythmic plantation melody as they began to unload cargo, the men clearly intent on earning their bonuses for singing—and advertising the *Belle*.

Aloysius Hatcher's brag boat, the *Spartan,* was docked just forward of the *Belle*. Her chimney stacks were higher this season, probably to gain a hotter fire in her boilers, making them just another one of Hatcher's efforts to keep the speed record he'd stolen from the *Belle*. Hal reminded himself to talk to Bellecourt about keeping a wary eye out for double tricks on the trip upriver; no telling what Hatcher would try on this voyage.

Wagons ambled down Front Street, and pedestrians bustled between the scattered buildings. Just outside a saloon, the local Pinkerton detective, Jonah Longbottom, earnestly questioned two men.

Hal idly wondered what they discussed; undoubtedly railroad business, but today was Monday, so Longbottom couldn't be hunting that missing heiress. The man was honest, diligent, and utterly predictable: Every Tuesday, he sought Miss Schuyler at every hotel and boardinghouse in Kansas City, as he'd been paid to do. No matter that it was a useless search, since any railroad man would have told him that she'd stay close to land and far away from water. Any riverman would have laughed in his face. No riverman would betray the one person who'd made the arrogant railroads look like fools.

Railroads had the nasty habit of lowering fares until they

stole all traffic, both passenger and freight, from the riverboats. After they'd killed every honest, independent riverboat, they'd raise rates to sky-high levels and take the profits home to New York.

So far, the only person who'd successfully mocked the railroads' omnipotence was that missing heiress. Second-largest stockholder in New York Central, Rosalind Schuyler had a fortune that could make Commodore Vanderbilt jealous. But she'd disappeared from her guardian's fancy Manhattan town house, setting off a frenzy of speculation in the press as the law and Pinkerton detectives hunted her.

Some folks said she was dead, like the big charities who stood to gain her money. They'd even filed suit to get their hands on it. But nobody paid much attention to them except their lawyers.

The railroads looked the hardest, of course. They'd scoured mile after mile of track without finding so much as a whiff of her French perfume. The orphaned little lady was winning the race, while every riverman cheered her on and laughed at the railroads.

Hal had met her once in New York, at his sister's house during a ball. She'd caught his eye immediately: It was rare to see a tall woman hold her head high, rather than slouch to appear shorter. Her enormous gray eyes, mobile mouth, and masses of honey brown curls had made his cock tighten with a hot-blooded man's need to stake an immediate claim. He'd wanted to drag her upstairs and bed her until all she could say was his name, then wake up in the morning to enjoy her again. She was the most dangerous woman he'd ever met because she'd made him want to stay.

Jerking his thoughts back to his original question, Hal gave a mental shrug at Longbottom's stubbornness and went to work on his logbook entry. He was tempted to compare railroads to works of Satan, especially when he considered how few first-class packets still docked at Westport Landing.

He shrugged off the idea, in favor of a fast departure for home, where he could freshen up before welcoming Viola and William. After years of writing his sister, he needed to be a good advertisement for the delights of Kansas City.

"*Félicitations*, Lindsay. You brought the *Belle* in very neatly." Antoine Bellecourt, the *Belle*'s other pilot, stepped into the pilothouse.

Hal smiled at his old mentor and shrugged off the praise. "Easy enough when the currents were the same direction as during last year's rise. A bit faster though—six miles an hour, I'd guess."

"*Vraiment?* Was that how you did it?" Bellecourt cocked his head to consider that news, as eager as any pilot to hear gossip about the river. Then he shifted easily to another topic, clearly having absorbed the implications of Hal's observation. "Ready to go ashore, *mon ami*? The Widow Cameron's loitering by the gangplank, watching for you."

Hal raised an eyebrow in disbelief and finished scribbling. "Why would I care what she's doing?"

"Given how you two flirted on the trip up from St. Louis . . ." the old matchmaker hinted.

"Are you sure about that, Bellecourt?" Hal tucked his logbook away into his suit pocket and gathered his blackthorn walking stick.

Bellecourt snorted. "A man would have to be blind not to see how she was looking you over, *mon ami*."

"I'm having dinner tonight with my sister and her husband, Bellecourt, not a woman hell-bent on marriage and children."

He resettled his Stetson on his head, bought in Tucson while he hunted for Viola a year ago. Given its completely different style from the uniform hats worn by the *Belle*'s officers, it also served to mark him as the boat's owner.

"Your objection to marriage, Lindsay, is really quite remarkable," Bellecourt probed gently, his black eyes quizzical. "You're more than comfortable with women."

Hal's mouth tightened for a moment. But Bellecourt had been his friend since he'd arrived on this river almost twenty years ago as a scruffy boy. In fact, he was the one who'd taught him how to read the river and be a pilot. If he'd waited this long to ask, then Hal could give him some of the truth.

He shifted the walking stick in his hand before speaking. "The widow is sister to Mrs. Bennett and Mrs. Turner. Would you want to marry into either of those families?"

"Where the fathers beat their sons as regular as spring thunderstorms? Then the boys grow up and do the same with their own get? *Merde,*" Bellecourt spat, his face alive with disgust. "I've lived in Kansas City for almost forty years and I've seen five generations of Bennetts and Turners shed their children's blood. And when the mothers stood idly by while their babies are whipped . . ."

Hal flinched at the all-too-accurate description of how a family repeated its mistakes, generation after generation.

His friend brooded for a moment, his black eyes as dangerous as an obsidian knife. "I wouldn't ally myself with those families if the Missouri was coming over the levee and they had the only boat in town, *mon ami.*"

Bellecourt glanced at him and smoothly switched gears. "*Les petites demoiselles* are a different matter—so pretty and sweet and charming, they are easy to guard and protect. Is your beautiful sister still married to Ross?"

Hal was glad to follow his old master's conversational lead. "That drunken jackass? He's been dead more than a year. But Viola caught a good man this time around, William Donovan of Donovan & Sons."

Bellecourt whistled. "*C'est vrai?* She did very well for herself."

Nodding agreement, Hal briefly considered the contrast

between Viola's two husbands. He'd never understood why she'd married Ross, and she'd never offered an explanation. Heaven knows he'd found enough reasons to quarrel with their father. But that ill-advised marriage had caused his sister's first fight with the old devil.

Turning from the old puzzle, he brought the conversation back to its original course. "Why don't you flirt with the widow? All you have to do is tell her my rules."

"No wife and no children?" Bellecourt laughed softly and followed Hal out of the pilothouse and down to the hurricane deck. "Or perhaps I'll simply attend Taylor's poker party, *mon ami,* rather than dance attendance on a lady."

Driven by habit, Hal reached up and tested one of the two hog chains' tension, making sure his boat was still stable. The *Cherokee Belle,* like all western riverboats, prized a shallow draft enough to dispense with a keel, such as oceangoing ships used. Instead, they used hog chains, which ran from stem to stern beside the texas, strong and taut to counterbalance the *Belle*'s heavy load in the hold below.

Just then, one of the Negro roustabouts trotted up to Hal with an envelope. "Telegram, boss. It's been waiting at the office for you."

"Thanks." Hal waved a dismissal and ripped open the envelope to read the message within. "Damn. Viola and Donovan were delayed leaving Washington. They won't reach Kansas City until dawn."

"Then they're still joining us tomorrow?"

Hal's head came up at a sharp bark, then he shrugged off the disturbance. It certainly hadn't come from his boat.

"Oh yes," he answered his friend. "But until then, maybe I'll go to Taylor's tonight." He brooded for a moment. He could visit Annie Chambers's bawdy house instead. He knew every parlor house and brothel on the Missouri—and most of those on the Mississippi and Ohio rivers as well. He could amuse himself with one of her women for an hour, or two. If she had anyone both interesting and clean, that is. Annie had teased him more than once about being too persnickety for his own good.

No, better to play poker; it would hold his attention far longer than any woman ever had.

"You could still chase the widow," Bellecourt offered, as they reached the boiler deck.

Another frantic bark, then another, sounded above the river's churning rush. Hal swung around to look for the source.

A clump of men and boys were gathered on the levee's edge near the railroad bridge, just above the river. Cudgels rose and fell. A knife flashed in the afternoon sun, then plunged downward. A dog yelped, almost a scream.

Hal clenched his fists, then forced himself to relax. He'd heard that sound before and always reacted far too passionately: rushing alone into battle to save a single animal. He reminded himself yet again that, with thousands of stray dogs around, the world wouldn't notice the death of one. He couldn't continue to rescue every beast that was being abused.

The dog wailed in anguish.

Cursing his own sentimentality, Hal swung over the railing and dropped onto the main deck. A moment later, he pounded across the wharf boat and leaped onto the muddy levee, Arkansas toothpick and walking stick in hand. No time to gather a policeman or a squad of men to help him, if he wanted to save that mutt.

Behind him, Bellecourt called two roustabouts to come along. The dog's barks and yelps were fewer now, boding ill.

The crowd of bullies was too absorbed in the dog's anguish to notice Hal's arrival. He dispatched the first one with a quick blow to the thigh, sending the lout tumbling down the embankment into Front Street. He dropped the second one with a sharp rap to the back of the head, leaving the fellow sprawling in the mud. Wielding the blackthorn like a windmill had a very salutary effect on the ruffians, much more so than using it like a sword would have.

The next blackguard spun to face him, brandishing a large bowie knife. Still gripping the blackthorn in the center, Hal quickly fell into the guard stance, drilled into him so many years ago in Cincinnati by a French fencing master. The ruffian charged, and Hal shoved the walking stick's head square into the fool's solar plexus. He fell down, gasping for air, as Bellecourt pounded along the railroad tracks atop the levee.

Most of the other bullies fled down the levee's side and into the alleys beyond Front Street.

Cowards.

Bellecourt and the roustabouts took up position across the railroad tracks to guard Hal's back, their own cudgels and knives at the ready. A crowd gathered to watch, some avidly gaping at the open display of violence, while others laid bets on the fight's outcome.

The biggest thug faced Hal alone now, a dirty knife in his hand and a Colt holstered on one hip. He was dark-haired and big-bellied, with a bulbous red nose, testifying to years spent wallowing in hard liquor. Just behind him, a small, bloody burlap bag twitched in the mud and lay still.

The thug's eyes widened as he took in the long steel blade on Hal's Arkansas toothpick and the equally deadly black-thorn walking stick. He grabbed for his Colt, and Hal charged. An instant later, the brute lay crumpled at the water's edge, his throat cut from ear to ear and the Colt sliding away from his dead fingers.

"Undoubtedly self-defense, *mon brave*," Bellecourt remarked, coming up to stand behind Hal. "The police will raise no fuss over his departure. They've been trying to get rid of that murderous fool for a year now."

"I'll have to talk to them about it, of course. And pay for his funeral."

Bellecourt shrugged. *"Mais certainement."*

Hal nodded agreement and knelt beside the ragged burlap bag, remembering all too well the first time he'd held a lifeless dog.

"Do you need any help, *mon ami*?" Bellecourt's voice brought him back to the present.

"No, I can manage."

Now what? As ever with an injured animal, it was best to start off by mimicking Viola.

"It's okay, fellow. It's okay," he mumbled, gently smoothing the coarse fabric to find the animal inside. The dog growled softly, then uttered a single, sharp warning bark.

Hal sliced the bag open carefully. Damn and blast, just how foul could one dog smell? Matted, rough, red fur brushed his fingers, a few more barks sounded, and he soon found the dog's head. Dark eyes blinked and the dog's lip curled in an almost silent growl.

"Good fellow," he crooned, petting the floppy ears, soothing words coming easier now. "That's my good, patient boy. Just rest easy while I look you over."

Hal grimaced at the sound of his voice, as he quickly cleaned his knife and sheathed it. This sort of cloying affection sounded so much better when coming from a woman. Still, frightened strays didn't bite females as often as they did men, so it was worth sounding like a fool. It wouldn't be for long, either, since this dog would quickly cling to his groom as all the others had.

The dog relaxed slowly and fell silent, except for an occasional yip as Hal gently checked him over for injuries. He never tried to bite Hal, but simply watched from half-closed dark eyes.

"Well, boy, looks like you're covered with bruises and a

few nicks but no broken bones. Nothing you can't recover from with rest and good food. And a bath," he added, gagging under another wave of the dog's aroma.

The dog woofed once in agreement and licked Hal's fingers. He'd rescued other stray dogs before, seen them back to health under his groom's care, and then given them away. None of them had ever tried to stay with him.

"Feel like eating, boy?" Chuckling softly, Hal slipped the bag completely off the battered little body.

The dog barked weakly and staggered to its feet, weaving from side to side. Hal steadied it, an aid that it seemed to just tolerate.

It looked like one of the terriers from Ireland, standing almost two feet high, with a long head, floppy ears instead of the more typical upright ones, and short fur. It raised its chin fearlessly as it considered the man, then wagged its tail slightly. The little fellow was game to the bone and could probably have successfully defended itself, except for being tied up in that burlap bag.

"Doing better now, fellow?"

The dog woofed again, its eyes still a little unfocused. It took a hesitant step forward toward Hal, staggered, and started to collapse.

Automatically, Hal reached out and caught the plucky beast before it landed in the mud, wincing at its prominent ribs. He'd never allow one of his horses to become this thin. "Let's get you home, boy," he soothed and picked it up in his arms, then stood up.

The long head turned to consider him from the new vantage point. Dark button eyes met blue eyes as the terrier took Hal's measure.

Hal blinked, startled by the intelligence in the dog's gaze. Then he looked back soberly, one eyebrow cocked as he waited for judgment.

The terrier stared at him for a long minute. Finally, he

woofed softly and laid his head against Hal's shoulder, his battered body snuggling into the man's warmth. Hal stiffened in surprise, then automatically cradled the little fellow. Hopefully, his valet would be able to save his suit.

A cop shouldered his way through the crowd then. He took a long look at the dead thug and raised an eyebrow at Hal. "Tried to kill one too many, didn't he? Just give me a statement before you leave town, both of you."

"Yes, sir," the two pilots agreed.

"I'll pay for the funeral," Hal added.

"I believe you have a dog now," Bellecourt remarked as they headed back to the boat.

Hal snorted. "Don't be absurd. Just like all the others, this one will happily trot off to a household filled with children."

"You can say what you like but will he believe it?" Bellecourt nodded at the muddy bundle in Hal's arms.

"He'll change his mind soon enough," Hal retorted as he absently fondled the small, furry head. "Give him a bath and dinner, then he'll be off to a dog lover's home before you could back the *Belle* off a sandbar."

Bellecourt grunted noncommittally. "So you say, *mon ami*. But I've got five dollars that says he comes onboard tomorrow at your heels."

"Done. I'll take the rest of your money tonight at the poker table."

Bellecourt laughed. "You can but try."

Still teasing each other about their poker skills, they headed back to the *Cherokee Belle* with the two roustabouts close behind.

The crowd had mostly dispersed by now, but one figure caught Hal's eye: a slender young man, with a carpetbag and a gold-headed cane, watching from the other side of Front Street. He was of average height, with brown hair and light-colored eyes that glinted under his broad-brimmed planter's hat.

He was probably a gambler, given his diamond stickpin, stylish clothing, and presence in this waterfront district. Judging by his muddy boots, he'd likely been stranded when the *Pretty Lady* sank this morning and was now looking for a new boat to ply his trade on.

The gambler touched his hat in salute to Hal, who nodded in response, then stepped back into the shadows. A minute later, Hal's attention returned to the dog in his arms.

Rosalind Schuyler cursed her own recklessness as she found shelter in a miserable little waterfront hotel's side doorway. She must discipline herself, forget her relief at escaping drowning one more time, and focus on staying free.

She shouldn't have watched the fight, not now, not when every instinct shrieked that her pursuers were close. She needed to find another boat to take her upriver, not stare at Hal Lindsay, even if he was given to rescuing small helpless beings like that terrier.

Why the devil did he have to be just as magnificent now as she remembered? Ever since she first met him, she'd hoped her reaction to him had been simply a woman's flutter over an attractive man in uniform. Then her father had died so suddenly in January, and David had broken off their engagement, and Lennox had . . .

Rosalind closed her eyes for a moment, forcing herself to calm down.

Nicholas Lennox might be handsome, but his heart was blacker than Hades. Her father had always said a gentleman should be judged by how he treated his inferiors. By that standard, Lindsay was the epitome of a gentleman, given his rescue of the wounded dog.

But he didn't—couldn't—matter to her now. Only staying away from Nicholas Lennox did. She had to keep running, if she was to stay free another year until her twenty-fifth birthday next April, when she'd come into her inheritance. Then, and only then, could she laugh at Nicholas Lennox and his vicious insistence on marriage. And after that, she'd marry and build a family to replace the one she'd lost.

All of which added up to Fort Benton, where neither train nor riverboat traveled in the winter. There, and only there, could she stay hidden long enough.

She took a deep breath, then another. Her stomach churned again, sending acid into her throat. Hiding for almost four months had taught her all too well how to ignore the feeling. Only the loneliness—the continual longing for someone to talk to, someone who'd understand and care about her—was harder to bear than her stomach's discomfort at the thought of boarding another boat.

And she'd never be able to pilot a boat as Hal Lindsay just did—dodging a drowned tree as if it were a toothpick. She was capable of daredevilry at the card table, but never on-board a boat.

Her father had left one other option: The trust ended when she married. But who'd marry a woman who wore men's clothing? She snorted as she visualized that wedding scene, where both bride and groom wore trousers. No, running and hiding was the only option.

A few steps remained to the packet line's office, where she could buy passage to Montana. And next spring, she could ride a train again. Those lovely marvels of technology that never, ever sank. She'd been born on a train, reared on trains, and fully intended to travel only by train as soon as she could stop hiding.

But for now, she had to keep moving. Her nerves were unsettled, as if Lennox were on the other side of this very door.

Suddenly, a woman sallied out of the hotel and tossed a smiling good-bye over her shoulder. "Bon voyage on the *Spartan,* my dearest!"

She bumped into Rosalind, sending them both staggering.

Rosalind automatically steadied her, her eyes searching the other for injury. An older woman, perhaps sixty years of age, with graying hair peeping around a close bonnet and a curved figure tightly corseted to maintain the illusion of a young girl's trim waist.

Desdemona Lindsay? Hal Lindsay's mother?

What had the woman, famous for her love of fine clothes and rich living, been doing in a grimy waterfront hotel? She was the matriarch of a wealthy and ancient naval family, not a gambler fleecing passersby with a game of three-card monte or a *nymph du pave* entertaining a dockworker for an hour. Could she have been visiting a lover, given the streak of semen high on her cheek? Rosalind had brushed similar streaks from her skin, after private times with David.

Lover? Dear God in heaven, could Lennox be here too?

"Are you all right, ma'am?" Rosalind inquired politely, careful to let only concern show on her face. Her heart raced frantically.

"Why, yes, thank you, sir." Deep blue eyes, so very similar to Hal Lindsay's, met hers and assessed Rosalind rapidly. Then she batted her eyelashes flirtatiously at Rosalind, who relaxed slightly when she realized she hadn't been recognized.

"It was nothing, ma'am, truly," Rosalind answered politely, easily keeping to a riverboat gambler's exquisitely—and meaninglessly—polite behavior. "May I escort you somewhere?"

Desdemona Lindsay froze as genuine horror flashed across her face. She recovered quickly, though her words sounded rushed. "Oh no, no, no, that's not necessary at all. I just need to walk another block or so. Please excuse me, sir, I must be going."

"Ma'am." Rosalind tipped her planter's hat and stepped

back into the shadows to let Desdemona pass. She had to get out of Kansas City fast, before Desdemona or her lover found her.

The dark clouds to the west echoed her mood as she studied the waterfront before her, looking for the recommended line's offices. Two steamboats, the *Spartan* and the *Cherokee Belle,* were docked along the levee next to the wharf boat, with their pilothouses and upper decks visible above the railroad embankment. The layers of crisp white decks, ornamented with lavishly carved wood, reminded some journalists of wedding cakes. Rosalind compared them to cheese and crackers on a plate, ready to be scattered to the winds.

The *Spartan* wore a broom on her pilothouse, silently bragging of her new status as the fastest boat from Kansas City to Sioux City. But she looked subtly unkempt, with faded gilding and dull paint, and her overly tall stacks made her seem slightly unbalanced.

In contrast, the *Belle* looked exactly what her reputation called her: a very fast packet, fully capable of setting a speed record from Kansas City to Fort Benton in Montana. Every bit of her two hundred-fifty-foot length was freshly painted in brilliant white, with crisp black and gold on her stacks and pipes. Her gingerbread was crisp and elegant and, even from this distance, Rosalind could see that her stained-glass windows displayed a wider range of colors than any other riverboat. Her golden initials, CB, hung between her tall stacks like a necklace around a society beauty's throat. Her name was proudly written high atop her pilothouse, as if challenging every other riverboat for the title of "fairest of them all."

Perfect for Rosalind's needs, even if she was a boat.

She sighed and headed for H.A. Lindsay & Company's headquarters. Risky business, riding one of Lindsay's boats. But what other choice did she have? Only the *Spartan* and Lindsay's boats sailed all the way from Kansas City to Fort Benton. And if Desdemona Lindsay's lover—*dear God, may that woman not have been speaking to Lennox*—was on the *Spartan,* then Rosalind would rather walk barefoot to Montana than step aboard that boat.

Lindsay & Company's offices were tidy and bustling with business, a good home for one of the best packet lines on the Missouri River.

"How can I help you, sir?" the clerk asked politely. His perceptive gaze and empty sleeve neatly pinned to his chest gave him the look of a wartime veteran.

"I'd like to book passage on the *Cherokee Belle* to Fort Benton. Single cabin, if you please," Rosalind answered briskly.

It never occurred to her that he might realize she was a woman. No clerk had looked askance at her since she was sixteen, the first time her brothers had taken her on the town in men's clothing. She was taller than most men, at eight inches over five feet, but it still surprised her that so many gentlemen made sexual advances to her when they thought she was a man. Of course, since she'd only once been courted by someone who wasn't a fortune hunter, any man taking a carnal interest in her femininity would be a surprise.

"Sorry, sir, but only deck passage is available on the *Belle.* Or you could wait till Friday when her sister boat, the *Cherokee Star,* leaves."

Wait four days for another boat? Four days of living in terror that Lennox or the Pinkertons would find her? Dear God, would her luck never turn? She did very well at the gaming tables, but winning a ten-thousand-dollar bankroll seemed a mocking balance for her inability to lose Lennox's hounds. She could feel that fiend breathing down her neck now, laughing at her attempts to escape.

Rosalind answered the clerk smoothly, grimly certain her inner panic didn't show in her voice. "A cabin on the *Star* will suffice, unless there's another boat leaving sooner."

"Hatcher's *Spartan* is leaving tomorrow for Fort Benton," the clerk suggested.

Rosalind shook her head briskly, barely repressing a shudder.

"Thank you but I'll sail on the *Star*."

"Very good, sir."

A few minutes later, armed with a ticket for the *Cherokee Star* and recommendations for local hotels, Rosalind headed back up the street, deliberately ignoring the churning river behind her. Staying close to water meant staying free. No one, even Lennox, would ever look for her on a boat.

What next? She needed to keep her card-playing skills polished while she waited for the *Star*. Perhaps she might be lucky enough to sit in on one of Taylor's famous poker games.

Chapter Two

"**Y**ou can also visit the girls at Annie Chambers's bawdy house, Monsieur Carstairs," Bellecourt continued his ode to the delights of Kansas City as he drove.

Rosalind blinked, but nodded politely. Taylor had promised her another player would give her a ride out to the game. He hadn't mentioned the man could tell better tales than a tour guide.

"Beautiful, lively, accomplished *demoiselles,* too," Bellecourt went on. "One can play 'La Marseillaise' on a man's balls."

Rosalind choked, pleased that Bellecourt obviously accepted her as a man but considerably startled by the latest boast. She'd heard a great deal of frank masculine conversation since she'd fled New York, including some very intriguing stories about what went on in houses of ill repute. Male gossip was fascinating, especially when they didn't realize a woman was listening, as she'd first learned from her brothers' chatter.

She hoped they'd reach Taylor's house before Bellecourt could invite her to accompany him on a visit to Annie Chambers's house. She'd never managed any good excuses for why she'd be so curious about parlor houses and brothels—and so completely unwilling to visit any such establishment.

Bellecourt fell silent as he neatly turned the horse and buggy into a graceful driveway, a ribbon of pale gravel in the twilight. Green grass flowed away on either side, with shade trees dotted across it. Rich beds of spring flowers marked pathways and ringed a gazebo. A fountain gurgled at the end of the drive, with a big white plantation house rising beyond.

"Incroyable, n'est-çe pas?" Bellecourt said softly. "Taylor came up from New Orleans before the war and built an estate he'd be proud to call home."

"Magnificent," Rosalind agreed simply, her voice huskier than usual.

Actually, the estate's elegant simplicity made her uncomfortable. She'd been prepared for a nouveau riche household's ostentatious lack of taste, not a mansion whose classic beauty reminded her of Oak Hill, her family's centuries-old estate on Long Island.

This was also the first time since she'd fled New York that she'd been in anyone's house. The Knickerbocker aristocracy that she'd grown up in allowed only family, close friends, and social superiors admission into their homes. According to their code, she didn't belong in Taylor's house, since she was both a stranger and a professional gambler.

She forced the reflexive discomfort out of her mind. She was simply attending an evening's poker game, something she'd done so many times since fleeing New York.

"Thanks for the lift, Monsieur Bellecourt," Rosalind said as she stepped down from the buggy. She drew in a deep breath of the humid evening air, rich with lilacs in full bloom.

"De rien. It was pleasant to have company on the drive out from town," Bellecourt answered as he handed the reins to a waiting groom. He was a tall, trim, older fellow, not as tall or as handsome as his friend with the Irish terrier, but riverboat gossip called him a clever poker player.

He'd also seen her only as a man, as had everyone else since her flight from New York. No sidelong glances at her chest, no lingering survey of her mouth, no quick lunge to open a door for her. Nothing like that from Bellecourt.

"*Bonsoir,* Taylor. As you suggested, I brought Monsieur Carstairs with me."

"Bellecourt." The two men shook hands before the host turned to Rosalind. He was a slender man, standing half a head shorter than Rosalind. But his black eyes saw and remembered every turn of a card, as she'd learned on the *Natchez* two months ago. "Glad you could join us, Carstairs. We can use a square player like yourself to keep the boys toeing the line."

"It's an honor to join you, sir," she answered, firmly returning his handshake. Her brother Richard had spent hours teaching her how to grip like a man. She missed him bitterly every time she shook hands. "I'm sure every player who enjoys your hospitality is a credit to the game."

"Kind of you to say so, Carstairs. But my wife's been waiting to make your acquaintance. Eleanor, my dear, allow me to introduce Frank Carstairs."

"Welcome to our home, Mr. Carstairs. Please consider it yours while you're in Kansas City," Mrs. Taylor murmured in a rich southern drawl, offering her hand. She was slightly shorter than her husband and as round as he was lean, with merry brown eyes.

Rosalind blinked at the generous welcome. Why on earth would a respectable woman offer a poker shark the freedom of her home? She'd heard of southern hospitality, but had never been its recipient before.

"It's an honor to be here, ma'am," she answered, keeping herself to the most masculine possible activity as she shook her hostess's hand. She was always afraid a woman's gaze would spot the clever tailoring that she hid behind. Thankfully, Mrs. Taylor was apparently yet another female who saw only Frank Carstairs.

"The honor is ours, Mr. Carstairs," the older woman responded easily before turning to Bellecourt. "Antoine, how good to see you here again. Thank you for that marvelous French champagne. It made toasting our youngest's betrothal very special."

Bellecourt bowed and waved off the thanks. For a moment, he seemed to be more a beloved uncle than the tough but jovial river pilot he'd been on the drive here.

Rosalind handed her hat and gloves to the Negro maid at the door, with only a moment's qualms. She'd gone without a hat's protective shadow at other games and had never been recognized as a woman. Surely, no one would notice this time.

A few minutes later, all four of them were passing through the house on their way to the card room. Taylor and Bellecourt led the way, while chatting amiably about horses. Mrs. Taylor had claimed Rosalind's arm, a service Rosalind was accustomed to providing in her role as unattached gentleman. It had taken years of mimicking her brothers to learn the social graces appropriate to a man.

"Were you on deck when the *Pretty Lady* struck the snag, Mr. Carstairs?" Mrs. Taylor asked.

"Yes, ma'am. I was taking my morning constitutional when it happened and saw the entire incident."

As she walked, Rosalind glanced briefly at the mansion's interior, whose spare white and gold elegance contrasted in so many ways to her family home's more modern dark lavishness. These furnishings were elegant but comfortable, with rich Oriental carpets covering the floors and family portraits gracing the walls, all shining in the soft lamplight.

"Was it a sawyer, Mr. Carstairs, or a planter?" Mrs. Taylor asked, as she automatically twitched her skirt around a child's pull toy.

Rosalind smiled privately. One day, she, too, would be happily and easily dodging her children's toys. She'd raise them as her parents had reared her: the center of the universe, not a social necessity. "Definitely a sawyer, Mrs. Taylor. I distinctly saw it swaying back and forth in the current, like a cat waiting to pounce."

Mrs. Taylor shuddered. "Dreadful things. I remember the first time I saw the Devil's Rake. All those barren branches reaching out for our boat, like the hands of the damned as they pass into hell. It was truly a horrifying sight and I was deeply grateful for the shelter of my husband's arms." She paused to compose herself. "Was there much panic on the *Pretty Lady* when she struck the snag?"

"Very little, ma'am. Captain Morris promptly beached her on a riverbank, allowing everyone to reach shore safely."

"Mr. Taylor said you were quite the hero and rescued a child."

Rosalind shrugged. "It was nothing, ma'am. A few little ones had returned to the *Pretty Lady* to watch the river, while their parents worked to save their few possessions. Most of them raced to their parents when summoned. I merely noticed the one remaining lad and returned him to his family."

Mrs. Taylor raised an eyebrow. "You're very modest, Mr. Carstairs. I heard you edged across shattered planking, barely an inch above the river, to save that little angel from the fast rising waters. As a mother, I must thank you."

Rosalind flushed bright red and bowed, unable to find words as she remembered how close the raging river had come to her and the boy. Every step she'd taken on those unsteady boards had reminded her of the last time she'd seen her brothers, when they'd fought the nor'easter to pull her from the yacht's cabin. And the hours afterward, when she'd struggled to stay alive despite the towering waves and winds.

Mrs. Taylor's next words brought her back to the present. "Now we've reached the card room and you need to think of more interesting matters than an old woman's conversation. Just remember that you're always welcome at James and Eleanor Taylor's house."

She patted Rosalind's arm and turned down another hallway, without waiting for an answer.

Rosalind's mouth twisted as she glanced after Mrs. Taylor's retreating back. Apparently she'd been accepted into the family, despite being a gambler.

She turned to follow Bellecourt and Taylor. After this morning and evening's surprises, she was more than ready for a poker game's familiar complexities.

Two more steps took her into the card room, a very serene place, with its pale green striped wallpaper and floral carpet. Three walls were almost entirely composed of modern screened windows, lightly veiled by sheer lace curtains, while a fireplace and the entrance door occupied the fourth wall. A round mahogany table held pride of place in the room's center, encircled by eight highly carved chairs upholstered in pale green velvet, which matched the wallpaper. Thankfully, the chairs looked sturdy and comfortable enough for a full night's card play.

A handful of gentlemen stood by a sideboard, chatting comfortably as a Negro houseman created a mint julep.

A shock slammed into Rosalind, harder than the *Pretty Lady* had hit the snag: Hal Lindsay was conversing with another gentleman by the window. Her pulse skipped a beat. For the first time, it betrayed her in a card room, as it had once before in a gilded Manhattan ballroom last Christmas.

Seen this close, he was just as appealing as he'd been in New York. He truly did enjoy a Viking's fierce beauty and coloring, highlighted by the knife scar on his jaw. He had the attractions of a self-made man, too, since he was famous for making his fortune without a penny from his wealthy family.

God forbid he should recognize her. If he returned her to New York . . . But she couldn't think about that, not and maintain her disguise.

Rosalind silently cursed her luck. She didn't need this sort of distraction when she was about to join the best private poker party in Kansas City. And she certainly couldn't afford to spend any time wondering what he'd look like without his exquisitely tailored clothes.

She wrenched her attention back to Taylor, who was now making an announcement to the room at large.

"Gentlemen, this is Frank Carstairs, a gentleman I met on the *Natchez* this winter. He's a square player and will be sailing on the *Cherokee Star* so you have a few days to take his measure."

The other men murmured their responses, as they looked the newcomer over. Rosalind bowed politely, privately amused at being introduced as an honest player. She did prefer legitimate methods of winning, even though Father had made sure she knew the dishonest ways as well.

"Let me introduce you to the other gentlemen, Carstairs. Starting on the left, Captain Peter Johnson of the *Osage Queen* and Mack Benton, his engineer. Phillip Logan, pilot of the *Palestine Belle*. Thomas Ratliff, a medical doctor who's our token landlubber."

Each man nodded as Taylor mentioned him, greetings Rosalind managed to return smoothly.

"Finally, Hal Lindsay, a licensed Missouri and Mississippi pilot and owner of a half-dozen first-class packets."

"Carstairs," Lindsay acknowledged the introduction. His voice was just as she remembered: a deep gravelly rumble that sent a delighted shiver down her spine.

"My pleasure, gentlemen." Rosalind bowed again. Thank God, Lindsay hadn't recognized her, and her reaction to the big pilot seemed to have gone unnoticed.

"Would you care for something to drink, Bellecourt? Carstairs? We have mint juleps, wine, or stronger spirits. There's also coffee or tea, if you'd prefer," Taylor invited.

Rosalind glanced around and saw that Benton was drinking coffee. She accepted the same from the houseman, pleased she'd been given the option to stay sober.

"How's the new dog, Lindsay?" Bellecourt asked, his voice carrying easily across the room.

Heads swiveled in interest.

Lindsay raised an eyebrow. "Sleeping at the house." He took a long swallow of his julep in its frosty silver mug.

Jaws dropped. The room, which had been softened by amiable chatter, was shocked and silent. Even the houseman froze, caught in the act of adding sugar to a silver drinking mug, as he stared at Lindsay.

Rosalind scanned the men's faces, trying to understand.

The doctor started to laugh. Others snickered. "Another stray? And this one is still with you? Thought they always left within an hour, Lindsay, same as your women."

Lindsay snorted. "He's just staying a little longer than most. Samuel will take him to that animal lover's farm in Independence tomorrow."

Bellecourt chuckled, his eyes dancing. "*Voyons,* this dog has lived with him for six hours, twice as long as the previous record. I've got five dollars that says the mongrel sails with him tomorrow."

Johnson laughed, and the rest quickly joined in. "You're losing your grip, Lindsay. You always said dogs, like children, were best avoided by men of sense."

Lindsay flushed slightly, but managed a response. "Just a small detour on my path to heaven, friends. By the time I return, the terrier will be gone and the sole topic of conversation will be you bemoaning your married states."

The men laughed at that prophecy and teased Lindsay a bit more before Taylor firmly brought them back to the business at hand.

The party took their seats at the table, chatting amiably, as gold and greenbacks emerged to be exchanged for ivory chips, all elegantly monogrammed with a "T" for Taylor. Rosalind adjusted her charcoal gray trousers automatically, the gesture well-practiced during her months of hiding from Lennox.

Then she settled her frock coat around her, so she could easily reach the Colts in her front waistband and the knife up her right sleeve. Just another set of movements she had performed hundreds of times since fleeing her guardian's Fifth Avenue mansion.

Finally settled, she glanced around the table to see the arrangement of players. Simple curiosity triggered that scan; she hadn't played with these men often enough to have any preferences for who would lead or follow her during a hand. Taylor to her left, then Bellecourt and Johnson. Benton, on her right, followed by Logan and Ratliff and—

Rosalind cursed silently, but kept her face masked: Lindsay would be directly opposite her. God willing, the cards would take her mind from him. As it was, he was far more interesting to her feminine side than David Rutherford had ever been, that coward who'd fled at the first sign of trouble.

Yet she'd once seen David as a marvel of masculinity. He'd enlisted after Ball's Bluff and served as a staff officer for three years, while other wealthy men bought substitutes and stayed fat and safe. She'd thought him a hero and enjoyed intimacies with him, in anticipation of their planned nuptials.

Hero. Bedroom.

Lindsay was a great wartime hero, as well as a very fine figure of a man. How would he treat the lucky woman in his bedroom?

A fiery lash jolted her, from throat to breasts to loins.

Her eyes widened. Her twin Colts shifted against her waist, reminding her of her masquerade.

She took a slow swallow of her hot coffee as she brought herself under control. She couldn't sleep with Lindsay, or anyone else, no matter how much her body clamored for the blinding, ecstatic release of physical pleasure.

"Seven-card stud is the game for tonight, gentlemen, and

the rules are posted on the wall," Taylor intoned with the ease of long habit as he shuffled a deck of cards.

Rosalind glanced at the professionally lettered placard that Taylor indicated. She'd seen its like more than once in gambling dens and quickly absorbed its guidance.

"Remember, there are no wild cards here; this is a game of skill, not chance," Taylor went on. "Ante is a half dollar; full bet is a quarter-eagle. All minimums will double at midnight, and again at two for those still playing. Any questions?" Taylor asked.

Rosalind shook her head and waited, chips neatly stacked in front of her. Two dollars and fifty cents for a full bet during a hand's first round of betting, doubling to five dollars when the fifth card was dealt. Doubling again at midnight, and once more in the early morning, to drive out casual players.

High stakes, but not the richest game she'd played as a professional gambler. Her two hundred dollars' worth of chips should be more than enough, without touching her hidden bankroll. Four months of running had taught her to always carry money, tucked away in more than one place.

Each man tossed a single chip, as ante, into the center and Taylor dealt the starting hand, two cards facedown to each player and the third card faceup.

Careful as ever not to let anyone else see her cards, Rosalind quickly checked her two hole cards and found a pair of queens. With the ten of diamonds as her door card, she had a splendid hand and an excellent chance at taking the pot. She could feel Father's ghost at her shoulder, beaming in anticipation of a win.

Her pleasure didn't show on her face as she set her hole cards neatly on the table before her, beyond suspicion of tampering, and waited for the betting to begin.

The two of hearts lay in front of Lindsay, the lowest card

visible, so he'd have to play—and bet—first. He studied his hole cards—his strong, elegant hands much too visible for Rosalind's comfort—then shrugged and tossed a quarter-eagle chip into the center.

Rosalind pondered Lindsay's move, given that a deuce was a surprising card to bring in a bet. Lindsay was either bluffing, had something very interesting hidden in his hole cards, or was simply a friendly guest, graciously betting in the first round. Since nothing about Lindsay struck her as either particularly gracious or inclined to bluff, she'd put her money that he held good cards.

Taylor handed Lindsay an elegant buckhorn-handled knife, acknowledging Lindsay's role as the first player to bet in this hand. "You've got the buck, Lindsay. Ratliff?"

The doctor, who sat to the left of Lindsay, shook his head and tossed his cards down. "Fold." He settled back in his chair with the comfortable air of someone intent on watching splendid entertainment.

Logan also quickly folded, but Benton considered the cards on the table with the calm surety of a seasoned gambler. He had a reputation for playing cards as aggressively as he built steam in his engines. Then he, too, tossed down a chip, betting a quarter-eagle on his jack of diamonds and hole cards.

Rosalind simply bet a quarter-eagle and waited for the other players to build up the pot so she could take it. The sheer contentment of being at a poker game once more wrapped around her like a sable cloak.

Hal folded on fifth street when Taylor dealt him his fifth card, yet another spade. He'd originally been dealt three hearts, hoping to see a flush if the gaming gods delivered him two more hearts. It hadn't happened, and now he settled back to

watch McKenzie and Benton—and the visiting poker shark—
battle over the pot.

Watching Bellecourt and Benton at a poker table was often
the best entertainment available in a Missouri River town.
Oh, Hal enjoyed poker well enough but not as much as those
two did. Sometimes in port, he would bathe, eat dinner, and
maybe have a woman at the local bawdy house. Then he'd return to the local gambling den to see the end of Benton and
Bellecourt's nightlong struggle.

Thank God, both of them were gracious losers, unlike
Nicholas Lennox. Losing a big poker game could drive that
dandy into a killing rage. Hal still carried a scar on his jaw
from stopping Lennox in New York, when that scum had
tried to carve up a *nymph du pave* after dropping five thousand dollars in a Tenderloin gambling den.

But tonight Carstairs was giving Bellecourt and Benton a
run for their money. He'd received a ten of hearts to match
his door card, the ten of diamonds, just in time for the doubled minimums at fifth street. His style now resembled the
clear-eyed aggression of a mountain lion stalking an ante-
lope.

Bellecourt matched Carstairs's wager, creating a larger
pot than usual for this early in the evening. Hal raised an
eyebrow, then returned to studying Carstairs.

The man had seemed spooked when he was introduced to
Hal, a familiar reaction. Many men were uneasy the first time
they met someone significantly taller than themselves. Now
that Carstairs's focus was on the cards, he was an entirely different fellow. Disciplined, aggressive, crisp in his speech and
movements. Calm even when a disappointing card was dealt,
like that trey of hearts on fourth street.

Altogether, he was exactly the sort Hal had sought for his
gunboat crew. He was a bit slender for naval duty but not too
much so. Many of those gangly ones could surprise you with

their stamina during action, despite seeming as weak as a woman.

Elegant hands, of course, with long, almost feminine fingers that handled the chips with the ease of long practice. He'd probably shuffle a deck like a magician.

He had unusual gray eyes, half veiled by thick dark lashes, which caught the light when he raised them to watch another player. Their bright color reminded Hal of the sun shining on the upper Missouri. He shrugged the fancy away as poetic and unrelated to card play.

Hal wondered idly how old Carstairs was, given his smooth cheeks. His skin was very fair, appropriate for his light-colored hair and eyes. But Hal would have expected to find some signs of age—at least the hint of a beard—given the gambler's obvious experience at a card table.

Then Carstairs turned his head to catch Bellecourt's latest quip. His profile was as pure as a Grecian statue, with a strand of light brown hair curling against his cheek. Another lock flowed down the nape of his neck like a woman's tresses.

Hal frowned. He'd seen a similar profile before, in a New York mansion. But there'd been an abundance of curls around the face and diamonds glinting in the woman's hair.

Ridiculous idea, to compare a man's looks to a woman's. And yet . . . Carstairs's build could be that of a tall, slender woman. The features were more suitable for a lady than a man, especially with the full lower lip. And those silver gray eyes with the long lashes were the very sort to inspire bad poetry.

Rosalind Schuyler, that runaway heiress, had gray eyes and honey brown hair.

But Carstairs couldn't be a woman. Female gamblers—professional ones, at least—made far more money than their male counterparts. They would joke, flirt, offer to play a private *game,* or two . . . then strip susceptible males of every penny.

Carstairs was doing no such thing. He hadn't flirted with any man at the table. In fact, he showed no awareness of the languishing glances Johnson had given him. He was simply playing a very good game of poker, as well or better than any man there.

Then Carstairs's eyes lit up as he laughed at Bellecourt's joke. A low, husky chuckle like the wonderful sound a woman makes when she's considering whether to join a man in the bedroom. It sent a frisson down Hal's spine and into his balls. He'd heard that laugh once before, from a tall beauty in a New York mansion.

Rosalind Schuyler, by all that was holy, had owned a sensual woman's husky voice. Deep enough to fool most men but unmistakable to someone who'd heard her before.

Carstairs was Rosalind Schuyler in disguise.

Hal shuddered slightly as his blood rushed south and into his cock.

By God, how did she pull off the masquerade? The sheer, blazing courage it took to travel alone for months at a time snatched his breath away. How had she managed to overcome her justifiable terror of boats?

He had to talk to her, win her confidence, and learn her secrets. His curiosity, his life's besetting sin, would accept nothing less. His cock vehemently agreed with his reasoning, as it eagerly pushed against his trousers.

Rosalind laid down her cards, showing two pairs of queens and tens, and gathered in her winnings.

"Two queens in the hole? No wonder you were pushing hard," Benton snorted as he tossed down his pair of jacks.

"Just lucky." She shrugged and started to stack her new chips before her.

Good winner, too. Hal would have expected that of someone with the sheer nerve to carry off a masquerade as big as hers.

"Well played," Hal said quietly.

"Thank you, sir," she returned, with a quick glance at him before she finished stacking her chips.

Carstairs was definitely Rosalind Schuyler. Her big gray eyes had glanced up at him, just like that, once before in his sister's Manhattan town house. Hal smiled privately as he waited for Bellecourt to deal the next hand. He might not be the best poker player on the Missouri, but he had always been able to put his hand on any woman he fancied.

Chapter Three

"And raise you ten," Lindsay said firmly, pushing the stack of chips into the center.

Baffled, Rosalind wondered what he could possibly be betting fifty dollars on, at fifth street. He might have a flush, if his hole cards were good. Or maybe a pair of aces in the hole. But no other possibilities came to mind, warranting such a large bet, especially with only two more rounds to be dealt. Surely, he had to be bluffing.

The elegant mantel clock struck midnight, every note as clear and true as the cards on the table.

"Minimums double on the next hand, gentlemen," Taylor announced. He'd already folded, as had Ratliff.

"Fold," Benton announced, walking away from an exposed pair of sevens. It would have won the last hand.

Rosalind quickly, and calmly, considered the chances of winning the pot with her ace and king. She could call Lindsay's bluff, if that's what he was doing. But it didn't seem likely; Lindsay was entirely too certain of himself, judging by how seldom he'd bluffed before. He had to have something solid. Besides, calling his bluff would cost her money rather than increase her chances of winning.

She, too, tossed in her cards.

Bellecourt, now the final player to oppose the big Viking,

eyed Lindsay suspiciously for a long moment. Finally, he spoke. "Fold."

Without a flicker, Lindsay gathered up the hundred-dollar pot. He never showed his winning hand, of course, not having been called on a bluff.

Then he pushed his chair back and stood up, triggering a general chorus of scraping chairs and grunts as others came to their feet. "That's it for me," he announced. "I'd best be off now, so I can reach the *Belle* early tomorrow."

"*Vous êtes sûr?* Perhaps you'll become even luckier when the bets double," Benton teased.

Lindsay chuckled. "You're just hoping to win back that fifty I took from you."

Benton laughed at that and the others joined in.

Rosalind smiled and stood up, careful not to stretch, lest the movement draw attention to her bosom.

"What are you carrying on this trip, Lindsay?" Johnson asked as he pushed his chair back. The other men began to mill about, clearly taking an expected break from the game.

Lindsay grimaced. "Spikes and some other supplies for the Northern Pacific."

"Those bastards!" Johnson snarled. "They expect us to carry their freight so they can build their damn railroads and put us out of business."

"Amen!" Benton agreed, his cup forgotten in his hand.

"Remember the *Effie Afton*? Fastest sidewheeler on the Mississippi until the Rock Island Bridge destroyed her. Goddamn railroads and the men who built them. They deliberately changed the currents to block riverboats," swore Logan, his first words not directed at poker.

There was a brief, reverent hush.

Rosalind watched curiously, surprised by the old pilot's anger. Rivermen on the Mississippi hated railroads, but they still managed to cooperate enough to divide up the cotton traffic.

"Remember the glory days before the war when you could see a dozen riverboats docked every day at Front Street?" Johnson growled. "When the hold was full every trip, passengers crowded the grand saloon, and men fought to sleep amidst the crates on the main deck? Now you're lucky to see half that many boats, thanks to those greedy railroad bastards. And wages are dropping like the temperatures during a Montana winter."

"Goddamn railroads and the men who own them. They steal freight, hijack passengers, and destroy the jobs of hardworking boatmen," Logan cursed.

"Amen." Johnson lifted his glass in salute, followed by the other men.

Rosalind blinked, touched her lips to her cup, but didn't drink. As a holder of New York Central and many other railroad stocks, she couldn't bring herself to join in a toast to the railroads' destruction.

"Peterkin sold the *Pride of St. Charles* for kindling last week," Lindsay said quietly, swirling the dregs in his silver mug. "God forbid I ever have to do anything like that to the *Belle*. I'd rather see her go down fighting, smashed against a railroad bridge."

Grief and anger rang through the room as men told stories of Peterkin's skills and the *Pride*'s travels. Rosalind had heard similar tales hundreds of times before on Mississippi riverboats, none of which had weakened her preference for railroads. Ignoring the heated words as much as possible, she considered whether she should convert any of her winnings to greenbacks while in Kansas City, rather than carry the gold's weight.

Eventually, Logan and Johnson left the room with Taylor, still fulminating about railroads, while Bellecourt asked the houseman for another cup of coffee.

"Care for a lift back to town, Carstairs?" Lindsay offered casually.

"You didn't ride Nelson?" Bellecourt asked, joining them.

"No, I've got Jones hitched to the buggy. I left Nelson at the farm since I expected to be spending time in town with my sister and her husband."

Bellecourt nodded. "You might take him up on it, Carstairs, if you want to leave any time soon. Benton and I always play until dawn, and Ratliff isn't likely to leave much earlier than that."

Rosalind considered the offer for a moment, then nodded. She'd prefer to get a little sleep before daylight and its increased chance of facing Lennox's hounds. "Thank you kindly, sir. I'd appreciate that."

"Good. See you tomorrow morning, Bellecourt."

"My thanks for your hospitality, sir," Rosalind said sincerely, as she shook Taylor's hand at the door. "Please convey my respects to your wife."

"Our pleasure, Carstairs. As she said, please consider our home your own whenever you're in Kansas City."

"Thank you, sir." She settled her hat back on her head and followed Lindsay down the stairs to his buggy, a very modern and elegant equipage, with a handsome gray hitched to it. The seat was extremely comfortable, beautifully upholstered in soft leather.

Lindsay was an excellent driver and not given to conversation, so she remained quiet as well. The heat of his big body, noticeable even on a humid spring night, and a faint sandalwood scent filled her senses, making her achingly conscious of his masculinity.

She took a deep breath, enjoying the aromas of fine leather and lilacs on the soft breeze. The buggy was superbly sprung and the horse had an uncommonly smooth gait, making the journey seem like a magic carpet ride. The road glimmered under a distant lightning flash, winding between cornfields and over the bluffs towards the town beyond. She had so many happy memories of driving home to Oak Hill on nights like this.

Rosalind was almost in a trance, as the buggy crested yet another hill, when he finally spoke. His voice was a deep, soft rumble that blended perfectly with the horse's hoofbeats and the wheels' quiet travel over the dusty road.

"Excellent tailoring you have. Disguises your womanly figure very well," he remarked gently.

"Thank you." She stifled a yawn, then realized what he'd said. And that she'd agreed. *Damn.*

Her fingers twitched, automatically reaching for her guns. She'd killed a man once before. Did she need to do so again? She tried to recover with a bluff. "Sorry, sir, but what did you say?"

Even in the faint light, she could see his smile. "You heard me, Carstairs. Or should I say Miss Schuyler?"

Blinding terror rose up, chilling her to the bone. Her limbs were leaden weights. But her blood raced through her veins, driven by the frantic beat of her heart. She considered jumping out of the buggy but where could she go? They were deep in farmland, too far to find help or quickly reach the city.

Gritting her teeth, she slid her hands over her guns. They gave her enough courage to beat her panic back. "Don't be ridiculous, Lindsay."

"Stop fretting, Rosalind," he said dryly, with a sidelong glance at her. "I won't expose your masquerade."

"Why not?"

He shrugged. "The longer the railroads hunt you, the more foolish they appear."

She stared at him, digesting his words. He looked relaxed and unafraid of her guns, even with his hands busy on the reins. Given how much rivermen hated the railroads, he just might be telling the truth.

Oddly, his brusqueness reassured her, where elegant

speeches would have been unnerving. Or perhaps it was the deep, velvety rumble of his voice—curt as before, but now offering support—that put her at ease.

The horse's gait changed, then steadied as the buggy began to climb a steep bluff. Lightning flashed again beyond the city.

She searched his face for a long moment, then yielded reluctantly. "You're very perceptive, Lindsay."

"Am I the first to realize you're a woman?"

She nodded slowly. As far as she knew, Lennox's hounds were still asking for Rosalind Schuyler, not Frank Carstairs. She suspected they'd come so close so many times due to bloody-minded thoroughness, not because they'd discovered her disguise.

"My lucky night then," Lindsay purred, casting an all-too-perceptive glance at her from under his fashionable bowler.

She remembered suddenly that he was a licensed Mississippi pilot, where boats regularly traveled by night. He must be able to see as well as any cat in the dark.

"Have a drink with me at my house," he invited. "Perhaps share a few tales of men you've fooled with that disguise."

She was silent. She could not—should not—agree to his offer. Yet she wanted to spend time with this man, more than with any other she'd ever met.

Her Colts' ivory handles pressed against her waist comfortingly. She'd killed a man before who'd tried to rob her. Surely, she could defend herself successfully again.

His voice rumbled again in the warm darkness. "My word that I mean no harm to you."

Hours spent at the card table with him had taught her something of his character, enough to be confident that he'd keep his word. And he had rescued that poor stray terrier, after all. Plus, it would be so pleasant to talk to someone who knew the truth.

Perhaps she could let down her guard a little, just this once. And if the worst happened, then she still had her guns for protection.

"Very well," she agreed slowly and ignored the warmth building between her legs at the thought of being with him.

Saying yes seemed a huge gamble. She stared straight ahead and tried to convince herself she'd come out a winner in the morning. All the while, the heat of his big, strong body seeped into her senses until she could barely breathe, let alone think.

A long roll of thunder echoed in the distance.

She'd driven with David more than once without losing her wits. But now strange thoughts crept into her mind, such as resting her hand on Lindsay's thigh to see if it was as hard with muscle as it looked. Or trailing her fingers over the back of his hand and then up his arm to test the varying textures of skin and linen. Or pressing a kiss to his cheek and filling her nostrils with his scent.

Or unbuttoning his shirt, leaning her head against his chest, and listening to the sound of his heartbeat. Then sleeping in his arms without worrying about detectives pounding on the door, shouting about a missing railroad heiress . . .

It had been so damned long since someone had held her close and safe. She'd almost sign away all her shares for someone who'd protect her, even for an hour.

The horse turned from the muddy road onto a long gravel driveway, finally stopping in front of a large house. It was a gracious house, solidly built as befitted a bachelor owner, with a limestone ground floor and a shingled second floor. A panel of pale limestone blocks rose above the gracious white columned front entry, crowned by an enormous fan window. A two-story white porch stood at each end of the house and neatly shingled gables popped up on the roof.

The grounds were spacious, notable for sweeping lawns,

lavishly blooming lilacs, and scattered shade trees. The gardens extended to the edge of a steep hill, with city buildings and the Missouri's broad expanse glimmering beyond. A conservatory's many glass panes glittered on the far side of the driveway.

Rosalind was stunned by the house's comfort and serenity. Despite its size, it was a home more than a mansion. She almost expected children to come running out the door, eager to welcome their father.

Instead, a sturdy Negro man emerged from the carriage house, at the back of the drive, and greeted Lindsay with the familiarity of an old servant. "Evenin', sir."

"Good evening, Samuel." Lindsay jumped down from the buggy and handed over the reins. Rosalind descended on the other side, trying not to think about her reaction to the house and its owner. She reminded herself that if she had to run, she could grab a horse from the carriage house and race toward the city.

"Will you want the buggy if you go out again tonight?" the servant asked. His eyes skimmed over Rosalind incuriously, then returned to his master.

She relaxed slightly. She'd been dismissed yet again as just another slender man.

A dog barked once from inside, and Lindsay stiffened before answering. "If we do, we'll ride instead of driving, Samuel, so you're free to go to bed."

The dog barked again, and again. Lindsay bit his lip and glanced at the big house.

Rosalind blinked. He'd been self-contained and silent while playing poker, even when he'd won that last big pot.

"Yes, sir. Good night, sir," Samuel added politely, nodding to Rosalind. Humming a plantation melody, he led the horse and buggy toward the big carriage house.

Lindsay headed for the house, with Rosalind at his side.

The dog was barking continuously now, so Lindsay's words were barely audible as he opened the front door. "Welcome to my home, Rosalind. What would you like to drink?"

Rosalind stepped inside but barely spared a glance at her surroundings. Her attention was fixed on the immaculate Irish terrier poking its head between the banister railings on the top floor. It was silent for a moment before it barked again, even louder than before, its eyes fixed on Lindsay.

"Devil take it, hasn't anyone been looking after that dog?" Lindsay grumbled, hanging his hat beside the door. "Ezra!"

He pounded his fist against his hand as he stared upward. The dog wagged its hind end violently, making its shoulders knock against the banisters. Then it pulled back and limped toward the stairs, trailing a man's red flannel undershirt behind it.

"Damnit, you should be in the carriage house," Lindsay growled. "What the devil was Ezra thinking of?" He started up the stairs slowly, grumbling threats at the absent Ezra under his breath, while Rosalind hung up her hat and watched.

The terrier was nearly frantic with excitement now, and its gait was very unsteady. It wobbled as it reached the carpet runner leading down the stairs, but didn't hesitate, its eyes still fixed on Lindsay. One foreleg stepped down, the other moved to follow . . . and the little fellow lost its balance, shoulders plunging forward as it started to tumble.

Lindsay lunged upward and caught the dog before it could roll down the stairs. His feet slipped and he fell full-length onto the carpeted oak treads. Twisting, he rolled to protect the rascal, landing on his back with the dog clutched to his chest. It wriggled, whined, and licked his face, vibrating with happiness.

"Damn," Lindsay muttered and sat up slowly, still holding his pet.

Rosalind coughed, trying to cover a giggle as she reached the landing. Lindsay glared at her as he hoisted the dog over his shoulder and up to the top of the stairs. The dog tried to turn around, but the flannel undershirt had become a tight knot between him and the man, keeping him immobile. He whined.

Lindsay cursed.

Rosalind giggled.

Lindsay glared at her as if he'd like to see her drawn and quartered.

Rosalind choked and helplessly giggled again.

A wizened Negro man burst into the foyer. "Did the dog . . . I'm sorry, sir. I thought he was asleep for the night." He didn't sound apologetic in the least.

Lindsay cast him a fulminating stare, but the other was unmoved. "What the devil is this dog doing in the house, Ezra?" He yanked at the flannel, but it was firmly caught on one of the brass rods holding the Oriental carpet against the oak stairs.

"He continued to bark after you left, sir. So I brought him in, gave him the shirt to guard, and he was quiet again. Do you need any help?"

"No," Lindsay said shortly, as he finally freed himself. The dog, however, was still bound to the carpet rods and whimpered plaintively. Lindsay said something quite rude under his breath.

Rosalind laughed out loud, and Lindsay's eyes promised her retribution even as he spoke to Ezra. "Just be ready to re-join the *Belle* tomorrow. I'll look after the dog. Good night."

"Good night, sir." Ezra, obviously an intelligent man, disappeared without a backward glance.

Choking down a giggle, Rosalind leaned down and quickly freed the shirt from the dog and the stairs.

Lindsay yanked her down across him and kissed her. Fast and hard, his tongue dived between her teeth.

She stiffened, affronted by the unexpected familiarity.

His mouth gentled. His tongue delicately caressed her lips as he rumbled something persuasive.

She sighed, captivated, and her jaw relaxed, admitting him. Then it was too late for objections as her sanity fled under his expert attentions.

He kissed like a devil intent on sweeping a woman's soul away. His neat goatee caressed her cheeks and chin as his tongue claimed hers. He tasted of bourbon and sugar . . . and man. She moaned, and her fingers caressed the whisker stubble on his cheeks. He was warm, and real, and infinitely better than any lonely dream.

Lindsay growled something and stood up, lifting her into his arms as if she were a petite demoiselle, not an overly tall Amazon. Fire flowed down her spine, from her throat to her core, at his easy mastery of her.

"What the devil do you think you're doing?" Rosalind gasped, stunned by how easily he carried her. Her breasts firmed, all too aware of the heat of his big body.

"What do you think?" Lindsay wasn't even slightly winded.

"Put me down!" she protested, trying to deny her own reaction to him.

"Not yet."

"What if Ezra thinks you're making love to a man? Won't he gossip?"

Lindsay laughed. "He knows me better than to think I prefer men. Besides, he'd keep his mouth shut, even if I slept with pigs."

She considered shouting for help but decided against it: Only his servants could hear her. Besides, the warmth building between her legs made it difficult to argue with him.

The terrier limped after them, his tail wagging jauntily. The undershirt was now just a distant lump on the carpet, an inconsequential oddity in the magnificent hallway.

* * *

Hal pushed open a door and dropped her on his big carved mahogany bed, taken by his godfather from a British merchantman during the War of 1812. The crystal lamps and brocade coverlet had come from France by way of New Orleans during the last war; legally paid for, unlike the bed. Winds from an approaching thunderstorm set the Irish lace curtains to dancing at the windows. Lightning sparked the sky in nature's fireworks.

But his prize was more unique than anything captured by his ancestors. He'd beguiled her into his house as neatly as he'd grabbed that last pot at Taylor's house with an unexpected bluff. And now he could savor her to the fullest.

She fascinated him. He had a million questions for her, ranging from how she'd managed to disguise herself to her opinions on lower Mississippi riverboat traffic. But none of them came to his lips, not once he'd felt her lovely ass as he carried her. He needed more of the woman hidden inside that far-too-concealing frock coat.

His cock lengthened at the prospect.

Hal caressed her jaw lightly, surprised at how his fingers trembled. "Where did you get the name Frank Carstairs from?" he asked hoarsely.

She tilted her head slightly to consider him. Hal smiled inwardly; of course, his little poker shark would want to think first. He'd enjoy burning all that cool consideration out of her. Damn, he'd like to see her knocked off balance and into overwhelming lust, after watching her icy control at the poker table.

"My mother's maiden name was Carstairs," she answered slowly. He continued to fondle her, wondering how he'd ever mistaken cheeks this smooth for a man's.

"And Frank?" His fingers trailed through the fine locks of hair at her temples.

"My second name is Frances." Her head turned slightly to follow his touch.

"Mine is Andronicus." Hal traced the outer curve of her ear and knew he deserved a medal for making conversation when his cock was this hard. But he needed to wait, needed to seduce her, his little poker shark, who was all too comfortable with the guns at her waist. Damn, she was a better challenge than piloting the *Belle* through the great rapids before Fort Benton.

"Henry is your first name?"

Hal's mouth thinned briefly. No one, except his father, had ever addressed him as Henry, and he'd never accepted that hated name from a lover.

Rosalind's breath caught as his fingers teased the pulse point under her jaw.

"Indeed. But you'll call me Hal tonight." He breathed the last syllables against her lips before he kissed her again.

And he'd wager a year's profits that this lady wouldn't bore him within an hour, unlike every other respectable woman he'd ever met.

Rosalind's willpower fled as soon as his lips met hers again. Her body had even less interest in maintaining sanity this time than it had exhibited on the stairs. Months of loneliness fled, banished by the hunger racing through her blood, fueled by his demanding mouth and hands.

His hand fondled her back and swept down over her ass, cupping it and pulling her close. She moaned and wiggled against him, driven half wild by the first feel of his magnificent hard cock, outlined by his trousers' rough wool. The scent of lilacs spilled into the room from the garden beyond, like a call to sensual delights.

He growled something and slid his hand inside the back of her waistband.

Rosalind jerked and stared up at Hal, panting for breath. How had he known she loved to have her backside fondled?

Her breasts ached for his touch, her pulse thundered through her veins, and heat pulsed and melted and then pooled between her thighs. "Hal," she moaned.

He stared down at her, his chest rising and falling rapidly. His eyes blazed blue fire, like a pirate gazing at golden treasure. "Damn, I need to see you."

Fire seared her at the hunger in his gaze and his fierce growl. She managed a weak nod, but he didn't wait for her permission as he lit a single lamp beside the bed.

Lightning scorched the air outside. The distant electrical storm was coming closer.

Hal's fingers made short work of undoing her string tie and crisp wing collar. He growled softly as he kissed the pulse at the base of her throat. The vibration ran through her blood, bringing more dew onto her thighs. She shuddered and arched under his kiss. She caught his head, her fingers plunging into his silky hair as her thumb brushed the scar on his jaw.

He kissed and licked her throat before slipping her collar aside to explore other sensitive spots. Rosalind jerked and moaned, her head tossing against the brocade coverlet. She clutched his shoulders desperately, her fingers digging into the hard muscle under the fine linen. His scent reached her, a mix of sandalwood and male musk.

He nipped her lightly, then licked the hurt until she sobbed for more. Her black wool vest yielded to his impatient fingers, and Rosalind gasped at her sudden ability to catch a deep breath.

"It's too damn stiff for a typical vest," he muttered and bent the edge over his hand. It stuck out awkwardly, like a breastplate and without the fluid grace of first-rate merino wool. "Is that how you do it? Built a corset inside your vest so no one can see your breasts?"

She licked her lip and tried to answer. But the hunger in his voice seemed to have snatched away her voice.

"Well, tonight this fellow is going to have a damn good time with your breasts," he growled, his eyes sweeping over her as if trying to decide what portion to taste first. "And you'll enjoy every minute of it."

Suddenly her clothes were too confining against the heated blaze of her skin.

Hal rapidly unbuttoned her shirt, somehow managing not to rip anything, made equally fast work of her undershirt's buttons, then pulled it open to expose her.

Rosalind stilled, her breath catching in her throat. Her breasts were flushed and pointed, surmounted by her nipples' hard little peaks. Would he find her lacking in feminine charms?

"Perfect," Hal growled and dived for her nipple.

Rosalind shrieked at the fiery lance that blasted through her body. She arched until her hips nearly came off the bed. His hand cupped her mound, perhaps for reassurance or to control her, as he suckled her. She sobbed her pleasure, unable to form words.

He paid equal attention to her other breast as he rubbed her woolen trousers against her mound. Rhythmically, again and again, matching the tempo of his mouth working her. The roughness incited her delicate skin to further gushes of dew.

She writhed under him, her hips moving to the beat he set. "Hal," she groaned. "Hal, do that again. Please."

"Beautiful. You are so goddamn beautiful," he muttered as he switched breasts.

She couldn't even think well enough to wonder why he said so. Instead, his deep rumble heated her veins like a glass of Scots whiskey. And she cursed him when he took his hands away, in language better suited for Mississippi levees, but he simply chuckled.

He removed her Colts from her waistband and laid them

on the bed, next to her hips. A few practiced moves by his strong hands saw her trousers open just enough to expose her canvas money belt.

She watched him, panting, unconcerned about anything except regaining those wicked fingers of his.

"Of course, your money's concealed but you wear your guns openly. Damn, but you're sexy with all these hidden surprises," he muttered. He shuddered slightly and his tongue ran out over his lips. He laid a kiss on her belly, where bare skin showed above the last button. She shivered, and her eyes fell shut.

He finished unbuttoning her trousers, pulled her shirt free, and paused to stare. "Men's drawers too? Christ, you're a special lady," he growled softly as he lightly touched her linen drawers.

His words triggered another gush of dew onto her thighs and she cursed. She'd claw his eyes out if he didn't do something, anything, to fill her.

He chuckled, a harsh broken sound, before his hand delved into her drawers, one callused finger finding her clit with arrogant ease. She moaned and her legs tightened around him. He fondled her, exploring her folds until she thought she'd scream. His hand left her, and she snarled, "Goddamnit, get your hand back there!"

Hal chuckled as he brought two fingers back to her pleasure. She groaned as he worked her, and she sobbed her gratitude when he circled her needy channel. One finger slipped in and she gasped.

"You're a tight one, aren't you, Rosalind? Will you take another finger for me?"

"Yes! Just finish me, damn you."

He chuckled and plunged two fingers into her channel.

Rosalind howled and arched at the invasion. She'd only taken David's member twice, and her body seemed to have forgotten the knack.

Hal's hand stayed motionless. "Not much accustomed to men, are you, sweet Rosalind? Take a deep breath."

He nuzzled her breast. "And another."

Heat shimmered through her skin.

He swirled his tongue around her nipple, then nibbled it gently. "And another . . ."

Her pulse speeded and she shuddered. Her inner muscles slowly melted around those strong digits inside her as he suckled her.

"Good girl. Now relax, then tighten." His fingers moved a fraction further in, then out. Her channel promptly clamped around him in protest.

"That's my girl," he praised hoarsely. "Now we go faster."

And he did. One hand thrust into her faster and faster, while the other squeezed her breast. She writhed and moaned, her hips rising and falling in a rhythm as old as time.

He added another finger until she was stretched wider than she'd ever been before. She wanted a climax, demanded a climax, couldn't believe there was anything else he could do that wouldn't provide a climax.

Yet still Hal pumped her, harder and faster, until her entire body was ablaze with heat and passion. Need built deep in her core, stoked by his wicked fingers pushing her into an agony of need.

Lightning burst from the skies, but Rosalind paid no heed. She flung her head back and cursed him, begged him, promised him anything, if he'd just finish her.

But his hand continued to ride her until she was a being of fire and hunger, completely focused on his touch and the agonizing pleasure he promised.

Her climax came closer and closer, but she couldn't quite reach it. She sobbed in frustration, thrashing against the coverlet.

Thunder crashed overhead and rain poured from the heavens.

"Take it, Rosalind. Come for me now," Hal snarled. He pressed down hard on her clit and waves exploded through her core and up her spine, like an engine's steam bringing the train's wheels to life. She howled soundlessly as the orgasm burst through every fiber of her being, changing her into a sensual being she'd barely glimpsed before.

Purring with delight afterward, Rosalind stretched and considered her prospects. She was still fully dressed except for her money belt and bow tie, both lying on the bedside table. Her frock coat was open, as was her shirt. She flexed her fingers and easily managed to touch her Colts.

Rain pounded on the roof and poured past the windows, filling the room with its delectable fresh-washed scent. Another lightning bolt flashed across the clouds, but farther away than before.

She turned her head toward the window and saw Hal beside his sea chest, stripping out of his clothes with ferocious haste. He was a magnificent sight, all broad shoulders and heavily muscled masculinity in the golden lamplight. Blond hair and a few puckered bullet scars marked his body, somehow adding to his attraction. A golden king of the beasts.

Mouth dry and guns forgotten, Rosalind rolled onto her side and leaned up on her elbow to see him better. Given his notorious distaste for good women, he was no candidate for a husband. But that was of no account now, only the chance to drown her senses in his arms.

Oddly, his shoulders and buttocks were completely covered by a network of silvery diamond-shaped scars, reminding her of an escaped slave's flogging scars. But these marks were very different. They were too regular, as opposed to the branching pattern left by a whip, and they were far more numerous on his buttocks, even marking the top of his thighs. Who could possibly have done that to him and why?

Then he turned around and her breath stopped. Dear God in heaven, he had an enormous cock. It neatly matched the rest of him, but would have seemed a monster on a smaller man. It was certainly longer and much thicker than David's member.

She stared, openmouthed. And moisture surged out of her core as if her previous climax had never happened.

Chapter Four

Hal tossed his drawers aside and began to don a condom. He'd barely managed the good sense to excavate a tin of those necessities from the sea chest, as protection against paternity. None of them lay anywhere else in this room, since he'd never brought a lover home before.

He always used condoms with a lover, whether friend or paid professional. He'd seen enough whores, grown rotten from syphilis, to rank pregnancy and disease as equal threats. Rosalind bore no signs of the pox, but he needed the sheath as defense against her fertility.

Something thumped against the carpet.

Hal glanced back at the bed and growled his appreciation. Blood raced into his cock, driving out any plans for leisurely seduction.

Damn, she was beautiful. Heavy-lidded eyes, tousled curls, mouth swollen and flushed—all evidence of her passion and an enticing contrast to her masculine attire. A single rosy nipple peeped out of her shirt.

Rosalind dropped another boot on the floor and yanked her suspenders off her shoulders. Her guns now rested on the bedside table, beyond easy reach. "Problem, sailor?"

"No, ma'am," Hal answered sincerely. "In fact, I'm mighty glad you decided to come aboard."

She tugged her shirt and undershirt over her head, muffling her response. "We're not there yet, sailor. And you're still overdressed."

He reached her just as she swung her feet down to the floor and stood up. "Just where the hell do you think you're going, little lady?" he purred as he tilted her chin up. A corner of his mind chortled that she hadn't looked at her guns once since she'd entered his bedroom.

"I love hearing you call me that," she purred. "It makes me feel fragile and eager to be protected." Long, slender fingers wrapped around his cock and squeezed. His eyes crossed as an ecstatic jolt blasted up his spine.

Wits fled and instinct took over. His mouth crashed down on hers and she surged upward into his kiss. He groaned encouragement and pulled her closer, shuddering slightly as one ruby-tipped breast tormented his chest. He kneaded her ass, rocking against her in anticipation.

Rosalind moaned into his mouth and wrapped one leg over his hip, opening herself further to his insistent cock. Her trousers' rough wool scratched his legs and his ass, in sharp counterpoint to their mouths' wet heat. His cock, dripping in eagerness, rubbed her belly's smooth skin and hardened further. Heat raged through his body, fueled by contact with her bold tongue and hard nipples. For someone who was as tight as a virgin, she had a delicious way of making her wants known.

She pulled away suddenly. He rumbled disapproval.

"Too much clothing," she answered succinctly, shoved her trousers and drawers off her hips, and sat down on the bed, clearly intent on her socks. Hal caught her slender, exquisitely feminine foot and lifted it for a kiss. She shrieked softly as she fell over backward.

A second later, both socks joined her boots on the floor and Hal stepped between her legs, his cock teasing her creamy folds. "Are you ready for me yet, my dear?"

"What do you mean? Of course, I'm ready."

"Or perhaps you could endure a bit of teasing," he murmured. He stroked her inner thighs' sensitive skin, watching her closely. No hardship that—an aroused woman was the most beautiful sight in the world, except for a fast riverboat.

"What on earth . . ." She quivered and her hips circled towards him. Dew gushed out of her core and over his cock. He stopped breathing for a moment before he could recover.

Later, he promised his inner hedonist, licking his lips. Later, I'll feast on her and explore her taste.

He fondled her again, finding his way through her womanly folds. Her petals, flushed raspberry pink to cherry red, dusted with golden brown hairs and glistening with dew, reminded him of a rare flower. Perhaps an orchid, captured in the jungle at great risk. And the way her clit stood bold and erect, scarlet with eagerness and free from its demure hood, made it a treasure to capture any man's eyes.

"Hal, are you planning to torture me?" Rosalind snarled and wrapped her legs around his hand. Her hips twisted against him, and her folds fluttered against his wrist.

His balls tightened in response. The need to confirm her comfort faded, washed away by the call of her musk and how her channel rippled around his fingers.

He stepped closer still and leaned over her. She reached up to him, their lips met, and his cockhead nudged her folds. She shifted restlessly, and his cock slipped inside her.

Hal froze, shuddering as her snug channel quivered around his cockhead. For a moment, he wished her dew could glide down his naked cock, then he put that folly aside. His cock didn't care about the chance of richer sensations; his cock simply wanted all of her. Now.

She moaned again. Her legs wrapped around his hips. Her fingers threaded through his hair. "Oh yes, sailor."

Hal pressed into her slowly, biting his lip against the urge to rush. Her beautiful gray eyes were half closed in bliss, as she arched and quivered. Her pussy rippled around his cock, dew flowing as she gradually accepted him. Damn, what a heady rapture she was, akin to finding a new path through a river's chutes.

He reminded himself fiercely she was only a brief diversion, not a longtime lover.

Finally, his cock was completely inside her. He shuddered again as his balls rubbed her satiny skin and her golden brown thatch caressed him. Rosalind moaned. Her hips circled, then pushed hard against him.

Hal gasped at how her channel tightened around his cock. Sanity frayed as he focused on her delights. His woman, the treasure that he alone had found and captured. Damn, she was beautiful as her cleft framed his cock.

He rode her slowly at first, letting her gasps and moans fill the air and make his pulse pound. Her sheath rippled and pulsed around his cock, spurring him on with heat. He varied his thrusts, trying different angles and strengths of approach. Some tightened her around him, some gave him more room to maneuver, some made her channel grab him like a gloved fist.

She trembled and sobbed his name. She wrapped her legs around his hips and threw back her head, moaning. Her rich voice grew huskier still as her orgasm's shimmering brilliance came closer and closer.

He shifted his grip, slipped his arms under and behind her shoulders. Pulled her down onto his cock with all the strength he could muster.

She shattered once, twice around him. Her muscles gripped him, seeking to pull him into passion's whirlpool.

Hal threw back his head and groaned, gritting his teeth as he fought to lengthen the pleasure spiraling between them. Sweat dripped down his face, his hunger for her driving his pulse into a frenzy. The wet slap of their flesh was louder than the rain against the windows. His harsh gasps for air raked his lungs. None of that mattered. Only the need to spill himself into the silken woman wrapped around his cock.

Rosalind started to climb again for the pinnacle. Her channel pulsed again and again, sending shockwaves into his cock. Hal bit his lip in agony, desperate to bring her with him one more time.

His thrusts' speed increased. Need built deep in his loins. Orgasm threatened, heedless of any demand for patience. Damn, but she was beautiful as she writhed under his pounding.

He nipped her earlobe. She gasped and climaxed with a shriek. Deep convulsions racked her body, from her neck down to her legs, and snatched him into orgasm. Rapture blazed through his spine and sprang from his balls through his cock. He poured himself out in a series of waves that shattered him like a spring tornado.

Finally he collapsed on her, too spent to move. Her breath caressed his shoulder, then settled into the smooth rhythms of sleep.

Dear God in heaven, how could a near-virgin wring him out like this? He knew his legs wouldn't hold him, a condition that usually resulted from ending a long abstinence by dalliance with a skillful lover. Neither circumstance held true tonight, given that he'd last enjoyed a woman two days ago.

What would it be like to frolic with her for a few days, or a week? His cock twitched at the images that question evoked. A definite vote in favor of a week with this lover, not the more typical few hours.

Hal snorted. She's only here for a night, he reminded his eager cock. Best make the most of it.

Rosalind roused to find herself still sprawled across the bed. A man's tongue circled her nipple. And again.

"What?" she mumbled and tried to blink her eyes open.

"Roll over on your side, my dear."

Strong, rough hands aided her. She muttered something uncomplimentary about anyone who'd demand movement from an exhausted woman but went where he indicated.

Then he bent her upper leg so her knee rose into the air.

"What the hell!" Rosalind half-reared up to look at him.

"Perfect." He laid his head on her thigh.

In the lamp's clear golden light, she could see them both all too clearly—including her utter nudity and complete availability to the man between her legs. What could possibly be his intentions? She gulped and tried to frame a question.

He trailed a single finger through her folds, then kissed her intimately.

"Hal!"

He nuzzled her, his goatee lightly brushing her delicate skin. Rosalind shivered at the rush of sensation.

"Try to keep your legs open as long as possible, Rosalind. I've a mind to feast on you."

She choked, stuttered something that didn't resemble words. She'd enjoyed mouthing David, performing fellatio as the books called it. And he'd been willing to tongue her, even though he preferred using his hand to pleasure her so that he'd stay ready. But it hadn't felt like this.

Nothing she'd heard or done before had prepared her for her lover feasting on her like a fruit sorbet. Especially when he was blatantly aroused and the clock suggested only a few minutes had passed since he'd so magnificently spent himself.

Rosalind moaned at one particularly devilish swirl of his tongue over her clit. And found herself wondering if she'd be able to walk in the morning, given this man's evident appetites.

It was a very long time, more filled with rapture than

she'd have deemed possible, before his mouth moved up her body. When he finally let sleep claim her, she did so restlessly, made uneasy by her first time sharing a bed with a man. She tossed and turned, slipping in and out of dreams. Then the nightmare returned, sending her back to her guardian's yacht on the afternoon everything changed. . . .

A few gleams of weak winter sunlight crept past the heavy velvet draperies but couldn't brighten the atmosphere within the yacht's grand saloon. Ornate rosewood and marble tables rose and fell as the boat crossed the restless sea, while the red brocade walls echoed her growing anger. She'd never tolerated Nicholas Lennox well, but this encounter bid fair to be worse than any other. Returning aboard her guardian's yacht to Manhattan from her father's funeral on Long Island was already her definition of a nightmare. She'd trembled and wept with every step as she forced herself up the gangplank. But this conversation threatened to turn her into a virago.

Lennox scowled at her, his hand resting on the brilliantly covered chair. Her obstinacy had worn away his usually smooth phrases until only the greedy predator remained. "You are absurd to cling to any hope that David Rutherford will return," he bit out.

Rosalind returned his glare just as ferociously, the multitude of pleats and frills on her black silk dress quivering with her anger. If nothing else, David's love of her late father's connections should bring him back to her side. "David Rutherford knows that I am the only woman for him."

Lennox laughed harshly. "Rutherford sleeps with his stepmother."

Rosalind's jaw dropped. "Impossible!" She rallied herself. "You are lying."

He sneered triumphantly. "I was with them more than

once. Do you want the details? How her bedroom is decorated? The crescent-shaped birthmark on his hip?"

Rosalind swallowed hard, recognizing the truth. Grief pierced her—and a strange lack of surprise.

"I told him to leave you or I'd spread the news of his liaison in every Manhattan club. I need your money far more than he does."

David might be gone forever, but she didn't have to accept Lennox. "Nonsense. I will never marry you."

He took a step toward her, and his hand lifted as if to strike her. Alarm skittered across her nerves, stronger than the caution she always felt when entering a wolf trap.

Rosalind raised her chin proudly, refusing to back down. He'd never touch her, not on her guardian's yacht.

His eyes narrowed, and he grabbed her by the shoulders. Two dots of hectic color appeared high on his cheekbones. "I have arranged the ceremony for Sunday, at my family estate," he snarled and shook her, repeating his prior announcement.

Affronted by his rough handling, Rosalind's temper snapped. "I'll never marry a bootlicker like you!" She tried to kick him in the balls, but her skirts muffled the blow.

He freed one hand and slapped her hard. Her ears rang as she staggered. Her heel caught in her dress's train, and she fell down. She landed hard on the scarlet Bokhara carpet, barely missing the sharp edge of a great, carved bureau.

Lennox stood over her with clenched fists. "You will marry me!"

She rolled onto her knees. She desperately wanted her Colts for this conflict, but they were locked away in her sea chest. Still, she fought on with words. "Never."

His booted foot crashed into her side and sent her crashing against the bureau. Rosalind screamed as agony slashed through her.

He kicked her again. Pain exploded in her chest. She

curled into a fetal position as another, and yet another blow smashed into her.

"Miss Rosalind?" Bridget O'Hara, Rosalind's maid and best friend, burst into the grand saloon just as Lennox kicked Rosalind once more.

Bridget wailed like a banshee, a long shrill cry that sounded like a summons of old Irish gods. Lennox whirled toward her.

"Damn you, be quiet, bitch!"

His tone sent a chill through Rosalind. "Bridget, no," she gasped.

Bridget screamed again. Lennox pulled a small revolver from his pocket and shot her in the forehead. The little maid collapsed onto the carpet, her sightless eyes staring at Rosalind from less than a yard away.

Rosalind's instinctive cry was choked off by the flaming agony in her sides. *Bridget, murdered by Lennox? Dear God, no.* She fought for air, trying to breathe as shallowly as possible. She swallowed cautiously, tasting what came into her mouth. No blood, praise God, but what now?

"Do you understand me, Miss Schuyler?"

Rosalind turned her head to look up at him, careful to move as little as possible.

Lennox stood poised on the balls of his feet, obviously willing to strike again. He smiled with the triumphant gleam of a jackal who'd stolen a lion's lawful catch. Bloodlust shone in his eyes and an eagerness to strike again. He didn't so much as glance at the girl he'd just slain.

Hatred bloomed, and physical terror ran through her veins in an icy torrent worse than a storm on Long Island Sound. She'd seen death before, but never murder.

"I understand," she whispered. She'd rather be dead than his wife. "I'll marry you Monday. After Miss O'Hara's church funeral."

Disappointment shimmered briefly in his face before he

settled back onto his heels. His expression shifted to a more conventional triumph.

A slight tap sounded, and the door opened quietly. Rosalind's heart sang for joy. Help, at last.

Silas Dunleavy, her guardian, walked in and stopped before Bridget's body, his long Yankee face disapproving. He curled his lip at the corpse, then looked Rosalind over. "You told me you were going to persuade her," he snapped at Lennox. "I hadn't expected a racket loud enough to disturb me in my cabin. At least the crew was smart enough not to speak up."

A cold wave ran down Rosalind's spine. She struggled onto her feet, leaning on the bureau for support.

Lennox shrugged carelessly. "Sorry. But she's agreed to marry me on Monday after burying her stupid servant."

"Good. We can start splitting the money then. It'll take time to go through all the stocks and bonds."

Dear God in heaven, Lennox and Dunleavy were working together.

"And my maid?" Rosalind gasped.

Dunleavy harrumphed. "I'll send the stewards in for her. Afterward, they can clean the carpet."

Rosalind closed her eyes and heard the two men walk away, chatting comfortably about how to rob her. She rather wished Lennox was lying about giving Dunleavy any of her money. Betraying her father's trust should not be rewarded.

"Don't think about going to the police, my dear," Lennox purred from the doorway. "I've already bribed them too."

Rosalind bared her teeth at him, wishing for her father's shotgun so that she could splatter both robbers across the wallpaper. She was never going unarmed again, even in women's clothing.

Lennox laughed. "Until Monday, my dear," he cooed. The door opened and closed. She heard a quiet conversation from the other room, then a cordial good-bye.

Rosalind closed Bridget's eyes and covered her with a tablecloth. Two stewards knocked on the door, then collected the body without a glance at Rosalind.

Rosalind limped to her cabin, more shaken than she wanted to admit. She was completely alone and defenseless for the first time since her near-drowning. She'd always had loving family, friends, and servants to protect her before, but not now.

Who could help her? Her family servants, now looking after the Schuyler estates? Dunleavy would fire them and destroy their reputations without a second glance.

Friends? She'd prided herself on having more friends amongst honest working folk than the idle rich. She could think of no one who would fight for her that Lennox and Dunleavy couldn't ruin—or kill.

Police? No shelter there. It would be far easier for them to take Lennox's cash than to take action against Dunleavy and Lennox—even if they believed she had been beaten, given that she was a female and therefore considered weak-minded and foolish.

For the first time, she felt the full weight of being alone in the world, with no family to protect her. No equivalent for her of the golden Lindsays, with their ferocious readiness to guard family members.

She sank into a chair. Fiery pain lanced into her sides from her abused ribs. She whimpered. But slowly she regained control of herself and began to plan.

She would never marry Lennox. She'd rather die and let all the charities named in her father's will have her inheritance.

She needed to hold on to the money. She had to be twenty-five or married to gain control of it. It was now January, and her twenty-fifth birthday was in April of 1873. Fifteen long months away.

How could she live in Dunleavy's house for that long and

not marry Lennox? She had a better chance of winning at three-card monte against a sharper. If she just had her Colts, she could have killed Lennox. She'd defended herself before with them, while playing poker with her father.

Poker. More than one man had told her she was good enough to be a professional gambler. Poker might be the answer.

Her men's clothes were in her cabin, locked in a small sea chest. She'd brought them as a reminder of good times with her father, when Dunleavy insisted she leave the Schuyler estate and live with him. She even had her money belt, still loaded with cash from that last evening with her father at a gambling house.

She could climb out the window at Dunleavy's mansion. Maybe Sunday after Bridget's funeral; nobody would expect her to run with these cracked ribs. She could cut off her hair in some back alley; thankfully, she'd kept it shorter than most ladies. It had first been cropped when she caught pneumonia after the near drowning.

And after that, where would she go? The railroads could take her to . . . But if Lennox questioned any of her friends, he could hurt them badly. No. She had to stay away from trains.

Then how could she travel?

Boats.

She shuddered, and a wave of pain slashed through her. She bit back a moan, unwilling to admit even that much weakness.

No one would look for her on a boat or near the water. She could take a train to Pittsburgh and board the first riverboat sailing down the Ohio.

Sailing down a river. Oh, dear God in heaven, she'd have to step on a boat and look at the greedy waters again. How could she do it?

But since her guardian was Lennox's fellow conspirator,

she had to leave. There was no safety for her in Dunleavy's house.

"Rosalind." The deep voice was far away.

Rosalind rolled over and pulled the sheet over her head.

A big hand shook her lightly. "Wake up, little lady."

Consciousness returned with a bolt of recognition. Lord have mercy, she'd spent the night with Hal Lindsay. She could feel the blush scorch her skin from the top of her head down to her breasts. She gulped.

Hal turned the sheet back gently and looked down at her. Freshly shaven and immaculate in shirt and trousers, he showed no signs of having indulged a satyr's hungers only a few hours ago.

She glared at him, longing for a cup of coffee and the nerve to simply pull him down and resume their dalliance. It was dark beyond the lamplight; surely there was time for more frolics.

Hal's eyes danced. "Sorry to disturb you but I thought you wouldn't want Ezra to see you like this. Here's coffee and there's a hot bath waiting."

"Bath?" Rosalind shot upright, clutching the sheet around her. *A genuine hot bath in complete privacy?*

Hal chuckled and turned to leave. "I'm leaving in an hour, just before dawn. You're welcome to ride with me or follow with Ezra."

"I'll travel with you. Thank you," Rosalind added as her hand closed around the coffee cup.

"My pleasure."

The door closed behind him with a soft click, leaving her to ponder his meaning. His pleasure that she had spent the night? Or was he so eager to hasten her departure? An unexpected pang shot through her.

She flinched, then shook off any regrets. She'd enjoyed a

night's diversion with a handsome, skillful lover who'd kept her distracted from her pursuers. She'd slept well, with only one nightmare. It had to be enough, despite her heart's yearning for a safe harbor.

An hour later, Rosalind sipped coffee as she pondered Hal's residence, given the insights from some exploration on her way downstairs. The furnishings were magnificent and eclectic—but sparse. Of five bedrooms, only two could accommodate sleepers. The library held a massive array of volumes but only one chair. The house would comfortably hold a single person, not a family.

She set down her cup as Hal looked into the dining room, the Irish terrier at his heels.

"Ready?" he queried.

"Of course." She touched the napkin to her lips and stood up. She was clean from the skin out and her hair was almost dry. Even her clothing had been sponged and pressed, thanks to Ezra. Mercifully, her body's aches and pains didn't show, at least if she was careful not to limp.

Hal, of course, looked magnificent in a superb white linen suit, which flattered his strong body and golden coloring like a king's coronation suit. After a quick farewell to Ezra, they reached the buggy before Rosalind looked back.

"What about the dog? He's a magnificent Irish terrier."

The little fellow wagged his tail as he gazed adoringly up at Hal. Samuel kept his face impassive from where he stood at the gelding's head.

"Ezra will take him to Asbury's farm," Hal answered curtly. "The man's a fool for dogs and will give him a good home."

Rosalind raised an eyebrow. "Are you sure? More to the point, does the terrier believe that?"

Pain chased briefly over Hal's face. "He will soon enough. There's no room in my life for him."

"Indeed." She forbore to say anything else, given Hal's distress and the dog's evident admiration. Hopefully, he would enjoy Asbury's farm. Better that than try to live somewhere he wasn't welcome.

Hal lifted the reins, Samuel stepped back from the gelding's head, and they were off. The terrier barked furiously and ran alongside.

Hal urged the gelding into a trot. The dog started to lag, but kept following, barking constantly.

Rosalind glanced back. "He's still with us."

"He'll go back to Samuel, as the other dogs did," Hal bit out and increased his speed.

The buggy jolted down the muddy road at an alarming rate, forcing Rosalind to hold on. The dog's barking grew more distant, but never disappeared. Hal pushed the horse faster and faster. Rosalind wasn't sure either of them would survive the ride.

Suddenly, one of the buggy's wheels caught the edge of a nasty pothole. The buggy bounced and started to roll. Cursing violently, Hal steered it to a safe stop. Rosalind swallowed hard and carefully uncurled her fingers from the grips.

The terrier barked from close by.

Hal looked around. "Dammit, fellow, don't you ever give up?"

"Apparently not. In fact, the gods would appear to be on his side," Rosalind remarked, watching the gallant dog limp toward the buggy.

Hal's mouth was a grim line. "I'll not take another dog, just to see him killed."

Her eyebrows went up in surprise before she recovered. "This lad looks well able to take care of himself."

"Perhaps."

The terrier paused, panting for breath, behind the buggy, as the two humans watched. Then he leaped up onto the luggage rack on the buggy's rear. He circled once and settled down, tongue lolling out in a canine grin. A single woof announced his readiness to continue the journey.

Hal turned back to the road ahead. "Perhaps he wants to stay with you."

Rosalind snorted. "He's never looked twice at me. Besides, I can't take a dog to Fort Benton with me. Too conspicuous."

"You haven't told me why you left New York."

She considered for a moment. He could probably guess, if he heard any gossip. And it would be such a blessed relief to have a confidant. "If I tell you, will you keep the dog?"

"Don't be absurd. Of course not."

"Then I have nothing further to say." Rosalind studied the scenery.

They rode in silence for a few more minutes before he spoke again.

"Guess I have a dog." He sounded more resigned than enthusiastic.

"Guess you do. What do you plan to call him?"

"Damn Dog? No, can't say that in front of my sister."

Rosalind chuckled. "Probably not. How about Cicero instead? He seems to be quite the orator."

"Cicero? Good enough."

Rosalind smiled a bit grimly and cautiously began her story. "My father died in January, of a bad heart."

"My condolences. He was a fine gentleman and an example to us all."

"Thank you." Her throat was tight, and she had to swallow before she could go on. "His will named his banker, Silas Dunleavy, as my guardian until I turn twenty-five and gain full control of his estate. At the funeral, Nicholas Lennox, a junior partner at Dunleavy & Livingston, paid me marked attention. I turned a cold shoulder, of course—"

"Of course," Hal murmured, effortlessly guiding the horse around a steep downhill corner.

"But he was importunate. I reminded him that I had a fiancé. He sneered at that and told me that barrier wasn't worth a snap of his fingers. The next day, David broke off the engagement, saying his family believed he was too young to tie himself down."

"Balderdash! He cared for you. And even if he hadn't, giving up your money on such a flimsy pretext is idiot's work. The David Rutherford I knew, who served three years on Grant's staff, would never be so stupid."

"I believe he was lying. There was a look in his eyes that spoke of terror. I did not press him for more of an explanation but simply returned his ring." *And cried myself to sleep yet another night.*

Hal patted her hand comfortingly. Rosalind went on more slowly.

"Lennox became more and more insistent, demanding an immediate marriage. I declined, repeatedly."

"Good for you. What then?"

"During the return to Manhattan, Lennox told me I needed a strong hand and he'd arranged for our wedding at his family estate. I refused emphatically. I'm afraid the language I used was not the most ladylike."

She stopped, remembering what had happened next.

"He beat you, didn't he?" Hal's voice was barely audible.

She nodded. Her flesh cringed at the memory of the boot heading towards her ribs. And when dear Bridget had burst in and screamed . . .

"The cold-hearted bastard. He should be castrated and made to run a gauntlet of armed women. He—"

Rosalind stared at Hal. "You don't think I caused it?"

"Of course not. You did exactly what any respectable woman would have done in those circumstances. He's the villain, not you, and it's a pity he's still alive." His voice gentled. "Don't fret, my dear."

"Thank you." Tears of relief blurred her eyes.

Hal curved his hand over hers, and she gripped it. To be accepted by him, and not considered stupid or deserving the punishment, set wings to her heart. She held her head up higher as she continued her tale.

"My brothers had taught me how to pose as a man for their own amusement. After they died, my father taught me how to pass as a male poker player, mostly to give us both an occupation other than grief. So I took my masculine clothing, and some cash, and fled Dunleavy's house. I cut my hair off and headed for Pittsburgh, thinking no one would ever hunt for me on riverboats."

"And you were right. You're very clever . . . and very brave."

"Thank you." She leaned her head against his shoulder for a fleeting moment. If she was to have only one night, and the scraps of this morning with him, it had to be enough. If nothing else, he'd given her the courage to continue.

Hal guided the buggy down Main Street toward the levee, Rosalind silent beside him. He always preferred peace and quiet in the morning, something he'd never found with a woman before. Damn, why did he have to enjoy her company so much when they'd part in a few minutes?

He shrugged off the fancy. "What hotel are you staying at?"

"Gillis House."

"Good choice."

The streets were nearly empty at this hour. A few drunks staggered home and a cop patrolled his beat, shoulders erect and brass buttons glimmering in the early morning mist. Just ahead, Jonah Longbottom came out of a seedy boarding-house, tucking something back into his leather portfolio.

Hal stiffened. Damn. Longbottom had started his hunt early. Since today was Tuesday, he had to be looking for Rosalind.

"That's the Pinkerton man, isn't it?" Rosalind hissed. "Put me down now before he spots me! I need to hide."

"No." Hal rapidly reviewed her options. What next? Railroads? He'd never give anything he cared a fig about to those bastards. Hide her in a seedy rooming house and hope she'd survive till the *Star* left? More than likely, Longbottom would find her before then. And to see her hauled back to Lennox, to be beaten into submission . . . A growl vibrated in his throat.

"I have money. I can buy a ticket on the *Spartan* and leave town today." Desperation threaded her voice. Longbottom was now only two buildings away.

Put her on Hatcher's packet? "Like hell."

He felt more than saw her stare at him. "Relax and look bored," he ordered.

A heartbeat later, she obeyed, falling back into a sleepy young man's posture beside him. He spared a brief thanks to the Almighty for her quick obedience. Now, if only her nerve would hold.

Longbottom touched his hat as they came alongside him. "Morning, Captain Lindsay. May I have a word?"

"Certainly." Hal drew up Jones, and the buggy stopped. Praise the Almighty, Rosalind was on the far side from the Pinkerton man. She eased further down on the seat, letting Hal's body block her from Longbottom's sight.

"Have you seen this woman, sir?" Longbottom handed up a leather portrait case. He cast an incurious eye at Hal's passenger, but said nothing.

The portrait was of Rosalind Schuyler, dressed for a ball. A woman would probably notice the pearls and diamonds embroidered on her gown. Any red-blooded man would see the bountiful cleavage, startling to one who'd seen her unclothed, and stop thinking with his brain. All in all, the picture was an effective red herring since few would pay attention to her face.

Hal passed the case over to Rosalind. She glanced at it

and handed it back. Gallant player that she was, her hands didn't shake.

Best give Longbottom some of the truth, at least what he could confirm elsewhere. "Miss Schuyler, is it? I met her in New York last year."

The man perked up. "And since then?"

"No, haven't seen the woman since," Hal lied cheerfully. Jones sidled briefly, setting his harness jingling. "What about you, Carstairs? Ever seen a female who looked like that around here?"

"Can't say as I have, sir." Her voice was as steady as if she was betting on a set of aces in a poker game.

Longbottom sighed. "Pity. But since you're an acquaintance, you'd recognize her, Captain Lindsay."

"I'd certainly notice anyone that beautiful."

"Indeed. I'll not keep you then. Good luck, Captain."

"Good day, Longbottom." A moment later, Jones was trotting down Main Street again. Hal heard Rosalind draw her first deep breath since they'd seen Longbottom.

Now to take her someplace safe from Pinkertons. "Ever consider becoming a riverboat pilot?"

She snorted in disbelief. "Have you lost your mind? Men will fly to the moon before I become a pilot."

"I can use a cub pilot, someone to teach the ways of the river. It'd give you a berth on the *Belle*."

"Do you know how much I hate water? The instant I set foot in the pilothouse, everyone would know I'm a fake."

"Nobody would say, or do, anything," Hal snapped back. "I own the *Cherokee Belle*. I hold a pilot's license for the upper and lower Missouri, plus the lower Mississippi. I also have my master's license. I can teach anyone I choose and do any damn thing I want on that steamer."

She shook her head. "It's crazy. Someone will realize I'm a woman."

"Has anyone—other than myself—seen through your disguise?"

"No. In all these months, only you did."

"And I'd met you before, an advantage no one else on the *Cherokee Belle* possesses." He paused. She managed a tight nod. At least she'd agreed with him so far. Now, onto the mechanics of how to pull this off.

"I'll have a cot set up in my stateroom, and I won't force my attentions on you. Ezra will fetch your luggage from Gillis House. No one will know. All the world will see is two men, two separate beds—not lovers."

She was silent, her shoulders shaking a little beside him. Her fingers clenched and unclenched on the rail.

He gentled his voice. "Do you have any other choice?"

"No." Her voice was a thin thread of sound.

"Then give it a chance, little poker player. If it doesn't work, you can transfer to the first boat we meet that's also heading upriver. Good enough?"

"It has to be, doesn't it? May God help us both," she finished softly.

Chapter Five

Hal stopped the buggy in front of his office and sprang down. His eyes flickered sideways but Rosalind didn't need the warning.

Less than a block away, dozens of people streamed over the levee and down to the *Cherokee Belle,* gleaming like a bank of lilies against the dawn sky. They were mostly men, with a few women and children to enliven the group. She could see some army uniforms mixed amongst the civilians' colorful attire, plus fringed buckskin jackets on others.

A groom coaxed a mare to the stable at the main deck's rear, while a roustabout carried a case of wine onboard. Freight covered the main deck and most of the guards, the main deck's extensions that stretched beyond the hull and nearly doubled the boat's width.

A trio of roustabouts sang something about long, hot summer days as they stacked barrels. The rhythmic rise and fall of their voices, with the mate's curses as counterpoint, sounded like a prophecy of times to come.

A steam whistle blew sharply once, twice, from the river to the west. The *Spartan* was passing through the Hannibal Bridge's opening, and making a great deal of noise about doing so. Thanks be to God that Desdemona Lindsay's lover—

the man she'd bidden farewell to at the hotel, who was hopefully not Nicholas Lennox—was leaving town.

"That Hatcher. He's just the biggest damn showoff in Kansas City," Hal snorted, Cicero circling happily next to him. "You'd think no other riverboat ever had a steam whistle, the way he carries on."

He shook his head and tossed a leather satchel at Rosalind. She caught it easily, as long-forgotten childhood games rose to help.

"Carstairs, take this to McPherson in the office," he ordered. "I'll watch for my sister from here."

"Yes, sir." Rosalind took the leather satchel inside the office, realizing Hal had given her one last chance to change her mind and run from both him and the detective.

It would be easier to hide, now that she'd seen that idiotic portrait, which bore almost no resemblance to her. It was only good as a memento of the expensive ball gown her godmother had chosen. That nonsensical dress had been heavier than a sack of coal, with its seed pearl and semiprecious stone embroideries. And utterly dependent on a fancy French corset and tight lacing to provide curves.

Hal Lindsay hadn't seemed to notice any lack. In fact, he'd been distinctly appreciative of her bosom after extricating it from her men's clothing. She blushed at the memory.

He'd also protected her from the detective and offered her a chance to escape Kansas City, where Lennox's tentacles crept closer and closer. She'd be a fool if she didn't take Hal up on it—whether or not it meant sharing his bed again. And she'd do her best to be a first-rate cub pilot, of course, no matter what she thought of boats and water.

"Mr. McPherson?" she asked inside the office, instinctively pitching her voice a little deeper.

The clerk frowned at her for a moment, then relaxed. "Carstairs, isn't it?"

"Yes, sir, but I now have the honor to be Mr. Lindsay's cub. He sent this packet for you."

McPherson accepted the satchel. "Thanks. I'll tell O'Neill, the *Belle*'s clerk, to refund your passage on the *Star*."

Rosalind touched her hat in gratitude. "Thank you, sir."

"Good luck."

"Good day to you, sir." She escaped into the open air, relieved that her costume and her new role had survived McPherson's inspection.

She found Hal talking to a short, stout, but very well-dressed man outside the office. Cicero paced along the board-walk, always within a few steps of his human. Rosalind took up her own station behind Hal's left shoulder, comforted by his closeness.

He acknowledged her presence with a single glance, but made no offer of introductions.

Rosalind listened patiently to the conversation—some-thing about buying Hal's land to build more stockyards in the "West Bottoms"—and watched the railroad track atop the levee. Better to study that than the water beyond.

Suddenly a whistle blew, lighter and sweeter than a river-boat's whistle. Rosalind's eyes lit up as a single Central Pacific railroad engine chugged into sight along the levee, from behind the railroad bridge. An elegant private railcar—custom-built by Pullman, insisted her expert eye—followed it, the small assemblage finished off by a single caboose.

A private train, the epitome of wealth and comfort. She hadn't had the pleasure of traveling on one of those since her father's death.

She sighed reminiscently, remembering the elegant seat-ing, the Brussels carpet, the soft bed that easily cradled even her long frame. And the personal chef and steward, the pri-vate telegrapher to capture the latest world and business news, and the engineer, who always delighted in showing her the

latest shiny brass gadget. Jeremy and Jackson playing yet
another prank as her mother laughed, Richard and her father
in long conversations about railroad routes, the long chess
games with her father or brother . . .

"Interesting proposition, Coates. But now, I have a sister
to meet and a boat to catch. We can speak again when I return from Fort Benton," Hal said briskly, shaking hands with
the stout gentleman. "Come along, Carstairs."

Rosalind shook off her reverie, touched her hat politely to
Coates, and followed Hal up the levee. He set a brisk pace
and reached the tracks on top, just as the little train halted,
exactly at the steps leading down to the wharf boat. A very
smooth stop, too, sign of an excellent engineer. A moment
later, a diminutive lady burst out of the private car. "Hal!"

Rosalind blinked. Cicero began to bark.

"Viola, my dear." Hal hugged the woman and spun her
around, grinning at her the entire time. Cicero barked again,
as if begging to join them.

Seen together, the family likeness was amazing, with
brother and sister sharing the same blond hair and dark blue
eyes. But each represented a very different gender. Viola
looked capable of dancing on water lilies, especially in a fine
Parisian carriage dress, which emphasized her delicate
beauty rather than overwhelming it. In contrast, Hal was the
epitome of masculinity, in his crisp linen suit, and he looked
more than capable of wrestling a bull to the ground.

A tall, lithe gentleman disembarked behind Hal's sister.
Black-haired and blue-eyed, he had the elegant beauty of a
Renaissance painting and had been clothed by the best English tailors. Even with those looks and clothing, he moved
with the easy grace of an experienced fighter.

Rosalind's poker-player instincts came alert. This fellow
was not someone to trifle with.

He smiled fondly at Hal and Viola and then glanced around,

assessing his surroundings like a wise man in a wolf trap. His eyes narrowed when they encountered Rosalind.

A chill ran up her spine. Had he recognized her as a woman? Surely not, since she was wearing her broad-brimmed planter's hat, which shadowed her face so well. She set her jaw and looked straight back at him.

His mouth quirked, and he saluted her with two fingers.

Rosalind nodded briefly and made a mental note to stay as far away as possible from him.

"William, my love, say hello to my brother." Viola caught the newcomer by the elbow and urged him forward. The two men shook hands and hugged. Finally, Hal stepped back and beckoned Rosalind forward.

"Viola, William, this is Frank Carstairs, my cub pilot. You can rely on him for assistance, should the need arise. Carstairs, this is my sister and her husband, Mr. and Mrs. William Donovan."

"Carstairs," Donovan acknowledged with a nod.

"Mr. Carstairs," Viola murmured and held out her hand. Her gaze was as direct as her husband's, but gentler.

Rosalind shook hands, careful to keep her grip as strong as possible, and tried to remember where she'd heard the name William Donovan before.

"Viola, this is Cicero, my new companion." Hal indicated the terrier, who was cautiously sniffing the lady's skirts.

"And very glad I am to meet him, too." Viola smiled at her brother, then squatted down. She crooned softly in a strange language. Cicero's ears came up, and his tail wagged briskly. A moment later, they were fast friends.

"Hal, you remember Abraham and Sarah Chang." Viola stood up and indicated two servants, soberly clad in black livery, who were rapidly transferring luggage from the private car to a cluster of roustabouts. "They were a great help to us when we were in London and Ireland."

"Of course, I do. Good morning, Abraham. Mrs. Chang." He gave the couple a quick, and very friendly, nod, which they answered with deep bows. Seen from the front, they were both of Oriental descent, piquing Rosalind's curiosity. She would have expected Negro servants or perhaps Irish, instead.

"And now, let me introduce you to my boat." Hal turned toward the *Cherokee Belle,* his face alight and Cicero prancing alongside. The stream of passengers had slowed to a trickle, as a few shabbily dressed men picked their way down the levee.

Suddenly, a woman's voice rang out from the street behind them. "Hal, my dear son!"

"Mother?" Hal spun around.

Viola stiffened, catching Rosalind's attention. Donovan took his wife's arm protectively and patted her hand, his expression severe.

"Dear God in heaven," Hal muttered. It sounded more like an invocation of the Almighty's aid than profanity.

A cold wave ran down Rosalind's spine. She turned to look.

Desdemona Lindsay was hastening up the levee, her smile broad under an ornately feathered hat.

Cicero growled.

Behind her, Captain Richard Lindsay oversaw a hack disgorging a pair of Negro servants and a multitude of expensive, perfectly matched steamer trunks and hatboxes. Goodness gracious, were the Lindsays planning to join the *Cherokee Belle*?

At that horrifying thought, Rosalind's gambler's nerves came to her rescue. Her countenance settled into the same impassive consideration she'd use for two wretched hole cards.

Hal's jaw tightened before he spoke again. "I'm sorry, Viola, I had no idea they were coming. Carstairs, escort my sister and her husband onboard the *Belle*. They're staying in the California stateroom. Starboard side, all the way aft. The Changs are in the Iowa stateroom, directly forward of the California."

"Yes, sir." Rosalind hoped her response didn't sing with relief. "This way, please."

"We'll look for you onboard, Hal," Viola said quietly, then went down the stairs quickly, with the surefooted ease of someone accustomed to unsteady footing. Her husband followed her after a last, long stare down the levee's other side. Rosalind brought up the rear, barely escaping ahead of Mrs. Lindsay's arrival.

Cicero barked with the unmistakable note of a dog that meant business. Hal sternly called him to attention, and the terrier quieted reluctantly, uttering a few reflexive growls.

"Mother dearest, how—pleasant to see you," Hal greeted her formally. "When did you arrive?"

"Darling son, we arrived yesterday afternoon after the most tedious journey from Chicago. I was so exhausted, I spent the rest of the day sleeping to recover my strength."

Desdemona's brazen lie so startled Rosalind that she missed a step on the uneven wooden planking leading down to the *Belle*. Donovan spun around, quick as a cat, but she recovered herself without his aid. He looked her over narrowly, then cast a single long, searing look up the levee. Finally, he nodded and went on again, without once saying a word.

Rosalind followed him, equally silent, only to stop dead when she reached the stage, the thin ribbon of wood and steel connecting the *Cherokee Belle* to the wharf boat and dry land.

Dear heavens, it was time to board another boat. She'd refused a London Season rather than endure an ocean voyage. Even months on Mississippi riverboats had barely made the species tolerable.

A first-class packet, a brag boat, a solid steamer . . . But all the compliments she'd heard couldn't make that white and gold pile of lumber enticing. It didn't matter whether they sailed an inland river or the Atlantic Ocean. Boats sank and people drowned.

For a long moment, Rosalind relived that fateful last voyage with her family, as they sailed for Manhattan to rejoin her father. The yacht pitching violently in the nor'easter as salt water poured in the door. Mother lying motionless on the cabin floor, her skull bloody and dented where she'd been thrown against a post. The twins, Jeremy and Jackson, pulling Rosalind out of the bulkhead's wreckage. Her older brother Richard lashing her to a mast, as Jeremy and Jackson tried to hold on to the lifelines. The icy water beating and tearing at all of them, while Richard made her swear that she'd survive. She had to tell Father, no matter what happened, how much they all loved him.

Then the mast had snapped and swept her brothers away in a cloud of canvas and sea foam.

She didn't remember much more of that long night, mostly how the water attacked her again and again. No stars, no moon—just the wind and rain and salt spray lifting her up, then dashing her into the depths.

The next thing she remembered was Father talking to her, his voice a hoarse thread of sound as he held her hand. He'd cried like a baby when she whispered his name. And they'd wept together when she gave him Richard's message.

"Carstairs." Donovan's voice was soft, very gentle, and subtly Irish, as if he were soothing a skittish horse.

A long shudder ran through Rosalind.

Then she stepped, very deliberately, onto the *Cherokee Belle,* and turned to look back at the levee. If nothing else, she would be farther away from Lennox on a riverboat than ashore.

*   *   *

Standing at the *Spartan*'s rail, Nick Lennox lowered his telescope and allowed himself one final glare at the *Cherokee Belle,* as he rubbed his throat. Overhead, the *Spartan*'s calliope roared out an arrogant military march.

"Boats," he muttered angrily, tapping his brother's swordstick on the deck. He silently damned Crédit Mobilier for firing him and later blackballing him from every Union Pacific train and any railroad doing business with the Union Pacific, simply because he'd been found in bed with two directors' wives at the same time. He'd managed to reach Kansas City through a combination of bribes and blackmail. But those options had run out, and the only way left to reach Omaha was by boat.

A slow, inefficient, dangerous boat.

"A train would be better. But at least Lindsay and Donovan are now where we can watch them," Eli Jenkins observed from beside him. He bore an uncanny likeness to Boss Tweed, with the same enormous belly, continuous cigar smoking, and frequent false smiles. His smiles concealed his thoughts, just as his gaudy clothing hid his rapacious appetite for drink.

He had been a superb advance man for the Central Pacific, where Nick had first heard of him, until they fired him for padding his accounts once too often. His fall from grace had inspired him to attack his former bosses as often as possible. He'd fallen on Nick's invitation to help destroy William Donovan, a major shareholder in the Central Pacific, with all the enthusiasm of a rat attacking a pound of cheese.

"And they should both be dead within the week, thanks to my new friend," he added with commendable enthusiasm.

"What a pity," Nick observed with mock piety and shared a smile of perfect understanding with Jenkins. If the two murderers weren't dead in a week, then he'd obtain that precious ledger, the key to ruining Donovan, once he reached Omaha.

"Any chance of more funds to gain other friends?" Jenkins asked quietly, contemplating the *Belle*'s main deck.

Nick snorted. "Perhaps if this one doesn't do the job. Finding one willing to help was hard enough and his price was ridiculous."

"True." Jenkins blew another smoke ring. "Or the Good Lord may look down and smite our enemies, hip and thigh instead, saving us the effort."

Nick smiled reluctantly. Divine intervention would be far cheaper than what had happened so far. He'd spent every penny he had to hound Donovan, then looked for more. As one of Rosalind Schuyler's bankers, Nick had sucked what he could from Cornelius Schuyler's estate. Then those greedy charities had insisted that the heiress was dead, given her long disappearance, and demanded Old Man Schuyler's estate as residual legatees. The courts hadn't agreed, but they had stopped all withdrawals from the estate until the clumsy female was proved dead.

He needed every last penny now, which meant marrying the Schuyler bitch before she turned twenty-five and gained control of her inheritance. *Foolish old man, permitting a mere female to manage that much money.*

Her inheritance was the best way to avenge Paul. Beloved Paul, the best brother any boy could hope for. And the O'Flaherty brothers as well, Paul's trusted bully boys. They had been Nick's good friends, especially the youngest brother, and could have found the Schuyler chit anywhere, even in the filthiest gutter. Now Paul and the O'Flahertys were six feet under, destroyed by Donovan and Lindsay in that isolated little Arizona mining town.

His throat tightened. "I'm going below," he announced.

Jenkins nodded peaceably. "And I. A poker game should have started by now."

Nick slammed his telescope shut and headed for the

stairs. A knot of men blocked his way, chatting leisurely as they strolled.

Nick shifted left, then right. No room to pass on either side. Jenkins cleared his throat. They paid no attention. Perhaps it was simply due to the loudness of the boat's rickety engine and paddlewheel. Still, Nick Lennox hadn't been ignored since he was at Columbia.

He thrust his swordstick between the hindmost man's legs. The fellow stumbled and lurched forward. His friends staggered then went down like ninepins, encouraged by a push from Jenkins. Nick and Jenkins stepped over and around them neatly, murmuring wholly insincere concern, as stewards and other passengers rushed forward.

Nick forgot them before he reached the grand saloon. Jenkins lifted a hand in farewell and turned toward the bar, where a dozen men were gathered around a table and a pack of cards.

Nick closed the door to his stateroom and poured himself a glass of brandy from the decanter. At least he still had enough money for a private stateroom. If the Schuyler chit were his wife, he'd be rich enough to travel like a king and order Donovan's death with a raised finger.

How could he find the bitch? None of the railroads, which supposedly knew her best, had had any luck. Pinkerton's men were bumbling, expensive fools, who bleated about unsuccessful visits to every rail stop, stage stop, and city. Nick had questioned her servants personally, but had learned nothing useful.

He'd searched the haunts of the gilded rich—Manhattan, Long Island, Newport, Saratoga—and found nothing. Advertising a fifty-thousand-dollar reward from Denver to California had harvested only con men, each promising, then failing, to produce the missing heiress.

Where the hell was she?

He'd hunt for her himself, of course, while he was on the *Spartan*. Inquire about her, post a reward in the local towns, and so on. No point in asking for her on the riverboats; her terror of waterborne transport was too deep-rooted to permit her to actually board one. He'd seen her near hysterics when tricked into stepping on a Brooklyn wharf.

Those steps would cover this Indian-infested wasteland only as far as Omaha, the furthest point in his journey through this benighted desert. Jenkins would search as far as Sioux City, the highest railroad crossing over the Missouri. One of them would find her; they had to.

And then he'd teach her exactly how she needed to behave, starting with a proper appreciation of his cock. Desdemona Lindsay had some excellent tricks; maybe he'd have her teach that young bitch how to honor him.

Purring at the image, Nick knocked back some brandy and allowed himself to remember exactly how and when he'd first had the pleasure of Desdemona's mouth.

It was a cold winter day in 1862 when eighteen-year-old Nick Lennox had boarded the *City of Thebes,* a Hudson River steamboat, to return to Columbia. Paul had flatly forbidden Nick to follow him into the Army, so Nick was compelled to do his best at school, while watching for chances to better his life after graduation.

His fellow passengers were the usual sort, at least on the boiler deck—mostly stolid merchants who'd have neither conversation nor connections to offer him.

Damn. He'd hoped to make a few contacts on the voyage downriver, men who could one day throw business to a young banker. He planned to take over Dunleavy & Livingston from his godfather, Silas Dunleavy, but needed money and connections to do so.

Although blackmailing Mrs. Pendleton—she of the adulterous liaison with a Negro carpenter—had paid his tuition, it wasn't enough to compete for top dog in New York banking against that sanctimonious idiot, J. Pierpont Morgan.

All in all, it looked like a boring trip, especially without a *nymph de fleuve* onboard, one of the harlots who specialized in amusing gentlemen on boat trips. He'd never understand why western riverboats barred them.

A whiff of his neighbors' conversation reached him, as they, too, watched the last passengers come onboard.

"I say Grant's the best of a bad lot," pontificated the man beside Nick. "He did damn well at Forts Henry and Donaldson. And his victory at Shiloh was very well fought, very well indeed."

"A tanner's son? It's McClellan for me. He's at least something of a gentleman," the other man said stubbornly. His words had the ring of an old argument, something that the two could repeat until they ran out of breath.

Nick paid them only the slightest heed, as he watched two women bid farewell on the dock. One was an exquisite little beauty, with creamy skin and pale gold hair starting to escape her bonnet. The other was probably her mother—taller, with dark hair, a splendid bosom, and a very trim waist. More importantly, both were wrapped in very expensive sable capes.

He smiled, smelling the sweet scent of money.

Unfortunately, only the mother came aboard; Nick would have enjoyed seducing the younger beauty. Still, older women often had a looser hand on the purse strings for a pretty male face.

"McClellan's a cowardly fool," said the first man.

"And Grant's a drunken sot," expostulated the other.

Nick's inner demon nudged him into becoming devil's advocate, and he turned to face them. "What about Robert

Lee, gentlemen? He's one of the Lees of Virginia and he married into George Washington's family. You can be sure he's one of the right sort of people."

The two men glared at him. The older woman, she of the splendid curves, stared at him as the purser collected her ticket. Hope blazed in her eyes for a moment but was quickly veiled. She went below after one quick glance at his companions, closely followed by a Negro maidservant.

Nick blinked, startled by the woman's reaction. He recovered himself and quipped, "If he wasn't a rebel, that is."

Grant's advocate laughed. "If Lee was fighting for the right side, he just might be the best general on the Continent." His friend joined in the laughter, and the brief *contretemps* was soon forgotten.

Nick found himself seated next to the woman at dinner, evidently a ploy by the steward to even up the numbers. Seen close up, she was a beauty of perhaps two score years, with dark blue eyes and raven hair. Their two dinner companions prattled on about cotton prices, with only the barest nods for Nick or the beauty.

"Nicholas Lennox, at your service, ma'am," Nick introduced himself as he passed a tureen of turtle soup.

"Desdemona Lindsay, sir," she answered in a soft southern drawl. "Are you related to the late Henry and Katherine Lennox?"

Curiosity reared its head. Wasn't one of the Lindsays married to a southern belle? He racked his brains for the connection, but managed to answer her. "My parents, ma'am."

"My condolences, sir. They were truly exemplars of the right sort of people. As is General Lee, God bless him." As her voice lingered over the last sentence, she glanced up at him through her thick lashes. A coquette's trick, but still damned effective.

Nick swallowed and silently cursed the color rising to his cheeks. Damn his lack of years; Paul never blushed. "Thank you, ma'am. That sentiment means a great deal, especially when coming from a lady like yourself."

She inclined her head, letting a single curl caress that long swan's throat. God help him, she was beautiful. But ladies were so tedious in the bedroom, good for nothing but breeding heirs.

Her voice was soft, pitched to reach only his ears. Her husky tones triggered a slow roll of heat through his veins. "You are very kind, sir. You must be alone now, as I am."

Nick shrugged and stirred his soup, watching a rich morsel rise to the top. He tried to think of something other than how her red mouth would look wrapped around his cock. "A fellow gets used to loneliness, ma'am."

"Still, it can be a burden on the soul to be without loved ones, as I know to my cost. Perhaps we can ease one another's pain. With private conversation, of course."

Nick blinked. He'd been the object of advances before but never made so openly, or in so public a space. Perhaps he'd misunderstood her.

Then a slim hand rested on his thigh—and his clothes were suddenly too damn tight. He barely stopped himself from loosening his collar. What the devil was she doing?

The soft, warm weight of her touch glided higher.

He choked. His woolen undervest rasped his nipples.

Her fingers drummed gently on his legs.

His cock wanted to lunge out of his trousers. His spoon clattered onto the table.

She cupped her hand over his balls. No fondling, just her steady warmth seeping through wool trousers and drawers and into his loins. His heart began to thud like a recruiting band's drum.

"Ma'am." He tried to find words that would gain him a reprieve. He wanted more but not here, not now.

"Yes, Mr. Lennox?" One finger—one finger only!—stroked the underside of his cock through his trousers.

His breath caught with an audible wheeze.

"Problem, sir? Anything I can do to help?" the waiter asked.

"Just take the soup away. I'll eat only plain foods tonight," Nick rasped.

"Yes, sir. And you, ma'am?"

"You can remove mine as well," she responded smoothly. Beneath the tablecloth, her hand began to glide slowly up and down his cock. Nick couldn't have moved if the Angel Gabriel had blown his horn.

"Congratulations, ma'am, on your husband's promotion to captain. Mighty clever work he did, down there in New Orleans," the steward said, as he neatly stacked their dishes.

Her hand froze. Nick's brain, never absent for long, lurched back into full life. *Husband? She must be Richard Lindsay's wife, the millionaire owner of that Ohio packet line.*

Another harsher thought struck him. Why was she making advances to another man? And could he possibly make some money from it?

"Thank you, waiter, you're very kind. Yes, the Lindsays are very proud of Richard." She almost spat the word "Lindsays."

Was she angry at them? What was going on?

Nick surreptitiously stroked the back of her hand under the tablecloth. With an almost painful jerk, her fingers returned to fondling him. Nick settled back to enjoy himself.

An hour later, the final course was removed from the table and diners stood up to stretch their legs. Nick's cock was as full and aching as he'd ever known it to be; Desdemona Lindsay had a damnable skill for arousing a man. Several times, he'd had to clamp his fingers around her wrist lest he spend in his trousers like a callow youth, not a strong fellow of eighteen.

He held her chair, grateful that the full cut of his trousers hid most of his arousal. "Excellent meal, ma'am."

"Indeed, although I think it might be improved by some meat. Lean young meat, fresh and tasty."

Nick prayed his ears weren't red. He was quite sure his cock was brilliantly crimson from the blood pounding in it. "Indeed? I'm sure any red-blooded man would be happy to provide you with a taste of such meat."

Her tongue strayed across her lips, raising images of how it could pleasure his loins. He forced himself to keep his breathing steady.

Mercifully, their dinner companions were still totally absorbed in the high price of cotton. They took their lamentations to the bar without a second glance at Nick and Desdemona's doings. The waiters also paid little attention as they rapidly cleared tables.

"Do you truly think so? I do hope you're right," she breathed. "Perhaps you could stop by my stateroom in, say, ten minutes, with a sample?"

"It would be a pleasure, ma'am," Nick said sincerely.

"You are so kind, sir." Her voice was honey smooth, an incitement to undreamed-of delights.

Nick inclined his head. Ten minutes later, to the second, he rapped softly on Desdemona's door. It opened immediately and he slipped inside, his cock at flagrant attention.

Wearing a heavy brocade peignoir and slippers, Desdemona closed the door quickly and turned to face him. She was as beautiful and mysterious as Delilah, with her black hair softly curling around her face. Her breasts rose and fell under the silk, drawing his attention to the valley between them where bare skin showed.

He'd make sure he saw all of her this night, enjoy any part of her he desired—after she explained what she really wanted. Carnal pleasures were quite enjoyable, but not nearly as important as the possibility of some lucrative blackmail. After all, the Lindsays were so very, very rich; they could afford to pay for silence about a matriarch's adultery.

"Thank you for coming," she breathed and leaned up against him. He took command of the kiss quickly, learning the taste of her lips and mouth until she moaned and leaned against him. Her nipples were full and hard, stabbing into his chest.

The slut.

He kissed her harder. He ran his hands down her back and squeezed her ass. She shuddered. Her legs spread. One leg wrapped around his thigh.

Nick tore his mouth away. He needed to climax so he could start thinking and make her beg for completion. Otherwise, he'd be the one promising anything, just so the witch would give him release.

"My cock—" he began and winced at how hoarse his voice sounded.

"Oh, your beautiful man meat." She smiled wickedly and licked her lips. "Does it ache?"

"You know it does."

She smiled again. Delilah must have worn the same look of carnal knowledge. She stepped away and dropped to her knees. She rubbed her cheek against his cock.

Nick's breath stopped. His cock, however, knew exactly what to do and somehow swelled even larger. If he didn't spend soon, he'd probably burst, given the pressure in his balls.

His brain, on the other hand, yammered something about how ladies never used their mouths on men. Never. So that couldn't be a possibility.

"Such strong man meat," she breathed. "Ripe and almost ready, rising from a man of fewer years than my youngest daughter. Perhaps it needs some help."

Nick's head fell back against the door as his hips pulsed against her cheek.

She unbuttoned his trousers swiftly, with a knowing chuckle. A moment later, his cock was in her hands. Her strong, knowledgeable hands.

His cock throbbed, as it wept pre-come over its length.

His balls tucked themselves even higher and tighter into his groin, desperate to release their heavy burden.

Nick bit his lip until it bled.

Desdemona's wicked tongue tasted his seed, teased his cock.

He groaned. His hips pushed again and again at her face.

Suddenly, her mouth swallowed his cockhead. She sucked hard.

Instantly, climax ripped through him. Seed boiled up from his balls, through his cock, and into her voracious mouth. He arched. He all but howled as she drank him dry.

He sagged against the door afterward.

She looked up at him and, very deliberately, cleaned her lips with her tongue. "Man meat. How delicious," she murmured and smiled confidently at him.

Self-preservation triggered his brain back into action. She was too self-assured.

"What do you want?"

Her eyelashes swept down, veiling the truth. "You, of course."

He gripped her chin and forced it up. "What else?"

She tried to jerk away.

His grip tightened; he didn't care if she bruised.

She stilled and glared at him.

Good. More wariness in her expression made him feel safer. "What else?" he repeated, more harshly.

She bit her lip, but finally answered him sullenly. "I have family in Kentucky. The war is difficult for them and they need the necessities of life—food, medicines, clothing."

"What of it?"

"Kentucky is troubled and half-lawless. Goods often disappear on the journey. I need someone reliable who can ensure my gifts arrive safely."

"Is that all?"

"Of course it is. What more could there be?" she spat back at him.

He studied her for a long time in the dim light. She glared back at him unflinchingly.

Finally, Nick nodded. Paul had said he could borrow the O'Flahertys if he needed help. "Three brothers work for me. They can deliver your goods."

Her eyes blazed with joy. "Thank you! Oh, thank you, kind sir!"

She sprang up and hugged him, her peignoir falling open.

He kissed her again. She responded eagerly, moaning a little as their tongues dueled.

Stuff and nonsense, how women worked themselves up over trifles. She obviously didn't know how to pay a simple bribe to get the food delivered.

Her leg rubbed his again. He groaned as his cock began to harden. Her errands were so trifling he wouldn't bother to tell Paul. He'd just tell the O'Flahertys to take care of matters. With that decision, Nick set himself to enjoying the rest of the night in Desdemona's bed.

Nick cursed himself for the callow fool he'd been. Desdemona Lindsay had been concerned with far more than food and medicines. Her nefarious schemes had risked Paul's life, and that of every other Union soldier, more than once.

He would never forgive her for that. He hadn't thought of a punishment good enough for her yet, although he enjoyed experimenting every time they met.

Desdemona was now his frequent lover, although she delighted in appearing the perfect society lady in public. A few months ago, she'd hesitated to set the Lindsay hounds on the Schuyler bitch. When she'd finally yielded, she'd given him a superb cocksucking, which had almost made him forget her previous reluctance.

Nick took a long, slow sip of brandy and stroked his cock as he considered his options.

If his arrangements came together, Donovan and Lindsay would be dead within the week. Then he wouldn't need the Schuyler chit's fortune to bury them.

Still, how could a man turn away from it? It would be a shame to waste all that beautiful money, which made even Commodore Vanderbilt turn polite, on a lanky female with no feminine graces.

She needed finding and taming and marrying—just so one lucky fellow could have the pleasure of spending every last dollar the Schuylers had ever made, while dancing on Donovan's and Lindsay's graves.

He'd find her. Somehow, somewhere, he'd have his hands on her again and this time, he wouldn't let go until his ring was on her finger.

Chapter Six

Hal dutifully kissed his mother's cheek as he listened, with only half an ear, to her laments about the journey from Chicago, while Cicero grumbled from behind his master's leg. Rosalind would be safe on the *Cherokee Belle* in a few minutes, far from his parents, who might recognize her and insist on returning her to that brutal bastard, Lennox.

Viola and William would also be better off onboard. Hal didn't know everything that had happened between Mother and Viola back in '65, just that Viola had turned steely in Mother's presence while Mother became tongue-tied, a most unusual state of affairs. Best to keep them separated as long as possible.

"I'm glad you made it here safely," he said finally, more to put an end to her complaints than because he'd truly been worried. Every child of Richard and Desdemona Lindsay had realized early in life that nothing in this world mattered as much to Mother as her own comfort. Heaven knows she'd never disturbed her routine long enough to nurse him through the aftermath of Father's lessons.

A roustabout nodded as he went past, easily balancing a ham on each shoulder. Hal returned the greeting casually, and Cicero barked automatically.

No sign of any other passengers except the Old Man, his

parents' servants, and now Ezra jumping down from the wagon, leaving Samuel to hold the reins.

"So why did you come if it makes you so wretched?" Hal asked bluntly, considering his father's presence. The Old Man had never, to his knowledge, come further upriver than Jefferson City, days below Kansas City.

She hesitated, catching his full attention. That ridiculous feathered hat shadowed her face so he couldn't read her.

"There are duties to be performed," Mother said finally, "which we need to discuss with you at length and in private."

She emphasized the last word as she eyed two approaching roustabouts with disfavor. They touched their hats, stepped around her carefully, and trotted toward Front Street.

Hal's eyebrows elevated. Mother wanted to discuss duty? The last time she'd mentioned that word was when she'd tried to talk him into joining the Confederate Army—preferably his uncle Beauregard's regiment—instead of the Union Navy.

"Indeed," he murmured noncommittally. Ezra, efficient as ever, dammit, was now organizing his parents' luggage, helped by Obadiah and Rebecca, his parents' longtime Negro servants, and the two roustabouts.

Richard Lindsay glanced up the levee at his only son, Henry—or Hal, as the boy preferred to call himself. He looked healthy, thank God, but his stance shouted that he expected trouble. Quite understandable; in the last eighteen years, they'd only met once without arguing, when the two fleets had joined at Vicksburg in '62.

Richard had stood tall on the *Anacostia*'s quarterdeck that day, proud to command the beautiful frigate. He'd known his father and grandfather's ghosts were with him, as they'd stood beside him during the nighttime inferno called the Battle of New Orleans. His father had labored long and hard to prepare him for this responsibility, including whipping him like a slovenly landsmen whenever his homework wasn't perfect.

Richard automatically flexed his shoulders at the painful memory. He'd hated those whippings with the cat, the way the rope wrapped around him so that the bits of embedded metal could tear his flesh. More than once, he'd bled through his shirt afterward. But he'd eventually learned his mathematics and he'd become a naval officer, back before he resigned from the Navy to make Desdemona happy.

Command of one's self, learned in blood and sweat if necessary, was required before one could lead men. How could any free spirit command a warship? He'd tried to teach his son as he'd been taught, and as his father and his father's father before that. He'd been soft with Hal and used a cane, instead of a cat, so there'd be fewer—albeit harsher—blows. But his efforts hadn't had the desired effect. Hal had grown wilder and wilder, more and more sentimental—the epitome of an unreliable officer. Then he'd disappeared.

Richard had worried a great deal when Hal ran away, until the first letter came for Viola. But he'd been terrified when Hal had enlisted in the Union Navy. As the younger brother, son, and grandson of naval officers, he had not believed that his wild son could successfully serve aboard a warship. But other men, uneducated and untrained but brilliant, had done well in the war. So perhaps Hal might one day competently command a stinkpot, one of the small wooden gunboats.

Then the West Gulf Blockading Squadron, victors of New Orleans, had met the Western Gunboat Flotilla, conquerors of Memphis, at Vicksburg. Richard had stood on his frigate and cheered, along with his seagoing tars, as the ironclad gunboats swept past.

And he'd cried unashamedly when he saw the *St. Paul,* fresh paint covering far too many battle scars, and his tall, blond son standing at attention with a skipper's blazing pride. Hal had seemed far too young to command a City-class gunboat, but he'd earned it when his stinkpot beat the rebels away from Grant's flank at Shiloh.

Dear God in heaven, how they'd hugged that evening. It had been a great day but it hadn't lasted. The old stubbornness and anger had flared up again and again between them, especially whenever he tried to persuade Hal to be cautious when taking the *St. Paul* into local swamps after guerrillas. But Hal had gone his own way, becoming extremely successful at all the fights a traditional navy never took on. He and his son had been ice-cold enemies again, by the time the Gulf Squadron returned to the ocean.

Since then, Richard had wondered if Hal's success with the *St. Paul* was a wartime fluke. Perhaps the time's martial spirit had swept away Hal's insouciance and turned him into a great officer, for a single moment, as it had made Grant into a great general, but left him an unreliable civilian.

He wished yet again he had someone to speak to about this. But he couldn't talk to Desdemona. She'd always insisted that Hal must follow in the family footsteps, and she had encouraged Richard more than once to cane their son, saying it was the same method her father had used on his sons, horses, and slaves.

And this voyage was the first time in ten years that he and Desdemona would share a bedroom. They hadn't had carnal relations since '61, when they'd fought over her demand that he go south into the Confederate Navy. She'd spent the war at their Cincinnati home, regularly reminding him of how close she was to the front lines. Since then, they treated each other like strangers, only coming together to see their daughter Juliet and her family, or attend social events. He'd considered sending her back to her family in Kentucky, after one of their more vicious fights, but that would be admitting failure.

Her desire to visit Montana on this voyage, rather than Saratoga or Newport, had shocked him. She'd prattled about needing to talk to Hal, but her facile words had rung false to him. The only other explanation was that she wanted to visit a lover . . .

A growl vibrated in the back of his throat. Oh, he'd wondered if his passionate wife had found a diversion elsewhere, when she'd locked him out of their bedroom. But she'd never shown any signs of having one; in fact, she'd always behaved perfectly in public. If he ever had any proof of infidelity, he'd divorce her. And then try to explain to his daughter and grandchildren why he'd treated their Grandmother Lindsay in such a fashion.

What about Viola and Hal? Viola was now married to a very successful man—who was unfortunately an Irish Papist. If Hal had become steadier, the *Cherokee Belle* would shine in his reflection and be a crack packet.

Richard didn't know whether he wanted Hal to have done well, or not. Naval discipline had been his family's backbone for far too many generations to be cast aside easily. But he still had nightmares of his sobbing son, with crimson stripes across his back, cowering away from the cane. Perhaps this voyage would at least take away those dreams.

Richard bit his lip in uncharacteristic hesitation. Then he drew himself up to his full height and marched up the levee, determined to discover the truth about his wife and his son.

The Old Man strode up the levee toward Hal, looking just as proud and erect as he had at Vicksburg. The intervening years had been kind to him, taking nothing from his height, which matched his son's. He still had the erect muscular build and direct eagle's eyes that had made him one of the most respected captains on the Ohio and Mississippi rivers. The greatest differences between him now and the man who'd so ferociously punished Hal eighteen years ago were white hair and the deep brackets around his tightly compressed mouth.

"Good day to you, son," the Old Man said calmly. He extended his hand, a greeting marred only by the slightest of twitches in his jaw.

Cicero barked lightly and began to sniff the Old Man's leg in a very friendly fashion. This earned him a tentative pat from the elder Lindsay, which Cicero leaned into blissfully.

Hal blinked at the terrier's preferences. What the devil was the dog thinking of? After snarling at Hal's mother and barking at every roustabout who passed, he was now willing to be friends with this hot-tempered, brutal old man? Shaking his head, Hal stepped forward, prepared to be polite.

"Good day, sir." He greeted his father and shook hands briefly. "I understand you and Mother plan to voyage with us. May I ask how far?"

"Sioux City, or perhaps Fort Benton." The Old Man took his wife's elbow, braced as if for a fight.

Weeks, perhaps months, onboard? Hal's eyes narrowed. "A significant voyage," he observed. "I presume you've booked a stateroom for that long?"

"Of course."

"In that case, let me expound on a few matters." He crossed his hands on his blackthorn walking stick, in a false semblance of ease. The Old Man inclined his head, watching Hal closely, his expression unreadable. Mother stirred, setting her train's ruffles into a swirl of lace.

"My sister Viola and her husband, William Donovan, are also traveling on the *Belle*. I expect all passengers to treat them, and any other passenger, with the utmost courtesy."

"Viola? Here?" Mother exploded into speech. "I will not have her around. Put her off immediately!"

"Impossible, Mother. She and her husband are my guests and they will be treated as such on my boat."

Cicero barked once, as if for emphasis.

"Richard, are you going to permit your son to dictate my behavior?" Mother spluttered, turning to her husband.

"Careful, my dear. He owns the *Cherokee Belle* and can order anything he pleases, unless it harms the boat or passengers' safety. Now let him finish." The Old Man's tone was very cool, his eyes guarded as he watched Hal, not his wife. He might have been discussing admiralty law, not mediating an argument between his wife and son.

She muttered something under her breath. Hal continued after a moment, slightly surprised that his father had spoken for Hal's position, even though tradition and the law justified it.

"Should they be discomfited—in any way—then the offending passenger shall be put ashore at the earliest opportunity. Whether that occurs at a large city or a sandbank is immaterial."

"A sandbank?" Mother gasped. "You wouldn't dare."

"I certainly would. Do not cross me, Mother."

"How dare you speak to me like that! Did you hear what he said, Richard?"

"Silence, Desdemona." The Old Man's hand clamped down on his wife's as he studied Hal. She fell into indignant murmurs.

Hal spared little attention for her as he faced his father, ready for a fight. Cicero brushed against his leg as he, too, assumed a fighting stance. He was as ready as Homer had ever been to go into battle alongside Hal.

A muscle ticked in the Old Man's jaw before he replied. "I am unaware of any daughter named Viola, or of any son by marriage named Donovan. I will, of course, give any strangers I should meet the full courtesy due them, starting with silence insofar as possible."

"Very well." Silence first, then cold courtesy. Not comfortable but better than Hal had hoped for. "You'd best board the *Belle* as quickly as possible. She'll sail within the hour.

I'll join you in a moment, after I give Ezra a few instructions."

Such as fetching Rosalind's luggage from Gillis House. She'd find it useful, especially if she had to depart suddenly, a step ahead of recognition.

Hal's heart twisted at the thought.

Thankfully, Mother and the Old Man didn't question him further. They started slowly down the levee, the Old Man assisting his wife on the uneven wooden steps as she held up her train, all the while complaining bitterly about the mud.

Hal caught up with them just as they crossed the wharf boat, Cicero frisking at his heels. The Old Man paused to study the *Cherokee Belle,* while Mother shook her skirts out and checked for mud stains. She also seemed to cast some quick glances upriver, where the *Spartan* had just disappeared from sight.

Hal waited, wary of what his father might say.

"Cincinnati Marine Ways built?"

"Hull and main deck, yes. Elias Ealer built the cabin decks."

Cicero sat down and briskly scratched his ear.

The Old Man grunted. "Good firms. Four boilers?"

"Six Dumont boilers, with five flues each. Niles engines, with twenty two-inch cylinders and seven-foot stroke."

"Plenty of power," his father observed neutrally.

"She holds the speed record from Sioux City to Fort Benton, and she's within an hour of the record from Kansas City to Omaha. She can beat any boat on the Missouri or Mississippi."

The Old Man lifted an eyebrow, but didn't challenge Hal's boasts.

"Five-foot draft so she can—"

"Go where the ground's a little damp," his father finished the old wartime saying. "Just as that gunboat of yours could."

"Exactly. But the *Belle*'s faster and more comfortable."

"Hardly difficult to be more inviting."

Hal chuckled reluctantly, surprised to find himself in agreement with the Old Man on anything. But those armored gunboats, where the sun never shone belowdecks, were worlds away from his tall, gleaming *Cherokee Belle*.

"Ted Sampson is the *Belle*'s captain; you may remember him as the *St. Paul*'s chaplain and one of her lieutenants. Antoine Bellecourt's her chief pilot, when I'm not on the watch list. Jake McKenzie is the assistant pilot on this voyage."

"You're not piloting?"

"I prefer to spend time with my sister and her husband."

The Old Man harrumphed and turned to his wife. "We'd best be going onboard, my dear."

"Finally." She turned her back on the *Spartan*'s wake and carefully picked her way across the stage and onto the *Belle*.

Hal escorted them up the stairs to the main deck and then up to the boiler deck, automatically checking that everything was shipshape. Cicero strutted at his heels, behaving more like a king entering his kingdom than a stray lucky enough to have a place to sleep.

Hal had taken the unusual step of having the *Cherokee Belle* repainted, in honor of Viola's visit. Given most riverboats' short lifespan of three or four years on the dangerous western rivers, few owners bothered with extra coats of paint. But the *Belle* deserved to look her best for family. Pure white throughout, of course, with jet-black trim and touches of gold. He'd even had the original artist touch up the stateroom doors' decorations.

"Black Jack Norton still your chief engineer?"

"Yes, sir, he's still with me. Best engineer on the Missouri." Hal cast a quick glance around for Rosalind. He was less worried about Viola. Nothing shy of a tornado could get past her Irishman.

"Good man. I remember him from your Navy days."

Hal relaxed as he spied Rosalind, calmly chatting with

Viola by the stern. Other passengers were scattered along the boat's port side, chattering like magpies as they watched the preparations to depart.

"Which stateroom do you have, sir?" Hal asked, as he held open the forward door to the grand saloon.

"Arkansas."

"A single wide," Mother sniffed as she sailed past the men, her nose high and her train almost swishing with disgust.

"The *Belle* is a very popular packet," Hal remarked. *Even in these days of declining passenger trade.*

Mother stopped abruptly, past the office, and barely three paces into the grand saloon. "Oh, my goodness gracious, she is magnificent."

She spun slowly as she took in the sight. Even the Old Man was wide-eyed as he inspected his surroundings. Hal barely stopped himself from grinning at their reaction.

The grand saloon extended over two hundred feet and was wide enough for a single row of dining tables, with mirrors at each end. The gleaming white bulkheads rose high on either side to the ceiling, where a series of Gothic arches spanned the grand saloon's narrow width. Stained-glass transoms ringed the ceiling, casting an ever-changing dance of light over the carved and gilded arches and the scene below. Crystal chandeliers stood ready to provide illumination after nightfall.

A massive, gilded bar covered the forward wall, in a symphony of carved rosewood, ebony, and mahogany, plus mirrors and expensive alcohol. The office faced forward on the port side, where O'Neill and his mud clerk conducted the boat's monetary business. At the opposite end, in a hymn to domestic virtues, lay the ladies' cabin, with its elegant Steinway grand piano. He'd ordered it freshly tuned so that it would be ready for Viola, a superb pianist.

Stateroom doors marched down both sides, each one

ornamented by a landscape representative of its namesake. Fine Brussels carpets flowed over the grand saloon's entire span, with a distinct change in color marking the start of the ladies' cabin. The furniture was equally lavish, with elegant marble-topped rosewood tables and matching chairs running down the grand saloon's center. Velvet settees and white wicker rockers invited passengers to take their leisure on either side.

"A most impressive first-class packet," the Old Man judged.

"Thank you, sir." Hal inclined his head, careful not to show too much elation at his father's surprising praise. He'd never done anything, except join the Navy, which the Old Man had approved of. "Staterooms are in order of the state's admission to the Union," he remarked. "Delaware, port side forward, and Pennsylvania, starboard side forward. Then New Jersey facing Georgia . . ."

"And so on, until Wisconsin faces California at the stern," the Old Man finished. Both of them ignored Texas, since its namesake was a block of cabins on the hurricane deck, not a single stateroom.

"Exactly." Viola and Donovan had the California stateroom, considered the safest, since it was furthest from any possible boiler explosion. "Bathrooms are full aft—just before the paddlewheel—with hot and cold running water. The water is filtered."

Mother blinked at the unusual luxury, but quickly recovered. "As should be expected on a Lindsay packet," she sniffed.

Hal forbore to mention that none of the Cincinnati-Louisville Packet Line boats filtered their water.

Obadiah stepped out of the Arkansas stateroom with a bow, his ebony face smiling as much as ever, and Rebecca bobbed a curtsy. He'd been a gift to the Old Man from Mother's parents when they married and had followed him ever since, even through naval service during the War. "Welcome, sir, ma'am. Just setting your things out."

The stateroom's eight-foot-wide space was a tart reminder of his parents' tardiness in booking passage. Two single berths rose up one side, with a neat washbasin in a corner. The stateroom's biggest advantage was its setting in the safer and more respectable ladies' cabin. Only women and married men were allowed back here, maintaining it as an area of strict gentility.

Hal's own double-wide stateroom was in the gentlemen's cabin, making it impossible to offer an exchange to his parents.

Mother heaved a heartfelt sigh and stepped inside, where Rebecca immediately began fussing over her. She'd been Mother's maid at Fair Oaks, Mother's family's plantation near Louisville, before being given as a wedding present. As long as Hal could remember, she'd been Mother's confidante. Today, her impassive face gave away nothing of her thoughts—or Mother's plans.

"Should a suitable double-wide stateroom become available during the voyage, I'll have you transferred immediately, of course," Hal remarked, backing away from the stateroom.

"I should hope so," his mother said as Rebecca began to rub her fingers. "Otherwise, what would people think of how the owner's parents were treated on his boat?"

Hal ignored her accusatory tone of voice, something only heard around her family. Other men were always greeted with a smooth, flirtatious lilt, redolent of her Kentucky childhood.

"I presume Obadiah and Rebecca have berths in the Freedmen's Bureau?" he inquired, keeping to basics. The texas was a set of cabins on the hurricane deck, directly below the pilothouse. It was reserved for officers and cabin crew (who were usually Negroes), plus the laundry room at the back. The Freedmen's Bureau was the nickname for the berthing area there, which was reserved solely for Negroes.

"Where else?" his father replied, raising an eyebrow as he watched Hal through the stateroom door.

Hal's mouth twisted. He'd fought to free the slaves, while the Old Man had made it more than clear that he fought to preserve the Union, not provide new liberties for "darkies."

Looking into his father's eyes, Hal forbore to mention that Donovan had booked a stateroom off the grand saloon for Abraham and Sarah Chang, his two servants. In fact, their Iowa stateroom was off the ladies' cabin—and directly across from his parents' Arkansas stateroom.

"If you need anything else, Roland Jones is the steward. I'm going on deck to visit with my guests."

The Old Man nodded. "I'm sure we'll see each other again shortly."

Hal returned the nod and turned away quickly. Five minutes with his parents had almost exhausted his meager store of courtesy. How was he going to get through the next weeks?

Chapter Seven

Rosalind froze when a big man stepped silently up behind her, then relaxed, easily recognizing Hal by his clean, slightly spicy, sandalwood scent. She'd sniffed every toiletry bottle in his bathroom after she'd bathed that morning, as she tried to build up a store of memories. Only about the carnal frolics, of course, and not the man, she reassured her wary brain.

"Is everything well?" Viola asked as she turned to face her brother.

He shrugged. "They'll be with us until Sioux City at least, perhaps even Fort Benton."

Rosalind's stomach plummeted.

Viola's soft mouth tightened. Her husband immediately wrapped his arm around her waist with a soft, wordless croon of reassurance. She smiled as she relaxed against him. "And we'll have a grand time visiting, as long as we're together. That should ruffle some feathers," she remarked with a tartness at odds with her affectionate posture.

A low vibration ran through the thin planks below them, then settled into a low steady hum. The *Belle*'s engines had just fired up and were ready to take her upriver.

Hal chuckled. "That we will. Care to come up to the pilothouse and watch my boat sail?"

Viola's face lit up. "Of course! Oh, Hal, to sail on your boat at last . . . It's the fulfillment of all those dreams we had while growing up."

She took her brother's arm eagerly and went upstairs with him. Cicero was close at their heels, near enough to make even Donovan give way. The big Irishman's eyes twinkled before he followed without a glance at Rosalind.

She went with them, of course, armored by her role as cub pilot. She had to talk to Hal as soon as possible. Spending weeks in close contact with people who could send her back to New York was clearly unthinkable.

Hal handed Viola into the pilothouse and tossed a gold coin at Bellecourt, Cicero wagging his tail happily beside him. Bellecourt caught the bright token and quickly tucked it away in a pocket. "So, you'll admit I was right, *oui*?" He laughed. "You've finally gained a dog."

Donovan stepped inside and Rosalind followed silently.

"No, I'll not admit you're correct. Your head would swell too much if I did," Hal retorted, his eyes dancing.

Rosalind took up station in a corner of the big square room, trying to be as invisible as possible. It was a workmanlike room, with windows on all sides and a door in the back. Dominated by the great wheel—almost twelve feet across—it was sparsely furnished with benches on the port and starboard sides and a rocking chair.

"Viola, William, this is Antoine Bellecourt, chief pilot of the *Cherokee Belle* when I'm not piloting. Bellecourt, Mr. and Mrs. William Donovan."

"*Monsieur. Madame.*" Bellecourt made a courtly bow and Viola curtsied briefly.

"Pleasure to meet you," Donovan observed and shook hands.

"You'll recognize Carstairs, of course," Hal added. "He's hired on as my cub pilot."

Bellecourt raised an eyebrow. "How much is he paying you to teach him the merits of honest labor?"

Hal laughed. "Poker lessons, in lieu of three hundred dollars."

"You are getting a bargain, *mon ami*. It will take more than three hundred dollars' worth of lessons to make you a great poker player."

Rosalind relaxed. At least Bellecourt accepted her as a cub pilot.

Hal laughed. "You'll soon find out just how good I am," he retorted. "If Benton left you any money."

"We both broke even last night." Bellecourt shrugged as he glanced out the window closest to land.

"All ready, sir!" O'Brien's voice was as clear as if he stood in the pilothouse, instead of on the main deck.

Bellecourt's jovial demeanor suddenly underwent a complete change to briskly efficient. "May I ask you to take a seat in the rocking chair, madame? The mate's signaled he's ready to get underway and the bridge is starting to open."

Rosalind cast a quick glance outside. No passengers were in sight. A single roustabout stood on the wharf boat, releasing the *Cherokee Belle*'s last link to land. Her mouth went dry.

The great bell sounded a single stroke from the hurricane deck.

"Oh, how splendid this is going to be," Viola chirped, settling into the indicated seat. Donovan took up station at her side.

"Step over here with me, Carstairs," Hal ordered. "You can still see everything."

Rosalind obeyed silently and moved to starboard, the side farthest away from land. Her hands clenched into fists before she slowly relaxed them, finger by finger. She couldn't afford any betraying signs of nervousness, no matter how much her stomach fidgeted and tumbled.

Hal shifted to stand between her and the wall, his sleeve just brushing hers. His warmth seeped into her chilled flesh.

Cicero circled the pilothouse, then sat down next to Hal, panting genially. Rosalind bitterly envied his composure.

Bellecourt blew the great steam whistle emphatically, sending its call roaring across the city again and again. Then he briskly rang down to summon the engines. Rosalind forced her attention to his movements, as he ordered the boat's mechanical core into motion.

The engine room's response came promptly, ringing the bell in an exact echo of Bellecourt's call. The boat shivered as the wonderful machines on the main deck, which would carry Rosalind away from the hunters, roared into full life. The vision of escape slightly relaxed her, as did Hal's silent presence beside her.

Bellecourt stepped behind the wheel and turned it cautiously, concentrating fiercely as he simultaneously watched the wharf boat from the port window.

The *Belle* began to slowly move forward, quivering as the great paddlewheel bit into the raging waters. The private train started to disappear from sight on the levee. Ahead, half of the Hannibal Bridge's iron span gradually swung open on the great stone pier.

A long minute later, Bellecourt rang down for more speed. The engine room's answer came faster this time. Bellecourt turned the immense wheel more strongly, urging the *Cherokee Belle* away from the wharf boat.

The boat's shudders increased.

Rosalind bit her lip against a whimper and closed her eyes. The river had to be moving as fast as Long Island Sound's waters on that dreadful night. If the *Belle*'s overworked boilers blew up, she and every other passenger would drown in that torrent.

"You're clear of the sandbars, Bellecourt," Hal observed. He stepped closer to Rosalind until their arms rested against each other. He smiled slightly, his blue eyes scanning the scene ahead.

Slowly, his wonderful scent and warmth crept into her and erased her panic. Somehow she regained the courage to look at the water again. The calliope began to play a gay dance tune.

Now the *Cherokee Belle* glided up the Missouri River, straight as a knife cutting through custard, with only the slightest vibrations. She sailed serenely between the bridge's stone piers, blowing her whistle and playing her calliope to celebrate her departure. Behind them, Kansas City's church spires slowly dropped out of sight, as if they were sailing beyond the reach of civilization.

The roustabouts' chant rose through the pilothouse windows, punctuated by the mate's orders to stow the lines, those great hawsers that had previously tied the *Belle* to land.

Rosalind took a deep breath. It was the first time she'd sailed since her mother's and brothers' deaths that she hadn't locked herself in a cabin and cried into a pillow.

Hal moved away from her as he turned to talk to Viola. His sister was full of questions about the boat, a curiosity Rosalind wished she shared. Still, she tucked the answers away in her mind, just in case she needed to know them as cub pilot.

Donovan watched his wife quietly, a smile teasing his hard mouth. Cicero began to sniff everything in the pilothouse, tail wagging as he investigated his new world.

Almost an hour later, the *Belle* had passed the Kansas River. Hal lounged against a side window, like an indolent lion, as he chatted with Viola. Donovan sipped coffee as he considered a hawk soaring ahead. Cicero was curled up in a corner.

Rosalind was wondering about the engines two decks below her. Far better to think about mechanical marvels than Hal's masculine potential, no matter how well he displayed it. She'd almost forgotten about being on a boat. A bell rang sweetly in the grand saloon below them.

"Time for breakfast," Hal remarked. "Are you hungry, Viola?"

"Hardly. You haven't told me about the rapids below Fort Benton yet, or—"

Donovan cleared his throat. "You promised you'd eat well on this trip, sweetheart."

Viola blushed.

Rosalind blinked, fascinated by Viola's reaction.

"Perhaps I'd do better in our stateroom, William, where you could feed me from a private tray," Viola suggested, her voice husky and redolent of carnal meanings.

Donovan smiled and kissed her fingers. "It would be a privilege, sweetheart. If you'll excuse us, gentlemen?"

Hal snorted. "Of course."

"*C'est magnifique* to see two lovebirds bill and coo," Bellecourt remarked after the Donovans left the pilothouse.

"True. It's a relief to see them like that," Hal agreed, "not squabbling like other married couples."

He watched the river go past for another minute before he spoke again. "Carstairs and I will be in my stateroom. He has a great deal to learn before I'll trust him near the wheel."

Bellecourt nodded, his eyes fixed on the river ahead. "*Très bien*. Don't worry yourself about the *Belle*; McKenzie and I will take care of her."

"Egotist." Hal chuckled and slapped Bellecourt on the shoulder. He whistled a Stephen Foster song about a riverboat as he went down the stairs to the hurricane deck. Cicero was close at his heels, giving happy little barks.

Rosalind silently followed them, all the while trying not to look at Hal's broad shoulders, narrow hips, and strong thighs parading before her. Difficult to say which sight discomfitted her more: Hal's superb body or the river flowing past.

Another flight of stairs later, the boiler deck was much warmer than the pilothouse, not surprising since it was directly above the great boilers. Sweat soon beaded on Rosalind's brow as she followed Hal along the elegant promenade around the grand saloon and staterooms. The boat's vibrations grew stronger as they moved aft, closer to where the great paddlewheel slammed into the water.

Even the heat and tremors weren't enough to stop Rosalind from thinking about the muscles under Hal's well-tailored suit. Hal opened his stateroom's door and jerked his head, indicating that she should precede him. She obeyed promptly but Cicero moved first, shooting into the cabin like an arrow.

The stateroom was spacious, almost sixteen feet across, with a large window on either side of the outer door. A washbasin occupied one corner, while an enormous brass bed, an elegant rosewood chair, and a matching dresser constituted the furnishings. A rich Oriental carpet covered the floor, and a row of clothes hooks paraded above the bed. The walls, curtains—now completely closed to hide the exterior shutters—and bed linens were all pure white. It was a most elegant stateroom, almost as splendid as her family's private railroad car, and fully worthy of being the owner's quarters on a first-class packet.

Hal shut the door firmly and tossed his hat onto a hook. "I ordered a cot for you," he began, turning to face her.

Rosalind giggled softly. "Ah, but did you explain that to Cicero?" She pointed.

Hal looked down and his eyebrows flew up. Cicero was ferociously scratching and kicking the cot's blanket and sheets into his idea of perfection.

Rosalind clapped her hand over her mouth to stifle her laughter.

"Why, you greedy little . . ." Hal began.

Cicero circled, then flopped down in the middle of his nest. He looked up at his human, yawned, and laid his head on his paws.

Rosalind was trying so hard not to laugh that she could

barely stand. Hal wrapped his arms around her waist, and she leaned back against him, shaking. He kissed her hair, then licked her neck.

She quivered in response.

He licked her again, a long caress that brought his mouth to just behind her ear.

Rosalind locked her knees desperately against the urge to melt into his arms. His fiery-hard cock rubbed against her backside through their trousers. Her nipples budded into aching points that rasped against her linen shirt.

"Will you mind sharing my bed instead of his?" Hal asked, his voice barely audible over the engines' noise.

"But—we can't," Rosalind stammered, fighting for sanity. "People would know."

Hal snorted. "A cub goes wherever and does whatever his master demands. That cot is the only open berth on this boat, installed by my order for you, when you came aboard as my cub. Everyone will think you're using it."

He nibbled her earlobe gently, sending a flash of lightning through her body. Despite her best intentions, Rosalind moaned.

"If you're quiet, which the boat's noise should conceal," Hal continued, sliding his arms around her. "And I don't kiss you on the mouth—a tempting prospect, although bruising might expose us as lovers—I'm sure we can continue our frolics together. The world will see what it expects to see: Frank Carstairs, the man—and not my lover."

He blew gently on the pulse beating in her neck and licked it again. Rosalind moaned as her eyes drifted shut and her legs opened for his knee.

"Well, Rosalind?"

"What of Ezra?"

"We're old friends. If I slept with Cleopatra, he'd say nothing." Hal cupped her breasts and framed her nipples with his fingers, kneading them gently.

Rosalind quivered as lust tightened her belly. Her head fell forward, giving him full access. He outlined her ear with his tongue.

"Do you agree?"

"Oh my goodness, how can I say no?" She groaned as his devilish tongue explored her vulnerable neck just inside her starched collar.

"Good girl." Hal turned her to face him and unbuttoned her collar. He kissed the hollow of her throat and sucked lightly on the delicate skin, where her clothing would conceal any mark.

Rosalind shuddered and grabbed his head, as her senses seemed to slip away. Her breasts were as firm and as aching as if he'd spent days arousing them.

"Best get your clothes off then, so we don't muss them."

Her womb clenched and dew gathered at his arrogant carnality. She must have said something, obviously an agreement since he didn't challenge it. He stripped her of her outer clothes, boots, and guns in remarkably little time.

"Someday, I'll have the opportunity to remove these at leisure," he observed, neatly hanging her clothing on the wall. "But today, I want to drink your nectar like my morning coffee."

Rosalind choked and blushed, unable to speak. She'd never expected to be reduced to such feminine incoherence.

He ran his finger down her cheek and over her lips. She kissed it instinctively, and he smiled—the slow, anticipatory grin of a male predator. Something inside her melted even more.

She thrust her hips toward him so that he could remove her drawers. Surprisingly, his hand cupped her mound through the fine linen. Fire jolted from his warm fingers through her loins and up her spine.

"You're growing wet, my dear. Will you give me enough to drink?" He fondled her intimately.

Her hips rocked toward him. She could barely breathe.

"Is that an answer?"

"Yes, please." She gulped.

"That's my little lady," he praised. Heavens, she liked being considered delicate. He tilted her back on the double bed, peeled off her drawers, and tossed them onto the chair. Her undershirt was the next to go.

Finally, she lay across the big brass bed's pristine quilted coverlet as he looked down on her. Any thought of hiding herself fled before the blatant hunger in his eyes.

Her breath caught. For the first time in her life, she felt the full power of being a woman. Tentatively, Rosalind arched to display herself for him.

He growled. The ridge behind his trousers grew more prominent.

Taking a chance, she toyed with her nipples, encouraging them until they were as plump and firm as berries.

He groaned and began to peel off his clothes. She purred at his eagerness, her eyelids drooping as she savored the sweet surge of pleasure through her loins.

Dressed only in his trousers, Hal dropped to his knees before her. He pulled her hips forward and spread her legs, opening her up like a peach. Then his tongue ran over her cleft in a long, smooth sweep that sent her surging against his mouth.

His fingers threaded her intimate folds, learning her. He toyed with her, stretching and squeezing and licking the delicate skin until the slightest touch made her shudder. Heat gathered there. Dew beaded and flowed for him.

He nuzzled her and licked her again. His tongue swirled around her clit. Her hips pushed against him eagerly. He scraped his teeth lightly over her mound until she sobbed. She flung her hand over her mouth lest she be heard over the engines and breakfast diners. And she wrapped her legs around his head to pull him closer.

His lips traced patterns on her folds that only he understood. She just knew that they drove her frantic. She'd never experienced, never imagined, anything like his leisurely enticements. Even the previous night didn't compare to this.

Then he sucked on her clit as if it were candy. Pleasure rocketed through her. She fought it, desperate not to shriek.

Hal growled something and continued. His wicked hands and mouth teased her, reminding her of how he'd feasted on her before. The engine's pounding seemed milder than the pulse beating in her veins.

He slipped a finger into her, teasing her inner nerves and muscles. Another finger circled her hidden entrance stealthily, enticing her more than any games she'd played there by herself, while teasing her clit. She'd always yearned for a lover who'd understand the lure of the forbidden. Still more dew slipped forth as her tension built stronger and stronger.

Somehow, she found the strength not to climax and scream, although it seemed the most desirable action imaginable.

Suddenly Hal stood up. She blinked up at him, confused and desperate.

"Stubborn lady, aren't you?" he remarked. His trousers stood out boldly, as if a tent pole lunged against them. She eyed the telltale bulge and instinctively licked her lips.

Hunger blazed in his blue eyes. He rolled her over onto her stomach and she shuddered in anticipation. Heaven knows she loved being treated as a fragile female, rather than an Amazon.

Chuckling hoarsely, he lifted up her shoulders and slid a pillow under her head. Another pillow went under her hips before he leaned over and caressed her ass, lingering over her spine and between her buttocks. His rough fingers slipped through her folds and lightly tugged her clit.

"Dear heavens, you could seduce a nun." Rosalind gasped.

"You flatter me," he bowed, but his voice was husky. He circled her needy entrance, teasing her with pleasures to come.

She moaned and hid her face in the pillow. If she had to look at the hunger and predatory intent in his eyes, she'd start begging him to hurry.

The big, blunt tip of his cock nudged her, veiled by the condom's membrane and framed by his woolen trousers.

She moaned again, a deep, aching sound. Her breasts ached, and she rubbed them against the quilted coverlet, greedy for the added sensation.

He gathered her legs up and opened her wide. She trembled with vulnerability and anticipation. He entered her with a long, heavy surge that drove him in to the hilt with the first sweet stroke. His fat, heavy balls pressed against her clit, their hairs teasing her intimately.

She was full almost to bursting, yet it wasn't enough.

Rosalind shuddered as hunger traveled through her again.

Her movement shattered his restraint. He rode her hard, grunting fiercely as he pounded her. His balls thudded against her, and his heart beat against her.

She groaned into the pillow again and again. Every inch of her body ached for him. Even the blood pounding through her veins wanted more. Her orgasm was closing in on her.

Her channel tightened rhythmically around him, slowly at first then more and more rapidly.

Hal growled, shuddered, then climaxed, spending himself in frantic jerks.

His delight was too much to resist. She climaxed as rapture burst through her bloodstream.

Chapter Eight

Hal rolled onto his side, taking Rosalind with him. She settled easily against him, still trembling a bit in passion's aftermath. Such a proud, controlled little lady she was—everywhere except the bedroom.

His arm tightened around her at the thought. Her surprise at how fast and deep sensuality could sweep her under had told him a great deal about her inexperience. Rutherford might have had her virginity, but he hadn't touched her essence. Hal smirked in pure masculine superiority.

Still, that didn't explain his reactions to her, since he'd never been interested in seducing virgins—even when they didn't seem likely to demand marriage and children.

He'd only indulged himself with experienced partners, in encounters pleasurable but brief. He'd carefully select his lover for looks, conversation, and sensuality, seduce them, and spend a day or two luxuriating in a flurry of lust. Afterward, he'd walk away, always disinclined to bed them again.

But Rosalind—hell, he couldn't have enough of her. They'd reach Omaha in ten days, Fort Benton six weeks after that. Surely he'd be bored by then. Surely.

In the meantime, he must protect her from that scum Lennox. So she'd need to do everything expected of a cub pilot—including dining at the officers' table, while he ate with Viola and Donovan. Damn.

He kissed her neck, swatted her hip lightly, and stood up.

"What the devil?" She started to sit up, glaring at him.

Hal chuckled and returned with a wet washcloth, the condom neatly disposed of. Thank heavens Ezra knew how to keep his mouth shut, and the chambermaid was his sister.

"Relax and let me tend to you. Then we can start teaching you how to pilot a riverboat." He pressed her back with a hand to her shoulder. She resisted for a moment, then leaned back on her elbows.

Hal began to carefully wash between her legs. She squeaked and closed her eyes. His mouth twitched, but stayed sober.

"Must I learn that?" Rosalind asked, a long moment later.

He nodded and rinsed out the washcloth. "You're here as a cub pilot so you need to act like one, or folks will suspect something's up."

"Damn." She closed her eyes for a moment, then came to her feet.

Brave little lady to take on piloting. He'd heard of how her family had died, and her own near drowning on the same night. No wonder she'd thrown a fit or two at the sight of a boat; something like that could spook the strongest man.

He pulled on his clothes, trying to think about how he could help her. "Your father liked mechanical things, didn't he?"

"Oh, yes, very much so." She smiled reminiscently as she buttoned her shirt.

"Do you have any similar interests?"

She grinned. "Yes, sir, I do. I enjoy the sound of a well-tuned locomotive engine, or—"

"How'd you like to meet a well-tuned, high-pressure steamboat engine?"

Rosalind's eyes lit up. "Could I? I've only been in the passenger compartments of a riverboat before. Father showed me train engines but never riverboats."

Hal's mouth quirked. The *Belle*'s magnificent pilothouse had left her terrified, rather than inspired, by a vantage point that many hoped to see. But offer her a visit to the cramped, dirty engine room, and she blazed like a furnace.

Rosalind gazed at the hubbub as if she'd just entered Sinbad's cavern. At last, something on a riverboat that she understood.

Freight was piled high all around, leaving just enough space for the boilers and firemen. Three thirty-foot-long cylindrical boilers stood on surprisingly small stands near the bow, each with a single door facing forward and a raging fire within. The metal around every door glowed red-hot, a sure sign that the boilers were being hard-fired. A bevy of ebony black firemen shoveled coal into each opening, working like men fighting to stay out of the bowels of hell. A bucket of pine knots stood by each boiler, ready for some unknown purpose. A few embers fell to the wood deck and were summarily dealt with.

It was, of course, quite hot and noisy, with the deck flexing subtly under her feet as the boat sailed upriver. Not the most stable foundation for mechanical contrivances.

Hal tapped her shoulder, then led her back under the line of pipes, with Cicero close against his leg. In a very small, confined space at the stern, they found a massive engine of the rather old-fashioned lever and poppet-valve style. It was coupled to a pitman—a type of connecting rod—which slid rhythmically back and forth through a deep channel on the deck. The brutal-looking engine and its twin, whose engine room was just visible past still more freight stacked down the middle of the main deck, obviously drove the great paddlewheel, visible through the stern windows.

The dominant beat in that cramped room was a steady whoosh-whoosh as the pitman walked up and down, and the water splashing down from the paddlewheel's blades. Or buckets, as the rivermen called them.

Everything was neat, tidy, and well organized. Even the firemen seemed calm as they flung coal through the grates, despite the danger. If a boiler exploded—as high-pressure boilers were all-too eager to do—those men would be the first to die. Every soul onboard could easily be destroyed in such a calamity, the way sixteen hundred men had died on the *Sultana* only seven years earlier.

Still, the biggest surprise was how dirty everything was, compared to the gleaming brasswork of a train engine. The only bright work to be seen here was the piston rod and throttle handle. In this engine room, everything was focused on work. Not on glory, not on beauty—just the overwhelming demand to drive the *Cherokee Belle* upstream.

A gray-haired man with startlingly young eyes came forward, sweating like the rest but much cleaner. He grinned at Hal with an easy familiarity, even as he looked over Rosalind. Competence oozed from his every pore. She was immediately glad she'd tidied up thoroughly before leaving Hal's stateroom.

"What brings you down here, Lindsay? Thought you were going to lounge about the boiler deck this trip."

"Showing my cub around the boat. He has some familiarity with engines so we're starting here. Black Jack, meet Frank Carstairs. Carstairs, this is Black Jack Norton, the *Belle*'s engineer."

"It's a pleasure to meet you, sir," Rosalind said sincerely as she shook hands. She might be able to trust the boilers run by this legendary engineer. He'd brought his gunboat safely through the Battle of Shiloh, despite an engine room filled with steam from shot-up pipes. Surely he could take these engines up a few hundred miles of river during peacetime.

She happily began to ask questions, starting with basics like the pressure gauge (an unfamiliar type to her, but Norton assured her it was the most useful on western rivers) and the safety valve on each boiler. A line was tied to each safety valve's lever, which could then pass through one of two pulleys. The lower one looked innocent enough, but the upper pulley led out of the boiler room to an unknown destination.

Norton told a few stories about his wartime service, including one in which he'd tied an anvil to the line, then threaded it through the upper pulley. He'd built the pressure particularly high during that escapade, confident that the boilers would have exploded a dozen times before the safety valve would open. After all, there was nothing like extra steam for more speed.

Rosalind nodded eagerly, quickly understanding both the risks and the benefits of the trick. She did so enjoy being treated as an equal by a man, instead of like a dim-witted broodmare. Conversations like this were the saving grace of her disguise.

An hour later—or perhaps more—Hal coughed. Rosalind flushed guiltily and stared at him, caught in the middle of a detailed discussion of the uses for different types of coal. Hardly a typical conversational gambit from a young pilot.

Norton snickered. "Don't be too afraid of boring him, Carstairs. Lindsay was my striker once, back when we took the old *Katy Anne* up to Fort Benton in '56, the second year a steamer made it through the rapids. He still remembers some of what I taught him."

Hal laughed. "And a hard taskmaster you were, too. Had me scraping out mud from the boilers twice a day. And you made me reverse the engines, lifting and resetting that damn club every time the pilot rang down, while you took your ease."

Norton's eyes twinkled. "Typical chores of a striker, my boy. And aren't you the better for doing 'em, just as I promised?"

Hal laughed and saluted his old friend, then left the engine room. Rosalind followed him up to the boiler deck, while Cicero raced ahead of them, barking happily at everyone in sight.

The few wisps of morning fog had completely burned off, and the day was glorious, sunny and clear with just a hint of spring's cool breezes. Most of the passengers were now strolling along the promenade, walking off their no-doubt hearty breakfasts. Some nodded or offered greetings to Hal, which he returned politely.

"I'm taking you up to the pilothouse now," Hal announced casually. "For a good view of the river."

Rosalind nodded, more relaxed than she would have expected. "Very well."

The big pilothouse was flooded with light and air, like a king's throne high atop the *Cherokee Belle*. Bellecourt still stood at the wheel, casually steering with one hand as he watched the Missouri ahead.

"*Ça va,* Bellecourt."

"*Ça va bien,* Lindsay," the older man responded, the French greeting sounding more like a casual reassurance. "*Bonjour,* Carstairs."

"*Bonjour, monsieur.*"

"Carstairs, Antoine Bellecourt learned the Missouri from his father, a French trapper who knew Lewis and Clark. He himself has traveled the Missouri in canoes, keelboats, and steamers before teaching me everything I know about piloting."

"You flatter me, *mon ami.*" Bellecourt bowed. "I am glad you came to join us, Carstairs. The river is still much the same as in my father's time, when Lewis and Clark first saw it, but the land—ah, that changes every day as more and more settlers come. Look around and see for yourself."

Rosalind nodded acknowledgment and turned to the world beyond the pilothouse.

Outside, Cicero trotted from the texas's roof down to the

hurricane deck and began to sniff busily at a water barrel in front of the pilothouse. As ever on a riverboat, the hurricane deck—with its hog chains running overhead for the length of the boat, plus poles, vents, and stairs—was designed for honest work, not idle perambulations by passengers.

Rosalind watched him for a moment, then looked at the river, which was clearly visible on all sides. The vibrations from the paddlewheel and Norton's engines were almost imperceptible here. A breeze caressed her cheek, bringing scents of green things reawakening. A swallow swooped out of the trees and snatched its prey just above the water, then circled back to safety.

Everything was so calm and rather mundane, almost like watching her favorite fishing hole on Long Island.

For the first time in the years since her mother's death, Rosalind's chest loosened onboard a boat. She cautiously allowed herself to watch the ripples dancing across the water, with little fear that they'd turn into towering waves.

There was silence for a few minutes. A great blue heron swept up from behind the *Belle* and flew on ahead, to disappear beyond the drowned oak trees ahead. Beyond them, the *Spartan*'s tall stacks belched smoke as Donovan stepped up onto the hurricane deck. He glanced around but made no effort to come up to the pilothouse.

"Your family is accumulating rapidly, Lindsay," Bellecourt remarked. "Your sister and her husband, then your parents, and now a cub. While my family sleeps in Kansas City, far from where I spend my days. You must feel tugged in many directions, whereas I have far too much time to contemplate my solitude."

Rosalind would have sworn Bellecourt's eyes were twinkling. What was he up to?

"Would you consider allowing me to tutor your cub? He seems an observant, steady lad. McKenzie can also help."

Rosalind's heart stopped beating for a moment. Learning

from Bellecourt would be a privilege—and not nearly as distracting as standing close to Hal.

Hal frowned thoughtfully before he looked at Rosalind. His blue eyes were more concerned than his voice's steadiness would indicate. "Is that agreeable to you, Carstairs?"

"Of course." She smiled back confidently, quite sure she'd be safe with Bellecourt and McKenzie. She'd learned a great deal about judging men in the past months, thanks to playing poker against them every day.

"Very well then, Bellecourt, and thank you."

"I am honored that you trust me with his education. He can stand all, or part, of my watches with me."

Hal studied her for a moment longer, then nodded. "In that case, I'll leave you two alone."

"And Lindsay . . ."

"Yes?"

"Ask Sampson if Carstairs can dine with me, or McKenzie, at the officers' table. He'll learn more from our company than the passengers'."

Hal nodded. "Of course."

Rosalind almost sighed with relief. If she ate with the officers, she'd be spared contact with Captain and Mrs. Lindsay, who knew her from New York.

Hal left and went down to the hurricane deck, where Cicero rushed to greet him while Donovan laughed. Rosalind was still smiling at the dog's joy as she turned back to the river.

"Have you fished, Carstairs? Hunted ducks or geese?" Bellecourt asked, easing the wheel into another turn. The Missouri's crookedness made the Minotaur's labyrinth seem as straight as a Roman road.

"Yes, sir, I did so often, with my father and brothers."

"Then relax and study the river. Study it the way you did when you hunted fish, Carstairs—when you looked for deep water or shallow, fast water or slow, depending on what you wanted to catch. Consider the birds and the bugs, what they can tell you about the currents."

Rosalind cocked her head as she considered the complexities involved in analyzing the river this way. It would be harder than playing seven-card stud with a tableful of drunks, when you'd no idea what they'd do next and any move could be violent. "Yes, sir. Then what?"

"Try to anticipate my movements as I steer the *Belle*."

"And then?"

"I will tell you when you reach that point, Carstairs. Learning this much will require several days."

Rosalind's eyebrows flew up. "Days?"

"Days." Bellecourt's tone brooked no argument.

"Yes, sir." *Days?* At that rate, she'd still be a cub pilot on the return voyage to Kansas City and never have stood a watch alone.

Rosalind stepped to the window and started looking for likely places to catch catfish or bass, the fish she judged most likely to be found in this shallow river. Black bass in clear quiet water, catfish in faster water.

Bellecourt's deep voice broke the silence. "See that bird on the bar there, off the starboard bow?"

She strained her eyes. It seemed a bit early in the year for a sandpiper, but the mincing gait was very distinctive. "The sandpiper, sir?"

"That's it. What does that bird tell you about the river?"

Rosalind reached back to childhood, when she'd tramped across Long Island's beaches with her brothers. "They like quiet water. So, uh, there's backwater there?" she ventured.

"Good. What else does it tell you about the river?"

She thought fast and gambled on her answer. "The strongest current is on the other side. Is that why there's a notch cut into the northern side, sir?"

"Excellent. Yes, the Missouri's getting ready to take that bar back. She creates islands and she eats them, just as fast."

Rosalind beamed inside at the praise, but managed a restrained, and hopefully manly, nod of acknowledgment.

"What type of craft have you steered before?" Bellecourt asked, as he casually took the *Belle* around the sandpiper's muddy scrap of land.

"A dinghy and rowboat, sir, on Long Island and in the Sound."

"Good training. You should learn the river rapidly then. The *Belle* is very responsive and well balanced, too. She may be easier to manage than your dinghy was."

Pride rumbled through the old man's voice, and Rosalind smiled. Heaven knows that dinghy had been a cantankerous pig, but she'd managed to steer it. Perhaps she could pull off this masquerade as a cub pilot. At least she understood the engines and the basics of piloting. Surely the rest would fall into place, at least well enough to see her to Fort Benton.

"Good to see you too, Cicero," Hal crooned, rubbing the dog's ears.

Cicero's eyes closed in an expression of canine bliss as his tail beat the air like a dragonfly's wings. He barked again but more softly.

"Fine dog you have there, Hal," William remarked as he stepped to within a foot of Cicero. "I knew his like when I was growing up in Ireland."

"Thanks. How was breakfast?" Hal asked, straightening up. "No, don't answer that. There are some matters brothers weren't meant to know."

William laughed and slapped Hal on the back.

Cicero growled.

"Don't be a damn fool, Cicero," Hal snapped. "He's my friend and yours too, if you have any sense."

Cicero rumbled something, then began to pace, clearly ready to defend Hal at any cost. Hal shook his head. "Dolt."

"They're usually loyal to only one man—or one family," William remarked. "Clever, courageous, good trackers, excellent fighters. You're lucky to have him."

"Yes, he's a brave one." Hal changed the subject, uncomfortable as ever in a discussion of dog ownership. "How's business?"

There was a long pause. Hal spun around to study his little sister's beloved husband, the man who had rescued her from starving on the dung heap called Rio Piedras. The man who'd risked his life to keep her safe from Paul Lennox. Hal's jaw tightened at the look he saw on William's face.

His fingers twitched, instinctively seeking the Colt at his waist.

"Profitable enough," William said slowly. He'd worn the same expression when he'd learned that Paul Lennox had kidnapped Viola, back in Rio Piedras.

"But?" Hal's voice was soft, quiet as he always was when facing a fight.

"Too many things are going wrong at the same time. Payments delayed, equipment damaged, supplies lost. Some of that could be chance."

"You don't think so."

Cicero growled, echoing Hal's tone.

William drummed his fingers on his bowie knife's hilt, then shook his head. "No, I'm afraid I can't pass it all off as bad luck. Especially not when the Army's canceling contracts, with no reason given."

"The devil you say!"

William nodded. "And the hell of it is that I can't discover any rhyme or reason for losing those contracts. They're just taken away when they reach the Secretary of War's desk. It's as if I've become a pariah, tainted by some crime too great to mention."

"Belknap's doing?" Hal asked, remembering gossip.

"Maybe. But surely he would know better than to disturb one of Sherman's longtime friends."

Hal grunted acknowledgment of that logic. "We'll straighten it out somehow."

"That's not necessary. I'm sure I can—"

"You're family and we stand together."

Surprise flashed across William's face. Hal lifted an eyebrow, daring William to object.

William blinked rapidly. Dust, or maybe a tear. "Thank you," he murmured before his expression returned to that of a smooth businessman.

"I have friends in Washington, at the Department of the Navy," Hal said briskly. "I can cable them—"

"That shouldn't be necessary. Belknap's likely the problem since he's the most corrupt man in Washington."

Hal whistled. "The Secretary of War? I'd heard some rumors but nothing solid."

William nodded. "He's dirtier than any of your firemen. Viola and I had to leave Washington before we could discover who bought him. So I asked Morgan Evans to learn what's happening, then report to me onboard the *Belle*."

Hal frowned. He'd known Evans back in Arizona as Donovan's local foreman and a good man in a saloon fight. Neither of those seemed like good training for a spy. "Can he accomplish that?"

William threw his head back and roared with laughter. Hal raised an eyebrow and waited for the explanation.

"He was one of Bedford Forrest's scouts during the War," William finally managed to say.

Hal whistled. He'd encountered Forrest's men more than once and had the scars to prove their competence. "Forrest? He was a frequent thorn in our side. So Evans was one of Forrest's devils. I almost feel sorry for those deskbound jackasses. When do you expect to see him?"

"Before Omaha."

"Ten days till we arrive," Hal mused. "So sometime in the next week or so, we should know who we're going to destroy."

"Destroy?"

"If I'd paid off Ross when he hinted at it. Or if I hadn't lost my temper and turned my back on Viola for marrying that coward, Viola wouldn't have been in that hut out in Arizona. That goddamn mud hut and the broken bottle with blood on its edges . . ." He broke off, fighting for control.

"Hal . . ." William took a step forward.

Hal waved him off. A minute later, he managed to speak again. "But you rescued her and made her happy. I'll stand by you two no matter what happens, even if it means killing the Secretary of War."

"Waste of time to kill a corrupt toad like Belknap," William observed in an overly businesslike tone. "The real question is who's pulling the strings."

Hal shrugged, glad to discuss actions rather than relive past agonies. "Sometimes you just have to hose the dirt off to get a clean boat."

The two men shared a long look of complete understanding.

"Thank you," William said quietly. "I've never gone into battle beside my brother before."

Hal slapped him on the shoulder. "Then we'll start by standing together at the bar. Barnes can fix you one of his famous lemonades and I'll have a real man's drink, a mint julep."

William hooted. "You call that a drink? Truly strong men turn aside from riotous spirits in favor of respectable beverages," he teased. "Perhaps you should confine yourself to milk."

Hal laughed.

Rosalind stepped inside the cabin and stretched, then lit the lamp. She began to close the shutters, glad of the privacy they offered.

Loud snoring came from the Alabama cabin next door, where the two farmers berthed. A merchant and his wife shared the Michigan cabin on the other side, empty now while they spent every waking minute at the bar.

The *Cherokee Belle* had laid up for the night an hour after dark. Like every other Missouri riverboat, she only traveled by daylight, when the river's vagaries could be properly appreciated and surmounted. So Rosalind had watched McKenzie find a solid tree on a bluff and guide the *Belle* through tying up alongside it.

After that, they'd eaten dinner at the officers' table before separating. Bellecourt and McKenzie had wanted to gauge the quality of the poker players aboard. Rosalind had simply announced the need for an early night.

She was truly tired. After the exertions of the previous night with Hal—Rosalind grinned at the memories—plus a long day spent watching the pilots as closely as if she were sitting at a poker table, it was hardly surprising that her eyes were dry and burning. Now she latched the shutters, yawned, and stripped off her coat.

The big brass bed beckoned her, with its crisp white linens and fluffy pillows. She could sleep there for hours in comfort. It was so big that she could fling her arms out. It was stable enough to dance on. In fact, it was so strong that it had barely creaked this morning when Hal made love to her.

Oh my, when Hal made love . . .

Her throat went dry and her breasts firmed. How magnificent he was and how skillful. One kiss from that firm mouth was enough to banish all thought and convert her into a raging inferno of lust.

She hung up her vest, smiling.

And he never hesitated, as David always had until she coaxed him into going farther than a kiss.

But Hal . . . He simply took and enjoyed. Without hesitation, without regrets, and with every fiber of his beautiful body, he hurtled into passion's dance.

Still, it would be lovely to explore him. The muscles in his shoulders, the crisp blond hairs on his chest crowned by those copper nipples . . . Were his man's nipples as sensitive as a woman's? Could they harden and thrust into the air when fondled or licked?

Dew trickled between her legs. Instinctively, she fondled her breasts through her linen shirt.

A dog barked. Another answered it from the riverbank. A man's footsteps sounded on the promenade outside, but the shutters hid his identity. Rosalind whirled around, her hand automatically reaching for her revolver.

"Silence, Cicero. Do you plan to gossip with every farm dog from here to Montana?" Hal growled and pushed open the door. Cicero strolled inside and leaped onto the cot.

Hal stepped in and stopped abruptly, his eyebrows lifting. His eyes blazed with lust, even as his hands went up. He kicked the door shut without looking at it. "Do you mean to shoot me with that, cub?" he drawled.

Her knees nearly buckled as an answering fire surged through her core. "No, sir. Of course not."

"Really? Then why is it cocked? Or did you have some other plans for this evening?" He stepped closer to her, crowding her with his warmth and scent. His mouth quirked under his crisp goatee.

Her nostrils flared and drank in the rich spice of male lust. Dear heavens, how she enjoyed that smell.

He wrapped his hand around the Colt's barrel and smiled at her. "I could take this, you know. Or perhaps I should insist that you pay attention to me, like a woman."

They were so close she could see the pulse beating in his neck. She glanced down and saw the hard bulge behind his fly. Her hand was shaking with the need to touch him and learn him and set fire to him.

She forced herself to speak calmly, or as calmly as one could when one's body was clamoring to grab a man. "I could demand something of you."

"Such as?" His tongue ran out over his lips.

He hadn't refused. "Take your clothes off, while I trim the lamp. The shutters are helpful but not a guarantee, especially if I'm to pay attention to you."

He gave her a quick kiss, totally ignoring her revolvers. "Damn, you're direct," he purred. "But I'll strive to deal with it."

Rosalind snorted as she holstered her gun. "You seem rather excited by my words."

"And the sight of you, half-dressed and aggressive, takes my breath away." He kissed her again. Her head was spinning when he stopped and started to strip.

Rosalind's hands shook as she trimmed the lamp to a more subdued glow. She was deeply grateful that she'd never played poker as his lover. She might not be able to form a coherent thought while distracted by his attractions. She could make some ridiculous wagers if he flirted with her across the table.

"And now?"

She choked at the sight of him, and her heart leaped in her breast. Hal stood, with his fists planted on his hips and his feet spread, wearing only his skin. His cock was scarlet with hunger as it reared toward the ceiling.

Dear heavens, he was magnificent.

A smile played around his lips. "What next?" he rumbled in a velvety growl, like a hungry gambler's approval of a fat pot.

Rosalind forced herself to think. "Lie down on your back. On the bed," she added hastily, lest he tease her by reclining on the cot with Cicero.

"As you wish." He disposed himself against the pristine white coverlet as if he knew he was a greater temptation than chocolate bonbons.

Hal smiled at Rosalind, more than willing to learn her intentions. A kiss perhaps? But no, that seemed too demure for his clear-headed lover.

In any case, it didn't matter what she planned, especially now that she'd put aside those Colts. She'd been damn brave today in the pilothouse—standing there stiff and straight, looking at the water, and never flinching. Her stiff-backed attitude had reminded him of Vicksburg, when a Confederate shell had beheaded his pilot. A young quartermaster, with no previous experience handling a boat, had leaped to the *St. Paul*'s wheel and somehow kept the gunboat on course, despite being half blinded by the pilot's blood and brains.

That young man had held himself just as painfully erect as Rosalind had today. And he'd grinned like a fool, when Hal ordered an extra ration of rum for him. Hal expected he'd enjoy Rosalind's idea of fun a good deal more.

Her voice brought him back to the present.

"Hands behind your head."

"What?"

"I don't want you to distract me. Put your hands behind your head."

"Very well." He did as she requested—and purred when she stared at his rearing cock. It bid fair to be an excellent evening's entertainment. Pity she'd be disembarking at Fort Benton.

She trailed her fingers down his arm to his shoulder. She traced his collarbone, then the line bisecting his chest. Hesitated—and lightly outlined his pectoral muscle.

Just how experienced was she? He hadn't given her much time before to display her skills. A slow circle brought her to his nipple. It promptly recreated itself as a stabbing point, flushed with blood and aching for her touch.

Praise the Almighty, she rubbed it. He gasped for breath as hunger swirled through his veins like a morning fog, clouding his judgment. She fondled it again, pinched it lightly. Scratched it just enough to teach his aching flesh a new sensation.

He bit back a groan.

Rosalind licked him, swirling over his chest in the same lazy circle her finger had followed. Circled his nipple and laved it. She was clumsier than other lovers he'd had but much more intent on him. Then she suckled him.

He groaned, the sound rising up through his body in rhythm with her long, slow pulls on his tit. His belly tightened, and his cock throbbed. Then she turned her attention to his other tit. She'd obviously learned from the first and soon found the most sensitive spots. She incited him with fingers, tongue, and teeth until he was groaning like a love-starved fool, his eyes slitted with pleasure. Lord have mercy, how he enjoyed being the center of her carnal attentions. All the while, Rosalind stroked his thighs idly, as if petting a restless horse. But she never touched his cock.

Hal tried to demand that she put her hand where it would do the most good. If he could just persuade her to pull on his cock once or twice, he was entirely sure he'd spend himself. Then he could regain his self-control from this fever of lust and tumble her as she deserved.

She cupped his balls gently. His hips damn near came off the bed as he arched toward her. "Damn it to hell, Rosalind," he gasped.

"Roll over."

What the devil? Hal blinked before he could focus on her. She was standing over him, arms akimbo and breast heaving. Her nipples thrust boldly against her white cotton shirt, and her cheeks were flushed. She ran her tongue over her lips.

Hal smiled deep inside. He was seducing her without lifting a finger, just by letting her play with him.

"Roll over," she growled.

"Yes, ma'am." He obeyed, taking a little longer than necessary so she'd see what she was losing. His rampant cock brushed against the coverlet's embroidery and the heavy cotton thread rubbed it like another hand.

Hal choked at the blast of sensation racing outward through his groin. He bit his lip until it bled, fighting not to erupt then and there.

A minute, or two, passed before he finally settled on a spot without too much embroidery to tantalize him. Then he remembered the old caning scars, which he'd never permitted a lover to touch before. *Damn.* Should he stop her? *No,* retorted his cock.

"Ready?"

"Of course." Dear God, what would she think of his scars?

She chuckled, then set to work exploring his back. Rational thought faded. Shoulders, spine, shoulder blades—she traced them all with her fingers then her mouth. She licked. She kissed the old bullet scar under his rib.

He shuddered. Lord have mercy, her lightest touch made his bones melt. He strained for breath as she charted his back, like a cub pilot learning a great river. His hips twisted and rubbed his cock against the coverlet. He almost howled, but managed to force himself to stillness. He was totally at her mercy, hungry to satisfy her slightest carnal whim.

She nuzzled a long arc from arm to arm, tracing where a cane had once blazed fire across his back. Her touch seemed a path to his back's most sensitive spots, as his blood heated and raced through his veins. He clenched his fists and bit the pillow when she nuzzled him again, then traced another arc and another until she'd explored every inch of his shoulders.

The sweet agony of her seduction burned away old memories, when his father's cane had etched scars into his flesh. His hips rocked against the bed, aching for more stimulation, desperate for release. His cock was hard and full, his balls tight against their roots. He groaned his approval into the smothering pillow and pushed himself back at her.

Rosalind's sweet mouth moved down his back to his ass. She stroked the muscles, traced his spine to where it disappeared, kissed the hollow just above the heavy muscle.

She licked and kissed his ass, then did the same to his thighs. Her finger slipped between his legs and petted his balls with the lightest possible touch.

His hips would not stay still. They pushed against the bed rhythmically, faster and faster, as lust demanded more and more of him. He had barely enough sense to keep his mouth hidden in the pillow.

She bit him delicately on the rump, barely setting her teeth against his flesh. Hal exploded. His body thrashed against the bed. His seed boiled out of his balls and up through his cock like steam rushing through a boiler. Stars burst behind his eyelids. He spent himself, howling her name into the forgiving pillow.

Chapter Nine

Rosalind's hand twitched, unconsciously echoing Belle-court's movements in the Cherokee Belle's pilothouse. Bellecourt guided the big riverboat along the water's silver ribbon between the islands as if he were following a straight flush. He had the height and coloring of his Nez Percé mother's family, with the affability of his French *coureur de bois* father, giving him both his mother's stories and his father's skill in telling them. After two days of watching him like a starving sharper in a gambling house, Rosalind was starting to learn a little of how the river looked to a pilot. Thankfully, there were no tall waves to alarm her.

"And so, we take the turn here, under the western bluff, where the current is deepest, *comprenez*? The jackstaff, that tall pole at the front of the hurricane deck, will show us where the *Belle* is aimed."

"Oui, monsieur," Rosalind answered absently as she checked to see how close they'd come to land. The river had undercut the cliff so steeply that oak trees leaned out over the water, as if trying to caress the passing boat.

Barking sounded from the hurricane deck, and Rosalind leaned forward to look. Viola Donovan was teasing Cicero with an old sock wrapped around a big bone. She passed it from one hand to the other behind her back, or tossed it from hand to hand, just enough to give the eager terrier a glimpse. All the while, Cicero danced in front of her and barked happily, tongue lolling out as he begged for the treat.

Her husband laughed indulgently as he watched their foolishness, while standing protectively between her and the edge.

Rosalind echoed the same smile, remembering how her old spaniel would play with her and her brothers, bouncing from side to side in readiness to chase the ball. Hal was very lucky to have family like that, and a childhood to cement the bond. She couldn't believe he'd gained those scars at the same time.

As if summoned by her thought, Hal stepped into the pilothouse and looked around. Rosalind snapped back to the present with a jerk.

"The next flood will likely take those oaks. *Quel dommage,*" Bellecourt prophesied, spinning the wheel as easily as any roulette dealer. He rang down for more speed, steadied the wheel, and nodded to Hal. "Any cables from the pilot's association?"

Hal frowned. "No, nothing from the association or anyone else about the Missouri. Why? Looking for news about river levels?"

Bellecourt nodded. "I think the spring rise will be long and high."

Hal whistled. "It was a hard winter, especially in the Rockies, and the weather's been changeable since then. But spring floods as well? That would be very dangerous."

"Less chance of running aground."

"Better chance of catching driftwood," Hal retorted. "And we'd need two men to handle her on every watch."

"*Mais certainement.* Will you take the wheel please? I'd like to cable some friends in Omaha and Nebraska City to hear their thoughts about the local rivers."

"My pleasure."

Hal stepped up to the big wheel. Rosalind's eyes widened at how easily and smoothly he took control, one big hand casually wrapped around a spoke and the other resting on the bell to the engine room.

"Ask Sampson to stop at the Brunson farm," Hal said, "whether or not they've got a flag up. We'll pay them a dollar if their eldest takes the cable to the nearest telegraph office."

"Bien." Bellecourt disappeared without a backward glance.

Rosalind blew out her breath and looked back at the river. She loved these quiet times with Hal in the pilothouse, close enough that his clean scent teased her nostrils. She wouldn't dream of intruding on him and the Donovans, of course, no matter how much she envied him the happiness he found with his sister. Strange that her happiest times this spring had been found atop a pile of inch-thick lumber, while floating on a wild river.

He stayed silent as he guided the *Belle* through a series of turns, dodging between barely visible sandbars, an island, and the tall bluffs to the west. He was as utterly competent as Bellecourt, his movements crisp and certain, yet relaxed even when he rang for a burst of full speed.

A broad, straight stretch opened up before them, surprisingly long for the Missouri, at almost two miles. Overhead, a great flock of pelicans flew steadily north, as if guided by the great river. Miles ahead, the *Spartan*'s tall stacks were just visible, twisting and turning as she worked her way through crooked water.

"Put your hands on the wheel, Carstairs."

"Yes, sir." Rosalind's heart leaped into her mouth. She hoped her voice sounded calm. Her fingers closed around a pair of spokes convulsively. *Think about the Belle, not what the water can do to you,* she admonished herself.

"Just get the sense of her coming through the wheel. We're in a deep channel, with no sandbars nearby, so you should only feel the water."

The *Belle* rumbled slightly as she moved upriver. Rosalind could easily find the vibrations from the paddlewheel. A little more concentration made her aware of the deep, heavy ripples lifting the hull.

"Care to take her?"

She gulped and nodded.

Hal lifted his hand, and the *Belle* belonged to Rosalind. She focused fiercely on the boat under her control.

A puff of wind pushed the *Belle* to the east, away from the channel. Hissing softly, Rosalind brought the steamer back to the center with white-knuckled hands—only to have her promptly veer to the left. The big white boat was far more responsive to the helm than her family's dinghy had ever been.

"See that big oak on the bluff ahead? Just keep the jackstaff lined up on it and you'll have a straight course."

She nodded, desperate to do exactly that. But every move seemed to make the *Belle* wallow across the river like a ferryboat.

"Use less wheel when you correct her. Two spokes are better than four."

Only spin the wheel two spokes past the center? Rosalind muttered a very improper bit of Latin under her breath as she fought the stubborn boat into something loosely approximating a straight line.

Hal chuckled. "Bet you can't hold a steady course for a full minute, using only one spoke in each turn."

Rosalind's competitiveness instantly flared into roaring life. She hadn't lost a bet in years, except to her father. "What do I win?"

He shrugged. "I'll stand first watch with you tomorrow. But if I win, then you have to bring me breakfast in bed."

"Done." Her mouth tightened, and she glared at the offending jackstaff. If it dared to stray far from that oak tree . . .

Hal took out his pocket watch. "Begin."

She squinted at the bluff and willed the *Cherokee Belle* to stay on a straight course. A mischievous breeze pushed the steamer to the east. Rosalind promptly corrected. One spoke went past . . .

Her hand tightened, and the wheel stopped just before a second spoke could go over the top. Praise to the Almighty, the river was deep and wide here, fed by a fat little stream. She needed the extra space to keep the *Belle* safe.

"Thirty seconds."

The jackstaff tried to saunter toward the oak tree's branches, rather than the trunk. Rosalind corrected it grimly, barely turning one spoke.

"Ten seconds." Hal's tone was conversational.

Rosalind prayed that the watch hands would move quickly as she hung onto the wheel.

"Done. Congratulations, Carstairs."

Rosalind's knees weakened in relief before she brought herself fiercely erect. "I always knew I could do it."

"Of course!" Hal slapped her on the shoulder. "But let me take her now."

"Yes, sir." Rosalind slowly relinquished the wheel, surprisingly eager to take it again.

She was still pondering that question when she entered the stateroom that evening. She'd played a few hands of poker after dinner, while Hal strolled the boiler deck with his sister and Donovan.

Captain and Mrs. Lindsay had been holding court in the grand saloon, as usual, where he told tall tales that rivaled the best Rosalind had ever heard and kept an eye on his wife. A group of like-minded gentlemen had gathered around him and spent much of their time trading stories about fish, wartime heroics, or business successes. Meanwhile, Mrs. Lindsay was flirting with the rest of the men.

Rosalind's mouth tightened. While she knew that not every couple had her parents' laughing delight in each other, it still scandalized her Knickerbocker heart to see a married woman encouraging strange men to leer at her.

Thankfully, her duties as cub pilot kept her away from the Lindsays during the day. At night, when the *Cherokee Belle* laid up, Rosalind dined at the officers' table—and kept her mouth tightly sealed as befitted the most junior officer on-board—then escaped to the stateroom she shared with Hal.

A light knock on the door made her jump. "Enter," she called, automatically deepening her voice.

Ezra poked his head around the door.

"Evenin', sir. Do you want me to turn down the covers before you retire?"

"Yes, thank you." She chastised herself for forgetting her disguise. If Ezra had arrived a few minutes later, she'd have been asleep in the big bed.

She leaned against the wall by the washbasin, careful to appear as indolently masculine as she could manage, while she watched Ezra. He was whistling softly as he worked and hadn't looked directly at her since he entered. How had Hal acquired such a discreet servant?

"When did you meet Mr. Lindsay, Ezra?"

"June of '62, sir."

"Ten years is a long time to work for the same man," Rosalind commented.

"He saved my life and I'll serve him as long as I live." Ezra glanced up at her from beside the cot, his hand smoothing its blanket. He was a thin man, barely five feet in height, but an indomitable spirit looked out from his raven black eyes.

Surprised at his response, Rosalind cocked an eyebrow. "What happened?"

"I was being caned on a plantation just outside Vicksburg, for having been two minutes late with the master's coffee. The master liked to teach new slaves the meaning of naval discipline, so he ordered one blow for every second I was late."

"The devil you say!" Rosalind came erect in anger at Ezra's mistreatment. *One blow for each second he'd been late? Intolerable!*

"First time I'd ever been caned and I knew right away, I'd rather have a hard whipping," Ezra said soberly, his eyes distant.

Rosalind choked at the thought of any punishment worse than a whipping.

"I'd had thirty of the promised hundred twenty blows, and my senses were fading. Suddenly, a fury broke through the trees like Gabriel's horn was leading the whole Yankee army."

"Was it Mr. Lindsay?"

"Lieutenant Lindsay, back then," Ezra corrected her gently. "He was leading a group of sailors from his gunboat, scouting for a passage through the swamp around the rebel guns."

The former slave smiled, past joy lighting his face.

"And?" Rosalind prompted.

He focused on her again. "He didn't have to save me. He could have waited an hour till the caning was over and all the watchers had left. Or he could have come back that night."

"Instead, Mr. Lindsay took action immediately." Rosalind probed gently.

"Yes, sir. He shot the overseer dead, dropping him into the dust like a bottle fly. Then he held that big gun to my master's head and told him he could either sell me or eat a bullet."

"The brute chose?"

"To sell me." Ezra's tone was mildly regretful.

"Pity."

Ezra shrugged. "Mr. Lindsay freed me, formally, as soon as he could. Said he wanted me to sleep at night, not have nightmares about my old master coming after me."

He paused for a moment before going on. "There's nothing I wouldn't do for Mr. Lindsay, nothing." His eyes drilled into hers, as if willing her to understand.

Realization swept over Rosalind. "His scars—they're from a caning, aren't they?"

"Yes, sir. Only a cane, used by an expert, leaves diamond-shaped marks like that."

"Yours must be worse," Rosalind said slowly, feeling her way through the implications.

Ezra shrugged. "No, sir. His are older, so they've faded more than mine. 'Sides, he's younger than I am and not bred to be beaten."

"God damn the vicious brutes to hell," Rosalind cursed, forgetting herself entirely.

"Yes, sir, that's what I think too, most of the time. Then I remember my mammy's teachings and I pray for God's forgiveness for them all."

"I'm sure the Almighty can forgive them, but I certainly have a hard time."

Ezra's teeth flashed in a grin. "I do too, sir. Will that be all for the night?"

"Yes, thank you. Good night, Ezra."

"Good night, sir." Ezra bowed, as polite as any English butler, and disappeared, leaving Rosalind to her thoughts. Who had beaten Hal? Had it been at his home or on a riverboat?

She shrugged off her futile questions and prepared for bed. Five o'clock came remarkably early, especially when accompanied by river mists and a cool spell. She fell asleep within minutes of climbing into the cot, lulled by the next-door farmers' incessant snoring.

Suddenly, she awoke with a violent start, to find herself

lifted into the air with the covers wrapped tightly around her. Instinctively, she started to fight. "What the devil—"

"Easy there, easy," Hal's voice crooned in her ear.

Rosalind stared up at him. A vagrant beam of gaslight crept through the shutters and lit his golden hair like an angel's halo. She wriggled again. "What are you doing? Put me down, please."

"All in good time, cub. All in good time. After all, Cicero deserves his bed, too."

"Hal, I can't move," Rosalind pointed out tartly and tried to free herself.

"True. And I can't touch your sweet breasts either. But I can reach your mouth."

Her arrogant lover kissed her, teasing her lips with his tongue. His breath hinted at brandy, while his goatee teased her. His scent was his own indefinable musk, a combination of sandalwood and Castile soap, and something uniquely Hal, masculine, and irresistible.

Rosalind sighed and opened her mouth so that she could twine her tongue with his. He played the game for long minutes, their tongues gliding together in a tempo that grew closer and closer to something more carnal.

She shuddered with hunger. Her breasts were hard, aching for his touch. Her nipples had tightened into engorged points, pressing anxiously toward him. The cot's covers were wrapped so closely around her that the blanket's wool reached through the sheet and nightshirt to rub her skin, like lust's sweet agony.

Two nights of sleeping with him had taught her body to hunger for him the way a poker player longed for a king to finish his royal straight.

"Hal, please. I need to touch you," she moaned, too desperate to refrain from begging.

He chuckled, although the sound was hoarse and broken. "But I have the better of you now. Surely, this is an opportunity to do what I like first. Such as kissing you again."

His mouth came down on hers hard this time and he kissed her like a devil, intent on creating pleasure without allowing any counterarguments.

Rosalind's brain, recognizing his greater skill and strength—and remembering past delights far too well—gave up the unequal contest. She became a creature of pure sensation, linked to the rest of the universe through his mouth, the warmth of his body through the cloth, and the strength of his arms holding her tenderly.

She wriggled again, eager to be closer to him.

He kissed her again and again until she nearly swooned, keeping her confined by his arms and the cot's bedding. At some point, he had sat down on the bed because his hard thighs supported her now. But still his arms cradled her, and his mouth taught her new paths to excitement.

Her core clenched again and again, in rhythm with his tongue's movements. Her dew dampened her thighs, then soaked her nightshirt and the sheet. Her skin was fiery hot, sensitive enough to feel every button's imprint on her skin, thanks to the pressure of his prison.

He nuzzled her face, teasing her with the contrast between his nighttime stubble and silken goatee. Rosalind mewed, too lost in his magic to form words. The cocoon's pressure forced her legs and intimate folds so closely together that every sensation was magnified a hundredfold, as if she were being rubbed everywhere. She could feel her lower lips unfurl and engorge, her clit swell and stand proud, her dew anoint them—all in readiness for him.

He nibbled her eyebrows, scraped his teeth down her nose, and sucked lightly on her lip. Rosalind arched up to him.

Hal kissed down her throat and licked the pulse at the base. At the same time, his hand slipped into the cocoon and stroked her leg. She groaned his name. Her hips pulsed in rhythm with his tongue. There was barely room for him to find a way between her legs, but he managed. He teased her clit very delicately.

Ecstasy surged through her, sweet and passionate, and she barely managed not to cry out. She started to relax, then gasped in shock as his finger entered her. He pumped her, urging her upward again mercilessly.

Helpless to resist, Rosalind arched and climaxed again, sobbing with pleasure. He stretched her with two fingers, then three, ruthlessly using his knowledge of her body's appetites. He took her mouth fiercely, swallowing her pleas for more. She shattered again and consciousness faded.

Cool air touched her thighs. Sweat trickled down her face. She blinked and stirred. "Hal?"

"Little lady," he muttered, rousing her senses with the verbal reminder of how fragile and precious she was to him, and spread her legs. Then he drove himself home between her legs in one ferocious stroke.

Rosalind gasped and reached for him. The cocoon's last remnants fell away and she was free to wrap herself around him. "Do it again."

He chuckled softly and kissed her hair. His coat's fine wool teased her gently, even through her nightshirt. His vest's buttons branded her, while his trousers scratched her thighs. The rich scent of his arousal filled her lungs.

"Again," she demanded and rocked her hips against him to emphasize her eagerness.

"Greedy," he teased hoarsely, then rode her. His speed quickly became that of a thoroughbred in a race's final furlongs, as passion sped faster and faster through them both.

Rosalind bit his shoulder, desperate not to beg louder, even though their neighbors' snores still sounded.

Hal grunted softly and tightened his grip on her hips. He shifted his angle slightly and thrust again. This time, his cock reached deeper into her, to where her muscles locked down on him like a poker player seizing the jackpot.

He growled and froze. His cock jerked again and again inside her as he came. She fell over the precipice, sobbing his name as passion swept her entire body.

Her sight grayed in the aftermath, then darkened as he rolled to cuddle her. Only his touch mattered now, and she fell asleep smiling.

Rosalind took another sip of her steaming coffee and reminded herself to thank Ezra. The hot drink was excellent, equal to anything she would have found in her father's house, and a splendid complement to the early morning scenery.

It was far better than the wretched stuff she'd drunk on the *Pretty Lady,* probably because of Norton's pet gadget, a water filtration system. No other boat on the Missouri had one, forcing their passengers to drink what Horace Greeley, the famous newspaperman, had called "the color and consistency of thick milk porridge."

The view was especially beautiful if she didn't look at the water itself. The air was clear and still, a suitable backdrop for the few white tendrils of mist that rose from the water or draped themselves over the trees. A handful of great blue herons stalked through an inlet and a bald eagle watched from high atop a drowned oak tree, all of them far enough away to ignore the boat. Far to the east, the skies danced with brilliant colors as hundreds of Carolina parakeets came for breakfast in an open field.

Or perhaps they'd heard Captain Sampson's inflexible rule that no firearms would be discharged at any time, lest the ladies aboard be discomfitted. Any man who violated that rule, or any other rule posted in the bar, would be put ashore immediately. Captain Sampson had only enforced it once, which apparently made this a very peaceable voyage.

Bellecourt was at the wheel, humming as he eased the

Belle past a side channel. Hal looked out the port window and muttered something under his breath.

"Any sign of them?" Bellecourt asked.

"Not yet." Hal picked up the telescope and began to scan the scene ahead.

Rosalind refrained from asking what they were discussing. Bellecourt was usually a very talkative sort, full of stories about the river, his French father, and his Indian mother's relatives. Rosalind hadn't been bored once. She was quite sure he'd explain the current conversation soon enough.

Cicero looked into the pilothouse, decided the humans there were completely uninteresting, and departed. A moment later, Rosalind saw him happily racing around the hurricane deck, apparently playing a game only he understood.

Hal froze and refocused the telescope. "There it is, in that elm tree off to starboard. See it?"

Straining her eyes, Rosalind could just make out a large bundle hanging high up in the tree.

"*Bien*," Bellecourt rumbled. "Now we shall have venison for dinner."

"Or wild turkey, or prairie chicken. Maybe bear."

Rosalind's eyebrows shot up. *Bear?*

Bellecourt shook his head. "They haven't taken a bear on this stretch of river for several years now. We'll have to go further north before we can taste that fine meat."

Hal lowered the telescope and caught Rosalind's surprise. "Didn't travel much on the upper Mississippi, eh, Carstairs?"

"No, sir. Are you talking about hunters?"

"Yes, the *Cherokee Belle* has two of the best working for her. They range ahead, take what game they can, and cache it for us to find."

"Does every boat have hunters working for them?"

"If they want fresh meat, they do. We buy where we can, of course, but the hunters are the surest source. And in Indian country, they also act as scouts."

"The *Spartan* doesn't have hunters this season," Bellecourt commented.

Hal's eyebrow lifted. "I thought she'd signed one on in Kansas City."

Bellecourt shook his head. "Not a one, *mon ami.*"

"Excuse me, sirs, but what are you talking about?" Rosalind asked.

Bellecourt shrugged, his expression turning grim. "Last season, the *Spartan's* stern knocked against a bluff and took down a Blackfoot burial ground."

Hal nodded. "Damn fool. He should have gone around like everyone else, instead of trying to shave an hour off his run."

"Word is that the *Spartan's* cursed and no hunter will accompany her into Indian country," Bellecourt finished.

"And Hatcher, being his usual arrogant self, wanted everything or nothing," Hal interpreted for Rosalind. "So unless a hunter signed on for the full voyage to Fort Benton, the *Spartan* wouldn't have him."

"*Précisément.* The last man he hired in Kansas City was too drunk to travel and the *Spartan* sailed without him."

There was silence after that as Bellecourt worked. He brought the *Cherokee Belle* into a wide stretch of river, almost calm enough to be called a lake. A broad, muddy bar stretched before the tree, holding the meat cache.

Rosalind frowned slightly, considering—as she'd been taught—how best to approach the tree. She'd seen many landings during her times on riverboats. All riverboats, except the vaunted packets of Captain Lindsay's Cincinnati-Louisville Packet Line, were so eager for business that they picked up passengers and freight as requested by any town, hamlet, or farm.

But every one of those landings had ended with the boat tied up to a tree or a dock. The closest tree to the river held the cached meat and it was too far, thanks to the sandbar, for the *Belle* to use it.

Rosalind was still puzzling over the landing when she sensed, rather than saw, Hal and Bellecourt look at each other. Then Bellecourt spoke. "Will you do the honors, Lindsay?"

"My pleasure." Hal took Bellecourt's position, with one hand on the wheel and the other ready to ring the engine room.

"Carstairs, take the helm."

"Yes, sir." She swallowed hard and obeyed. She was supposed to land the *Belle*?

"Just take her straight in to the sandbar," Hal ordered quietly and let go of the wheel.

"There isn't a tree to tie up to," Rosalind pointed out.

"The *Belle* has a spoonbill prow so she's stable on any bit of muddy land, without a tree's assistance."

"Very well." Her hands were sweating even more than on her first visit to a gambling house. She forced herself to be calm. She'd played poker alone and won. Here, she had friends and teachers. She could do this.

"All you have to do is steer. I'll give the calls to the engine room," Hal added.

"Thank you, sir," Rosalind said with considerable feeling. She'd had visions of herself mistakenly ringing for full-speed ahead.

"It's how I was taught. Bellecourt was always very careful of his boat."

The old master chuckled wickedly from where he leaned against a window.

She lined the jackstaff up on the elm tree and prayed. An eddy tried to divert the *Belle*, but Rosalind held her steady. Her knuckles were white as she gripped the wheel, desperately holding a straight course. She didn't dare take her eyes away from the jackstaff and the tree.

"You can land her anywhere along that sandbar," Hal commented. "O'Brien's men will just have a little further to run."

Rosalind nodded without looking at him. Calm swept over her at his words, the same peace she'd felt before at a poker table. Vibrantly alive, aware of anything and everything, in command of herself and her surroundings.

Hal rang down for half speed ahead, which the engine room promptly answered. The great wheel eased under Rosalind's hands as the sound of churning waters lessened.

"Signal that you're landing, Carstairs," Hal prompted.

"Of course." The correct whistle popped into her head, as if she'd been doing this for years.

She pulled the line. The *Belle*'s sweet three-note whistle blew as requested, ringing over the silent waters like the cry of a great white songbird: one long and two short.

Hal rang down for quarter-speed ahead. There was very little sound coming from the *Belle*'s stern now. Rosalind kept the boat on course, praying hard. The muddy stretch of shoreline was coming closer and closer—and looking smaller and smaller. She could carry this out.

Just before they struck, Hal rang for quarter-speed back. The *Belle*'s momentum eased her onto the sandbar as gracefully as a swan. She glided a few feet up the muddy slope, then stopped with only a slight lurch.

Immediately, O'Brien's shout sent a pair of roustabouts over the side and running to the tree. All the while, the *Belle* idled on the sandbar.

The roustabouts returned in less than five minutes, grinning with accomplishment as they held up two large bags. They jumped aboard and O'Brien promptly rang the boat's bell.

Hal glanced over at Rosalind, and she nodded. She blew the whistle, signaling departure, just as he rang down for half speed astern. The *Belle* eased off the sandbar as gracefully as she'd alighted on it. The current caught her stern and smoothly turned her. Rosalind accepted the change, letting the boat head back into the main channel.

Hal rang for half speed ahead, then full speed ahead as the *Belle* proudly returned to her course. Rosalind's breath eased out for what felt like the first time in hours.

"*Très bien*, Carstairs!" Bellecourt slapped her on the back. "Very neat indeed. Far better than Lindsay's first try," he added slyly.

Hal laughed. "In a swamp, with river pirates shooting at us? I still say my landing was the least of that day's excitement."

Rosalind laughed with the two men, giddy with delight. Boats, at least this one, might be fun from time to time.

"Congratulations, Carstairs."

Hal immediately stiffened, and Bellecourt fell silent. Rosalind dared a glance over her shoulder.

Captain Lindsay stood in the pilothouse's door, immaculate as ever in an elegant black wool coat. He might have spoken to her, but his eyes were on his son.

The ship's gossip was full of speculation as to why the father and son so seldom spoke to each other. The only item New York gossip could contribute was that it was very unusual to see a breach between two Lindsays. The clan was notorious for how tightly they stood together.

"Thank you, sir." She was relieved that her voice was even huskier than usual.

"Would you care to join me for breakfast to celebrate your first landing as a pilot? With your mentor, of course. The chef has promised my wife brioche, thanks to yesterday's purchase of fresh butter."

So Captain Lindsay's invitation was really for Hal.

Hal's face was a cold mask of meaningless politeness. The proud confidence, fitting in the pilot who'd guided Rosalind through her first landing, was now almost totally eclipsed by wariness. He opened his mouth, but Bellecourt spoke first as he stepped to the wheel.

"I'll take the *Belle* now, Carstairs. No need to task your beginner's luck with the next stretch of crooked water. Captain Lindsay is a famous pilot, and I'm sure you can learn much from him. I'll keep an eye on the *Spartan* as well, since she seems to be dropping back."

Rosalind relinquished the helm just as Hal spoke. Reluctance lurked in every note. "Thank you for the invitation, sir. We'd be honored to join you."

Captain Lindsay bowed his head in acknowledgement and led the way after one last, sweeping glance at Hal. Rosalind could have sworn she saw longing and frustrated pride in the older man's eyes.

Chapter Ten

Rosalind trailed Hal and his father, slowly down the stairs, thinking back to when she'd last seen Desdemona Lindsay. In Kansas City, with semen drying on Desdemona's face, and before that, on a frosty winter night in Manhattan two days before Cornelius Schuyler's death . . .

Rosalind and her father, Cornelius Schuyler, came out of the gambling den and paused to button up their overcoats against the January cold.

Her family had always spent Wednesday night playing cards, with poker the game of choice by the time she turned ten. When she was seventeen, Father had used it to coax her back into life after Mother and her brothers died in the '65 nor'easter. He'd played endless games of cards with her, diverted her by dressing her as a man, and taken her to gambling resorts, where no one would recognize her. By now in early 1872, such masquerades were their favorite sport as they sought to challenge each other with more skillful crooks or dangerous surroundings.

New York's Tenderloin district was a suitable scene for such adventures, with the snow providing a spurious cloak of innocence. Even after midnight, men prowled in the fitful light from taverns looking for prey or to celebrate a success, while loose women hunted for one last customer before seeking shelter.

Further down the street at the corner, Rosalind could see their footmen, Clark and Matthews. Clark touched his hat, and Rosalind smiled. Their carriage would be ready and waiting, as soon as she and her father reached the corner.

"What did you think of that last deck of cards?" her father asked. One of his revolvers bumped against her hip.

Despite all the generations of wealth and stolidity behind him, Cornelius Schuyler enjoyed taking chances. He gambled in some of the roughest dens in North America, and he invested in railroads, pitting his judgment of men and technology against some of the most ruthlessly corrupt men in the world.

He frequently joked that a faro game in a Cincinnati wolf trap was more honest than the stock market; at least in a wolf trap, you had some hope of finding honest men in the crowd. Wolf traps, those lowest forms of gambling den, were always startling because violence could come at any time for any reason. The game itself was usually a square one, simply because otherwise the dealer would be dead within seconds. They were splendid places to gamble, if you were honest and kept a cool head.

"Shaved," Rosalind shrugged as she moved her pair of pocket Navy Colts into her overcoat, where they could be reached easily. The coat sagged a bit, but it would be more surprising in this rough neighborhood not to be armed. "The edges were very smooth but I could still feel how much narrower the cards' centers were."

The guns had been a present from her older brother Richard on their last Christmas together, a more delicate version of the deadly accurate Navy Colts he had carried. They'd practiced together for days before he'd let her carry them in a public place. Now she wore them whenever she visited rough neighborhoods.

"Good observation."

"Thank you."

By mutual consent, neither spoke about the five hundred dollars she'd won by recognizing the cards' deception. The den's proprietor had probably alerted a thief to the win, offering to split the take from robbing the two Schuylers.

Lawson and McNamara came out of the gambling den behind them, squabbling amiably about a faro dealer's honesty. Rosalind ignored them, pulled her broad-brimmed planter's hat further down over her face, and started down the street with her father.

Cornelius Schuyler usually frequented establishments where the gamblers were bourgeois and unacquainted with him or his daughter. But when he wanted to pit their expertise against skilled professionals, he'd take her to more risky locales. Still, he always took a few trusted servants for protection, with some entering the gambling den to stay close at hand. Lawson and McNamara, for example, were Union Army veterans, excellent pugilists—and gardeners.

"David's taking me to lunch with his grandmother tomorrow," Rosalind remarked, as she carefully stepped around a leaning fence post.

Her father grunted an acknowledgment. "Have you told him about your masquerades?"

Rosalind sighed. "No, not yet."

"He's a good man. He'll understand." He didn't sound completely confident.

She shrugged. "Maybe."

She left her greatest fear unsaid, that David would leave if he found out she was unconventional enough to pose as a man. He had extremely high standards for behavior, given his plans for public office. And he was a perfect fiancé from so many angles: quite wealthy in his own right, happy to converse with her as a rational human being, a graceful flirt, and her occasional bed partner.

A drunk staggered past them in the street, reeking of gin and sweat and urine and worse. Rosalind gagged slightly and wished she were home. She'd never quite become accustomed to the smells in the rough districts. And she always prayed heartily that she wouldn't step in something too foul to be easily scraped off and forgotten.

A bit of white flashed in an alley, and Rosalind glanced over. A man stood in the shadows next to a small tavern, while a cloaked woman knelt before him. Rosalind could hear him groan as he pulled her blond head closer to his hips. The sight drew little attention from the drunks, only a profane comment about hogging a good spot from one of the loose women.

Rosalind blushed scarlet and walked on. She doubted she'd ever grow accustomed to seeing people taking their carnal pleasures on a public street.

Something odd about the couple nagged at her, and Rosalind looked back. The woman's cloak was edged in fur, shimmering with sealskin's expensive luster. A wealthy woman? Here?

The laboring female pulled back from the man, letting his cock slip from her mouth and illuminating her profile. The man growled something, and leaned forward to pull the woman back to him. For a moment, both their faces were fully visible.

Rosalind immediately recognized them. Her jaw dropped.

Her father choked, then gripped her arm. "Come along. Quickly now."

Rosalind speedily obeyed, glad that neither the man nor the woman seemed remotely aware of their watchers.

Minutes later and safe in the warm carriage, she stared at her father, still stunned by what she'd seen. "That was Mrs. Richard Lindsay, wasn't it? With Nicholas Lennox?"

He nodded grimly. "It was. And it would not be polite to speak of it again."

"Of course."

She'd tried her best to forget. But Lennox's marriage proposal had brought it back to mind. It had been easy to decide against his suit, even when she was bruised and bloody from his beating. She would not tolerate an adulterous bastard—a violent, murderous beast—for a husband.

Hal looked back from the door for his missing cub and spotted her along the promenade. Dammit, he needed her with him.

"Carstairs," he snapped, and Cicero barked an echo.

Rosalind looked up, startled.

He frowned at her and held the door open. Guilt flashed across her face.

"Sorry, sir. Just thinking about that new channel outside St. Joseph."

Hal raised an eyebrow at that spurious excuse and let the door fall shut behind them, as he followed his father. He was sure she'd concentrate once they sat down at the table. Still, the risk was too great that his parents would recognize her; he needed to keep their attention as much as possible.

It was too early for many passengers to be down for breakfast. Still, the tables were set with white linen and gleaming china as precisely as in a first-class hotel, while waiters stood by silently, in their crisp black livery and white aprons, almost hovering over the few diners present. All was done as well—or better—than in a dining room on one of the Old Man's boats.

Mother rose from a table halfway down the long room. She was dressed to the nines, surprising for a woman who'd taught her children never to disturb her before noon, and beamed at the approaching trio like a pilot seeing straight water ahead.

"My dear boy," Desdemona gushed and leaned up to kiss Hal on the cheek. "How good of you to join us for breakfast."

"Mother." He returned the salutation formally. He had no idea why she was up this early, let alone dressed so well. "May I present Frank Carstairs, my cub? Carstairs, this is my mother, Mrs. Richard Lindsay."

Rosalind bowed formally. "Ma'am."

No surprise, or recognition of Rosalind, showed on Mother's face. "Mr. Carstairs, such a pleasure to have a handsome young face onboard. You must sit next to me, where you can tell me all the boat's gossip."

Good God, is Mother going to flirt as she usually did with a new male acquaintance? She'd regularly done so with his junior officers during the War.

"And, Hal, darling, you'll sit at my right."

Darling??? Why was she buttering him up? Hal took the indicated seat with little appetite and no comment, as he silently signaled Roland Jones, his steward. Roland nodded, almost imperceptibly, and moved forward. He'd serve this meal himself, his expertise sure to satisfy Mother's demanding—and very vocal—standards.

The Old Man held his wife's chair, then sat opposite her, flanking Hal—and Rosalind. Hal kept his face impassive: he wouldn't be able to privately warn Rosalind, or vice versa, should the conversation head into dangerous waters. Cicero slid into his accustomed position beside Hal's chair. Thankfully, he was a dignified dining companion, who was quieter at the table than Mother was likely to be.

A basket of brioche was the first food to appear, presented by Roland to Mother with great panache.

"Remember, Hal?" she cooed, waving the offering toward him. "You swore you'd eat brioche on your boat, just as your great-grandfather did when he escaped from the British prison ship."

Mother mentioning a Lindsay as someone to be admired? She'd always held up only her Davies relatives for admiration.

"The Commodore also enjoyed brioche every morning," the Old Man added. "As do I, on my boat."

Mother and Father working together? Good God Almighty, they only did that when there was money or power at stake.

Hal nodded, his expression a mask of formality. "Will you join me?"

"Thank you, dear. And your father, as well."

"Of course," Hal said as smoothly as possible. "Sir?"

"Thank you." The Old Man seemed to relax a trifle as the food quickly appeared. Both men ate heartily of their ham and eggs, while Mother picked at her soft-boiled egg.

"Tell me, Mr. Carstairs, have you been a pilot long? You're a very well set-up young man and must have been quite an asset to your previous employer." Mother batted her eyelashes.

Hal's mouth tightened.

"I'm honored that the *Cherokee Belle* accepted me as a cub pilot, ma'am." Rosalind calmly buttered her brioche and completely ignored the attempted flirtation. "Would you care for some butter or salt for your egg?"

Mother's smile slipped slightly at the rebuff. "Thank you, no. I had such a dreadful night's sleep that I must confine myself to only the blandest of foods."

"How terrible for you, Mrs. Lindsay. What exactly was the difficulty?"

Rosalind had found one of the two perfect lures for Mother, a topic Hal had heard far too many times before, but one that always galvanized her. Within a minute, she was off and running on a litany of complaints about her berth, the sheets, the inadequate stove, and so on. The only alternative would have been to compliment Mother on a social success.

"I tell you, sir, the worst of it comes every night when the boat ties up."

Mother leaned forward to emphasize her point, and Hal flinched at her proximity to Rosalind. He had to change the subject at the first opportunity.

"The stillness—the utter lack of any reassuring civilized noise, such as the engines driving the paddlewheel—makes it totally impossible for me to sleep."

"I am sorry that you find it so discomfiting, ma'am," Rosalind said soberly, her face as composed as when she played poker. "You must be a very courageous woman, to brave such privations and dangers, in order to see your son."

Mother preened. "It is a situation that must be borne with fortitude," she intoned. "We must also consider that poor lost orphan, who wanders the western wilderness alone."

"What orphan, Mother?" Hal asked.

"Rosalind Schuyler, of course. You may remember her from your dear sister Juliet's party last Christmas. Tall and gawky but from an excellent family."

"It is our duty to find her and return her to her fiancé, Nicholas Lennox," the Old Man added.

Rosalind began to cut her ham into very small pieces. Very deliberately and very thoroughly.

Hal's mouth tightened. *How dare they threaten to return Rosalind to Lennox . . .* He managed to quell his rising anger long enough to demand an explanation. "Why, in heaven's name, are you so concerned with that runaway?"

"It is our Christian duty to care for the lost souls of this world," Mother intoned sanctimoniously. "Miss Schuyler must be found immediately, at all costs."

Hal's eyebrows flew up. Mother had never given a fig about anyone except herself.

"Think about her fiancé," the Old Man inserted quietly.

"Consider how agonized you would be, if your fiancée was missing."

"I don't have a fiancée," Hal retorted, more than willing to lead the conversation away from the missing heiress.

"Or your wife. Or your daughter. The agony of a parent, when their beloved child is missing, rends the heart worse than a sword blow." Deep lines were graven into his father's face.

The old anger flared up in Hal, as hot and fierce as if he'd been caned yesterday, instead of years ago. If the Old Man had been unhappy when Hal disappeared, then he shouldn't have terrified Viola and nearly killed Hal.

Mother watched placidly, her eyes traveling between the two combatants, as she always did when her husband and children fought. Rosalind was also quiet, but hers was the patience of the gambler waiting to make a move. She had enough gumption to go up against his father, a combat Hal had never won.

He couldn't let her intervene. He had to stop his parents from thinking about the missing heiress while Rosalind was at the table.

Hal spoke the truth publicly for the first time, the one statement that would command his parents' full attention. "I am not married, nor will I ever be. And I will never bring children into this world."

Mother's eyes narrowed briefly, then she dabbed at them with her napkin. "But, Hal, how can you deprive me of the joy of grandchildren? Their sweet prattle and pretty ways . . ." Her voice was far too calculating for the sentimental words she uttered.

The Old Man's voice rose over hers as he pounded on the table. "Who will tend you when you are ill? Or comfort you in your old age?"

"I will never risk subjecting a child to my temper, sir," Hal enunciated his long-held decision.

"Nonsense! You were an excellent naval officer and clearly have a well-disciplined temperament. No, you must have children soon."

"Or else what? You'll cane me—again?" Hal's voice was very soft. He knew exactly where his Colt and Arkansas toothpick were at this moment. He could physically defend himself now against his sire, as he couldn't years ago.

The Old Man stared at Hal. Mother dropped her spoon, then hastily looked around for listeners.

"Cane?" Rosalind whispered.

Roland Jones coughed. "Captain would like to speak to you, sir."

Hal glared at his father, daring him to answer. The Old Man's eyes narrowed and seemed to look into the distance. He said nothing.

Satisfied that he'd protected Rosalind and finally stopped his father's continual demands for grandchildren, Hal tossed down his napkin and stood up. "Please excuse us, Mother. Sir."

A minute later, he entered the starboard boiler room, with Rosalind close behind him. The engines' usual steady beat sounded healthy enough. Sampson was pacing the aisle between the engines, his strong body preventing Hal from seeing what was wrong.

"What is it?" Hal asked, raising his voice to be heard.

"You'll have to see for yourself," Sampson replied and stepped aside, a drop of blood on his lip from where he'd been gnawing it.

Sampson, worried enough to show it? Hal nodded and moved forward.

Norton and Brady, the assistant engineer, were staring at the safety valve. Beyond them, William also watched the safety valve, his expression as sober as when he'd followed Viola's kidnappers into a collapsing silver mine.

Hell and damnation, was it broken? Were the boilers

about to overheat and explode? Terror ran its icy fingers through Hal, triggered by the one calamity every western riverboat crewman or passenger feared.

He had witnessed the *Sultana's* terrible explosion and had helped recover some of the sixteen hundred dead. Those poor devils, so recently freed from the hellish prison at Andersonville, had deserved far better than to be killed only a few hundred miles from home. He still had nightmares about the charred, emaciated corpses floating in the Mississippi.

"What is it?" He recognized his level tone of voice as the same one he'd used at Shiloh when he'd taken his stinkpot into action against an overwhelming Rebel army.

"Brady found the blacksmith's anvil in the engine room, hanging from a line to the boiler's safety valve, while he was showing the engines to Mr. Donovan," Sampson said quietly. "The boilers could have blown up a hundred times before the safety valve would have acted."

Sabotage? Rosalind could have been killed. "Do you know who was responsible?"

Norton handed him a circular cap, such as every poor boy wore, but now grimy beyond almost all recognition. "Brady also found this hanging over the safety valve so we couldn't see the pressure."

"Harrison's cap," Rosalind said quietly, from over Hal's shoulder. The fellow had rigged the *Belle* to explode the first time she built up a full head of steam—killing everyone onboard.

Hal marveled at her calm. Internally, he was comparing the relative merits of gutting Harrison or tossing the brute into the nearest boiler and shutting the grate.

"Yes, he was the only fireman who always wore a cap," Norton agreed.

"But he's gone now—went over the side less than an hour ago and swam to that last island. The devil thumbed his nose at us!" Sampson snarled the uncharacteristic blasphemy.

"Do you think he did it on a lark?" Brady asked, probably hoping for an innocent explanation. Harrison had served on his watch.

William shook his head and spoke for the first time. "I found a half-eagle in Harrison's blankets when we searched his berth."

Brady whistled.

"Who would want to murder everyone on a boat?" Rosalind asked hoarsely.

"Or just kill one person and not care if anyone else was hurt," William suggested. His eyes promised Hal a later meeting.

"We'll have to keep this from the passengers as much as possible," Sampson said slowly.

Hal nodded, his jaw set. He hoped William's attacker wasn't reaching out to destroy the *Belle,* just because William was aboard. But if someone was trying to hurt Viola's husband, then he'd see them destroyed, no matter what it took.

"I can ground the *Belle* by McLerndon's farm," Bellecourt offered from behind Rosalind. "We could use the opportunity to check for any other problems, *mes amis.*"

Surprise scampered across the others' faces. Hal and Norton were the first to nod agreement.

"Good idea," Hal said.

"We can shift cargo to the shore," contributed Sampson.

Hal nodded. "Which will give us the chance to search it, as well."

Everything went as planned. Bellecourt took the wheel, deliberately missed a channel, and ran the *Cherokee Belle* aground on a sandbank just below a bluff. Roland promptly set the passengers ashore, to study the vista or fish, and ordered the waiters to serve a lavish picnic lunch.

Bellecourt and Sampson then spent four hours pretending to get the *Belle* off, while actually hunting through every nook and cranny onboard. The remaining crew members were rightfully horrified and worked like demons to search the boat. Thankfully, they found no other attempts at sabotage.

By the time the passengers started straggling back, the search was over, and the *Belle* once again looked and behaved like a first-class packet, not the scene of attempted murder. The *Spartan,* which had been so close that morning, was now almost out of sight.

After dinner, the waiters cleared the tables away and prepared the grand saloon for a dance. Mother preened and fluttered her fan faster, as she surveyed the available men. The orchestra started tuning up, and Viola walked her fingers over William's sleeve. He smiled down at her, the contented smirk of a man who knows he will enjoy whatever happens next.

"Will you dance with me, kind sir?" she asked softly, her eyes glowing with carnal invitation.

William kissed her hand. "It would be my very great pleasure, dear lady."

Damn, they looked ready to cuddle in public. Hal cleared his throat with unnecessary emphasis. "If you'll excuse me, Viola, I have business to attend to in the pilothouse."

"Of course. Sleep well, dear brother."

He kissed her on the cheek. "Good night, sweet sister. Brother." He slapped William on the arm and turned to go.

"Good night, Hal." William's voice changed tone. "Now, sweetheart, would you prefer to dance in the grand saloon or . . ."

Hal fled. The *Cherokee Belle* was tied up, but if he knew Bellecourt, he'd be teaching Rosalind some of his Indian mother's stories about the stars. Hal needed to congratulate her on how well she had conducted herself during that damn breakfast with his parents.

As he'd suspected, he found Bellecourt and Rosalind on the hurricane deck, just aft of the jackstaff. The night was dark, except for the colored light streaming from the grand saloon's skylights. As ever, Rosalind was watching Belle-court and the stars. She only eyed the river while standing watch as a cub pilot.

The only sounds were Bellecourt's elegant tale and the dance music from inside. Sampson had doubled the anchor watch and armed them. After this morning's alarm, they patrolled the main deck with the same silent, deadly vigilance they'd use a few weeks later in Indian country.

Bellecourt cast a quick glance at Hal, then continued recounting his story. Hal's nose quickly found Rosalind's distinctive scent, soap with a very light trace of lemon. His cock promptly hardened. Hal froze and ordered his unruly tool to behave. It was not impressed by his command.

Hal cursed silently and started drawing the lower Mississippi near Vicksburg from memory, paying particular attention to how it would look in the dark. Every light on the boat would be doused then, even the mate's pipe, so that he could pick out landmarks as different shades of black when compared to the river's pale glimmer. His cock slowly, and sullenly, subsided until it lay against his thigh, rather than the iron-hard rod it had been.

Bellecourt finished his speech with a flourish. "And so, *mon ami*, you should always be wary of Coyote, the trickster."

"Indeed, sir, I will remember," Rosalind said warmly. "Thank you for telling me some of Coyote's exploits. Good evening, Lindsay."

"Evening, Carstairs, Bellecourt. Satisfied with today's outcome?"

Bellecourt shrugged, a very Gallic movement visible in a bit of golden light. "For now, *oui*. But who knows what tomorrow will bring?"

"Do you think—" Hal stopped short. He trusted Bellecourt with his life, but he didn't want to discuss the possibility of further attack in public.

Bellecourt's mouth tightened, but his voice was steady. "It is too late at night for thinking, *mon ami*. I am for bed so I will be prepared for whatever tomorrow brings. *Bonsoir, mes amis*."

"Good night, Bellecourt."

"Good night," Hal echoed as he watched the older man go inside. He turned to study the river, immensely aware of the woman beside him. She was close enough to touch, and her scent wreathed him.

Below them on the boiler deck, men laid wagers on the *Belle*'s perpetual poker game, while a polka's rollicking tune came from the grand saloon. He didn't want to join either gathering, not when Rosalind stood near him in the dark. Perhaps they could play something else, something carnal.

"Care for a private game of cards, Carstairs?"

"Of course, sir." Her enthusiasm came ringing through. He'd rather suspected his little gambler would compete in any game offered.

"Come back to the cabin then."

She followed him with a little bounce, almost as pleased as Cicero. The dog, however, immediately dived onto the cot, circled, and yawned. Having thus expressed his opinion of what behavior should be, Cicero curled up and closed his eyes.

Rosalind chuckled. "I suspect we're about to disappoint him again. What card game do you want to play? Whist, perhaps?"

"Poker, of course. Five-card draw, I think." He hunted through his sea chest.

Rosalind raised an eyebrow. "Draw poker? Very well; it's a better game for two people. What's the minimum bet?"

"We'll play for clothing," Hal announced, then tossed a deck of cards onto the bed and palmed a condom. He'd hide it under the pillow when she wasn't looking. Her reaction was everything he could have wished.

"Clothing?" She cast a guilty glance at the very loud polka coming from the grand saloon next door, then went on more moderately. "How can we compete for clothing? We can't play poker if we're naked."

Hal chuckled. He'd hoped bare bodies would distract her keen brain. "We'll make each article the equal of a chip. You can bet one, two, three, or more articles, as you would gamble with chips. They'll have to be taken off and put into the pot, of course."

She pursed her lips, then nodded. "Very well. And the winner of a hand can resume wearing whatever articles he wins."

Hal's bright vision of Rosalind wearing nothing but a handful of cards faded. He gritted his teeth.

"Nonsense," he snapped. "You cannot put an article back on. And, you can only wager articles adorning the body. The winner is the last one still wearing a piece of clothing."

She stared. Her pulse beat in her throat. "Your objective is to see me naked," she whispered.

He shrugged elaborately. "Afraid you'll lose?" he taunted. "Of course, if you'd prefer to play something simpler—cribbage perhaps, or pinochle . . ."

Rosalind choked. Color blazed on her cheekbones. "I am not afraid. I'll play, and win, any game you name."

Hal bowed. Had she realized that both would be the winner in this game? "Very well. Strip poker, it is. You can deal first." He definitely thought he should be the first to bet.

"Thank you." She sat down on the bed and turned to face him. Her hand flexed nervously on her thigh, then relaxed. "How many cards can we exchange?"

"Why not five? No need to save cards for other players."

Rosalind nodded agreement and shuffled. She dealt five cards to both of them, then studied her hand with the intensity of the professional she was. His hand contained a pair of fours, which gave him a solid starting point.

She looked at him and waited. He smiled to himself.

"I'll wager my watch and chain, as two chips. Plus my Colt, with its holster, as the third chip." He dropped them neatly on the cot beside Cicero. The dog eyed the articles, then studied Hal quizzically.

"Three? Very well then, my watch, watch chain, and stickpin." She briskly deposited her wager beside Cicero. "How many cards do you want?"

"Three."

She dealt him the requested number and took two for herself. Nothing worth mentioning in the new cards. Still, the objective was to overwhelm Rosalind with lust, not acquire clothing.

"My coat and weapons belt." Hal stood up and slowly shrugged off his coat. Rosalind stared at him and swallowed, which his cock thought was a very good omen. He removed his weapons belt with equal deliberation, allowing her as much time as possible to contemplate what waited behind his fly.

"Ah, my two Colts to call. Plus, my tie to raise you." She didn't quite stammer.

Hal pretended to consult his cards. "My vest, to call."

He removed his vest with even more delays than for his coat, deeming it best to stop betting while he still had his shirt on. Women's appetites heated best when they could guess about the future, rather than see it clearly. Given how her eyes dwelt on his chest, he rather thought his strategy was working.

She laid down her hand. "A pair of sevens."

"That beats my fours," Hal said calmly, pleased with himself, but unwilling to show it. She'd need to remove some clothing during the next hand.

He shuffled and dealt. Four cards could be the start of a jack-high straight. Anticipation burned through him. Rosalind hesitated. He lifted an eyebrow. "I believe it's your turn to wager, unless you wish to fold."

Her eyes flashed, and she stood up. "My coat and collar." She took the coat off quickly and dropped it on the other side of Cicero and sat down. She found it harder to separate the collar from the soft collar band, but finally managed to remove it. She hadn't looked at him once while she took them off.

"My boots, as two chips, don't you think?"

Her eyes flashed to his, and she nodded jerkily.

He took them off, careful to flex his back and shoulders, then tossed them down beside her coat. The look on her face, of fascination and curiosity and lust, almost made him purr. He deepened and softened his voice to keep the mood as carnal as possible. "How many cards?"

"Three, please." She quickly sorted them into the others.

The single card he drew was the delightful completion to his straight. Hal waited happily for her next move.

"My boots. And my socks, as two." Rosalind made her wager a little too calmly.

Hal was impatient. "My socks. Plus my cuff links, as two chips." He'd raised the stakes by one chip and quickly went further. "My shirt."

He eased the linen off with the coyness of a king's mistress. Rosalind's eyes were enormous, and she nervously licked her lips. By the Almighty, she was enticing. His chest tightened and his cock ached. Pre-come dampened his drawers.

"My vest." Her voice was a hoarse croak. She swallowed hard and took it off. Her breasts were suddenly richly apparent behind her shirt's fine linen, while her nipples were hard peaks. She blushed fiercely, not looking at him.

"Dear heavens, you're a beauty," he whispered.

Rosalind's head snapped around. "What?" she whispered.

"You're beautiful," Hal repeated. "Didn't you know?"

She shook her head, still staring at him.

"Good God, look at yourself in the mirror. Tall, curved in all the right places, a mouth to fill a man's brain with fantasies . . ."

"Me?"

He nodded. How could she not realize? Had that fool fiancé not shown her how irresistible a woman she was? "You know you're a delight to talk to," he said impatiently.

Rosalind shrugged. "Men don't usually consider intelligence attractive. Or at least, they don't find both the brain and its package to be interesting."

"Are you saying that men either ogled or talked to you, but not both?"

Her mouth twisted. "Exactly. Except for David Rutherford but he ran at the first sign of trouble."

"Dolt. And as for the rest of those men, you can wash them out of your memory," Hal said roughly, wanting to break some well-bred New York heads. "You're a stunning woman. You've the body of Venus, Athena's brain, and Diana's courage. How could any man resist?"

"You're serious."

He shook his head, trying to find a way to convince her. "Tease me with your body and see how well I play."

She cocked her head. He waited, unable to breathe. The orchestra next door swung into a slow, sensual waltz. But he heard it as camouflage for the doings in his cabin.

"My shirt, to call." Her voice was a husky croak that lanced through his body.

Hal closed his eyes briefly. His chest was as tight as if he'd run a race, while his trouser buttons were carving themselves into his cock. None of that mattered.

Rosalind slipped one brace over her shoulder. He quivered but kept himself in check. Another brace went down, freeing her shirt. She pulled it out of her trousers, and Hal moaned.

She smiled, her eyes alight with dawning power. She undid the first button slowly while his pulse pounded. The second button seemed to take an age before it came free, as his loins tightened. Her slender fingers lingered over each of the subsequent buttons. Hal's balls lifted high and tight into his groin, desperate for release. He could not have named his cards to save his life.

She slowly peeled the shirt over her head. Her breasts shifted under her fine cotton undershirt, then settled, ripe and ready. Her nipples were dark, stabbing against the cloth, and, oh, so very eager. Would she enjoy being taken from behind, so he could fill his hands with those ripe mounds while riding her?

Hal groaned. Could he survive another hand of this game?

"You told me the truth," she whispered, searching his face.

He snorted. "How could I deny it? Just look at my cock."

She surveyed him below the waist for the first time. His cock somehow managed to grow fuller still under her gaze, becoming a rock-hard instrument of torture.

"Raise you." He stood up and stripped off his trousers. Two seconds later he flung his undershirt and drawers down on Cicero. He planted his hands on his hips and faced her, his cock bobbing with eagerness.

"Oh yes," she whispered. "Oh yes, you are magnificent and very, very truthful. Now sit down and let me play."

Hal wondered what demon had crept into his brain to birth this form of torture. He sat down, legs spread well apart to give his swollen cock and balls some ease.

"Call you," Rosalind said firmly. She shucked her trousers and drawers, letting her undershirt fall freely over her hips. He could see every detail of her form underneath the fine cotton. Her flushed, swollen breasts, the dark pebbles of her nipples, the dew sliding down her thigh in a delicate trail . . .

The scent of her musk hung ripe and inviting.

His breath caught. Pre-come glided freely down his cock, as if begging for the opportunity to taste her.

She flipped her cards over with an unsteady hand. "Three tens."

"Jack-high straight."

"You won." One slender fingertip swirled over his cock-head. She touched it to her tongue lightly. Her eyes closed, and she moaned. "Salty. And delicious."

"Lean back on the bed." His voice was a harsh growl. She promptly obeyed him, watching him through her lashes.

"Now spread your legs so I can see what I won."

She blushed and obeyed. He stepped up to her and stroked the inside of her thighs lightly, enjoying the light sheen of dew. She trembled as he traced the delicate blue veins. He slipped one index finger, then the other, between her folds and teased her gently. She moaned and arched, head falling back as her eyes closed. The pose lifted her breasts toward him, like a pagan sacrifice.

"Beautiful," he murmured and tasted her offering. A very delicate lick over one nipple, then he swirled his tongue over it. A light nibble then a slow suckle . . . He groaned at the taste.

Greedily, he savored her with deep pulls that made her writhe like a cat under him. And how she gasped his name when he turned his attentions to her other breast.

He cupped her breasts together so that he could attend to them both more easily. Lick, lick, nibble, suck, mixed with long swipes of his tongue or deep pulls inside the hungry cavern of his mouth. She was wet and gleaming, flushed with passion, and sobbing for more.

Her hand wrapped around the nape of his neck and pulled him closer. He rumbled approval and slid up her to take her mouth. They kissed in deep, slow tastes, his goatee framing her lips perfectly while his chest hair rubbed her nipples until she turned frantic. Her hands threaded into his hair and her slender legs embraced his hips. She was as open to him as if they were already joined. Her hot, creamy folds teased his cock until he could barely think. His seed boiled into his cock and demanded to erupt.

Instinct and the habits of years guided him now. Somehow he managed to find the condom and don it without leaving her. He gripped her hips, adjusted his stance, and thrust. His cock slid into her easily. He groaned as the demanding rhythm of approaching orgasm pulsed through him.

"Hal." Rosalind shifted under him slightly, and he slid into her to the hilt. "Hal," she repeated with blatant satisfaction and clenched herself around him.

Wits fled. Instinct older than the Missouri swept in. He growled and rode her like a frenzied beast, intent on covering his mate. The room was filled with the wet slaps of their heated flesh pounding against each other, taking and giving in equal measure, while the music next door grew louder and louder.

Rosalind raked his back with her nails like a wildcat. He sobbed into her hair and shattered, pumping out his essence as she gasped his name while finding her own climax.

The waltz finished with a loud flourish. People laughed and applauded, then began to chatter. Hal shuddered, but managed to roll over, taking her with him to cuddle close.

"You won," she whispered.

"You did. You still have clothes on so you have your grubstake."

Rosalind kissed his shoulder, where she'd bitten him. "Guess we'll just have to play this again, and again, until we can reach a conclusion."

Hal groaned. "If we live that long."

She chuckled and snuggled down against him. "We will," she answered confidently. "We have plenty of time."

His heart stopped. *Time.* How long would they be together? They had to grow tired of this game before Fort Benton, when she left the *Cherokee Belle*. He could not, dare not, think they'd be together longer than that.

* * *

"Idiot," Nick snorted as he and Jenkins strolled back to the *Spartan* after dark. "It's hard to believe Harrison was the best man available."

Jenkins wisely stayed silent.

"And then to return to us and demand—demand!—more money to complete the job." Disgusted, he whacked a nearby willow with his swordstick, then smiled. "Still, he was useful in one way at least. I'd never scalped a man before."

"Stupid fool," Jenkins agreed. "But the next fellow will do better."

"If not, then we'll toss for who scalps that one." It would be so much more enjoyable to kill Donovan and Lindsay personally, when those two brutes would know exactly who was responsible for their destruction.

"Of course." Jenkins bowed. The two men smiled at each other in perfect accord.

Chapter Eleven

"Mornin', Bellecourt. Carstairs," Hal sang out his greeting as he stepped into the pilothouse, Cicero at his heels.

Rosalind nodded a response, a faint smile in her eyes before she looked back at the river. He was damn proud of how fast she'd calmed down in the pilothouse and steered a few easy passages, with only a faint tremor in her hands betraying her old fear of water.

She'd helped bring the *Belle* in to pick up a local farmer, his betrothed, and their families so that Sampson could celebrate the wedding during the riverboat's regular Sunday services.

She'd gone white when she'd helped Bellecourt steer through the Devil's Rake, whose maze of driftwood, snags, and *embarrasses* —where drowned trees came together to form an impenetrable thicket—made for unpredictable currents and a pilot's nightmare.

A week's journey hadn't lessened his attraction to her. Instead, his passion seemed to grow every night they spent in bed. Worse still, he enjoyed her company in daylight—the quick intelligence, the keen observations, the flashes of wry humor . . .

Still, they'd say good-bye in six weeks when she disembarked at Fort Benton. She was meant for a stable, loving home, like the one she'd grown up in—with an adoring husband and a brood of rambunctious, happy children, every one of them confident of her protection. Blessings he couldn't give her, lest he pass on the Lindsay heritage of beatings.

"*Bonjour,* Lindsay. Have you come to watch the animals greet the sun?" Bellecourt spun the wheel, danced the *Belle* through a tight turn, and steadied her, while a pair of deer watched from the shadows under the bluff's oaks. A great blue heron sailed past and settled near a pair of egrets at the water's edge.

"Of course. I'd like to see how that orchard looks, now that it's become a rake where the river sliced through the land."

"Orchard, sir?" Rosalind questioned softly.

"Yup. Just before the war, Bickford planted an apple orchard on a bluff overlooking the Missouri," Hal explained. "Some folks said he was too close to the edge; others said it didn't matter because the river could take anything it wanted."

"And the Missouri grabbed it."

Hal nodded, pouring himself a cup of coffee from the ever-present pot. Cicero had considered the pilothouse's familiar space, then departed it for the hurricane deck's open expanses. He was now racing around the texas on the hurricane deck, enjoying the morning's freedom and uttering occasional barks of pure joy. Homer had chased leaves with equal delight long ago.

"The spring rise carved it away, about a week ago. Now the entire orchard's at the bottom of the river."

"Still standing upright with the branches pointing up, out of the water," Rosalind finished the description.

"Depends on how high the water is. If we're lucky, the branches and leaves are obvious. If not, we'll have to dodge them somehow and keep a solid hull on the *Belle*."

"*Heureusement,* it's a smaller hazard than the Devil's Rake we passed a few days ago," Bellecourt commented. "That place brings hell so close that a Protestant will go to confession."

Hal and Rosalind chuckled at his description, just before a woman's voice interrupted.

"Good morning, Hal. May we join you?"

"Of course. There's a rocking chair in the back, if you'd like to sit down." Hal smiled at his sister and William, as Cicero happily barked again. Today was a far better morning than the last one he and Viola had shared with his dog. . . .

Fourteen-year-old Hal walked home, cradling Homer's body in his arms. Tears streaked the dirt and blood on his face. The Carter boys had snatched Homer, probably by an appeal to his appetite, and then they'd tortured him.

Hal had attacked as soon as he heard Homer's barks, but it had been too late. He'd outfought the two older boys, but their black eyes and broken noses, even their retreating backs as they'd run away, were little consolation, when compared to Homer's death.

Dear God in heaven, who'd have thought so much blood could come from one little body. And the broken limbs had flopped so much when he picked Homer up that he'd made his coat into a burial shroud, just to provide more dignity for the gallant dog.

Oh, Homer, Homer, what will I do without you? You and Viola have been my only confidants.

Piano music floated out the window and down the long line of mansions in the fashionable Cincinnati district. It reached Hal's ears, lightening his burden a little.

Good, Viola was home. She'd understand how much Homer had meant, even if Father always called him "a sentimental attachment unworthy of a future naval officer." And she wouldn't scold, as Mother would, for disgracing the family by appearing in public in his shirtsleeves.

He gulped for breath and wiped his eyes one last time. Then he started up the stairs to the big town house.

The front door flew open, and his father glared at him.

Oh, no. Heaven only knew what punishment his father would deal out.

"Where the hell have you been?"

The music stopped.

Damn, the Old Man was swearing. This was going to be bad.

Hal straightened his shoulders, still sore from the last beating, and stepped inside.

His father slammed the door. "You weakling, have you been crying in public? About a dog?"

Hal glared back. He clutched Homer's body closer.

The Old Man shouted again, within inches of Hal's face. "What woman would want to bear your sons, if she knew you were a sniveling brat?"

Twelve-year-old Viola ran into the foyer. Hal instinctively yelled a warning, knowing all too well the penalty for surprising their father.

Without looking around, the Old Man flung out his hand to stop the newcomer.

Viola skidded to a stop less than an inch from her father's fist. Her blue eyes were enormous with shock and fear.

"Viola," Hal whispered, his body cold with terror for the first time that day. The Old Man had never lifted a hand to his daughter before.

Mother glided into the room, came to a stop by her favorite Ming vase, and folded her hands. She must have been receiving calls from other matrons, since she was wearing her best. "Has your son been sniveling in front of the neighbors, Captain Lindsay? Intolerable."

The Old Man glanced around. "Take your daughter away, Mrs. Lindsay. This is men's business."

Mother nodded without hesitation. But then, she'd never argued with her husband about how to discipline their children—nor comforted her offspring afterwards. "Come along, Viola."

The girl hesitated, searching her brother's face. "What about Hal?"

"Your father will deal with him," Mother snapped. "Come along."

"Hal—"

"I'll be all right." And he would be, as long as she was happy. He wouldn't make a sound, no matter what the Old Man did. She'd be frightened if she heard him scream. He couldn't think about the Old Man almost striking her, Hal's dear companion on so many explorations through the woods or along the river.

Viola searched Hal's eyes. He kept his face calm, hoping to persuade her that nothing painful would happen. She'd never seen the Old Man punish him, so she might believe it.

She finally yielded. "Let me take Homer."

The Old Man harrumphed but, for once, said nothing about sentimental weakness.

Hal passed over the little corpse.

"Oh, Homer . . ." Viola started to cry.

"Come along now." Mother gripped Viola's elbow and steered her out of the room.

"It is beyond my comprehension," the Old Man said quietly and savagely, "how you can be such a milksop. You'd lose your entire crew by weeping over a scratch on the ship's mascot."

Hal's mouth tightened at the insult, but he knew better than to respond. Words only increased his father's anger, magnifying Hal's danger. The Old Man was deadly with a cane or a rope, as befitted a man who'd learned from the Navy's stern disciplinarians. He preferred to use a cane—the more silent and more deadly of the two—on his son, citing his desire not to disturb the ladies in his house.

The Old Man's mouth twisted as the silence stretched between them. "Upstairs to your room, mister."

Hal went as ordered, his father barely a step behind him. The room was painfully neat, good enough to withstand inspection, but making Hal's personal disarray more apparent.

"Attention!" the Old Man barked.

Hal struck the naval pose and waited, breathing hard and fast. His terror was fading, now that Viola was safe, but his anger at yet another argument with his father was building.

The Old Man sneered. "Trying to pretend you're a sailor? You wouldn't pass inspection by a blind chaplain in those muddy rags. Anything to say for yourself, mister?"

"What good would it do? You've already tried and condemned me," Hal retorted, his control snapping at last. "You don't care that I want to be a riverboat pilot, not a naval officer. You want me to be exactly like you—a clean-shaven bully like all the other Lindsay men."

"Why, you insolent wretch!" The Old Man slapped him across the face and Hal punched him in the jaw.

The Old Man staggered slightly, staring at Hal. Then he came after the younger man with all of his superior strength and speed—and far better fighting skills. Hal realized that his father had done more than stand watch while serving in the Navy; he must have engaged in numerous dockside brawls before he'd married Mother and moved to Cincinnati.

Two minutes later, Hal was stretched facedown across his bed, his hands and feet tied to the rails with the ropes kept for practicing knots. He struggled anyway, cursing the Old Man with every expletive he'd learned while exploring Cincinnati's back alleys.

The Old Man shoved a leather strap into Hal's mouth and buckled it behind his head. He unbuckled Hal's pants and yanked them down to the knees, then pulled Hal's jacket and shirt up, exposing Hal's shoulders.

Terror, instilled in him by past canings, touched Hal again and he fought it back with rage. He was not ashamed of fighting for Homer or crying for him, his confidant, who'd heard all of Hal's anger and fears, but loved him anyway.

The Old Man stepped back, his face scarlet with anger, and reached for the cane kept in Hal's room for exactly these occasions. "By God, I'll teach you not to strike your betters, mister. And you will learn enough discipline to lead your men and raise your sons, no matter how long it takes to beat it into you."

He lifted the cane, and Hal caught a glimpse of himself in the small mirror above his chest. He looked exactly like his father—skin flushed red and eyes blazing.

The Old Man brought the cane down hard and fast, striking Hal across the buttocks. The familiar two-edged jolt of a caning blossomed—the thud of the cane's weight then the fiery burn.

Hal waited for his father to deliberately pause and let the anguish build, as had always happened before. Instead, the second stroke came quickly, its thud blending into the previous stroke and increasing the pain.

In a single blinding flash, he realized that the Old Man hadn't announced the number of strokes to be given, as on every prior beating. Instead, the Old Man was beating him like a madman, the strokes coming faster and faster as he cursed Hal's stubbornness and inadequacies as a son.

Hal closed his eyes and promised the Almighty that if he survived this caning, he would never have children. Half choking on the leather gag, he fought the waves of agony for as long as possible, until he finally fainted.

He woke up later to find his hands and legs free, although his clothing was still disarranged. He started to turn over, then screamed into the coverlet, as agony burst across his back like wildfire. Overwhelmed by more pain than he'd ever felt before, he yielded to merciful unconsciousness.

"How could he do this to his own son?"

A girl was crying. Viola.

Hal tried to answer, but his voice came out as a croak. He tried to move, but a small hand lightly touched his arm, careful not to cause any more pain.

"Be still, Hal. You shouldn't move when your back is like this." Her voice was thick with tears. "Just let me clean you up."

She began to gently wash his back. Hal buried his face in the pillow to muffle his shrieks. Agony ripped through him when the washcloth brushed one blood clot and he passed out again.

It seemed a very long time before he drifted back to reality. Viola was now washing the backs of his knees, which thankfully hadn't been harmed.

"You shouldn't see me like this," Hal protested feebly.

"There's no one else to take care of you. Father—" She stopped. Tears choked her voice when she went on. "Before Mother and Juliet left for Louisville with him, Father told us that Obadiah would look after you. But Obadiah is at the farm until tomorrow night, and I couldn't let you wait that long. So I stole the key and came in . . . And I'm glad I did."

"Thank you." Hal hissed slightly at another lance of pain.

"Oh, Hal, what are we going to do? Should I fetch the doctor?"

"Wouldn't do any good. He'd just call me a weakling, say it's a father's right to teach his son a lesson, and refuse to treat me without Father's permission. That's what he said before, after the Old Man beat me for not knowing those Latin conjugations."

"Father has no right to hurt you like this!" Viola insisted.

"I've learned a few things from Rebecca and listening to the slaves on Grandfather's plantation, but I can't heal anything like this."

"I won't die, Viola. Not from this."

She hesitated. "Well, if you have a fever before Obadiah returns, I'll fetch the doctor."

Hal grunted something. Mercifully, she took it as assent.

"He's beaten you before, hasn't he?"

Hal was silent, unwilling to tell her the truth. His back would tell a tale, if she looked.

"Damn him!"

"Viola!"

"It's not a curse; it's a wish," she said stubbornly, her hands as light as angels' wings as she worked. "He may be a great shipowner but he's not handy at raising you. You need to leave."

"What happens to you if I go? Juliet will be gone as soon as she finds a rich husband. Then there'll be no one to protect you."

"Don't worry about me. I know how to stay out of trouble."

Hal gritted his teeth against a particularly nasty stab of pain.

"Do you have any money?" Viola asked, as calmly as if they were discussing buying candy.

"No, he's confiscated my allowance for the past six months."

"I can give you fifty dollars, which Grandmother Lindsay sent me for sheet music. That should see you to Independence and give you a grubstake. The Missouri River is so far away that he won't look for you there."

"I won't take your money!"

"Hal, I can't just stand by and watch the next time you two become angry. He'll kill you—or you'll kill him."

Hal couldn't bring himself to agree with her forecast. "I'll pay you back."

"Don't be silly. Just stay safe and write me when you can."

"I'll always do my best for you, sis."

She dropped a kiss on the top of his head.

But he'd failed Viola in '65 and she'd married Ross. The knowledge of his failure ate Hal's soul worse than his father's cane had ever cut his back.

"Hal, my dear boy," the woman's voice purred from behind him.

Hal stopped in midstride, then turned slowly, schooling his face into the usual polite mask he wore around his mother. "Good evening, Mother. What can I do for you?"

She looked around the grand saloon, which was full of passengers taking seats for the evening musicale and waiters bustling to fill last-minute orders. At the piano, Viola played a medley of popular songs. William leaned down to say something, and she laughed up at him, her face so full of joy and contentment that Hal's heart skipped a beat. Not for him, the comfort of a happy marriage—and the attendant risk of children.

"Shall we step outside where we can speak privately?" Mother's Kentucky drawl was very thick, boding ill for their discussion.

"Certainly." He glanced at William, a silent promise to return later. William nodded calmly.

But Viola's head came up, and she saw him and Mother. Her expression changed from the carefree joy of a moment earlier to a cold wariness, like a pilot studying a whirlpool. Her mouth tightened as she studied Mother, and she missed a beat.

Her husband touched her shoulder, capturing her attention. She glanced up at him, and a silent message passed between them, too veiled for Hal to decode. A moment later, she had resumed her pleasant mask as a musician.

The air outside was crisp and clean, washed fresh by the afternoon's rainstorm. Hal leaned against the rail and watched his mother pace, waiting for her to start talking. It never helped to suggest things to her; she'd simply take everything offered and then ask for more. So he, like all of her children, had learned early to let her start any conversation.

"Hal, my dearest boy, I am deeply concerned about Miss Schuyler."

Inwardly, every nerve came to full alert, but nothing showed on his face. "Rest easy, Mother. I'm sure the Pinkertons are doing their best to find her."

"But it would be better if you found her, my dear. Then you could marry her immediately and become a railroad baron, thanks to her inheritance."

Hal stopped this train of thought ruthlessly. "Isn't there a fiancé or suitor in New York with a prior claim?"

Mother dismissed the man with an airy wave. "Nothing binding."

"I'd heard someone else, besides her guardian, was pushing the Pinkertons to find her. Nicholas Lennox, perhaps, who's called himself her fiancé?"

She went white. Hal's eyes narrowed, and he frowned, studying her. What the devil had caused that reaction?

"Nicholas Lennox," she said stiffly, "is a junior partner at her father's bankers. Of course, he is concerned." She went on, recovering her earlier fluency. "But he is not formally betrothed to her and you could be."

He shook his head. "No."

She put her hand on his arm and gazed at him earnestly. He raised an eyebrow and waited.

"My dearest boy, think of yourself. The riverboat business is dying on the Missouri. In five years, there will be nothing left but barges, which is hardly a fit setting for your skills. Oh, there may still be riverboats on the Mississippi but they have cotton, which the railroads don't handle as well. There's no cotton on the Missouri and the railroads will soon take everything."

Hal inwardly winced at her logic, which he couldn't refute.

"In order to survive, my son, you must enter another realm of affairs. Miss Schuyler has a vast inheritance of railroad stocks and shares in related businesses. As her husband, you would be a great railroad baron, who even Commodore Vanderbilt or Jay Fisk would respect. So you must find her and marry her, as quickly as can be, for your own good."

Unable to counter her demand that he find another source of income, Hal fell back on stubbornness. "No. I will not marry Miss Schuyler nor anyone else, as I have said many times before."

"I understand your anger at your father, dear Hal."

Dear? Why was this so important that she'd use an endearment when talking to him alone? His hackles raised.

"Sons always quarrel with their *paterfamilias,*" she continued, her voice honey-rich with spurious concern. "But you must do this for yourself, not for him."

"Impossible. I will not marry." His voice was as implacable as a frozen river.

She blinked, clearly surprised, then she came back to her original request. "Hal dearest, please forget about the past and start thinking. With your long experience of the Missouri, you must know how to lay hands on that missing heiress."

Would she never stop trying to persuade him? Dammit, if she went on much longer, she'd start discussing ways to find Rosalind. And Mother was a very clever woman; some of those ideas could succeed in finding a clever gambler posing as a man—especially if she started him pointing out the advantages and disadvantages of her ideas. He had to end this conversation now.

"Do you have any other topic to discuss, Mother? If not, I must return inside and join my sister."

Fear flashed across her face. She swallowed hard, dropping the thread of her argument. Hal's eyes narrowed. Why would the mention of Viola cause such a strong reaction?

His mother shrugged elaborately. "Go then, if you must. We can continue our conversation later."

"Good evening, Mother." He bowed and went in. He would think more about this later.

Rosalind glanced up from where she was leaning against a wall, as Hal entered the grand saloon. Bellecourt had started teaching her to read charts, before they joined the evening's musicale. It would be a pleasure to listen, instead of straining her eyes. And here she was surrounded by wooden walls, not the pilothouse's windows with their watery views.

At the opposite end, Donovan was singing "Oh! Susanna," as Viola accompanied him on the grand piano. Cicero was seated in front of an empty chair, as if daring any man other than his master to try for it. Hal headed for them, also singing, like a black bass drawn to a fisherman's lure.

Most of the passengers had settled into the rows of chairs that stretched across the grand saloon to face the piano. There they happily clapped and sang along, stomping their feet for emphasis during the chorus. The *Belle*'s cabin crew stood along the walls, humming the same lively tune while staying alert for any summons.

Mrs. Lindsay followed Hal less than a minute later and quickly gathered her usual coterie of young men around her. She held court near the bar and kept her back carefully turned to the ladies' cabin, laughing and flirting as if she was an eighteen-year-old girl.

Captain Lindsay was in the *Belle*'s perpetual poker game, currently limited to a handful of players including McKenzie. He glanced over the cards at his wife, his face a granite mask.

Rosalind's fingers curled into claws. Even a week after hearing he'd been the one who scarred Hal, she still wanted to shoot him. Or drown him. Or . . .

She slipped into a chair a few rows back from the piano, where she could see but not be easily seen—and could quickly depart, should the need arise.

Hal, Donovan, and Viola finished the song and bowed to the chorus of applause. Then Hal claimed the seat guarded by Cicero, as Donovan began to sing "Jeannie with the Light Brown Hair," his deep tenor voice effortlessly evoking the passion he felt for his wife. Viola accompanied him with a concert pianist's skill, and the crowd quickly quieted. As he listened, Hal idly rubbed Cicero's ear between his fingers, evoking an expression of complete bliss on the dog's face.

Rosalind smiled privately at the sight. Hal would make a splendid father someday, judging by his patience with the energetic dog and how much the *Belle*'s crew loved him. Genetics be damned; his character proved it, not his parentage. She could wish he had a dozen children, to teach how to slide down the stairs on the family's best silver platter or make their homework into an exciting game. He'd be a superb husband for some lucky woman, too. Loving, protective, respectful. Passionate and daring.

For a moment, Rosalind allowed herself to dream of what it would be like to be married to him. . . .

"Do you want to see Sherman's inauguration next year?" Rosalind asked Hal, as they left the big gambling resort late one summer night.

"Sherman?" She didn't need daylight to know that he'd

arched one elegant blond eyebrow. "I thought the general had refused to run."

Rosalind shrugged that detail off as she settled into their buggy for the drive home, glad to be wearing trousers rather than heavy skirts. Judging by his expression when he'd seen her come down the stairs, Hal was pleased too. She'd been thinking all evening about exploring his reaction later, which had so distracted her that she'd actually lost money. Now she rushed back into speech, trying not to think about just how her breasts had tightened when his arm brushed them. She did so enjoy a lighthearted family argument. "He'll run and he'll be president. He's the obvious choice, now that Grant is finishing his second term. And he's honest, too."

"A rare quality in Washington," Hal agreed. He took the first corner a trifle too fast, causing the buggy to lean and his body to press against hers.

Rosalind's breath stopped, and she shivered helplessly. Four years of marriage, and she still reacted like a lovesick girl.

"Still, I'd say that he won't run," Hal continued, "because there aren't enough wild horses on this continent to make William Tecumseh Sherman do anything he's promised not to do. My money's on Hayes."

"Hayes?" Rosalind's voice squeaked a little as Hal's leg rubbed hers. She brought it back to a deeper pitch, more befitting her attire. "Do you mean Rutherford Hayes, the governor of Ohio?"

"Yes. He's a war veteran, honest, promised to work with southern Democrats to end Reconstruction. What more could you want?"

"Sherman and honest elections in the South, with the Negro as a welcome member of society." She wondered what Hal would do next. Two children and she still couldn't predict his moves.

"You're dreaming," Hal said calmly. "That won't happen in our lifetimes. No, I expect to vote for Hayes in November."

His big warm fingers began to stroke the inside of her thigh. Rosalind closed her eyes as dew eased from between her nether lips. He'd never before made carnal advances outside their home, not when she was wearing men's clothing.

"How much would you care to bet on it?" he asked, cupping her mound through the fine wool. She gasped and arched involuntarily, pressing herself against him.

If anyone should happen to see them like this . . .

"Five thousand," she managed. The only thing keeping her from slapping his face—or jumping astride his thighs—was the sound of his breathing, which was as uneven as hers.

"That's a large sum of money. Do you think you're good for it?"

"Dear heavens, Hal." She shuddered. Somehow he'd managed to slip his fingers down the front of her trousers. If she survived the next block without begging him to take her, she'd be eternally grateful to the Almighty.

He chuckled, a little harshly. She wished she could see if he had an erection.

"Can you manage that large a bet?" he asked and eased his fingers into her drawers.

"Of course." She sighed as she slid down on the seat and spread her legs slightly, shamelessly making herself available.

"In that case, maybe. Or maybe not." His hand left her just before it would have slid between her folds.

Rosalind somehow managed not to whimper. The buggy stopped, and she opened her eyes slowly. Home already, drat it.

Hal sprang down and handed the reins to Samuel. She followed more slowly as the two men exchanged quiet greetings. Then Samuel took the equipage to the stables and Hal made for the garden, not the house.

"Hal, why are we going this way?"

"Because we still need to talk."

"About the presidential election?" She was completely baffled as she closed the gate behind them. She thought they'd finished that minor argument. "Don't you want to look in on the children before going to bed?"

"We can take a few minutes for ourselves first." He faced her from the middle of the herb garden, hands propped on his hips. Rich scents arose from the well-tended plants around them, while a high hedge ensured their privacy. Crushed oyster shells gleamed white from the paths underfoot. A fountain gurgled softly in the background, and marble benches invited them to enjoy the scene.

A marble satyr danced on a plinth with blankets and pillows spread at his feet, as if ready to watch bacchantes lose themselves in amorous delights. A small clay pot rested in a steaming pan of water above a small brazier.

Rosalind's core tightened in instant recognition. The pot held thick oil, warming for use in her intimate regions. Her nipples tightened into aching points and rubbed against her linen undershirt with every breath.

"Five thousand is a very large sum to wager," Hal remarked. His calm demeanor was even more impressive now that she could see how his cock tented his trousers. Her hand reached for it involuntarily, and his eyes gleamed. "I say I need a sign of your good intent, before I agree to such a bet."

"What do you have in mind?" She hoped for something intimate, something that would take them quickly back to the house so she could obtain release.

His smile deepened, matching the mythical figure behind him in carnal knowledge. Rosalind quivered as heat lanced her from her womb to her breasts.

"A kiss perhaps? Or more?"

"Anything," she sighed, a heartfelt plea.

He cupped her face in his hands, and she rubbed her cheek against him. "Well, perhaps as a start . . ."

He slanted his head and tasted her mouth. She promptly

wrapped her arms around his neck and gave herself totally up to him. His tongue stroked her lips and teased her tongue until she was maddened by hunger. She pressed against him, moaning a wordless demand. He chuckled, a little brokenly, and claimed her with all the forcefulness she could have wished. She tightened her grip and yielded to him.

Hal pulled her closer and kneaded her ass, setting off waves of need throughout her body. Her legs seemed weak and unable to hold her, so she wrapped one leg around his hip to open herself further to him.

Then his hand was inside her trousers, inside her drawers. He rubbed her clit from behind with all the expertise of long familiarity, then squeezed it in just the stroke that always brought her to her knees.

Rosalind shrieked and climaxed helplessly.

He kissed her again, while teasing her nether folds. She moaned his name, recognizing his determination not to let her relax.

"Do you need a ride, darling?"

He fondled her intimately, triggering another rush of sensation through her loins. Her channel clenched, and dew gushed over his hand.

"Yes. Please. How can you ask?" she groaned.

"Then kneel over the pillow, darling, and unfasten your braces."

Rosalind went simultaneously hot and cold as she realized his intentions. "Thank heavens," she breathed and kneeled on the thick blanket. She fumbled with her braces' buttons, cursing them until they came away and freed her. An instant later, and she'd assumed her favorite position, ass lifted to the watching moon, as her beloved husband ran his finger down her spine.

"Damn, you're beautiful like this," he breathed. "We should do this more often in the moonlight."

"People could see," she protested weakly as he caressed

her under her shirt. Her breasts plumped and fitted themselves into his knowing fingers. She sighed, trembling, barely able to stay up.

"Or maybe daylight."

"Daylight?" She could barely think, but somehow managed to protest. Although she'd likely enjoy anything he wanted to do.

"Daylight," he insisted and plucked her nipples. She keened her encouragement, her hips thrusting back against him. He rumbled approval and plunged one hand back between her legs. His big fingers found her clit, and she moaned again.

"Are you very aroused, darling?"

She mumbled something, wishing he'd put that big rough finger inside her. Or better still, his cock.

"Do you know that your folds are pulsing in invitation, darling?"

"Are they? Then why are you waiting?" she managed to ask, desperate for fulfillment. He always took forever to arouse her before he rode her ass. Ridiculous to wait so long for an activity she enjoyed so much.

He chuckled but rewarded her by reaching for the clay pot. An instant later, he was smoothing thick, warm oil around and around her anus, causing her to groan with delight. Closer and closer his hand came, frequently replenishing the supply of oil, until by the time he dipped into her rump, she was writhing against his hand. She was as desperate to be filled by him as if he hadn't ridden her in days, instead of the few hours since teatime.

He kissed her shoulder as he worked a second finger into her. She groaned again, breathing out as he'd taught her, so she could stretch to hold him. The third finger entered, setting off small pinwheels of delight up her spine and through her loins, as his other hand teased her clit. She was pliable with sensuality, eager to accept him.

"Dammit, darling, you're too eager. You're not letting me take this slow." His voice was hoarse with effort.

"Please, just take me," Rosalind begged and tightened herself around his fingers.

He gasped and froze. She panted, her hips twitching with the effort to keep them still. If she pushed him too hard, he might ride her cunt—immensely pleasurable, but not what she wanted now.

He groaned, and his finger teased her insides. "Witch." He took his hand away. Before she could voice her disappointment, she felt him fumble with his trousers, heard a button, then a second, rip free. Answering urgency blazed in her.

He rose up behind her, his jutting cock rubbing against her backside. She moaned her willingness, her lust, as she pressed back against him. He took her hips with a grip of iron, and his cockhead pressed into her rump.

She moaned his name, her body opening and welcoming him as he entered on one long, sure stroke that quickly saw him hilted. He stayed poised exactly there—without moving, damn him—for a long moment. She was stuffed full of him, his lust blazing up her spine like steam from a boiler. She groaned, desperate for release, and her hips pressed against him, shifting his cock inside her so that it teased her most hidden channel.

He shuddered and gasped her name. Then he rode her, pounding into her with the hard demands of a powerful man taking his pleasure in the woman he loved.

Every fiber in her approved and gloried in his possession. She bucked against him, urging him on. Faster and faster, harder and harder, they drove each other toward the approaching pinnacle.

Suddenly he stiffened, gasping her name as his hips pounded her frantically, releasing his essence deep into her. She climaxed, sobbing with pleasure as rapture simultaneously raced up her spine and through her womb.

Rosalind slid down the stateroom door, shaking in orgasm's last waves. Mercifully, she'd managed to escape from the grand saloon and return here before reaching an end to her fantasy.

It was all nonsense, of course, especially the dream of two children sleeping in the nursery. Hal refused to have children, a decision she could understand after seeing him with his father. So she'd best think of him as just a boon companion and protector on her way to Montana, not as a potential husband.

A tear slid down her cheek.

Chapter Twelve

Rosalind came quietly down the stairs from the hurricane deck, glad to stretch her legs as she fetched beignets for Bellecourt. When Hal had finally come to bed after the long musicale, he had ridden her like a man possessed of demons. She was still stiff and sore and sated—and eager for more.

The promenade deck was almost empty at this hour, with most passengers inside eating breakfast. She could hear feminine skirts and footsteps near the bow, although their identities were screened by the stairs and the cabin's bulk. A woman's voice reached her—Viola Donovan's?

"A word with you, Mrs. Lindsay, if you please."

Compelled by curiosity, Rosalind crept forward to peer around the corner. A superbly dressed Viola Donovan had her back to Rosalind as she confronted Desdemona Lindsay. Viola started to glance over her shoulder as Rosalind brushed a barrel, then quickly returned her full attention to her mother.

Could she have heard Rosalind? Surely not. Rosalind settled herself to listen.

"We have nothing to say to each other, Mrs. Donovan," Desdemona said coldly, watching her daughter like a duchess facing a scullery maid.

"If you won't talk to me, then I'll have to speak to Captain Lindsay." Viola was dispassionate, as if comparing apples at a market.

Horror flashed across Desdemona's face, to be replaced by hauteur. "What nonsense. Even if you had something to say, he'd never listen to you."

"Can you afford to take that chance?"

Desdemona raised a single eyebrow. She was facing Rosalind, but her attention was focused on her daughter, who was standing between her and Rosalind. They were greatly alike in height, but Viola was sleek and svelte, where her mother was curvaceous.

"My dear child, has the western sun hurt your head?" Desdemona asked finally, her expression now a neat blend of pity and superiority. "What do you want from me? Acceptance by polite society? Perhaps admitting your Irish husband into the Pericles Club, the *ne plus ultra* of masculine society? Impossible, even with Captain Lindsay as a member. People would never forgive a solecism like that, especially from a descendant of Virginia's first families like myself."

Viola laughed mirthlessly. "You only consider social success, don't you, Mother? Have you ever wondered about anything else?"

"What else could there be? If you'd ever stood friendless and alone in front of a taunting mob, you wouldn't question the need for social status."

Viola's mouth twisted. "Honor perhaps? Or love for your children?"

Desdemona shrugged. "Of course, honor is important but it won't protect you. Power and money and success will keep you safe. And it could all be yours again, as a daughter of Richard Lindsay."

Viola shook her head. "Impossible. Father disinherited me years ago."

Concern, as false as it was blatant, covered Desdemona's

face. "Wouldn't you like to be invited to the best parties? Have the best people clamoring for an invitation to your house? Dine with the president or hear the latest piano sonata from Europe? Doesn't that sound marvelous? As soon as I persuade Captain Lindsay to forgive you and you divorce . . ."

Viola stomped her foot. "Enough of this. I'm here to talk to you about Hal."

"Hal? Why him?"

"Don't ask him for anything he's not willing to give."

"What on earth are you talking about? Hal is a grown man with a mind of his own."

"I saw you two together last night. If you try to cozen him into anything, I'll tell Father about your goings-on during the war."

Desdemona's eyes widened. Rosalind held her breath.

"You wouldn't dare," Desdemona said hoarsely.

"Wouldn't I?"

Rosalind was quite certain that Viola could make a fortune at the poker table. Bluffing or not, she was playing her hand with all the assurance of someone holding a royal flush.

"He'd never believe you," Desdemona stammered hoarsely,

Viola shrugged. "Can you take the chance that Edward Ross didn't leave me—his widow—his evidence of your misdeeds? Or that Father will listen to me?"

Desdemona closed her eyes. "What do you want?"

"Let Hal make his own choices. Believe that I will do anything, and everything, to see that he has a happy life of his own making."

Desdemona mumbled something under her breath, her face twisted and angry. Finally, she nodded. "Very well."

"If you think to renege on this agreement, Mother, don't. Because I can tell Father at any time, should the need arise."

Desdemona hissed like an angry goose before she cleared

her expression. "That won't be necessary. I'm sure our under-standing will hold. But don't think you'll ever be welcome in my house."

She tossed her head and flounced into the grand saloon, banging the great doors.

Viola sighed then squared her shoulders. "You can come out now, Mr. Carstairs."

Rosalind took a deep breath before walking around the corner with all the nonchalance she could muster. She should have known Viola, who'd lived on the frontier for years, would realize she was there. "Good morning, Mrs. Donovan."

Viola raised an eyebrow at Rosalind. "Mr. Carstairs, I am well aware you heard every word that just passed. I am equally certain that, as Mr. Lindsay's cub"—*was there a slight emphasis on the last word?*—"you will behave with the utmost discretion."

Rosalind didn't know all the secrets in the Lindsay family, nor did she want to learn them. But she was certain that she wanted Hal to be happy. She bowed formally. "You have my word, Mrs. Donovan."

"Thank you." Viola looked somewhat mollified. "Then I bid you adieu, Mr. Carstairs, while I rejoin my husband."

Rosalind touched her hat respectfully. Personally, she would not care to have Viola Donovan as an enemy. "Good day, Mrs. Donovan."

Her heart pounding with rage, Desdemona Lindsay managed a smile and a wave for the two young officers. She declined their offer of breakfast with a shake of her head and another smile, this one genuinely regretful. Young military men frequently left the army and went into a truly important field, like politics or railroads, making it advantageous to keep their friendship. Similar officers had provided such interesting, and useful, gossip during the recent unpleasantness.

Besides, their handsome young bodies were such a pleasant relief for tired eyes, after days of looking at the boring river.

One last nod for the steward—a most polite fellow who definitely understood the homage due his betters—and she finally regained the sanctuary of her stateroom. Her ornate toiletries set gleamed on the dresser, the heavy Georgian silver a silent reminder of her true position in society.

How dare Viola speak to her own mother like that? Intolerable! And to suggest that she'd speak to her father about her mother's long-ago behavior—ridiculous! Anyone who had married that ill-bred drunk, Edward Ross, just to keep his mouth shut, would hardly start chattering now.

Hopefully, Nicky's men would kill that upstart Irishman soon. Then she'd make sure Viola would use his money to buy an important husband, preferably someone in politics. It would be very useful to have a persuadable politician in the family, unlike those arrogant and ridiculously upright Lindsays. And once Hal found that silly Schuyler chit and married her, the family would rival the Vanderbilts.

With that logic, Desdemona felt able to draw a deep breath for the first time. She closed her eyes and concentrated on calming down. In and out, very slowly, very evenly. She was barely conscious of the limits set by her tight corset, after so many years of wearing one. She caressed her silver hand mirror with a reminiscent smile, remembering how her cousins had flown into a jealousy flurry years ago when they saw this wedding present.

A light tap on the door spun her around with an irritated jerk. Who on earth would disturb her?

Her husband closed the door behind him. He carried a small tray, covered with brioche and the necessities for tea.

Desdemona, who'd opened her mouth to complain, shut it again. Why was Richard serving her tea? He always left that sort of task to servants.

"Tea, Desdemona?"

"Of course." She watched him manage the fine details of removing the used leaves, stirring in cream and sugar—all in a small space that barely gave her room to shake out her skirts. "How do you do that?"

"Do what?" He didn't glance around.

"Be so neat and clever in such a small space."

"It's far larger than my midshipman's berth on the *Constitution*," he observed as he gave her the cup of tea, fixed precisely the way she preferred and accompanied by a small brioche, which smelled deliciously of butter. His expression was the courteous mask he frequently wore in public, revealing nothing of his thinking.

The tea and brioche smelled heavenly, reminding her of how little she'd eaten for breakfast. She bit into the rich treat, savoring how it melted on her tongue.

"Did you have a good constitutional this morning?"

Desdemona barely managed not to drop her cup. Instead, she lifted her eyes, keeping them as innocent as possible, to him. "It was perfectly acceptable, thank you. I saw a number of egrets, whose feathers could be most profitable if sold for hats. And—"

"How is Mrs. Donovan?" His tone sharpened.

So he wanted to play it that way, did he? No more ignoring their daughter's presence onboard, at least in private.

"She seemed quite well."

Richard's eyes searched hers. He had amazing eyes: gleaming gray like noonday sun on a sword blade, as her brother had once said. She kept her expression guileless, although inside every sense had come to quivering alertness. What did he truly want?

"Do you think so?"

"Of course. What could be wrong?"

"Indeed. How could there be trouble?" His tone was firm and authoritative, yet she sensed wariness. She was deeply relieved when his eyes released hers. He rose and began to pace with his hands clasped behind his back, his teacup left behind on the tray.

"We've done very well for ourselves, haven't we, Desdemona?" he observed. "You bore me three beautiful children who lived to adulthood and we already have four handsome grandchildren. We have two magnificent houses, besides our estate in Cincinnati. Our health is excellent. Yet—"

"What more could we ask for?" she asked lightly. "A castle in Spain?"

He spun to face her. "Our children's happiness?" he countered, his eyes intent on her face.

Desdemona blinked, honestly startled. Why on earth was he thinking about that? "What do you mean?"

"Despite our quarrels, Desdemona—"

Such as the one where you cut off my dress allowance for six months?

"You've always been very concerned with our children's future. So let's discuss something important to both of us."

"Juliet is extremely successful," Desdemona answered, keeping to a safe topic. "She has a wealthy husband, four children, and five—or is it six?—houses. She's also a leader of New York society with entrée into every important gathering. In short, she has everything she's always wanted."

"True, that's exactly what Juliet sought. But what of Hal? Or Viola?" He seemed pensive, an unusual emotion in a man whose overwhelming self-confidence had once attracted her. Nicky might have a pretty face—and a beautiful body—but his manners were so smooth as to lack that arrogant edge of self-assurance that Richard wielded so well.

"We only have one daughter now," Desdemona reminded her husband. He was the one, after all, who'd disinherited their youngest daughter and forbidden her name to be spoken in his house. Seven years later, Desdemona still wasn't ready to talk about Viola, even if her husband was. Too much conversation might reveal why Viola had married Edward Ross.

Richard's eyes bored into hers. "Let us speak the truth here, Desdemona, where no one else can hear us."

Desdemona covered her involuntary shiver by buttering another brioche. Once Richard took a notion into his head, it would be easier to turn the Ohio River from its course than change his mind. And if he decided to ask the reasons for Viola's actions, what could she say? So many years had passed; could she persuade him that she didn't remember?

She chose her words carefully. "Viola Donovan seems very content with her lot."

"Yes, she does. And the way that big Irishman watches her, as if she were the sun and moon." He drummed his fingers on the windowsill. "We looked at each other the same way, when we were first married."

She smiled, remembering those long-ago days. She'd been sixteen and visiting her cousins' rich James River plantation when she'd met him. Wretchedly lonely and angrily conscious of her low status as a poor relation from uncivilized Kentucky, she'd been instantly attracted to Lieutenant Richard Lindsay's size and animal magnetism at the Norfolk naval base. She'd immediately practiced her first come-hither glances on him.

When she'd learned he was from a wealthy New York family, she'd made a determined play for him, planning only to rub her cousins' disparaging noses in her success. But what had started as a pretense of passion turned into truth as she spent more and more time with him. When he proposed—and offered to resign from the Navy so that they could live near her family—she'd thought herself the luckiest woman in America. Thirty-five years later and the founder and owner of the second largest packet company in the United States, an empire that even Commodore Vanderbilt hadn't been able to conquer, Richard was still a very impressive parti.

"Yes, we were happy then," she agreed, more to herself than to him.

"We've had arguments from time to time but we're still together," he remarked, his eyes resting on hers.

Together? She nodded agreeably, carefully masking her expression as she'd learned to do during the war. She'd hated him when he enlisted in the Union Navy, while her brothers and nephews had served the Southern cause. To this day, she regretted none of her actions during that unpleasantness, and she certainly saw no need to welcome him back into her bed. Unless he decided to send her back in disgrace to Kentucky and her family, of course. In that case, she'd use whatever means were necessary—including seducing him—to maintain her status.

Richard's mouth tightened, making her uneasily aware of just how often he'd successfully read others' expressions. Then he moved away to the window.

"But Hal is different." A tic throbbed in his cheek before he spoke again. "He's not happy, Desdemona."

"He's a very wealthy man," Desdemona protested. "He's also well-respected and has excellent connections."

"Especially with the military," Richard agreed.

Desdemona's mouth thinned. Hal should have obeyed her and fought for the South. On the other hand, if he and Richard had gone south, she'd be living off others' charity, as her cousins were.

Still, cream always rises to the top, as her grandmother always said. She'd send her cousins some hand-me-downs when she returned to Cincinnati and civilization. By then, it would be time for her new fall wardrobe from Paris. Pleased by the vision of her cousins' frustrated envy, she listened to Richard's bragging about the war with equanimity.

"I always tried to mold him into a valorous officer. The feats Hal pulled off with that stinkpot and later with the *St. Paul* made him a legend in both the Mississippi Squadron and the Atlantic Fleet."

"And you did help him," she snapped, irritated by his continuous talk of Hal's service in the Union Navy.

"Do you think so? Or do you think I used the cane too often and too hard? He ran away so soon after the last caning that I've always wondered if it was my fault."

Desdemona stared at him, totally shocked. Richard had always been a model father—stern but fair towards all his children. So what if Hal had been punished more often than his sisters? He'd been naughty far more often. "Caned him too often? What are you talking about? You did no more than a father's right and duty to a disobedient, unruly son!"

"I lost my temper the last time. He looked so small and fragile lying there in the bed afterwards," he muttered. "And when he said, last week, that another caning . . ."

Desdemona rose and wrapped her arms around him, the first time she'd willingly sought him out since the war. Perhaps her proximity would distract him from this nonsense. "Hush now, hush. You were always a very gentle father. Why, you wouldn't even permit me to spank Viola, no matter how often she accompanied Hal's escapades."

"Are you sure?" His eyes searched hers, which irritated her. She wanted to shake some sense into her idiot husband. "Tradition said to use stern discipline, but I've always wondered if my son's happiness was more important."

"Of course, I'm sure," she purred, forcing herself to gentle her tone. "Mothers know these things. Hal is a good man today because of you."

He leaned his chin against her hair, hiding his expression and mussing her elegant coiffure. She bit her lip against a reproof; Rebecca would have to rebraid it later.

"Thank you, my dear, for supporting me." His voice was steadier now so, hopefully, he had put aside any worries about Hal's upbringing. Better for him to focus on more important things, such as finding and marrying Hal to the Schuyler chit.

Hal paced the hurricane deck, happily standing anchor watch at one of his favorite spots on the Missouri, and watched the setting sun paint the western bluffs in shades of crimson and gold. The *Cherokee Belle* had tied up for the night where a small stream, its path edged by cottonwoods, joined the river. This anchorage gave a good view of the higher ground to the west and the river's sandbars and scrubby islands, now slowly disappearing under the spring rise's high waters. A large oak grove topped the bluffs here, while just visible to the southeast lay the old mountain man's woodyard.

A barred owl, the only owl who liked fish, swooped down and snatched his dinner out of the river. It headed west for the grove—then suddenly banked and flew south, past the trees and out of sight. Had something—or someone—disturbed it?

From below Hal's feet, he could smell coffee and hear the string orchestra tuning up for the evening's concert. Rosalind and Bellecourt were down there, playing cribbage in the bar. A smile played over his mouth at the thought. Bellecourt was unlikely to bowl her over as quickly as he did others.

A flash of bright light, like the sun shining off a mirror or polished metal, caught Hal's eye from one of the oaks atop the bluff. Old instincts stirred, then relaxed at the lack of any other hint of human presence there.

The flash was unlikely to come from a sniper sitting in a tree. Only white men would fire on the vulnerable pilot in the glass-walled pilothouse, as Hal's wartime experiences in guerrilla territory had taught him. But there'd been no talk of river pirates or road agents, nor any sightings of skulkers along the bluffs.

Still, he studied the high ground to see what had caused that flash, too experienced in rough country to overlook the prickling at the nape of his neck.

"May I join you, Hal?" Viola interrupted his survey as she ascended the stairs to the hurricane deck.

"Of course." He sprang forward and assisted her up the last few steps. She spared barely a glance for the hurricane deck, with its workmanlike assortment of steps down from the Texas's cabins, pipes for the *Belle*'s innards, the hog chains overhead that stabilized the riverboat's trim, and the knee-high railing. Wrapped in her elegant sealskin cape against the spring evening's almost wintry chill, she dodged the obstacles neatly, then turned to look downstream.

"Can we still see the woodyard?" she asked as she produced a small telescope and began to scan the Missouri's eastern edge, beyond the *Belle*'s starboard side.

"Over there, just beyond that big cottonwood . . . See?"

"Ah, there it is!" She focused the telescope and studied the woodyard. "Amazing. People in San Francisco will never believe such a place exists."

"You mean they've never seen a woodyard surrounded by skulls on tall stakes? Why, I thought you could see and do anything in San Francisco," Hal teased gently, keeping his face straight with an effort.

"Exactly. Woodyards in San Francisco are much more civilized. They rely on dogs, or perhaps honking geese, to keep trespassers out, not evidence of long-dead Indians," Viola said firmly. "At any rate, those mortal remains should be properly disposed of in a manner sympathetic to their people's beliefs."

"But they do keep savage Indians away from that woodyard," Hal argued mildly. A little further north, and he'd openly wear his Colts, as would most of the other men on-board. Sampson's prohibition against the display and usage of firearms, lest the ladies be disturbed, was lifted in Indian country.

Viola sniffed and shut the telescope with a loud snap. "The Indians are rightly wary of anyone who'd kill so many and display their heads as a reminder."

"Very perceptive of them," Hal agreed and quickly gave his sister a one-armed hug. "I'm glad you're here. I always wanted to show you the Missouri."

"And I'll always treasure my memories of these days. It's like standing in the Garden of Eden, a time before man cleared the trees and plowed furrows into the ground."

"Some would consider that progress."

She sniffed and pointed at a dozen small lumps of human waste floating down the river, past the *Belle*. "And I suppose those are a sign of civilization?"

Hal wrinkled his nose at the all-too-familiar sight of human waste. Such sights had been rare before the war, when there were few white men living this far up the Missouri. "Sure sign of a big town just ahead. We'll visit Omaha tomorrow—where civilization hasn't yet proclaimed itself with a sewer."

Viola snorted. "Omaha, is it?"

"Yup."

"No wonder railroad agents often help their clients to travel around Omaha, rather than through it."

Hal shrugged. "The town will soon be great, given its beautiful site and the railroad yards there."

Viola gave him a sideways look, which he ignored. "Rail-roads?"

"Railroads," Hal agreed flatly. He might not like those iron horses, but he had to respect their potential. "Enough of that. Is William coming up here?"

She smiled, so happily that it sent a stab of envy through him. "Of course, my husband is joining us."

"Then let's promenade until he arrives." He extended his arm with a bow. She accepted it with a laughing curtsy, and they began to stroll along the hurricane deck's port side.

"Viola."

"Yes?"

"Never mind."

"Go ahead and ask."

Hal hesitated.

"Scaredy cat," she teased. "I'm a married woman now. I can talk about anything. And if I don't like your topic, my husband can teach you a lesson, if need be."

"He can try," Hal retorted, falling back on the old joke. The one time he and William had fought had ended in a draw. But she was right: She didn't have to answer any question if she didn't want to. "You've never answered this question before but maybe you will now, since you're married to William." He took a deep breath before continuing. "Why did you marry Ross? Had he served the Union in some secret way and gained your admiration?"

Viola didn't speak for several minutes. Finally, "It's not my secret to tell, Hal. I'm sorry."

"You weren't in love with him?"

"Great God, no! I could hardly abide him."

Hal swore, the single blasphemous phrase perfectly summing up his opinion of his late brother-in-law. "Damn him. Excuse my language but I wish you hadn't felt that necessity, Viola. I could have helped you."

She shook her head vehemently. "No, I was the only one who could manage Ross back then. Not you, not Father. But it's over now, thank God, and I have William."

"Did I hear my name called?" Her husband stepped out on deck beside them, his black hair edged in scarlet by the setting sun. Viola immediately blazed into life, smiling like a gambler holding all the cards.

Crack! A rifle shot broke through the twilight's peace and a bullet buried itself in the texas's wall.

Hal scooped Viola up with one arm and ran for the far side of the texas, with William barely a step behind.

Crack! Crack! Crack! Bullets ricocheted off the hurricane deck's tin roof, barely missing William. All three humans leaned against the texas's wall and Cicero tucked himself against Hal's leg.

Hal instinctively checked the land within sight, off the *Belle*'s starboard. Only sandbanks lay there, and none of them had enough greenery to hide a rabbit, let alone a sniper. All of the shots so far had come from the oak grove on the bluffs, just north of that fat little stream.

Cicero started to growl. Below them, the *Belle*'s men began to stir in angry response. "Who's shooting at my boat?" roared Sampson. O'Brien's and Norton's shouts were equally loud and far more profane. None of them could do much though, since the sniper controlled the only stairs leading to this deck.

"William, you're hurt!"

Hal's head snapped around at Viola's cry. A stream of blood was running down William's cheek.

He touched his face carefully. "Just a scratch. He must have clipped me with that last bullet."

Viola leaned up to look.

Crack! The bullet cut through the texas's edge less than an inch from William's shoulder. Splinters flew.

How could they escape safely? The only chance was to climb over the side and down to the boiler deck. It would be a tricky maneuver, with Viola in skirts, but worth it to save her and William.

Another bullet carved the texas's wall beside them.

Hal opened his mouth to order . . .

Then a second gun roared out the distinctive flat note of a

Henry rifle from the south side of that little stream. Tree branches cracked and broke atop the bluff. Then still more shattered. A body splashed loudly into the river.

Hal, William, and Viola stayed completely still, waiting for the successful shooter to announce himself.

Then a man's voice shouted, his Mississippi drawl very apparent, "All clear, Donovan! That bastard won't be troubling you again."

Hal recognized the voice immediately and began to laugh. "Morgan Evans," he muttered. "Of course, it would have to be one of Bedford Forrest's hand-picked men who killed a sniper and rescued us. The man will be intolerable now that he's saved the life of a Union officer."

Chapter Thirteen

"All clear," Hal announced as he stepped inside Sampson's cabin. Evans whirled to face him, his two Army Colts appearing in his hands faster than any draw Hal had ever seen. Hal raised an eyebrow and waited, his overcoat dripping on the Brussels carpet. A warm drizzle had started to fall a few minutes ago, and mist was rising from the river.

Evans holstered the two big revolvers. "Sorry."

"No offense taken. I'd have done the same." Hal closed the door, all too aware of Rosalind standing guard outside. Damn, but she'd been white when she rushed up on deck behind Bellecourt. He hoped he hadn't been as pale during the attack, when he'd thought he might not see her again. A weakness for a woman could hog-tie a man within days, especially if they had a family together.

"We've changed anchorage," Hal added as he took off his coat and hung it up on a wall hook, followed by his hat. "We're now tied up off a small island, in the middle of the river. It's the safest spot we could find before full darkness."

Two hours after the sniper attack, the *Cherokee Belle*'s passengers and crew were still buzzing. Four armed men—every one a crack shot—now patrolled her, eager to shoot any evildoer, while others waited eagerly to take the remaining watches. Abraham Chang, William's manservant and a deadly fighter, had the stern end of the hurricane deck, while Rosalind patrolled the bow end, near the captain's cabin. It had seemed the easiest way to keep her close.

Hal had asked Sampson for the loan of his cabin so that he and those most directly affected by the attack—Hal, Evans, William, and Viola—could talk privately. Sampson, who was no fool despite being an ordained minister, had given him a hard look, then nodded.

Sampson's cabin was the largest onboard, as befitted the captain of the *Cherokee Belle*. It lay directly underneath the pilothouse and stretched the full width of the texas. Windows took up three walls, now covered by heavy white brocade draperies, and permitted Sampson to easily monitor the *Belle*'s activities. The furnishings were expensive but highly functional, including a desk, two chairs, and a large bed. Like the passengers' staterooms, a rich Brussels carpet covered the floor, a vivid contrast to the crisp white walls with their Biblical engravings.

The only jarring note was the small circles of raw wood in the walls, where the ship's carpenter had plugged the fresh bullet holes. They'd be painted tomorrow.

"Ready to talk now, Morgan?" William asked from his seat on Sampson's bed, where he had his arm around Viola and a bandage around his head. Bloodstains on her lace cuffs showed how carefully she'd tended him. Hal would have called them almost inseparable before; now he saw them as two halves of one whole.

Morgan Evans was still dressed in the same dusty flannel shirt and canvas trousers he'd worn to hunt the sniper, a marked contrast to his usual elegant tailoring and aristocratic Mississippi manners. His chestnut hair and cavalry mustache were neatly trimmed, although a day's growth of beard darkened his chin. A few raw scratches on his cheek showed where he'd met branches while creeping up on the sniper. With two Colts at his waist and a Henry rifle against the wall behind him, he looked as lethal as a mountain lion on the prowl, and his drawl held the same deadly intent. "Are you sure your cub won't talk? You can hear through these thin walls easier than through my grandmother's velvet drapes."

"I'll vouch for Carstairs," Hal snapped.

"And I," William agreed. "Let's get down to business. Start at the beginning, for Hal's sake."

Evans's gray eyes narrowed briefly. "Carstairs is that reliable? Hell of a recommendation, coming from you two. Take a seat, Lindsay, and make yourself comfortable; this may take a while."

Hal raised an eyebrow, poured himself a cup of coffee from Sampson's omnipresent carafe, and leaned against the door. It was a useful prop, but he also needed the warmth. He was still chilled to the bone by how close Viola and William had come to dying.

Evans took a few quick turns in the large cabin, then began to talk. "William placed me in charge of all of Donovan & Sons' business when he and Mrs. Donovan went to Ireland and England last fall on their honeymoon. Gradually, I noticed that we weren't winning as many Army contracts as we should have. Plus, the Army was canceling some existing contracts. But when these problems stopped in February, I figured it'd just been a temporary glitch, maybe caused by some quartermaster idiocy. Still, I should have investigated it at that time."

February? Wasn't that when the charities filed suit to gain Rosalind's inheritance and the courts froze all access to the Schuyler fortune?

"We've spoken about this before, so stop kicking yourself. Go on," William prodded.

"I reported this to you, William, when you returned in late March. You went to Washington to investigate, using your longtime contacts, while I went on a buying trip for Donovan & Sons."

"But none of my sources knew anything," William picked up the thread. "Or, if they knew, they weren't talking. When Viola and I needed to leave, so we could join the *Cherokee Belle* in Kansas City, I asked Morgan to look into it, using any methods he thought useful."

Viola snorted. "Any methods useful? May I be blunt, Morgan?"

He bowed. "Certainly, ma'am."

"Morgan served in Bedford Forrest's escort during the war, Hal. In other words," Viola continued, "Morgan learned how to spy from one of the best."

"Congratulations," Hal said sincerely. "Remind me not to try to keep a secret from you."

Evans flushed slightly and resumed his report. "I spoke to the War Department clerk responsible for our contracts, as one Southerner to another. He would say little but did indicate that a look at certain bank records might prove enlightening."

"Fascinating." William's Irish accent briefly showed itself.

"The deposits came from a New York bank and the clerk there was most informative, once I greased his palms. William Worth Belknap, the Secretary of War, has been bought by your enemy. His personal accounts show a substantial deposit immediately before every cancellation of a Donovan & Sons contract."

Viola snorted. "That's no surprise. He's being investigated by the Senate now, for selling arms to the French."

"And he'll probably get off scot-free. The man can spin lies faster than a tornado," Hal commented.

"Do you know him?" Evans asked.

Hal shrugged. "I've met him a half-dozen times. Handsome fellow, did well during the war. Just buried a beautiful wife with rich tastes and is expected to marry her sister, who has even more expensive tastes."

"That could be costly," Viola observed. "Paris wardrobes are not cheap."

"No, and then there's his entertaining, which is on a scale to impress even the French ambassador," Hal agreed. "More to the point, during the three years when he was a tax collector in Iowa, he was famous for having paid off all his debts—*and* acquiring land and stocks worth more than four times his salary."

Evans whistled.

"He's doing the same in Washington, has been since the day he arrived. It's open talk there that you've got to bribe him if you want to do business with the Army," William growled. "Hell, John Hedrick's making a fortune just selling introductions to Belknap, given all the men who want a piece of the fat army pie."

"Which you haven't paid," Viola added, stroking her husband's hand affectionately.

"I'm not a saint, sweetheart," William answered ruefully. She chuckled and his mouth quirked. They shared an intimate look before he looked back at the two men. "I've paid him but not so much that I'd have to raise my rates."

Evans pounced on that tidbit. "Less than he wanted."

"Much less. But I figured Belknap couldn't take everything away because Sherman's an old friend of mine, going back to the California Gold Rush. And I'll haul freight where no other company will go."

"So he didn't stop the Army's contracts with Donovan & Sons," Hal said slowly, considering the implications.

"Not at first, no. Just in the last four months."

"What changed?" Hal probed.

"Nicholas Lennox," Evans answered. "I followed the deposits back to the New York bank where they originated. That clerk was also very talkative after some golden incentives."

There was an appalled silence, then Hal slapped the door frame. "Goddamn son of a slimy bitch, I should have killed him back in New York. Two chances and he slipped through my fingers both times." He caught his sister's eye and flushed. "Sorry for the language, Viola."

She waved off his apology. "If we're speaking of Paul Lennox's younger brother, I'm sure you were speaking the truth."

"Oh, he's Paul Lennox's brother, all right. A banker and a snake with a vicious temper." *Who should be gelded for beating Rosalind.* He rubbed the old scar on his jaw.

"He's been paying Belknap to run Donovan & Sons out of doing business with the Army. Apparently, he first tried to attack William directly. Then he spread lies about William, hoping to destroy his reputation. When that didn't work, he found some money and headed for Belknap. What advantages does he have? A fortune perhaps?" Evans asked.

Hal shook his head. "No. Just his salary and what he inherited from his brother. I don't know what the Golconda Mine brought when he sold it but—"

"Not enough to buy Belknap for four months. He charges top dollar to be corrupted," William snapped. "Nicholas Lennox was scared by the Golconda's flooding and sold cheap. The California buyers were able to restart full production within a month, with most of the same miners."

"Lennox is a banker, correct? Perhaps he was robbing one of his clients," Evans suggested.

Rosalind's father had died almost four months ago, just after New Year's. *Could Lennox have been robbing Rosalind's inheritance?* Once again chilled to the bone, Hal wrapped both hands around his mug. If so, no wonder he was desperate to marry her and gain everything, especially after those charities talked the courts into freezing Cornelius Schuyler's estate.

"Could be," William answered Evans thoughtfully. "But can he find enough money that way?"

"Probably not, not at five thousand to stop a contract."

An awed silence greeted Evans's revelation. The tall Mississippian looked around his audience, a wry smile growing under his cavalry mustache.

Hal recovered himself first and began to pace. "Nobody can keep paying out that kind of money for long. Even Commodore Vanderbilt would find it taxing."

"I can counter it," William said slowly.

His wife snorted. "When pigs fly! You're too stubborn to pay blood money like that. You're more likely to let Belknap try to find someone else to haul that freight—then enjoy watching him grovel as he begs you to come back."

"Your prediction contains a good deal of logic, Mrs. Donovan. But what if it's not money but something else?" Evans asked. "Something that would terrify Belknap into obedience?"

"Such as?" William demanded.

"Jebediah Etheridge's ledger book."

"Who?" Viola asked.

"Jebediah Etheridge was Grant's favorite sutler during the war. Even followed him east, just so the general could have his coffee exactly the way he liked," Hal answered, watching Evans intently. "More recently, Etheridge was appointed sutler at Fort McGowan, selling food, tobacco, alcohol, and such to soldiers and Indians there."

The aristocratic Mississippian nodded encouragingly at Hal.

"But didn't Etheridge die a month ago, during that Indian raid?" Hal probed.

"Certainly did," Evans agreed.

"Belknap's been selling those positions ever since he came into office," William observed slowly. "A fat sum at first to be appointed, then monthly or quarterly payments. If Etheridge's ledger book contains details of those payments—"

"Then President Grant could hardly overlook his friend's testimony coming, as it were, from beyond the grave. And the man holding Etheridge's ledger book could blackmail Belknap into doing anything," Viola finished her husband's thought.

Evans beamed at her like a proud schoolmaster. "Precisely. According to the clerk, Lennox learned of the ledger book from his railroad acquaintances and immediately tried to acquire it."

"Does he have it?" Hal demanded.

"Not yet. Etheridge's replacement, James Ripley, has come east with the ledger book and the sale should take place this week. He has relatives in Council Bluffs and Sioux City, so the meeting will occur along the Missouri."

"Where?"

"Probably Sioux City," Evans answered William.

"Probably?" Viola exclaimed. "We have to stop Lennox from buying that book and you don't know where to go?"

Evans spread his hands. "My informant said either Sioux City or Omaha. I favor Sioux City since Omaha is a Union Pacific town. The U.P.'s backed by the Crédit Mobilier, who fired Lennox three years ago."

"Why?" Viola whispered to Hal.

"Cousin Duncan says Lennox was found in bed with two of the directors' wives. At the same time," Hal answered absently, considering the distance to Sioux City. With the Missouri running so high, it would take longer than usual to reach.

Viola choked. "Greedy fool."

Hal realized what he'd said and tried to divert her. "He also has a clever tongue."

Viola raised an eyebrow at that, then turned her attention to the others' debate.

"Omaha is closer to Fort McGowan so it might be more convenient for Ripley," William said, countering Evans's suggestion.

"My money's on Sioux City, which Lennox can easily reach without taking a U.P. train," Evans said. "Afterwards, he can return to Washington—and Belknap—in less than a week."

"That does sound the likeliest option," William said slowly.

"Given that, the *Belle* should make Omaha late tomorrow afternoon but she'll have to tie up there overnight." Hal made plans briskly. "So, tomorrow night, we can look for Lennox and Ripley, just in case they stopped there. If not, we sail for Sioux City at first light. They're unlikely to try another attack in a city."

"And when we find them—"

"We take the ledger book," Viola finished for her husband. "By force, if necessary."

Hal's mouth slowly settled into the same mirthless smile he'd worn when chasing guerrillas out of swamps. *Force. Oh yes, we'll fight.* And this time, unlike that dustup outside the Tenderloin gambling hell or the duel at his sister's house, Hal would not let Lennox walk away. Any threat to Viola and her family, or to Rosalind, must end immediately.

Hal's heart leapt when he saw Rosalind, waiting patiently in her borrowed oilskins on the hurricane deck outside Sampson's cabin. It was ridiculous to be so exhilarated by the sight of one female. She glanced at him briefly, then looked back at the river, with the same bored but alert posture he'd seen from so many sentries during the war: her gray eyes continually sweeping her surroundings, her body relaxed but ready to use a gun on a moment's notice.

"Anything happen?" Hal asked quietly, coming down the half-dozen steps to join her on the hurricane deck. The rain had stopped, but the boat was now shrouded in a thick river fog.

She shook her head. "They identified the sniper, a drifter who's known for his mean streak and love of money. Not a particularly good marksman, thank God."

"Amen," Hal echoed, thinking of the blood running down William's cheek and the terror on Viola's face when she saw it. A crack shot would have killed William with the first bullet, then taken Viola—or him—with the next.

Dear God, he could have died and never seen Rosalind again. He took off his hat and ran his fingers through his hair. To his surprise, they were shaking. Worse, a cold lump of ice sat in his stomach. He'd been steady as a rock when he'd guided the squadron past Vicksburg. But the thought of never seeing one tall, long-legged, high-bosomed female with a clever mind had almost undone him.

Utter foolishness. He'd lived through worse than being shot at by one man with a gun. But logic didn't rule his emotions tonight.

Hal jammed his hat back on and turned for the stairs.

"Are you finished for the night, sir?" she asked.

"Yes. Come along." He had to touch her. He had to reassure himself he was still alive and she was still his. He tried to make conversation while his feet led them toward his cabin. "Did you hear all of it?"

"Most of it, I think." She kept pace with him easily.

"Any thoughts?"

"It's very credible, sir. Lennox assisted in many of his bank's Washington dealings. He'd know who to talk to, if he wanted to injure someone who did business with the Army."

Hal grunted. "Figures. Do you think Lennox would go to Omaha or Sioux City?"

"Sioux City," she said promptly and stepped onto the boiler deck with him.

Hal raised an eyebrow as he turned down the promenade for their cabin.

She answered his unspoken question. "Sir, several of the Crédit Mobilier directors hate Lennox and have done their best to ruin him. Appearing in Omaha, and thumbing his nose at the U.P., would likely infuriate them beyond all restraint. It might be enough of an insult to force Dunleavy & Livingston to fire him. Sioux City is much safer."

"I agree. But we'll make the rounds of the hotels and gambling dens in Omaha, in case he's there." He entered his stateroom and hung up his hat and coat. Cicero brushed past them, heading for his cot.

She was frowning as she pulled the door shut behind her. Damn, but she was beautiful, even in men's clothing.

"I could help you search," she offered, her gray eyes thoughtful as she hung up her coat and hat. "I've seen him more often than you have so I should recognize him easily."

"Too dangerous." His voice was thick. The air was laden with her scent—the light, clean smell of soap and something uniquely hers. He would never have known it again if he'd been killed.

Nonsense. Any man who thought about being killed would be dead very soon. He'd seen that happen often enough during the war. No, what he had to focus on was saving Viola and William. Do something concrete, not dwell on what could be lost.

Still, his hands were shaking slightly when he cupped her face and his chest was tight. "Let's think about this instead." The one sure way to stop her talking and keep him from thinking.

He bent his head towards hers. She immediately tilted her head back, slanting it to meet his approach. He kissed her lightly, his lips teasing her. The tips of his whiskers brushed her skin, sending an echoing frisson into his bones.

He groaned, a harsh needy sound even to his own ears. He cared nothing now, in the aftermath of nearly losing his life, for the danger of their discovery as lovers. Her hands slipped up into his hair and pulled him closer. A shudder ran down his spine and into his loins.

His tongue probed her more deeply, finding and savoring the contrast between her agile tongue and strong teeth. She moaned something as she leaned into him, her long elegant body now a warm caress along his entire length. Need spiked him wherever she touched, making his skin prickle in hungry awareness. His hands slipped down to her shoulders—so slender and strong—then down her back, pulling her closer to him.

He fondled her ass. . . . Damn, but she was beautiful, firm and curving so perfectly into his hands. She moaned again and wrapped her leg around his, inviting more caresses. He readily obliged her, enjoying every warm curve and sinew as much as the taste of her mouth. His cock swelled until his drawers were a prison.

He lifted his head from hers. She looked back up at him, eyes dazed. "Too many clothes," he answered her unspoken question.

"Ah." She started to unbutton her frock coat.

Hal smiled, certain that he looked like a lion anticipating his next meal, and followed her example. He was undressed well before she was, thanks to carelessly tossing his garments over the chair. A fine sheen of sweat coated him, emphasizing his cock's eagerness.

Next door, in the grand saloon, men's voices swelled and flowed as they discussed the attack. Someone started to sing one of the old wartime campfire songs, providing a lonely underpinning to the others' harsh phrases. It was a song Hal had heard before, in the swamps during the siege of Vicksburg. Many men had died during those days, and he'd written more than one letter of condolence to a mother.

He shook himself. Tonight was for the living, not the dead.

His legs trembled slightly, but he stiffened them until he stood steady again.

Hal stepped up behind her and nuzzled the nape of her neck. Such a long, elegant sweep of white skin and sinew and bone. With all those wonderful hidden nerves and delicate pulse points to inflame a lover's senses. Pity that more women didn't cut their hair short.

Rosalind shivered and moaned, bending her neck forward in wordless invitation. Only her undershirt and drawers hid the rest of her temptations.

Despite his throbbing cock, Hal took his time before moving down to her shoulders, pulling aside her undershirt to expose the fragile skin. He was careful to touch her only with his hands, trying to keep himself under control by somehow limiting his contact with her.

He licked and kissed and nibbled lightly until she was shaking like a leaf. She started to turn towards him, but he tightened his hold on her shoulders. "Not yet."

"I can barely stand up." Her hoarse voice, probably meant to be tart, sounded needy.

"Put your hands on the door to steady yourself. After you take off your undershirt," he added. A risky move but he needed to feel more than fine linen.

"Hal," she protested weakly, then gasped.

Hal licked the pulse point he'd just nipped, enjoying the fine tremors running through her skin. And if he stayed behind her, she wouldn't see how his hands still shook. Dear God in heaven, he'd come so close to losing her.

Mumbling something under her breath, she yanked the undershirt over her head and threw it onto the chair. Hal grinned at the disorder she'd caused, so untypical of his little lady gambler. And so redolent of inner turmoil—and arousal.

Muttering, Rosalind turned back to the outside door and placed her palms flat on it. Light from the grand saloon filtered in through the transom on the opposite wall, highlighting the clean sweep of her spine and long legs. Her position also had the most enticing result of thrusting her ass out at him.

Hal gave himself a moment to enjoy the view. His cock surged appreciatively to a damned uncomfortable size.

"Hal, please . . ." she gritted.

"Damn, but you're beautiful."

"And you're entirely too far away," she retorted.

He chuckled and ran his finger lightly down her spine, enjoying the faint bumps indicating each vertebra. Then he laid his palms flat on her shoulder blades and glided them up to her collarbone. "Lovely," he said hoarsely and bent to delicately nibble. Who was he torturing more, him or her, as he cupped her sweet breasts, with their taut nipples?

"Hal. Oh, dear heavens. Hal." Her head fell forward.

He worked his way down her back, exploring and laying claim to every inch with lips and teeth and tongue. His fingertips and palms also mapped her, noting every point, every caress that made her shudder and moan his name. From time to time, he'd play with her breasts and her sweet belly, enjoying how she arched and wiggled under him.

He wondered once if anyone could hear them, then thrust the thought away. No one and nothing else mattered, only searing this woman into his memory.

Her hips twisted and pushed toward him, triggering jolts of hunger through him. His cock burned and throbbed for her, sending matching pulses through his body until he could barely think. Hal tried to remember why he'd wanted to take his time, but couldn't think of a reason to counter the hot, tight swell of his desperate balls.

He sank to his knees behind her and nipped the ripe curve of her rump through her drawers. Rosalind jumped and shrieked, barely managing to muffle the sound against her arm.

Hal would have smiled except need rode him too hard for such softness. He rubbed his cheek against the spot to soothe her, crooning her name. She steadied slightly under him, moaning and trembling like a horse ready to bolt. The rich scent of her musk was clearer now, so close to its source.

He slipped a finger between her legs. Dear heavens, she was very wet indeed. He groaned his appreciation and pressed the seam up into her, rubbing her sensitive folds. Her knees buckled until she rested on the edge of his hand, gasping and shaking as dew flowed down her leg.

"Hal, please. You're killing me." Her voice was a hoarse thread of sound. Her thighs trembled against him in the desperate pulses of near-orgasm.

He ran his tongue down the seam in her drawers, from her spine past the sweet hidden delights of her rosebud, until it met his hand. She sobbed his name as more dew gushed and he sucked it through the linen. Her clit throbbed against his thumb.

He pressed the seam hard against her clit. She wailed and climaxed in a wild spasm that left her sagging against him.

Hands trembling, Hal lifted her and laid her facedown across the bed, with her feet on the ground. A moment later, he had her drawers unbuttoned and yanked to the floor.

He stepped up between her legs and rubbed his cock against her sweet inner flesh, from thigh to thigh and through her folds. He slid it up the crack in her ass until it nudged her spine and rocked his hips, enjoying how his cockhead rippled over the varying muscles and bones. She was so heartbreakingly perfect.

She moaned again. Her hips circled restlessly, and more dew glided down to anoint his thighs.

He took his cock in his hand—his shaking hand, dammit— and guided it into her, barely steadying himself enough to find her on the first touch. And he trembled like a colt when her intimate hairs rubbed his loins, setting off sparks throughout his entire body.

The contact banished all discipline, turning him into little more than a rutting stallion. He thrust into her hard and fast, barely sane enough to be glad her channel clasped and welcomed him. She was hot and moist deep inside, the epitome of the cauldron of life and exactly what he needed.

She gasped his name when he locked his arms under her armpits and gripped her shoulders, the better to ride her harder. Her dew flowed over his cock and through her folds until they seemed linked by both his cock's desperate rigidity and her fluid welcome.

But it didn't—couldn't—last long. All too soon, his seed burned out of his balls and up his cock, poised on the brink of an eruption. He tried to hold it back, enjoy one more deep delicious lunge into her, but couldn't.

Rosalind shuddered and bit her arm, groaning as the first hard wave of orgasm rocked her channel and ripped the last vestiges of self-control from Hal.

Lips and teeth locked in a grimace of pleasure and pain, he surrendered to passion and poured himself into her. He filled the condom in a series of spasms that rattled his bones.

Afterward, he lay on top of her for a long time before he could breathe again. He started to shift, to free her of his weight. A single, delicate snore greeted his ears, and he smiled ruefully. No more riding her tonight, even if his loins were willing. He took a moment to savor how her breathing traveled through her ribs and rippled against his chest.

Finally, Hal stood up, his legs barely able to hold him, and studied his lover. She was so beautiful, lying there in the dim light filtering through the transom. Enticing as Aphrodite, with the beautiful curves of her rump below that narrow waist. And those long legs so perfectly made to draw a man in and hold him close while taking pleasure.

He reached toward her—then yanked his hand back. She

would be leaving at Fort Benton, walking out of his life as she had walked into it.

His lips curled in a snarl. *No.* He would do something, anything to keep her. Marriage perhaps, but not children. Dear God in heaven, even with Rosalind as their mother, he couldn't risk subjecting children to the hot Lindsay temper.

Chapter Fourteen

"So that's the capital of Nebraska," Nick Lennox commented, as he leaned on the Spartan's boiler deck's rail and looked across the Missouri River. Below him, he could hear the deck crew busily letting down the stage on the other side so that passengers and cargo could enjoy the uncertain attractions of Council Bluffs. Downriver, the *Cherokee Belle*'s stacks glinted as the riverboat worked her way up to Omaha. "A big bridge, a wide river that wants to sweep the bridge away, and a few buildings—some of them solid. Has anyone there considered paving their streets?"

"'Some towns are famed for beauty, and others for deeds of blood. But say what you may of Omaha, it beats them all for mud,'" Jenkins declaimed in between puffs on his astonishingly foul-smelling cigar. "Or, so said the local paper a few years back."

"And it still sounds like a good description, at least in springtime. Where did you learn to quote poetry?" He kept the conversation innocent, given the few passengers still on the boiler deck. The smell of coffee and fried bacon drifted past him, reminders of the breakfast being served in the grand saloon.

Jenkins shrugged. "My dad was a preacher and made all

his sons memorize poetry when we disappointed him. It still comes in handy when I want to fire up a crowd."

No wonder Jenkins could start a riot faster than any other rabble-rouser. A quick look confirmed that their listeners had finally left. "Is everything ready?"

Jenkins's eyes, small and cold in his seemingly jovial face, shifted to meet his. He smiled closemouthed, not displaying any of his foul teeth. "All you have to do is say the word, sir, and the problem will be, ah, dispatched, faster than you can snap your fingers. I've also got some plans for that riverboat, in case we get another chance at her."

"Excellent." He'd offered a ten thousand dollar bounty for both Donovan's and Lindsay's heads, just to ensure Jenkins's strongest efforts this time. Then a wave of overripe perfume identified another entrant to the conversation. Best be polite, at least while he was still on this pretentious tub. "Good afternoon, Captain Hatcher."

Like his boat, Aloysius Hatcher was going soft. The bull chest typical of riverboat pilots was echoed by an expanding waistline. Where the *Spartan* was in desperate want of a fresh coat of paint, Hatcher's once-fashionable clothing badly needed mending and cleaning. But the sidewheeler had brought them here in excellent time, given the heavy waters, and Hatcher's eyes were still sharp and steady when he watched the river.

"Afternoon, gentlemen. As you see, we're offloading cargo and passengers now, so we'll be ready for tomorrow's run. Do you have any plans for tonight, Mr. Lennox?"

"Yes, I have friends to meet in town." Good God, was Hatcher still trying to finagle his way into Nick's confidence? He'd been told from the beginning that Nick expected to spend the entire night in Omaha. Nick controlled his irritation with an effort.

Hatcher seemed to realize he'd irritated his golden goose and rushed into overly cordial speech. "There's a great deal you and your friends can do here, sir. Omaha's quite a sporting town. Prizefighting, cockfighting, dogfighting, whatever you like. And there's some bagnios where the women fight too. Afterward, you can buy one, even if they do frequently have the French pox. Perhaps you and your friend would like to—"

"Enough," Nick snapped. The women had started to interest him until the mention of syphilis, or the French pox. He'd never knowingly touched such a female and never would.

Red rose in Hatcher's face as he clamped his lips shut. Jenkins's honeyed tones broke the hostile silence. "Your suggestions are very interesting, but I suspect Mr. Lennox and his friend already have plans."

"Of course," Hatcher said stiffly. "I hope you'll have an excellent time ashore." He nodded to them both and mercifully removed himself quickly.

Damn, he'd be glad when he left this boat and its captain. Nick raised an eyebrow at Jenkins. "Your plans?"

"Keep an eye on Donovan and move as soon as a chance presents itself. Should he dine ashore alone, say at the Cozzens Hotel, we'll have him in a trice."

"Splendid. I'll cross the river at sundown when it's quieter and I'll stay until dawn." Nick considered his options for filling the time between meeting Ripley and his predawn rendezvous. Find a likely woman to bed down with? Interesting thought but not if he had to pay; he had little enough cash, as it was. Perhaps he could rebuild his purse by playing cards. "Any suggestions for where I can find a good game of poker?"

"Allen's gambling house, if you want a square game. Or Clapper Bill's for a more raucous one."

"Thank you. And good luck."

Jenkins grinned, this time showing his stained teeth. "Same to you, sir."

* * *

Squinting slightly against the sunset, Rosalind kept her eyes firmly fixed on Omaha rather than the Missouri River. The *Cherokee Belle* was the only first-class packet docked here, since the *Spartan* was tied up across the river at Council Bluffs. After a long day of watching the *Belle* fight its way upstream, she'd much rather consider Omaha's notorious sights than the raging brown waters pummeling their way south behind her.

She'd last visited it two years ago—in high summer, when all the talk was of dust and dust storms. She'd also stayed on the high bluffs as much as possible and avoided the riverfront, as was appropriate for an unmarried young lady traveling with her father. From today's vantage point, she could see the low ridge of mud that marked the levee, then the town's warehouses and saloons. Beyond them, trees marked the more respectable streets, providing some shade against the end of a surprisingly warm spring day.

Horses and mules pulled wagons along the streets, sometimes visibly struggling to shift heavily laden drays. Pedestrians were easily spotted, especially when they crossed intersections as warily as a gambler picking his way through a rigged game. A few open carriages trotted past the saloons, while their gaily clad female occupants waved at male passersby or stopped to greet them warmly.

All in all a prosperous city, but a rougher one than she'd visited on her own. Even with her pair of Colts snug against her waist, she was very glad she'd be going ashore with Hal. Besides, in his company, she rarely remembered water's dangers.

A soberly dressed Viola Donovan was also studying the town, while William Donovan observed from his wife's side. Morgan Evans was considering Omaha with a hunter's dispassionate—and merciless—eye, while Bellecourt and McKenzie discussed the recent local floods over a sheaf of telegrams.

Hal's voice cut across their conversation, and Rosalind's heart leaped. A leashed Cicero paced beside him, dark eyes alert and ears pricked as if he, too, was desperate to find a villain. "Ready to go ashore, my dear? Gentlemen?"

"Of course," Viola answered.

"Everyone know where they're searching?" Morgan asked.

William nodded. "Certainly. Viola and I will take the better hotels, starting with the Cozzens. Hal and Carstairs will search the business district, while you and McKenzie will take the waterfront. Bellecourt will sieve through the local gossip."

"As we agreed," Morgan added briskly, "if you locate him, don't confront him; just send a message to the Donovan & Sons warehouse. Gillespie, the local manager, will find William and then the others. If Lennox isn't here, we meet in two hours at the Wyoming."

"Afterward, William and I will have dinner with Gillespie, at his home," Viola added. "He has a new baby and wishes William to be godfather."

"A most important engagement," Hal commented. He'd never allowed himself to take on a godparent's duties; they seemed too painfully close to a parent's.

There was a general murmur of agreement before they made their way down the stairs and across the stage to Omaha. A few minutes later, the Donovans had departed in a hack, while Bellecourt had been greeted enthusiastically and borne off by a pair of older gentlemen. Evans and McKenzie had disappeared into the closest warehouse.

Cicero growled at a pair of mongrels sniffing under a nearby boardwalk. They answered him loudly, and he promptly loosed his own slanderous challenge.

"Quiet, Cicero." The dog glanced up at his master's order, sounded one more warning, then sat down beside Hal with the air of having won a tough battle. The two curs barked repeatedly before reluctantly returning to their explorations.

"Ready?" Rosalind asked.

"Of course." Hal silently led the way up Farnam Street, his blackthorn walking stick tapping out each step, and paid little heed to Cicero's frequent libels of the local canines. Rosalind raised an eyebrow and decided to try her hand at recalling his attention.

"Prosperous town."

"Indeed."

Best try another topic. "What on earth is that smell?"

"Probably a dead hog."

"It's coming from under the boardwalk, Lindsay."

Hal shrugged. "Hogs take shelter there from winter storms, Carstairs, then die of the cold. Spring's warmer temperatures bring putrefaction."

Rosalind repressed an involuntary shudder. But at least he was talking to her, and she wasn't looking at the river. "And Omaha isn't one of the ablest towns at removing such garbage."

"No. On the other hand, they're talking about a big celebration in June to honor trees."

Her jaw dropped. "Trees?"

"They think more people should plant and cherish them."

Rosalind closed her mouth. *A party for trees?* Still, orchards and groves would certainly reduce the amount of mud and dust found here.

Hal stopped on the boardwalk's edge, in front of a large saloon, to look back down the street. Standing beside him, Rosalind could see the levee, the *Cherokee Belle*, and the Missouri's angry waters rushing past. Four miles away, Council Bluffs' steeples rose on the Missouri's eastern shore.

Four miles. She'd nearly drowned in the Long Island Sound,

less than two miles from land. Her skin went cold at the memory.

Hal turned around and started walking again, shouldering past two drunks without a second glance. "Hurry up," he called back over his shoulder. "We need to reach the church before sundown."

Church? Why would he want to go to church? Her heart leaped into her throat. Could he possibly mean a permanent union? Impossible. He had to be hunting for Lennox.

Cicero growled at two dogs standing in a doorway, both twice his size and scarred from past battles.

Rosalind swallowed hard before she spoke, as she hastened to catch up with Hal. "I thought we were going to the business section," she questioned carefully, scarcely daring to hope.

"After we're done at the church. We must arrive there before the minister leaves for dinner."

Rosalind stopped cold, forcing Hal to turn toward her. She wanted her marriage proposal to be delivered properly, not from a man walking so fast she could barely hear him.

The piano inside the saloon struck up a sentimental ditty about lost love. An open carriage carrying a pair of gaudily dressed and painted soiled doves swept past, pulled by a team of high-stepping horses and scattering dirt clods right and left. Neither Hal nor Rosalind spared it or the mud a single glance.

"Why are we going to the church?" she demanded.

Hal's mouth tightened. His blue eyes, usually so brilliant, looked haunted.

The two dogs snarled at Cicero, but Rosalind paid them no heed.

Hal glanced around, but they were momentarily isolated on the boardwalk. He looked back at her and spoke with obvious reluctance. "Marriage."

No words of love? It was a public street, and she was dressed as a man. Still, some declaration of affection could, and should, be provided. "Why?"

"It's the only way to protect Viola and William. Your money can permanently buy Belknap's benevolence and stop Lennox."

Cicero launched into a torrent of canine calumnies, which were quickly returned by the other dogs.

Money? All he wants is my money? Rosalind flinched as if she'd been struck in the stomach. That was all Lennox had wanted from her, too. She forced herself to look for another explanation. "Is that the only reason?"

Color rose in his face. "What else? We're good friends and deal well together."

Just friends? Cold pierced her veins as if she were trying to walk through a Montana blizzard. She wrapped her arms around herself and tried to think. This wasn't Lennox, who'd ordered her to marry him, then killed her best friend for objecting.

This was Hal, talking about marriage to her. Gallant, gentlemanly Hal. The epitome of what any woman would want for a husband, if he just had a sentimental attachment to her. She desperately looked for a reason to accept. If she couldn't have his love, perhaps she could be happy adoring his children. "What about children?"

"I will do my best never to sire any." His eyes were as implacable as a stone statue.

Something inside her broke at his denial of her dream. Lord have mercy, this was worse than Nicholas Lennox's offer. "No," she croaked.

Yapping fiercely, Cicero lunged at his canine tormentors, but Hal yanked him back.

"What the hell do you mean by that?" he demanded.

"No marriage."

He grabbed her by the shoulders, his strong fingers biting

into her. Lennox had gripped her like this, just before Bridget died. Hal's blackthorn walking stick clattered to the board-walk, like the pieces of her heart.

"You have to do it," he insisted, staring down at her as if he could compel her with just a look. "It's the only way to keep Viola and William safe."

Cicero strained against the leash, barking so loudly that Rosalind could barely hear Hal.

"Never." She wouldn't agree. She couldn't accept a love-less marriage with him, without even the hope of children. She tried to twist free of him. "Let me go!"

"Dammit, Carstairs, you'll marry me if I have to drag you to the church!" He shook her fiercely. Her knee came up in-stinctively to counterattack. Unlike Lennox's proposal, this time she was dressed to fight.

Cicero charged at his tormentors, jerking the leash through Hal's fingers and pulling one hand away from Rosalind.

"Cicero!" Hal snapped and tried to grab the strip of leather.

The two local dogs sprang on Cicero. Suddenly, a whirling mass of barking, biting dogs erupted in the middle of the boardwalk.

Rosalind ground her boot heel into Hal's foot. Caught off balance, he briefly loosened his grip on her. Not for long, but long enough. She wrenched herself away and took to her heels.

Hal lunged for her. The dogfight crashed into him and sent him staggering.

She ran hard, shrugging her coat back onto her shoulder. She couldn't be trapped, yet again, by a man who only wanted her money.

"Carstairs!" he bellowed.

Heaven help her, if he'd said "Rosalind" just once, she might have returned to him. Just one sign that he saw her as a woman, instead of a walking bank account.

Instead, she turned the corner and ran as if the devil were at her heels. Ran as she had run once before, after Nicholas Lennox's proposal. Ran as she'd wanted to when the yacht sank, destroying her mother and brothers, sending an ocean of saltwater pouring over her.

She dodged mudholes, carriages, and gaps in the boardwalk. She raced down alleys and behind warehouses. And all the while, her brain screamed, "No, not him too!"

Eventually, Rosalind came to a stop in a dark alley. She leaned against the wall, gasping for breath. Slowly, the voice inside her head faded until all she could hear was her heart pounding in her chest and her agonized breathing.

Hal, her aching heart moaned. *Hal*.

Rosalind gradually became aware of other things, like a patch of icy ground in the deepest shade next to the building. The sunlight was almost gone, lighting clearly only the rooftop above and sending a few faint gleams into the alley below. Crates and barrels were stacked behind one building, with rancid cheese spilling from a splintered box. Loud, drunken voices reached her from inside.

A large brown rat studied her curiously, whiskers rippling, as if considering how best to bite her. A pocket Navy Colt appeared in her hand. Rosalind blinked, trying to remember why she held it.

The answer came slowly to her shaken reasoning. She'd been on the *Cherokee Belle* long enough—slept with Hal Lindsay often enough—that she'd forgotten the need to defend herself against the predators found in poorer lodgings. A Colt would kill rats, which was how she'd perfected her shooting in the past few months. It wouldn't stop lice or cockroaches or mosquitoes or . . .

She shuddered. She'd need to hide for almost twelve months more, among vermin like these, if she was to evade Nicholas Lennox without Hal's aid.

Twelve months. That rat had to be at least a foot long. How many more like him would she meet? Nausea rose in her throat, but she forced it back. She would survive this, too, and build her own life. And one day, please God, she'd cherish a loving husband and children.

She cocked the revolver and aimed it at the rat. It was time to start fighting.

The big brown varmint, which had been only a few feet away from her feet, froze. It blinked at her, its nose twitching furiously.

She glared back. Her finger tightened on the trigger. She'd bet a thousand dollars that no one nearby would find a gunshot disturbing.

Abruptly, the rat turned and ran for the safety of the jumbled barrels. Before she could so much as blink, even its tail had disappeared. Rosalind slowly relaxed. *What next?* The answer to that seemed simple: Take passage to Montana.

The voices came clearer from inside the saloon, now that she paid them more heed. While most were obnoxiously discordant, two were reasonably polite—although probably followers of Demon Rum—with one man definitely from New York.

"The deal was for two hundred dollars, not five," the New Yorker snapped. He sounded furious, an unusual note for someone negotiating a deal.

Rosalind stiffened at the all-too-familiar voice. *Could it be?* She slid along the wall, trying to move closer to the speakers.

"That was before I read the ledger book, mister. But I know what's in it now. You'll pay me five hundred right smartly or I'll shop this l'il beauty round to the highest bidder," a westerner retorted.

Ledger book? Rosalind looked cautiously around the corner. A muddy street, an uncovered boardwalk running between it and the saloon—and a slightly ajar window, next to a narrow door. Gaslight's harsh glare spilled onto the boardwalk, and a scrap of curtain fluttered, as if agitated by the argument within.

She gulped, but she had to hear more. Slowly, she crept onto the boardwalk and into the doorway's shelter. From here, she could even hear one man drumming his fingers on the table.

"Very well. Five hundred, it is," the New Yorker conceded reluctantly.

Dear God in heaven, it was Lennox. Rosalind's breath caught in her throat and her heart seemed to stop beating. She lifted her revolver, ready to fight.

Paper rustled and coins clanked. One man—probably Ripley as the successful purveyor of Etheridge's ledger book—grunted approval. A muffled thud, then he spoke again. "Pleased with what you see, mister?"

"Quite." Lennox's voice purred like a gambler collecting a fat pot. "In fact, it's better than I hoped for."

Rosalind bit her lip against the urge to shoot the smirk off his face. Just once, she'd like to see that nasty man flattened by defeat. Just once.

"Good." Ripley sounded just as satisfied as Lennox.

There was a pause, during which she heard glasses being drained. Lennox was less than a yard away. If she stepped around the barrels and shot him through the window, she could probably escape afterward. But that would be cold-blooded murder. No. What else could she do to him?

"Any good gambling houses in town?" Lennox asked. "I'd like to celebrate our acquaintance with a game of poker."

Rosalind almost snickered. Lennox must want to win back his five hundred dollars. Could he be pinching pennies or just greedy? How much had it cost him to bribe Belknap? Lennox's salary as a junior partner at Dunleavy & Livingston probably barely provided for his clothes. His family had been in straitened circumstances for years, with his brother's slum housing as the only sizable source of income. Donovan had said Lennox had inherited little money from his brother's silver mine. Could money be his weakness?

"Dan Allen's saloon is where the top-notch sporting men go. Or there's Clapper Bill's, for something rowdier," Ripley answered.

"Dan Allen's house, it is. Would you care to join me?"

Lennox at a gambling resort? He had a reputation among New York sporting men for enjoying poker, although he wasn't reckoned as one of the best. She might be the better player, especially since she never willingly imbibed at the card table. And large sums of money changed hands at gambling houses. . . .

"No, I'm eating with friends. But I wish you luck."

"Pity," Lennox returned, with a strong edge of disappointment. For that much emotion, perhaps he truly was feeling pinched.

"Good day to you, mister."

"Good day to you, sir." Rosalind could almost see Lennox gritting his teeth. A glass clanked down on the table, a chair scraped along the floor, and booted feet moved away.

Rosalind thought hard. If Lennox lost every penny he carried at the card table tonight, his schemes would be crippled. He wouldn't be able to hire another crewman to sabotage the *Belle* or another sniper. If she were truly lucky, he'd have every dime he owned with him. If she stripped him of every penny, he couldn't attack Hal or Donovan again.

Etheridge's ledger book was the key. If Lennox held it, he could still blackmail Belknap into ruining Donovan. He'd fight to keep it with everything he had. If she held it, then she'd control Belknap, and Lennox wouldn't be a threat again.

If she defeated Lennox at poker, she could take it away from him. She'd have to ruin him tonight at Dan Allen's house, where play was notoriously honest, so Lennox couldn't win by trickery. She'd need to keep her head and play a good, tight game. With a little luck and her big bankroll, she'd gain that ledger book, and Lennox would have to crawl back to New York.

Then she could give the book to Donovan and sail to Montana, not return home to New York. While she might be able to stop Lennox from attacking Hal and Donovan again, she couldn't stop Dunleavy from marrying her off to Lennox. So she'd still have to hide until next spring.

A simple plan with one major flaw. If Lennox recognized her, he could demand that she accompany him back to New York and marry him. Marriage to that murderous thug. Chills raced across her skin.

If he recognized her. Unlikely, since only Hal had realized she was actually a woman under those man's clothes. And the delights he'd shown her in a bedroom had made her woman's body seem more attractive than ever before.

She gasped, wrenching her mind away from those memories and back to confronting Lennox. Her stomach hurled itself into a Gordian knot at the danger.

She forced the panic back with logic. She would be wearing a hat, which would shield her features. He wouldn't be looking for a woman in such a place, least of all her, since the town lay on the water. Her clothing concealed any hint of bosom or hips, so he wouldn't consider her a target for lascivious glances, only the typical fast assessments of hands and eyes that gamblers exchanged.

It could work. And he'd be ruined if she succeeded. Surely inflicting such a defeat on him was worth the chance. And if the worst came to pass, and he carried her back to New York, she could always kill him later, even if it took years.

Rosalind smiled mirthlessly and returned her Colt to its holster. One way or another, she'd destroy Lennox, no matter what her stomach thought of her chances.

Desdemona considered her husband Richard sourly, although her expression of warm concern never altered as she listened to her neighbor's complaints about the weather. What did she care if this spring's weather was particularly changeable and flooding threatened to take the fool's spring wheat crop? She'd forgotten how immeasurably dull dinner parties in these provincial towns could be, when she'd agreed to dine ashore with some of Richard's business acquaintances. After all, she hadn't traveled further west or north than St. Louis since before the war.

But Richard had promised her the chance to sleep ashore in the luxury of a private bedroom. With him snoring next door, she'd be free to slip away and meet Nick Lennox.

Dear, handsome Nicky, of the wicked hands and tongue. She loved the secret of their liaison, the delight of having such a handsome—and young—cavalier, when all the other women of her generation only had their husbands.

He did have a few faults, such as how he'd reminded her of their relationship when he'd insisted she send Hal to find the Schuyler heiress. He'd become quite nasty when she'd hesitated, uncertain whether Hal would obey her as he ought. Why, Nicky had even sworn to tell Richard she'd been a spy.

Obnoxious brat! He'd be well served when Hal married the chit.

She accepted more champagne with a coquettish flutter of her eyelashes. Her boring neighbor immediately preened and redoubled his efforts to describe his lost wheat in greater and greater detail. His knee swung wide and brushed hers, an unmistakable invitation despite the layers of cloth between their skin.

Desdemona was affronted. Submissive, eager glances were one thing but a stranger forcing physical contact on her? She immediately cloaked herself in the full armor of a high society matron. She raised an eyebrow and silently demanded that her neighbor withdraw. Even if he'd been as pretty as Nicky, she wouldn't have been tempted. The real delight of her life, after all, was in society's admiration. Everything else was either a path to greater acclaim or the slightest of passing fancies.

Her neighbor choked on his wine. His leg snapped back to its proper location with an almost audible click. He began to speak of charity work for orphaned children.

Desdemona nodded approval and thought of more exciting matters. Tonight, she and Nicky would be lovers again. A few moments' talk of how easily Hal had agreed to find the girl and then they could enjoy themselves. She just had to survive this dreary party and meet Nicky an hour before dawn, while Richard slept unknowingly in the other hotel room.

She sipped champagne to hide her smirk.

Hal scraped the last mud off his boots' soles and entered the Wyoming Hotel, broad-brimmed hat tilted at a deceptively careless angle and Cicero strutting beside him. The lobby was expensively furnished in brown and gold, with polished brass spittoons and heavy chocolate-colored drapes to keep out drafts. The large room was full of westerners and dudes, most of them eyeing the restaurant's big dinner bell in anticipation.

He was much more in sympathy with the Arkansas toothpick at his back or the deadly blackthorn walking stick at his side, given his desire to break things, than the fools concerned solely with their stomachs.

Rosalind was gone. Dear God in heaven, he'd frightened

her into running again. He'd spoken the truth, but his tongue had tied itself into knots rather than express his feelings for her. He simply couldn't be that vulnerable to anyone.

Perhaps it was for the better. Surely she'd soon find another man, who'd cherish her as she deserved and never lift a hand to their children. His fists clenched at the thought of the unnamed fellow who'd share her bed, then slowly relaxed. She'd be happier away from him. The best thing he could do for her now was to find and destroy Lennox.

William waved from where he sat with Viola and the others in a corner of the hotel's lobby. They had a small group of ornate, plush chairs and an expansive sofa, from which they could observe the entire room.

Hal nodded and made his way to them, careful to step around the clumps of men covertly eyeing Viola. He didn't envy anyone who tried to take her away from her husband.

His sister's eyes swept over him and took in every detail of his expression and clothing, just as she had when they were children. Concern appeared, but was quickly replaced by a hostess's politeness. She shifted closer to her husband and patted the velvet-covered sofa.

"Come sit here, next to me," she invited. "We've almost taught the waiter how to provide a proper cup of tea. Or Morgan and Mr. Bellecourt can vouch for the coffee, if you'd prefer that."

"Tea, thank you." Hal kept his head erect and his face calm as he sat down. Cicero curled up next to him on the floor, with an almost audible yawn.

She poured, adding cream and sugar as he preferred, and passed it to him silently. The fragrant brew's heat and sweetness reminded him of the delights of Rosalind's bed. Ah, the hot, moist clamp of her inner muscles when she was lost in passion. . . .

"Will Carstairs be joining us?" William asked.

Hal stiffened, then managed a shrug. "No, he's left my employ."

William's eyebrows lifted, and Bellecourt started to expostulate.

"I offered him a different job, one that would have kept him with the *Cherokee Belle* after this voyage. He refused and felt it best to leave," Hal continued. He was ruefully proud of his even tone of voice, a complete contrast to the pain stabbing his heart.

Cicero whined softly and rubbed his head against Hal's leg. Hal patted him absently and looked straight back at William, daring him to question the explanation.

"I understand," William said smoothly. "We will miss him."

Hal wondered uneasily just how much William did understand.

"*Quel dommage,*" Bellecourt murmured. "He could have become a great pilot once he was fully at home on the water."

Evans stirred restlessly. "Enough of that. Did you see Lennox?"

Hal shook his head. "Not a trace of him."

"No one else found him either," William announced quietly.

Damn. He would have enjoyed smashing that bastard's head.

"Will we visit Gillespie tonight?" Viola asked. "I'd like to see the new baby, if we can."

William smiled down at her fondly and kissed her hand. "Of course." She answered him with an intimate look that twisted Hal's heart. To share that kind of loving confidence with Rosalind . . .

He slurped his tea loudly. William stiffened, and Viola chuckled.

"Doesn't Gillespie and his wife live a few miles outside town?" Evans asked. "Will you spend the night with him?"

"That was our plan," William agreed. "I'd prefer to stay until just after dawn, so Viola won't be disturbed by road agents on the drive back."

"Good idea," Hal agreed. "The better light will also make it easier to spot snags and driftwood on the river, when we sail to Sioux City." *Where we'll finally destroy Lennox.*

"It will also give me time to receive answers from those telegrams to Sioux City," Bellecourt added.

"Can Abraham stand watch tonight on the *Belle*?" Evans was clearly considering options.

Viola chuckled. "I pity anyone who tries to attack a boat that he's guarding!"

Her husband laughed. "Amen to that, my dear. Of course, he can stand guard, Morgan, if Hal will have him."

"My pleasure." He'd seen Abraham Chang once before in a fight, when Paul Lennox kidnapped Viola. He, too, pitied anyone who tried to sneak past that Chinese warrior.

"What of the rest of you? Would you care to join us?" William asked, his eyes lingering on Hal. "Gillespie and his wife are very hospitable and very proud of their first son. I'm sure they'd welcome you."

Hal winced. *A happy couple with a newborn child? No.* He barely noticed Evans's equally reflexive flinch beside him.

"Ah, you young people." Bellecourt harrumphed. "You can coo at babies but I will play poker and share stories with old friends."

"That sounds very pleasant too. Morgan?" Viola invited.

"I'd thought to stay in town, close by the *Cherokee Belle*. Eat dinner, have a few drinks." He shrugged carelessly.

"Masculine pastimes," Viola ruthlessly summed up his plans.

Evans bowed in acknowledgement. "Exactly. Perhaps Hal will care to join me."

"Glad to." Far better to spend time with a fellow bachelor than in a house full of what he'd never have.

"Then we'll all meet tomorrow morning at the *Cherokee Belle,* an hour after dawn." Viola summed up the arrangements briskly.

William lifted his teacup in salute. "Until tomorrow."

The first day without Rosalind. Hal's mouth tightened, but he managed to join the others' salute. "Tomorrow."

Chapter Fifteen

Rosalind studied Dan Allen's gambling house from the shelter of the hotel across the street. Warm rain fell gently from the skies, softening a lawless scene and promising more water for the Missouri River.

A noisy saloon occupied the first floor with the gambling rooms above, judging by the silhouettes moving at the windows. A very interesting element was the pawnshop in back—located directly below the gambling rooms. Clearly, players suffering from the absence of Lady Luck could procure some additional time at the tables by pawning their belongings. The entire complex was tidy and bustling, albeit with a rough clientele.

She'd seen Lennox enter the saloon, swaggering like Napoleon as he shoved his way through the doors. Then she'd stopped at the neighboring hotel to clean up, while a local ragamuffin kept watch on the saloon.

Now her boots and charcoal gray trousers were once again immaculate, her coat was smoothly pressed, and her diamond stickpin shone like the expensive jewel it was. Her hair shone with Macassar oil, which darkened and disguised its natural color, and the faint scent of sandalwood rose from her cheeks, as if she'd recently shaved. All steps necessary to brand her as worthy of a high-stakes game in the town's top establishment. Her Colts were tucked neatly at her waist, visual warnings that she wasn't a pigeon ripe for the plucking. She'd moved a thousand dollars from her bankroll into her coat pocket, ready for use. More waited in the canvas belt, ready to break Lennox.

What lay underneath the gambler's immaculate outer shell was another matter. She'd nibbled a little boiled chicken and bread while the hotel staff pressed her coat. Now her heart was hurling itself against her ribs, as if considering how best to return that chicken to the farm.

It was a worse reaction than the first time she'd visited a gambling resort with her father. Then, she'd still been shaken by her mother's and brothers' deaths, and grateful to her father for the diversion of learning to play cards like a professional. She'd taken comfort in her short hair, cropped during the pneumonia that had nearly killed her, her polished men's clothing, and, most importantly, her father's presence at her side. He'd given her the diamond stickpin that night.

She ran her thumb over the diamond, remembering all the times she'd worn it around her father. She could almost feel him winking at her and standing behind her, ready to coach her if necessary. She'd always won when he was in the room.

But now she was alone. She'd have to fight this battle without Hal or her father beside her. If she failed or was exposed as a woman, she'd be imprisoned in Dunleavy's isolated country estate until she married Lennox.

Rosalind shivered. The cabin of a sinking boat during a gale would be a far friendlier place. But enough of that. The only way to eliminate Lennox as a threat was to strip him of money and blackmail material, a campaign only she could win.

She tapped her broad-brimmed planter's hat firmly into place. Time to play poker and ruin Lennox.

* * *

Hal set his plate, half full of uneaten beefsteak, down on the floor and turned to his coffee. Cicero rumbled happily then dived into the treat. Hal envied his dog's simple enjoyment of food. Even good wine had lost its flavor without Rosalind, so he'd returned to coffee, an old friend from his Navy days.

Evans raised an eyebrow, but said nothing while the waiter cleared their plates. Here in a private room in Omaha's best restaurant, service was fast and discreet, especially when the waiter was tipped in advance.

"What do you want for dessert?" Hal thumbed through the menu left behind on the table, contemplating the list of puddings and *glacées* with very little interest. None of them were a *tarte tatin,* Bellecourt's beloved upside-down apple pie that Rosalind had enjoyed with such wholehearted enthusiasm.

His friend didn't answer immediately, and Hal looked up, ready to offer the menu.

Then Evans spoke quietly, his eyes very steady on Hal's face. "I heard there's a house in town where one can enact fantasies. I'd planned to visit it, should time permit."

Hal blinked. *Fantasies?* Morgan must be talking about brothels, where one could play very imaginative, very carnal games with experienced women. Curiosity reared its head, and his cock filled slightly.

He drummed his fingers on the table as he considered the possibilities. He'd heard of such expensive brothels, which catered to a network of carefully vetted, highly sensual men and women. He'd played games before, of course, but only as brief diversions with a partner he already knew and trusted.

God in heaven, he could imagine enacting such fantasies with Rosalind. But the little minx would probably insist on playing a hand of poker first, just to decide who would be on top. He bit his lip and tried to shake off that image. Best to get on with his life without her and start seeing other women.

"Would you care to come along, Lindsay? I'd be proud to stand surety for you," Evans offered.

Surety? Were these fantasies so intense that introductions and guarantees were needed? His ever-present imagination leapt into full life, producing the image of Rosalind in a harem slave's fragile silks. His cock all but roared at the thought.

But she wouldn't be there. Hal bit his lip and firmly ordered his cock to consider other possibilities. Perhaps a petite raven-haired beauty with breasts that filled a man's hand. He forced himself to see every detail of the girl's curves, including the fit of her rump against his cock while her head barely reached his chest. He tried to imagine how her intimate folds would be shaped, but all he could see was Rosalind. Gray-eyed and high-breasted, long legs wrapped around his waist as she encouraged him to thrust harder.

His chest tightened at the memory. His cock somehow hardened further until every button in his fly seemed branded on it.

"No, thank you, Evans. I am deeply appreciative of the honor you've given me by this invitation but I must return to my boat." At least he'd managed a reasonable excuse, rather than saying he'd be useless with any woman other than Rosalind.

Evans spread his hands politely. "A pity. Perhaps another time when matters are more settled."

Settled? The best resolution would be Rosalind as his wife, and that was an impossibility. She was gone now, and perhaps soon she'd marry someone else.

"Perhaps," Hal said noncommittally. He couldn't bring himself to consider Rosalind enacting fantasies with another man. He signaled the waiter for the check.

Rosalind sauntered across the street, careful to stay on the planks that bridged the mud. Pushing through the doors, she was immediately hit by the reek of alcohol, tobacco, and unwashed men. But she didn't break stride: She'd been in similar gambling resorts too often to be taken aback by a stench that would have sent her mother into hysterics.

A solidly built, blue-uniformed guard stopped her with a silent request for her guns, the standard method for reducing fights in respectable saloons. She handed them over calmly, saw them stowed in a large, locked cabinet drawer, and accepted the numbered receipt. Then she was free to view the setting for her confrontation with Lennox.

An immense bar covered the far wall, with mirrors on the few flat surfaces and bottles in every carved niche. Four bartenders served beer or poured whiskey, as fast as they could, to the men standing five deep in front of it. Negro waiters, all in neat black uniforms with white aprons, carried trays loaded with glasses and bottles to patrons at the tables.

Immense gaslight candelabras hung overhead, and elegant sconces on the red brocade-covered walls brightly lit Dan Allen's saloon. The floor was wood, of course, with sawdust scattered across it. There were no bloodstains on the threshold or immediately inside, so Allen either demanded gentlemanly behavior from his rough clientele, or his staff was very fast at cleaning up after dust-ups. She'd bet a golden eagle that the answer lay somewhere in between.

An elegant staircase rose beside the bar, with two narrow-eyed, uniformed gentlemen standing at the base. The private gambling rooms, where poker or whist were played, must lie beyond, their sanctity preserved by those guards.

Roughly dressed men crowded the saloon, all with drinks in their hand. Many stood three and four deep around the faro tables, calling out bets or yelling encouragement to the cards. The few poker players seemed more intent on imbibing than playing a game of skill.

Underneath the roar of voices, a piano pounded out something that might be called music. It was pleasant enough for a place like this, but nothing like the Chopin or Beethoven songs that Hal's sister loved to play.

A dozen gaudily dressed loose women loudly encouraged the betting, while simultaneously displaying their own wares to all comers. Rosalind paid little heed to the whores, an attitude that had more than once earned her a reputation as a man who loved men. She'd laughed before at the truth in that, but not tonight. She had other business to attend to.

She forged her way through the crowd as she searched for her quarry, politely excusing herself whenever a ruffian was disturbed by her passage. As she'd expected, Lennox was nowhere to be found in the very public and noisy saloon.

To find him, she'd have to gain admission to the private rooms above. She could do that either by working her way up from one of the few poker tables in the saloon or by simply bribing her way in. Eager to attack, she opted for the faster method and approached the guards at the staircase.

"Good evening, men. Can you tell me where I can find a good game of skill in this town?" She rolled a half eagle across her knuckles.

One of the guards swallowed hard, watching the half eagle as if it were his hope for heaven. "There are private rooms upstairs, sir, for short cards. Stud poker, draw poker, whist . . ."

"And the high-stakes game?"

"That'd be the regular stud poker game, sir, which is just setting up now. Up the stairs and all the way to the back," the other answered, his eyes flickering back to her face from the coin.

"Thank you." She quietly tipped each man a half eagle and headed up the stairs.

"Thank you, sir. Just tell Brittain that Charlie and Bill sent you," the first guard responded as his gold vanished from sight.

Rosalind found a long corridor at the top, decorated in the same red brocade wallpaper as below. Wall sconces lit the way brightly, permitting few shadows in their harsh gaslight. Four doors dotted the corridor, making this a substantial gambling resort, but not the largest she'd ever seen. Of course, the size of the game rarely matched the scale of its setting. She'd once played for two thousand dollars on a muddy levee outside Memphis, for example.

A very muscular bald man with an immense mustache coldly watched her approach. He was superbly dressed in the best frock coat she'd seen since New York, quite possibly tailored by the same genius who'd created her own suit.

She stopped in front of him, a golden eagle barely visible between her fingers. "Mr. Brittain? Charlie and Bill sent me."

He relaxed slightly, although he was still a very intimidating figure. "Which game are you looking for, sir?" he asked politely, watching her face and not the coin.

His acceptance of her as a gambler and a man sent the old pregame confidence rising in her veins. She understood houses like this far better than the Missouri River. "High-stakes stud, if you please," she answered calmly.

"Right this way, sir." He pushed open the door beside him, and she entered, slipping the golden coin into his waiting hand. "Good luck, sir."

"Thank you, Brittain."

"Your eighth player, gentlemen," he announced and closed the door behind her.

The room was surprisingly large, with the air of a men's clubroom, rather than a tavern's back room. Heavily carved walnut wainscoting lined the walls, with striped red velvet wallpaper rising above it. The wallpaper was almost totally covered by pictures of famous racehorses and trotters, creating an impression of good luck and good cheer. The furniture matched the paneling—carved walnut with luxurious burgundy leather upholstery. A large round table occupied the center of the room, with nine chairs around it. A few scattered side tables and chairs rested against the walls, providing sanctuary for any spectators.

An immense etched glass chandelier hung directly over the central table, providing brilliant light for play. It also eliminated any shadows, in which a dishonest player might attempt to fudge the cards. A dumbwaiter and bellpull lurked in the far corner, probably directly over the pawnshop, while a sideboard held decanters and glasses.

Eight men glanced up at her entrance. Or, to be more precise, one dealer in the same dark blue livery as the guards, six well-dressed men—and Lennox.

Her heart lurched, but she kept her head up and her voice calm and deep. "Good evening, gentlemen."

A chorus of "good evenings" answered her from everyone except Lennox. "Come to lose your money to your betters, Mr. Sharper?" He sneered.

Rosalind raised an eyebrow at his rudeness, but kept her voice calm. "Sir, I'm here to play a game of skill with gentlemen," she answered with a slight emphasis on the last word. Did the fool rely on derogatory talk to win hands for him by distracting the other players?

Lennox's mouth tightened, and color mounted in his cheek at her counterattack. He started to say something even more impolite, but a tall well-dressed fellow coughed, his green eyes twinkling under his Stetson. Lennox bit his lip and contented himself with a loud snort. He hadn't recognized her.

Suppressing a grin at his blindness, Rosalind greeted the tall man, recognizing him from her time on the *Natchez*. "Good evening, Bristow."

"Carstairs, isn't it?" Bristow touched his hat in acknowledgment. Rosalind bowed politely, glad to see at least one honest poker player present.

"I'm glad you finally made it to Nebraska for a frontier

game of poker," Bristow went on. "May I introduce you to
our fellow players?"

Exultation surged in her, hot and bright, as he named the
other men and she returned their greetings. She could have
shouted her relief to the skies, but she forced it back fiercely.
Round one might be hers, with Lennox's lack of recognition,
but the game's end would come only when she plucked
every feather he had.

She seated herself at the round table with the others and
purchased her chips, a large sum but not enough to send up
warning flags—certainly less than Lennox's or Bristow's stakes.
She'd keep the size of her bankroll hidden for as long as possible.

With the casual ease of long experience, the other players
finished counting and stacking their ivory chips, all emblazoned with Dan Allen's initials. Bristow was the most prominent, still exhibiting the graceful, clean-limbed frame of the
famous wartime cavalryman. He was always willing to talk a
man's ear off with tales of his beloved shorthorn cattle or his
prize horses, and was an excellent poker player, who'd spent
a large amount of time at the *Natchez*'s tables. At the time,
Rosalind had wondered if he'd simply sought to avoid the
unmarried women who clamored for his company.

Given the diamond stickpin he wore, another player appeared to be another professional gambler, although she didn't
recognize him by name. The others seemed to be wealthy
townsmen, comfortable with each other and the game.

Hamilton, the dealer, a sturdy middle-aged fellow with the
stolid demeanor and all-seeing eyes of a first-rank faro dealer,
calmly announced the house's rules. Quarter eagle ante, half
eagle for a full bet. All minimums doubling at midnight, and
again at two, for those still playing. It would definitely be a
high-stakes game, played for serious gamblers and not ama-
teurs. He expertly dealt the first three cards as soon as every
player had paid the ante to enter the hand.

Rosalind quickly checked her hole cards—a mismatched three and six. It would be very difficult to build a winning hand from them and the ten looking at her from the table, although the ten and six were both diamonds. She'd need to fold and wait for a better chance at Lennox.

That decision made, she studied the other players, eager to start learning their tells. Lennox grinned at the three of hearts displayed before him, then caressed his chips, obviously eager to bring in the first bet.

Bristow glanced at Lennox and yawned, a definite sign he thought he had an excellent chance. His visible jack had to be matched by something else in his hand.

"Five dollars, gentlemen," Lennox announced, pushing the chips into the center. "Anyone brave enough to try to claim them?"

A slight rustle ran around the room at Lennox's bravado, but no one spoke. The next player folded quietly, which was what Rosalind had expected. Then it was Bristow's turn.

"I'm in," he announced, matching Lennox's large wager. But Rosalind had played him before and knew him as a tight player. If Bristow was willing to bet like this, he must be very confident of winning the hand.

Two more players folded, probably unwilling to match their cards against the two men already jostling for the pot.

Then it was Rosalind's turn. She started to fold, but hesitated, strategies flashing through her brain.

What did it matter who took Lennox's money, so long as he was empty-handed at the game's end? She had a good card visible, so no one would be surprised if she wagered aggressively. Perhaps she could build up the pot by raising the stakes, then fold on fourth or fifth street, which would still minimize her risk. If Bristow took the pot after that, Lennox would have lost more money than if she played conservatively.

It was a very unusual strategy, one that required deep

pockets and was far different from a professional's tactic of only chasing the hands that seemed winnable. But her bankroll was substantial, mute testimony to how well she'd done on the Mississippi riverboats. Now was the time to use her winnings to defeat her enemy—and protect Hal.

"I'll see you—and raise you two," she announced, increasing the minimum bet to seven dollars. Bristow and Lennox would each have to add two more dollars to stay in. She could lose her wager if anyone called it, since she had no cards to back it. Her stomach was doing cartwheels behind her stiff vest.

Bristow stretched slightly, so he'd stay in. Good.

"How generous of you to fatten the pot for me." Lennox sneered. She ignored him. He stroked his mustache, mouth pursed, then relaxed. He'd definitely stay in.

The remaining players quickly folded. Lennox matched her bet, as did Bristow. Rosalind relaxed subtly, careful to show none of her tension. Her strategy had worked. Lennox would lose more money, thanks to her, if Bristow took the pot.

Hamilton dealt the next round of cards, for fourth street. Surprisingly, Rosalind received a seven of diamonds, matching her six and ten. Could this be the start of a straight flush? It would be an amateur's gamble to stay in, hoping to be dealt that exceedingly desirable hand.

Lennox raised again, Bristow matched him, as did Rosalind.

She received the eight of diamonds on fifth street, moving her a step closer to a straight flush. She wondered what Bristow was holding; his board cards hardly seemed worthy of serious play, from where they lay exposed to sight on the table.

The usual murmurs were barely audible now, as the other players watched the game. Bets doubled on fifth street, and any player who stayed in now would probably see the hand through to the end.

Lennox now had two pairs showing, all black aces and eights. "Dead Man's hand," whispered the fellow who'd been standing behind him. He edged away from the table.

Lennox wagered fifty dollars, all the while sneering at Bristow.

Bristow ostentatiously doubled Lennox's bet—and yawned when Lennox lectured him about the superiority of Lennox's hand. While Lennox vilified Bristow's logic, Rosalind silently matched Bristow's bet.

Lennox then matched Bristow's bet, after the briefest glance at Rosalind's board cards. His exposed two pair were still far better than hers.

Bristow shot her a quick, searching look, but said nothing. Did he suspect that she wanted to fleece Lennox for personal reasons? Heaven knows her board cards were no more worthy of this much action than his were.

On sixth street, Rosalind received a four of diamonds. If she received a nine of diamonds on the river, she'd have her straight flush and take Lennox's money. Her mouth quirked at the unlikely prospect.

But she could feel a current flowing her way, luck carrying her forward. If she'd learned one thing from Hal on his beloved *Cherokee Belle,* it was to trust the river. Her fingers flexed, as if searching for a riverboat's wheel.

Lennox was definitely showing all the cockiness of someone holding a full house. Bristow might have three of a kind, if his hole cards were a pair and matched one of his otherwise pitiable board cards.

Lennox wagered a hundred and fifty dollars. Bristow matched him coolly. Rosalind doubled their bets, as calmly as if she'd been sitting in her parlor on Long Island, then she took a sip of coffee.

"Why, you foolish puppy, to give me your money so easily." Lennox sneered.

Rosalind shrugged. "Are you going to match my bet or fold?"

Grumbling loudly about insolent fools, Lennox matched her bet. Bristow silently did the same.

The room was now so quiet that Rosalind could hear everyone's river sliding onto the table. The last card of the hand, dealt facedown as one card per player. She quickly turned up an edge to see: The nine of diamonds had come to her on the river. She waited.

Lennox stared at her, his handsome face finally thoughtful. "One hundred to call," he announced. Of course he wanted to see her hand.

"Fold," said Bristow with a sigh.

Rosalind peacefully matched Lennox's wager, then turned over her cards. "Straight flush, gentlemen, ten high."

Lennox's language descended into the gutter as he watched the dealer gather the chips and pass them to Rosalind. But he stayed in the game. She still had a chance to empty his pockets and take the ledger book, too. And on that hope, she tipped Hamilton a larger sum than might have been expected.

Hal walked briskly down the boardwalk, alert and wary amidst the swirling mist. The earlier warm drizzle had stopped, and fog was building now, shrouding buildings and streets in swathes of damp gray. When he'd left Morgan, he could see fifteen or twenty paces away in the brilliant light from any saloon's windows. Closer to the Missouri now, he could see only ten paces away in the glimpses of gaslight from the grubby taverns. His steps were muffled, and it was difficult to tell where other sounds came from, or how far distant their origin.

Cicero was equally silent as he trotted beside Hal.

There were far fewer people on the streets here, so close to the levee, than there had been just after the war, when the Missouri was covered with men racing west and wild men and women crowded the levees to take their money. He'd have been jostled every step back then, but now he simply exchanged glances with the few passersby and ignored the loose women. Far away, he could hear the rail yards and their attendant saloons—where money grew fast on the Union Pacific payroll, and the sporting men and whores now gathered.

He was alone, bitterly alone in this world of swirling mist and shabby wooden buildings. Oh, the *Cherokee Belle* was waiting a few blocks ahead, and his friends would search for him, if he went missing. But here and now, where a footstep could be blocks away or just a few feet, he was a solitary human being.

If Lennox had paid someone to attack him, he wouldn't be able to see a blow coming as easily as on the *Belle*. But he had his blackthorn, his knives, and his gun—more than enough to discourage any paid thug, or two. Still, he kept his head up and his eyes alert, although his heart ached for Rosalind and the excitement of bygone days.

For the first time, he faced the inevitability of loss. He'd dreamed from earliest childhood of becoming a riverboat pilot, the king of all he surveyed on the river. He'd achieved that and more. He owned the *Cherokee Belle,* the *Cherokee Star,* and others. He held sizable chunks of land in many river towns—hell, even in Chicago.

But the riverboats were dying, as his mother had so irrefutably argued. In ten years—or even five—the only work on the Missouri River would be pushing barges, because the railroads would have taken everything else. It would be enough to keep his boats running, but when they inevitably succumbed to the Missouri's wild caprices, would he be able to rebuild them? Not as they were now, he couldn't, not with their fine staterooms and gilded carvings. Only a fool would deny that passenger traffic was disappearing faster than a summer rise.

What then? Other men had wives and families waiting for them, who'd welcome them no matter what monies came from the river. But he had no one, now that he'd lost Rosalind.

He was a very wealthy man, and he was alone. He was losing the great love of his youth—the power and prestige of ruling a riverboat. He wouldn't have a pilothouse to stand in, with the wind in his face and a fine boat trembling under his command.

And he'd lost the woman who could be the great love of his maturity, the one woman who'd ever made him want to stay. He'd never again see those brilliant gray eyes of hers, which could gleam with intelligence or blaze with passion.

He came to the last corner before the levee, which was vividly marked by the big white barrel in the middle of the intersection. NO BOTTOM, it announced accurately and succinctly. A thin film of ice, making it look deceptively welcoming, covered the road. He'd seen more than one arrogant fool try to cross it in years past, only to speedily sink into chest-deep mud, a peril undoubtedly worsened by this spring's wet and changeable weather. The boardwalk here was uncovered and as wide as many rooms, silent testimony to the locals' willingness to work hard for dry feet even in this rough neighborhood.

In a small tavern just ahead, its entrance distinguished by a tumble of barrels and crates, men sang loudly and drunkenly. A single oil lamp glowed in an upstairs window, then disappeared.

Hal turned up the collar of his overcoat and marched on. He'd welcome a cup of coffee as soon as he rejoined the *Belle*. Or perhaps whiskey, which might be better suited to blocking thoughts of Rosalind in another man's arms.

Cicero growled.

Strange footsteps sounded in the fog. The planks underneath his feet quivered. Hal stiffened, every sense alert.

Suddenly, a crate hurtled out of the fog at his head, propelled by a running man. Hal ducked and twisted away. The crate missed him by mere inches.

As his attacker went past, Hal whacked him across one knee with his blackthorn. The additional energy was just enough to send the fellow pell-mell off the boardwalk and well into the street before he could recover. Ice cracked and mud slurped. The man hollered in pain and disgust as he tried to free himself from the morass.

Cicero erupted into a torrent of barks.

A whistling blow came out of the fog at Hal. He instinctively snapped his blackthorn sideways to block it and heard the solid thump of his well-made cane striking another.

He whirled to meet his new attacker and swore inwardly. He faced a square-set brute holding a shepherd's crook with the ease of an experienced fighter. The brute attacked again, thrusting at Hal with his crook's blunt end. Hal parried, pushing it aside.

Cicero jumped at the thug, but grabbed only a mouthful of cloth. The man was able to easily shake him off, at the expense of a torn pants leg. He struck at Hal again, clearly planning to stand off and cause damage.

Hal snapped his blackthorn to block the strike and charged, simultaneously shifting to a two-handed grip. Now he could punch with his stick as if he were boxing. He landed a punishing blow to the other's ribs.

The thug snarled, and a new respect entered his eyes, shown by the fitful light from the saloon.

Cicero barked as if his life depended on making noise, circling behind the thug.

Hal closed in, his blackthorn punching hard and fast from

both directions. The thug blocked and counterpunched, using the classic one-handed grip of the stick fighter. Their fight became a windmill of violence on the boardwalk. The only sounds were the rattle of their sticks or the muffled thuds of wood against flesh, all backed by the men's grunts and the dog's incessant barking.

Some strikes reached their targets, including many to the ribs. Hal's blackthorn tore the thug's scalp open, sending blood gushing. The brute counterattacked furiously, as if desperate to win quickly. Hal sidestepped, but his boot caught a loose nail, and he stumbled slightly.

A long narrow knife dropped into the thug's free hand. He lunged forward, bringing the gleaming blade up to rip Hal's face. Hal pivoted his blackthorn, desperate to stop the sharp edge.

The thug staggered abruptly. Cicero's jaws were locked in the brute's leg, just above the knee. "Damn cur," he swore, but his knife never wavered in its rush at Hal.

But Cicero's attack had given Hal just enough time to block the blow. Then he kicked his attacker twice in the balls, the high left-right dance step called the jig kick.

The thug gurgled with pain and dropped his shepherd's crook. But he didn't give up: He kept the deadly knife coming straight at Hal's face.

The sharp edge nicked Hal's ear as he skillfully sidestepped. He slapped his blackthorn across the other's unprotected ribs below the knife. And, as the thug went past, Hal reversed his blackthorn and whacked him over the head with the knob.

The brute grunted once and collapsed, his head and shoulders hanging off the boardwalk, inches from the frozen mud.

Cicero snarled at the vanquished foe, then sniffed him warily. The man stirred slightly, then went limp again.

The first attacker had finally crawled free of the mud to stand on the opposite side of the street, teetering on his one solid leg. Hal brushed back his coat to show his revolver. The man turned and quickly hobbled off, using the building's wall to support himself, and moving as if the devil were at his heels.

Satisfied, Cicero let loose a string of triumphant barks and yips, while his tail wagged like an admiral's flag.

Hal had won, thanks to some timely help from the stray dog he'd rescued during another waterfront fight. The time had definitely come to admit that having a family was advantageous. He reached down and patted his terrier on the head. Cicero promptly arched into the caress and barked again.

Hal pulled out his handkerchief and pressed it to his ear to stanch the stream of blood. Hopefully, his ribs weren't broken; they'd certainly need to be wrapped when he returned to the ship. Ten years ago, he would have gloried in this fight and happily retold it in tavern after tavern. Now he just wanted a snifter of brandy, a hot bath, and Rosalind.

"Come along, Cicero. You're starting to sound vainglorious," he ordered. "Let's go home."

The dog looked at him, then uttered a few more barks, clearly trumpeting his clan's superiority. Ears high and tail wagging, he strutted down the boardwalk beside his human.

Hal grinned and fixed the sight firmly in his memory, to recount to Rosalind later. Perhaps this tale of Cicero's prowess would coax her into listening to him long enough to hear his apology. He could live without the *Cherokee Belle,* and all she stood for, if he just had his lady at his side.

He had to find her. He had friends in Omaha, and further upstream, who'd help. Then he'd court her properly with flowers and every pretty word he could manage. Women liked that. He'd also make damn good and sure no other man ever came close enough to whisper honeyed words in her ears.

And one day, when she smiled freely at him again, he'd ask her to marry him. He couldn't promise her children, but he'd give her anything else she wanted.

Chapter Sixteen

Rosalind leaned back in her chair, careful to keep her hole cards—with her pair of queens—far from prying eyes. Two aces rested in plain sight on the table, as part of her board cards. The private room, which had once seemed spacious, now had spectators in every corner, not surprising given the size of the pot and the game's length.

Half past four in the morning and the minimum bets had doubled twice, as warned. More than twenty-five thousand dollars in chips rested in the pot, waiting to be claimed by one of three players: Lennox, Bristow, or herself.

All the other players had left the table, their money gone to either Bristow or herself. Now they dallied nearby, watching and whispering as they eyed the game. She suspected they were saving up stories to tell their friends, and possibly grandchildren. One of them had already called this the richest poker game in Omaha's history.

Other sporting men and a few loose women had come to watch, many arriving at two, when the bets doubled for the last time. Rosalind had overheard more than one side bet on who would win tonight.

One of the soiled doves was very tall, an almost perfect match for Rosalind's height. She'd arrived with two other females and seemed more intent on the winning players than any of the spectators. She was a beautiful willowy creature, superbly dressed in a spectacular creation of rose pink watered silk, decorated by rows of roses and matching pink flounces. Back in New York, Rosalind would have envied her both the dress and the self-assurance to wear it.

Bristow stacked and restacked his remaining chips, his green eyes occasionally flickering from Lennox to Rosalind.

Rosalind had a scant twenty dollars in chips before her, the remains of her bankroll and pawning her stickpin. If she won, she'd be able to reclaim her reminder of her father's wisdom. But that meant little to her. Only the game, and defeating Lennox, mattered now.

Lennox also had twenty dollars of chips remaining. He'd pawned his gold watch, ruby stickpin, and swordstick to come this far.

"Get ready to read 'em and weep, gentlemen," he challenged and took another swig of whiskey. He'd grown more and more frantic as the evening had progressed and the cards had turned further against him. This hand, with its potential for a straight, was his best chance of winning in the past hour.

Rosalind ignored his chatter, as did Bristow.

And Hamilton imperturbably dealt each of them their river card facedown. The room was very quiet, except for the saloon's piano music reverberating through the walls.

Rosalind serenely checked her river. It was the queen of diamonds, giving her a full house. An excellent hand, even if Bristow held an entirely possible four-of-a-kind.

She took a slow breath, careful not to show any emotion. But she could feel the current running strongly in her favor, the way the Missouri River had felt from the *Cherokee Belle*'s pilothouse.

Lennox chortled as he stared at his hand. Then he pushed his remaining chips into the center, with a triumphant, "I'm all-in and I'll send you to hell."

Rosalind raised an eyebrow at his cockiness, but said nothing.

Now it was Bristow's turn.

"Fold," he announced calmly and set his cards down. He pushed back from the table, but didn't stand up, his eyes steady on Lennox.

Rosalind glimpsed his left hand, away from Lennox, resting on his wrist, as if ready to draw a knife. Surely, Lennox wouldn't try anything, not with so many watchers, but his temper was wearing so thin as to be capable of almost any affront.

"I'm in," Rosalind announced with preternatural calm and pushed in enough chips to match Lennox's final wager. Her stomach's earlier shenanigans had long since given way to an icy detachment, familiar but more acute than anything she'd previously experienced at a card table.

The room seemed to hold its collective breath.

Lennox flipped over his hand—a straight. Five cards in sequence, from three suits.

Rosalind revealed hers: full house, queens over aces. Now she held every penny he'd owned when he walked in. But she still wanted the ledger book.

Lennox flushed hard as he stared at her cards. His mouth worked, but he said nothing as he drummed his fingers on the table.

Hamilton began to gather up the chips as the spectators erupted into a chattering horde. Lennox threw Rosalind a last, fulminating glare and pushed back his chair.

"Congratulations, Carstairs," a former player gushed, charging towards her chair through the crowd. "May I buy you a drink to celebrate?"

She held up a hand to forestall him. "One moment, sir. Mr. Lennox," she called. One last gamble to take and pray that the river's current held true. "May I offer you one more bet?"

Lennox spun on his heel and stared at her, the swordstick held tightly in his hand. The room was abruptly silent again, full of goggling eyes. "What are you thinking of?" he answered warily.

"Everything on the table against a single item from your pockets, chosen by me. The winner to be decided by cutting the cards."

The spectators gasped. Lennox's tongue ran out across his lips, and he swallowed, his Adam's apple bobbing. His face was transfigured by lust, savaging his Narcissus-like beauty.

"Very well," he agreed. He tossed a gold card case onto the table and sat back down.

"Remember, Mr. Lennox, I choose the item," Rosalind corrected him. Her voice was low and harsh, like the growl of the *Cherokee Belle*'s engines taking her through crooked water.

Lennox's mouth tightened. He glanced around the room, as if looking for support. No one spoke. "As you wish," he said finally. Reluctantly.

"Turn your pockets out on the table," Rosalind ordered. *Great God in heaven, may he not have hidden the ledger book anywhere else, while I wasn't present.*

Lennox obeyed, muttering all the while. A small, flat, leather wallet. A toothpick case. Keys.

"Coat pockets, too," Bristow drawled before she could mention Lennox's omission.

Rosalind's mouth quirked. She was glad he was helping her, rather than hindering her. Especially since she should pretend to be a gentleman of superior manners.

Lennox glared at Bristow, then reached into his coat's breast pocket. A handkerchief fluttered down. Finally, he set a small leather-bound volume on the table, its edges stained with water and blood. It had to be Etheridge's ledger book.

Rosalind ran her fingers over the various articles on the table and managed to pretend an interest in the gold card case, while their audience whispered and pointed. Finally she picked up the ledger book and flipped through the pages, which mostly recorded the purchase of supplies, such as tobacco, and their later sale to Fort McGowan's soldiers. Every receipt of money and every expenditure were neatly noted, with the resulting account balance entered in the right column.

Two entries sprang off the pages at her.

"June 8, 1871. Withdrew $1,500.00 in cash from my account at the National Bank of C—"

And the next line said, damningly:

"June 8, 1871. Paid $1,500.00 in cash, by hand, to Wm. W. Belknap at West Point, New York."

The initials J. E. sat beside each entry, conclusive proof that Jebediah Etheridge had been openly paying off the Secretary of War. Once she held this and all of his money, Lennox would no longer be able to blackmail or bribe Belknap into destroying the reputation and livelihood of Hal's brother-in-law.

If she lost, and Lennox took this book, plus all the money on the table, he'd have a fortune with which to make further attacks.

She set her jaw and looked back at Lennox. "This will do," she said, pretending a carelessness she didn't feel. "It's a handsome book and will serve me well."

Someone whispered and was quickly hushed.

"Not the book, not that," Lennox objected. He shook his head vehemently, his eyes wide and appalled. "Surely, you'd prefer the card case, or my wallet."

"Are you reneging on your bet?" Rosalind asked. "One item from your pocket, of my choosing, against everything else on the table. Do you wish to withdraw?"

"No, damn your eyes. I'll see this through to the end. And buy everyone here a drink with my winnings," he asserted with an attempt at his previous arrogance.

"Very well. Mr. Allen, will you please shuffle a fresh deck for us?"

"You can't—" Lennox started to object, then hurriedly stopped as the crowd muttered.

She'd known from the beginning that he'd been marking the cards, nicking them with his gold pinky ring. The old technique had given him little advantage; her father had taught her and her brothers the same method when she was seven. So she'd read the cards as easily as he had and used the knowledge against him. But she wasn't about to let him attempt the same trickery again.

And their audience knew that past chicanery was the only possible excuse for refusing a fresh deck. Their surprise— and the unspoken threat of frontier justice for cardsharps— had clearly shut his mouth.

Allen slid smoothly into Hamilton's seat and ostentatiously opened the new deck. He shuffled with a great professional's elegance and speed, and riffled the cards until they flowed like a river between his hands.

Hal had had the same relaxed mastery of his environment when he stood in his pilothouse, his fair hair shining in the sun and his blue eyes gleaming as he studied the water. Dear, beautiful Hal . . .

Allen slid the cards over to Lennox.

He swallowed hard, rubbed his fingers together, then quickly split the deck into two sections. He turned over the top section, showing the bottom card.

Jack of clubs. Only a queen, king, or ace could bring her victory. Without hesitating, Rosalind picked up the other section and exposed the bottom card.

A blond king, in elegant red robes emblazoned with hearts. The king of hearts had defeated Lennox.

Etheridge's ledger book—and its ability to create, or block, threats to William—now belonged to Rosalind. Lennox could no longer threaten Hal or his kinsman.

"No!" Lennox exploded. "You can't win! I must have the book and the money!" He started to pull a knife from his sleeve.

Rosalind promptly drew hers, a second after Allen, Bristow, and most of the male spectators. Lennox growled in frustration as he measured his opponents.

The female spectators crooned their delight at the unexpected display of force. The tall blonde fluttered her fan as she stared at Rosalind.

"Would you care to repeat yourself, sir?" Bristow asked coldly. "Allen's house is famous for guaranteeing a square deal to every sporting man. To suggest otherwise is to impugn the honor of Omaha's finest establishment." His voice implied that only death would wipe out such an insult.

"Dammit," Lennox snarled. His eyes darted around the room, visibly measuring the number of knives and the distance to the door. But only a fool would start a fight under these conditions, and Lennox had never been called stupid.

"What did you say?" Rosalind asked coldly. Life would be so much simpler if she could kill Lennox now and not worry about any future depredations. Then she could dream of seeing Hal again or tasting his mouth or sleeping with him. . . .

"Nothing. A misunderstanding, that's all," Lennox answered. He sheathed his knife and brought his hands up to his lapels, in a grudging sign of restraint. He shifted his boiling gaze to Allen. "Many thanks for your hospitality but I must depart for another appointment."

He tipped his hat and was gone, the crowd parting before him as if disgusted by the risk of touching him.

Rosalind prayed that his "appointment" was a social fiction, designed to cover his escape from the room, and not a meeting to somehow arrange further trouble.

"Well played, Bristow," she said sincerely. "My thanks."

"Congratulations on winning, Carstairs." Bristow shook her hand. "You played a magnificent game, far better than my efforts."

The crowd surged forward to offer their congratulations, while Allen quietly converted the chips into cash. She conversed with them somehow, politely discussing details of her strategy and encouraging compliments for Bristow's play.

The king of hearts stared up at her from the table, as if reminding her of what she'd won and lost that day. Lured closer and closer, she finally slipped it into her pocket and smoothed it as if stroking Hal's face.

Folly. Pure folly. She'd never see Hal again, feel his hand caress her cheek, or taste his lips on her mouth. She'd never again lie in his arms, too sated to move, and hear him chuckle as his dog began to snore loudly.

A stab of pain closed her throat just as Bristow launched into a wordy explanation of a particular bluff. Once she'd have valued such chatter and the game that sustained it. But not now. She needed Hal, just to make life worth living. That would never change, no matter how far she ran or how long she stayed away.

What could she do? Fight for his love, but how? She couldn't win his heart if she dwelt in Montana while he lived in Missouri. So she'd have to go back to him. Should she accept his offer?

Her mouth twisted. It would be a loveless marriage with little hope of children. No toddlers to cling to her skirts or prattle about their father. No namesakes for her brothers or parents to share memories of her lost family with.

But she'd have Hal. She could laugh with him over breakfast, squabble lightly with him in the pilothouse, and make passionate love after dinner. Or maybe before teatime, if they were married. After all, married couples didn't have to leave the bedroom unless they chose to. She shivered at the possibilities.

Marriage to him would be a delight but without love or children? She chewed her lip as she considered her options, then made up her mind. Hal respected and liked her now, so there was a sporting chance that he'd fall in love with her, if they were continuously around each other. If he didn't fall in love with her, then she'd have to content herself with the crumbs of his affections. Either way, she had far better odds of being happy with Hal—and making him happy—than married to another man. And children would have to remain a dream, not reality.

She deliberately caught the eye of the tall blonde. "May I have the honor of procuring refreshments for you?" she asked, society's formal phrases coming clumsily to her lips.

"But of course," the beauty cooed and took the proffered arm.

Rosalind nodded to Bristow and the others, then steered the blonde toward the exit. If she was going to fight for Hal, she wanted no further deceptions between them. So the next thing she needed was a woman's wardrobe—after she reclaimed her diamond stickpin.

Lennox flung out of the saloon in a fury into the foggy night. No one, dammit, had the right to take his money—or Etheridge's ledger book from him, least of all a young weed of a gambler. He'd have to cable the office in New York and demand more cash. And if they complained yet again that it was the middle of the month and they'd already sent him all the rent monies—why, he'd just have them raise the damn rents and collect the cash immediately from the damn Irish in his tenements. Damn fools. And damn greedy gamblers.

He strode down the boardwalk, his boots pounding the

planks like drums. Yes, he was noisy, as superior beings should be. And if anyone gave him any trouble, he'd be more than happy to return the favor and send him permanently to the local cemetery. He was rather disappointed that the local whores gave him the shoulder. He'd have enjoyed working off his temper with a knife on one of those sluts.

His anger gradually faded as he walked through the cool mists, leaving room to think of other matters.

Desdemona. He was supposed to meet her at five. But what the hell did he care about her? She hadn't found the Schuyler termagant for him.

But Desdemona was rich, or at least her husband was. If the two of them killed that pompous old bear—he ground his teeth at the memory of how the old man had humiliated him last Christmas—then he could enjoy her money, and use it to destroy Donovan and Lindsay.

Divorce might work as well. Scandalous, of course, but cuckolded husbands had paid well before to avoid letting the world know the full details of how they'd been duped.

Murder, though, would be simpler and much more satisfying. To see the old bear lying in a pool of blood at his feet . . . His cock twitched hard at the thought.

Nick checked his watch—less than ten minutes till he was supposed to meet Desdemona at a warehouse, three blocks from where he stood in this abysmal neighborhood. Thank-fully, Desdemona's fondness for rough environments and a bit of exhibitionism had led her to suggest the place. He'd never reach a respectable locale in time.

Desdemona regarded her surroundings with an approving eye. The night watchman's office was small and stark, with only a table, chair, and cot inside the bare wooden walls. A damp mist from the river permeated the room, as if seeping through cracks in the walls. At least the cot had blankets, far more than their last rendezvous had offered in Pittsburgh.

A light knock sounded, and she spun to face the door. "Come in," she breathed, and Nick entered with a smile. She'd once seen him as a golden boy to be wrapped around her finger, then sent off to do her errands. And his efforts to blackmail her, for aiding the Confederate cause during the late war, just made him more dangerous—and more exciting.

Throughout all the years since the war's start, the secret of her liaison with beautiful Nick had kept her sane while she listened to those northern biddies boast of their menfolk's doings. They had pallid merchants to snore in their bedrooms, while she had stunning, talented Nick to spur her to the heights.

And the danger of being his lover fired her blood as nothing else ever had. No matter where the risk came from— someone discovering her adultery or Nick turning on her—she was always excited to meet him. He was temptation and jeopardy in a single, irresistible package.

He held out his hand and she went into his arms in a rush. He nipped her earlobe—a caress easily hidden by her long hair—and she shivered with delight. He was so much better now at arousing a woman than when they'd first met. Soon he'd open her dress and play games with her breasts, suckling and fondling and kneading them.

They'd have to be more circumspect in their play than usual. With Richard waiting for her at the hotel, she couldn't stay in seclusion for a few days until time, and her maid's skill, removed all traces of illicit dalliance.

So tonight she wouldn't be able to kiss dear, wicked Nick. Or taste his cock—a true pity, since that caress always tested his self-control. But he could still lift her skirts and bring his fingers and cock to dance against her intimate folds . . .

Hot cream moistened her folds at the thought. She clung to Nick's shoulders, sighing in anticipation, as he licked her neck.

Richard Lindsay was colder than he could remember ever being, colder than when he'd stood watch above an ocean of ice floes. Desdemona had awoken him when she'd crept from their suite and he'd followed her. Now he stood in a dank alley amidst a stack of barrels reeking of salt fish—and knew his worst fears had been realized.

He'd lived his entire life according to family and naval tradition, and the rules of polite society. Desdemona had always set an equally high value on the customs of polite society, enjoying more than anything else the acclaim of her peers. She'd demanded that her children—including Hal and Viola— follow the same rules. When they didn't, she'd been as ferocious as a Greek fury, insisting that the full punishment be meted out for the transgression. In private, though, she'd denied her husband his conjugal rights—while carrying herself with the smug certainty of a woman who's been well-ridden.

In some ways, he'd been relieved when he found a spyhole, knowing that at last he'd learn whether or not his wife truly was an adulteress. Then he'd heard masculine footsteps and looked out from his hiding place, only to see a man knock on his wife's door.

There'd been hints before of her adultery but no proof. Whatever the faults in their marriage, he'd always thought her snobbery—her passion for society's praise—would keep her faithful. He'd thought it at least possible that she'd never risk her role as a leader of society on an illicit affair. But now he knew better. Whoever was with her was obviously confident of her welcome.

Moans and gasps came from the room, along with the rustle of silken skirts. Gritting his teeth against the urge to kill, Richard put his eye to the spyhole.

His wife was in the arms of the most notorious black-mailer in New York, Nicholas Lennox. *Damn and blast. Couldn't she have chosen a better paramour than him?*

"Nick," Desdemona whispered, her voice a needy thread.

"Eager, my bitch? Is your dew dripping down your thigh yet?"

Richard's hands clenched.

"But before I take my pleasure with your breasts—or your cunt—have you found the heiress yet?" Lennox squeezed her breasts and she gasped with pleasure.

"No, but I'm sure Hal will find her," Desdemona groaned, then gasped again when he worked her breasts.

Lennox smiled at her knowingly. Pressed between him and the wall by the door, she still managed to rub herself over him like a cat in heat.

His wife of thirty-five years fondled the bastard's ass with both hands. A silent growl rose in Richard's throat. His wife of thirty-five years, dammit. His woman, not Lennox's.

"You're beautiful like this, writhing against my hands as I heat you for my bed. How many times have you danced like this for me in the past ten years—a hundred? Two hundred?"

Ten years? She'd been sleeping with Lennox while he'd been at war? And afterwards, as well? All this time, their marriage had been a lie?

"Not often enough!" Desdemona groaned.

Damn her. After I get my hands on her, she won't be able to sit down for a week.

"So true, my bitch, so true. You are the most magnificent lover I've ever had. Perhaps we should make our attachment permanent."

What the hell . . .

Desdemona frowned and her hands dropped away. "What do you mean?"

"Marry me and we could enjoy each other every night."

Marriage to my wife?

"We could travel to Europe, roam Italy, and delight our-selves as the Romans did. Or—"

"Nonsense. I'd be a social pariah if I divorced my hus-band and married you." She took a step away and propped her hands on her hips to glare at him, her usual behavior when aggravated. It was certainly not a sign of fear. But she hadn't refused out of love, or respect, for her husband.

Lennox's eyes narrowed, but she was too affronted to under-stand the danger.

Richard left the barrels' shelter and headed for the office. He would not lose his wife to this louse. He'd keep her—and then he'd teach her how to be a true wife.

"Is that all you can say?" Lennox inquired, silky soft but completely audible through the thin walls, as Richard crept to the door. "Just no? What if I tell your husband about your wartime doings, especially those rifles you sent to the Con-federate Army. Hundreds of weapons that wounded or killed Union soldiers and sailors such as your son. Do you think he'd want you after he heard that? No, he'd divorce you and leave you penniless. Surely, you'd be better off as my wife— and I wouldn't tell him everything I know."

The words stopped Richard at the door more effectively than a salvo of cannon fire. *Treason? Desdemona Davies Lindsay, the wife and mother of Union sailors, had sold ri-fles to the enemy?* Men had died because of her. Because he hadn't controlled his wife well enough.

"Why, you—you blackmailing scoundrel!" she spat at Lennox.

Blessed Jesus, she didn't deny it. She was guilty of a crime for which death was the only proper penalty. He might have forgiven adultery, but not treason. Three generations of naval officers roared behind his eyes, and a red mist dark-ened his vision as he drew his old Navy Colt.

"I still have the receipt for those guns, and for their ammunition," Nick purred. Then his voice turned to pure steel. "Choose, bitch. You can come easily or else I'll destroy you."

Richard kicked in the door, breaking the lock. First he'd kill Lennox for aiding treason, and then he'd deal with his wife.

Gun drawn, Lennox pushed Desdemona away from the door, her skirts sweeping along the wall, and fired a shot.

Instantly recognizing the danger, Richard pulled the trigger. The sound of the two, almost simultaneous shots rocked the small room.

Fire burned across Richard's temple and his knees went weak. Blood streamed down his face. Reflexively, he fought to cock the gun again as he slid down the doorjamb. He had to destroy the traitor.

"My God, look what you've done!" Desdemona peered over Lennox's shoulder. "You killed my husband!" And she screamed as loudly as any riverboat's whistle.

Hell and damnation, Desdemona, don't turn hysterical now. Not when there's shooting going on.

"Goddamnit, bitch. Be quiet!" Lennox snarled.

She screamed again, an even more earsplitting note.

Another shot blasted through the room.

Desdemona crumpled to the floor beside Richard, as Lennox stepped away just in time to avoid her.

"Good riddance," Lennox grunted.

Dear God, no! Blood and brains covered the wall, then began to drip slowly down on Richard. His vision was graying from loss of blood until all he could see was Desdemona's hair and Lennox's boots. He had to shoot the bastard. He gritted his teeth, cupped his left hand around his right, and managed to aim at her killer's head.

Lennox kicked the gun out of Richard's hand. From the sound, it skittered under the narrow cot, too far for him to reach. He could barely see Lennox's boots now, with the splitting agony in his head and the blood running into his eyes.

Think, he told himself, struggling to remain conscious. *Think.* He still had the bowie knife on his hip. His fingers moved slowly, agonizingly slowly, toward the sharp blade.

Lennox laughed and kicked Richard's hand away from his coat. "You fool. You stubborn, honorable fool."

Lennox kicked him hard in the ribs. Pain exploded in Richard's side, sweeping thought before it. Air raced out of his lungs, and he gasped for breath.

Lennox set his Colt's muzzle sharply against Richard's ear and cocked it. Still gasping for breath, the old captain managed not to flinch.

Then two drunks staggered by outside, trying to sing the old Scottish chorus, "I'll lay me down and die." Richard flinched at the words and prayed they weren't a prophecy. He tried to shout, but could do no better than a harsh gasp.

Lennox froze, then slowly took the gun away. "Best not shoot you, lest someone hear it and investigate. Still, you'll be dead within fifteen minutes, old man, at the rate you're bleeding."

He shoved Richard's feet clear, rolling him onto his back and kicked Desdemona's head away from the door. Her warm corpse settled against Richard's chest, blue eyes still open. She shouldn't have died like this, no matter what she'd done. Not Juliet and Hal and Viola's mother.

Lennox paused as he stepped into the doorway. "At least I won one fight tonight," he purred. "I killed the old bear."

The door closed behind him softly.

Richard fought for consciousness. He tried to free himself but couldn't move Desdemona. All he had to show for thirty-five years of marriage was his wife's treason and her corpse weighing him down. All his life, he had tried to be honorable, tried to do what was expected of him, and it ended like this. There had to be another way. . . .

Then the door closed behind Lennox.

If he lived, he was going to hug his children and grand-children and tell them, over and over again, how much he loved them. He'd apologize to Hal, and Viola. And every extra day the Lord gave him, he'd thank the Lord and he'd do his best for his children and grandchildren.

All he had to do was live. Somehow. He began to pray, with a greater desperation than he'd felt in combat.

Chapter Seventeen

Hal paced along the *Cherokee Belle*'s roof as he studied Omaha, its buildings little more than shifting shadows against the great sweep of plains running west. The river fog embraced it like a lover, rolling along the roads and wrapping itself around every plank. The few scattered bits of gaslight, as inhabitants rose to go about their business, seemed distant and unimportant.

It was almost impossible to see across the river behind him. Then the *Spartan* sounded her bell, its note memorized by every riverside dweller, to warn of imminent departure from Council Bluffs on the eastern edge of the Missouri.

Sounds of town life were muffled and changeable, their source often impossible to determine. Clear and yet eerily attuned to the river's rushing waters, a line of roustabouts sang of rising early in the morning, as they passed barrels of nails across the levee to be stowed onboard the *Belle*.

But Hal could feel the sun shining on his head and shoulders, stronger this dawn than typical for an April morning. It was likely to banish the fog in short order and bring a warm, almost summerlike day. And it might bring spring thunderstorms this afternoon, which would send still more water pouring into the Missouri. The *Belle* would need two men to handle her wheel, in that case, just to fight her upstream against the current.

Inside the pilothouse, Bellecourt was humming as he prepared to sail, while the purring of Norton's engines made the *Belle* vibrate like a thoroughbred at a derby, eager to begin the sprint to Sioux City. O'Brien's voice rose from the main deck, where he oversaw the last pieces of luggage and freight coming aboard. Sampson shared coffee and talk of Indian depredations with two army officers on the hurricane deck.

The *Cherokee Belle* would sail for Sioux City as soon as William and Viola came aboard. And leave Rosalind behind.

Hal closed his eyes in pain. Damn, how he wanted to stay behind in Omaha and look for her. If he waited until after the trip to Sioux City, she might be gone forever. The risk of never seeing her again—or worse, losing her to Lennox—was almost intolerable, sending chills through his body such as he'd never felt in combat.

He made an abrupt decision and stepped up into the pilothouse. "I'm going ashore, Bellecourt, to look for Carstairs. I'll return within an hour, before Mr. and Mrs. Donovan arrive and the *Belle* sails."

Bellecourt glanced up and shrugged. "*Très bien,* Lindsay. Please try not to enjoy too much trouble."

Hal chuckled at their old joke and flipped a fast salute. With Cicero happily trotting at his heels, he quickly went down to the boiler deck, where Ezra caught him on the promenade.

"Sir, do you know what Captain and Mrs. Lindsay's plans were?"

Hal blinked in surprise; his father never discussed social engagements with his children. "No, they hadn't spoken to me." He continued reluctantly, spurred by an instinctive unease, "Why do you ask?"

"They spent the night ashore at the Cozzens Hotel, sir.

But Obadiah just sent a runner to ask if we'd seen them. He took coffee into their room but neither Captain nor Mrs. Lindsay was there. He's asked around but no one's seen them."

Hal frowned. *Mother wasn't in her bed at dawn?* She liked her comforts, beginning with sleeping late. *And the Old Man would never miss a sailing time.* "I'm afraid I didn't see them. My compliments to Sampson and ask him to send a steady man to help search."

"Yes, sir."

Hal went ashore, still frowning. If his parents didn't appear shortly, he'd have to help look for them, although he had no idea where to start, besides their hotel. He shook off that worry when he crossed the levee and headed up the street into town, with Cicero uttering occasional yaps of disdain for the local canines.

Unlike the hunt for his parents, he had a list of places where he could hunt for Rosalind. Only the *Cherokee Belle* and the *Spartan* were sailing upriver today. She'd already refused passage on both of those boats. He couldn't imagine why she'd bought passage on the *Cherokee Star,* instead of the *Spartan*, back in Kansas City. But he doubted her reasons would have changed during the trip upriver. So he'd look for her first in the gambling halls, then broaden the hunt to boardinghouses. High-class gambling halls should remember an elegant and highly competent young poker player. And if the Pinkerton detectives had already flushed her out, then he'd simply have to buy them off or break her loose.

The fog was thicker in the streets of Omaha than it had been at the *Belle*'s highest point, cutting visibility down to less than twenty-five feet. The sounds of horses and wagons were both muffled and stronger now, hinting at a town coming to life.

"Lindsay!" a stranger hailed from the alley to his left.

Hal spun, instinctively reaching for his gun. His hand froze inches away from the trigger's comfort. The stranger held a double-barreled shotgun pointed at his chest. At twenty feet, it was unlikely he'd miss.

Cicero growled, deep and low.

Hal lifted an eyebrow. He'd always been good at bluffing. Perhaps he could stretch this encounter out until someone would take notice and help him. "I'm afraid I don't know you, Mr. . . . ?"

The big-bellied dandy laughed. "You're a cool one, aren't you? I'm Eli Jenkins, an associate of Nicholas Lennox."

Shit. "How do you do," Hal returned politely, calculating his odds. If Cicero attacked, he might distract Jenkins long enough for Hal to draw his Colt. But Cicero would probably die in the attempt. *Stall.* "And to what do I owe the honor of this meeting, Mr. Jenkins?"

"There's a price of ten thousand dollars on your head, Lindsay, and I mean to claim it."

Hell and damnation, the devil's to pay now. And he'd never see Rosalind again. Cicero growled again and edged forward.

"Mr. Jenkins—"

"I'm really not interested in talking to you, Lindsay, since the *Spartan*'s waiting for me. I need to claim my money now, before I follow Donovan's casket to Boot Hill."

The feathers of a lady's hat appeared over Jenkins's shoulder. "Watch out, ma'am!" Hal yelled and leaped forward. Cicero jumped for Jenkins's arm.

Two Colts barked, almost as one. The shotgun jerked upward and fired into the sky. Then Jenkins's neck disappeared in a cloud of blood and flesh. He crumpled slowly into the mud, facedown. The *Spartan*'s bell rang again, summoning its last passengers.

Hal jerked to a stop, mud and blood splattering his boots. Cicero howled in surprise and backed up to the safety of Hal's boots.

At the alley's other end, a lady slowly lowered her two

pocket Navy Colts, holstered them under the skirts of her jacket, and folded back her veil. She stared at Jenkins's body and swallowed hard, her complexion turning green. "Dear God in heaven, forgive me," Rosalind Schuyler murmured. Hal could almost see the effort of will it took for her to remain upright.

The truth rushed out of his mouth in a torrent. "Damn, but I love you, Miss Schuyler. Will you marry me?"

She looked at him then and smiled faintly. She was an incredible sight, in her highly fashionable green carriage gown with bell sleeves and a deep flounce in front. It emphasized her superb figure, caressing her breasts and waist like a lover's glance.

Her hat provided the finishing touch. A high-crowned velvet affair, its feathers rose over the crown before dancing down the rear. The black face veil, trimmed with point lace and jet beads, was folded back to the hat's brim, then fell in neat pleats down her back.

Her appearance was sophisticated, feminine, and worlds away from a New York debutante or riverboat gambler. None of Pinkerton's men would recognize her. If Hal hadn't slept with her, he doubted he would have known her.

"Yes, I'll marry you." Rosalind nodded, her smile playing around her mouth. She rummaged in her reticule for a handkerchief, which she held in front of her nose and mouth, as if warding off the stench of death. "We need to warn Mr. and Mrs. Donovan of their peril."

Cicero curled his lip at the enemy's remains, then frisked ahead to Rosalind. She patted him and rubbed his ears in his favorite caress. He leaned against her in pure adoration, displaying an ease Hal wished he could emulate.

Hal followed Cicero and stopped in front of her, carefully blocking her view of Jenkins's body. "They spent the night with friends and should be returning within the hour."

He hesitated, embarrassed about his clumsy declaration

of love. William had told him once that women needed to hear the words. Heaven knows the man told Viola often enough that he adored her. But flowery words weren't for him. "I came to find you first, before looking for them or for my parents. I found it intolerable to live a day without you."

Joy broke across her face, and she reached out to him. He swept her into his arms then, and held her close. She buried her face against his chest and shook as if she would shatter. He wrapped his arms around her fiercely. He would never let her go again.

As her tremors slowed, Hal backed her out of the alley and onto Farnam Street's boardwalk, the next street over; he needed to enjoy this moment without any thought of death or enmity. He had a little time for Rosalind before finding, and warning, William.

Cicero sat down beside him, scratched his ear briskly, then yawned. A few men, mostly laborers, gathered to point and stare at Jenkins's corpse. A uniformed driver, sitting at the reins of a very elegant brougham with a large trunk strapped on behind, tipped his hat to Hal and waited. That must be how Rosalind had arrived.

Someday, he'd ask her where she had obtained it. But not yet. Holding her gave him so much joy he had little use for such mundane details as transport.

Hoofbeats announced the arrival of another carriage. Hal glanced over casually, then cursed under his breath. Rosalind stirred in his arms.

"Lindsay. And perhaps the lady is Miss Schuyler?" William Donovan asked, a Sharps carbine in his hands and Viola at the reins. Bullet holes laced his buggy's hood and body, as well as his hat. The feathers on Viola's bonnet were singed and torn. Dried blood marked a long graze on the horse's flank.

Hal snarled, instinctively baring his teeth. There would be no peace or safety for any of them until Lennox was dead.

His grip tightened reflexively on Rosalind. She looked at the buggy and hissed.

"Correct. Although she's actually soon to become Mrs. Lindsay," Hal answered as she turned to face the newcomers. He was more than willing to follow William's lead and not remind the ladies of their peril. However, he did keep an arm around Rosalind's waist to reassure himself that she was still there. "How did you recognize her?"

"She reminds me of a young gentleman I met, the former cub pilot on the *Cherokee Belle,*" William said blandly.

Hal snorted. He might have guessed William would see through a woman's disguise.

"What happened to you two?" Rosalind demanded, totally ignoring the men's chatter. He should have known she'd insist on the truth.

"A half-dozen brigands interrupted us on the drive back into town. The sheriff is talking to the two who survived," William answered briefly. He looked more than willing to gut the next man who disturbed him.

Hal jerked his head over his shoulder. "Eli Jenkins met the same fate back there."

"Jenkins was Lennox's man?" William's eyebrows shot up. "That explains a good deal, since he'd have known how to cause trouble for my freight trains. Thank you for disposing of him."

"Miss Schuyler managed it. Jenkins had the drop on me and she saved my life."

Rosalind shuddered.

"Thank you, darling, for saving my brother's life," Viola declared and launched herself out of the buggy at Rosalind. "Congratulations on your betrothal, my dears. I always knew you two were meant for each other."

"You knew?" Rosalind's voice rose to a squeak as the smaller woman hugged her. She stopped, coughed, and tried again. "When did you realize I was a woman?"

Eyes glistening with tears, Viola waved off the question.

"William knew the moment he first saw you but he made me promise not to speak of it." She drew Hal close to her and Rosalind. "I am so very glad for you both."

Hal wrapped his arms around the two most important women in his life. Joy rose up in him, tempered by the need to protect them from Lennox.

"I gather that felicitations are in order?" a man drawled, and Morgan Evans strolled down the boardwalk to meet them. He looked remarkably dapper, freshly shaved and his coat neatly pressed. There were few signs, except for his heavy-lidded eyes and a somewhat sated look about his mouth, of someone who'd spent the night in an expensive brothel. He had the courtesy to show only genial curiosity and no recognition of Rosalind.

Viola chuckled and the little circle broke apart. Viola rejoined her husband, but Rosalind held Hal's hand as he answered Evans. "Certainly they are. Miss Schuyler, may I present Morgan Evans, top hand for my brother-in-law? Evans, this is Miss Rosalind Schuyler, my fiancée."

"Mr. Evans." His little gambler gave Evans a very formal nod. Hal would wager a day's receipts she was enjoying this charade.

Viola glanced at her husband, who winked back at her.

Evans hesitated briefly, searching Rosalind's face under the very fashionable hat and veil. Then he smiled, a genuine show of acknowledgment and approval. "It is a very great pleasure to meet you at last, Miss Schuyler."

He bowed over her hand with a flourish, and she accepted his homage like a queen. Hal knew he was grinning like a fool and didn't much care. Evans stepped back to stand with Donovan, just as Ezra arrived with an armful of coats to gape at the assembly.

Interrupting the general air of relaxation, Rosalind gave Hal her gambler's all-encompassing scrutiny. "You said you needed to search for your parents. Why?"

Hal shrugged uncomfortably. "They've disappeared. Obadiah went to wake them, but they weren't there, nor could he find them at their hotel."

"Mother was gone from her bed at dawn?" Viola's jaw dropped open. "Impossible. Even during the war, she preferred to sleep the morning away."

"It's equally unimaginable for the Old Man to miss his boat's sailing time," Hal agreed soberly. "I sent some of the *Belle*'s men to help search for them. But we can't linger for long, since we have to reach Sioux City before Lennox does."

"Sioux City? Oh yes, I forgot something." Rosalind dug in her reticule and produced a battered little leather-bound book, which she handed to William. "I believe you may find it useful."

William's eyebrows shot up in surprise, a rare sight in itself. "Etheridge's book?"

"The same," Rosalind answered.

"How did you come by it?" He flipped through pages as he spoke, while Viola leaned over to watch.

"Poker, wasn't it?" Hal suggested.

Good Lord, she'd taken away Lennox's most potent weapon, using that little book to blackmail the Secretary of War into attacking William. William's business and reputation were now safe from destruction by the corrupt bureaucrat.

His fiancée nodded, a smile playing around her mouth. "So now you can search for your parents, Hal," she said pointedly, pulling away slightly to look at him.

He frowned, unwilling to be without her for any time. He certainly couldn't take this elegant creature with him while he prowled the roughest part of Omaha. "A simple misunderstanding between the Old Man and Obadiah is the most likely explanation, Rosalind. The *Cherokee Belle* has a schedule to keep and I'm sure the Old Man will appear."

She tapped her toe as she watched him. "But now you have time to be certain of that, since you don't have to immediately chase Lennox, correct? After all, he'll need some time to frame another attack, with Jenkins and the ledger book gone."

"Correct," Hal said reluctantly.

She smiled at him. Hal had the unsettling feeling that he was going to see the same sweetly triumphant look on her face a great many times in the future.

"Excellent. And Cicero can help us hunt," she said briskly.

"Cicero? Help *us*? You should return to the *Belle* at once with Viola."

"Well, of course, I'm going to help you with Cicero, not wring my hands."

Hal acknowledged to himself that any description of helplessness sounded nothing like his little gambler.

"And you know how fond Cicero is of Captain Lindsay," Rosalind continued, "and how clever he is. My old spaniel did similar tricks on many occasions so I'm certain Cicero will find it very easy to find the captain. Won't you, dear?"

The besotted dog sat up straight and barked enthusiastically. Hal shot him a jaundiced look, then caught William's eye.

His brother-in-law shrugged sympathetically. "Viola and I will accompany you," he offered. "Donovan & Sons' depot is a block from here and I'll have one of my men deal with Jenkins's body."

"Thank you." Hal bit his lip against suggesting that Viola wait safely aboard the *Belle*. If her very protective husband wouldn't utter those words, what could a mere brother say? He grasped at straws to get either of the two women safely away. "What about the carriage?"

"A friend loaned it to me for a morning's use. It can accompany us, in case Captain or Mrs. Lindsay prefers to ride in comfort," Rosalind answered firmly.

Realizing that he was boxed in, Hal glanced at the mountain of cloth in Ezra's arms. "Are those for Captain and Mrs. Lindsay?"

"Yes, sir. I brought the coats from the *Belle,* in case they were chilled. Their gloves, too."

"Give me Captain Lindsay's gloves."

Hal took the proffered leather and squatted down beside Cicero. Homer had been more inclined to chase rabbits than track humans. But for Rosalind's sake, he'd try her suggestion.

"You know who Captain Lindsay is, don't you?" He held out the gloves as he watched the dog he'd rescued from the streets.

The terrier sniffed the fine leather. Then bright dark eyes looked back at him earnestly, head cocked as if understanding every word. He barked once, sharply.

A shiver went down Hal's spine at the unexpected answer, almost a communication. Perhaps if he behaved as if this would work, it might do so. Uncertain of how to give the order, he addressed Cicero as if he were a military scout.

"Excellent! Now find Captain Lindsay, Cicero. Find Captain Lindsay." He emphasized the last two words, staring at the dog.

"Woof!" Cicero responded and sprang up. He trotted out into the street and began sniffing intently, casting about as if trying to find the scent.

The *Spartan's* whistle sounded through the fog. Two long, one short in her signal for departure. Lennox was leaving town. Hal gritted his teeth rather than think about all the trouble that blackguard could cause now.

Cicero barked, as if summoning his humans, and headed up Farnam Street.

"He's found something!" Rosalind exclaimed.

"He's following the road to the Cozzens Hotel, a route

taken by many," Hal felt obliged to point out. "He could be trailing a female dog, for all we know."

"But that's the hotel where they stayed, isn't it?" Rosalind retorted.

"Yes."

"Then he's a very good boy."

Hal surrendered to her confidence and offered her his arm. "Yes, he is. Shall we?"

Hal, Rosalind, and Evans followed Cicero from the board-walk's relative comfort, with William and Viola in the buggy, while Ezra and the carriage brought up the rear. The small crowd trailed them from a distance, slowly growing in numbers. Hal suspected they were the best show this part of Omaha had seen in years.

At the first corner, they paused to let an open carriage pass, apparently headed for the levee. Two women sat inside, both shabbily dressed in mourning black, although lacking the heavy veils of recent bereavement. They appeared related, given their patrician features, but of very different ages, with the youngest not yet thirty and the other clearly past sixty.

Evans broke stride. Hal looked back to find the man, who had casually hunted snipers and spoken offhandedly about pleasuring women, now gaping at the carriage's occupants. Then he started to smile, a very predatory smile that raised Hal's ire. He would not care for such a look to be directed at his kinfolk.

The youngest female's hand tightened on her carriage as she stared at Evans. She swallowed, her eyes as wide as if she gazed upon a cottonmouth snake. Hal spared a look at William, who shrugged his ignorance. Then William's buggy passed between the carriage and the boardwalk, breaking the spell.

Evans visibly shook himself and moved quickly to catch up. Glancing backwards Hal saw the young female still eye-ing Evans as her carriage turned the corner.

Cicero trotted steadily uphill, ignoring all other traffic. The drivers stared at the cocky dog, then paused or made room for him, all allowing him to pass unhindered. A few even turned their rigs around and followed, forming a small procession behind Rosalind's carriage.

The *Spartan*'s calliope began to play, fading as she moved past. Hal missed a step. *Why the devil was the Spartan heading downstream? Was she rushing Lennox back to Kansas City and the railroad east?* Given how fast the Missouri River was running, she could have him there in a handful of days. Perhaps the fog's remnants had muffled the sound too well for him to read, and she was continuing upstream.

Cicero kept on, steadily surging along city blocks and across intersections as he followed a carriage's typical route to the Cozzens Hotel. Rosalind murmured approval and Hal added his voice to hers, as he became more and more convinced that Cicero did indeed know where he was going. Their trail of followers continued to grow, now numbering more than a dozen men with a handful of vehicles.

And the *Spartan* was definitely sailing downstream. . . .

Suddenly, Cicero halted in the middle of a corner. His head came up, and he sniffed rapidly, turning around and around as he tested the air.

Hal's mouth tightened. Homer had always done the same thing when he lost the rabbit's trail. But he'd always found the rabbit.

"Has he lost the captain?" Rosalind murmured.

"No. He's found the point where the Old Man came down the hill but departed from his former route," Hal answered. He did not want to consider why his parents might leave a main road in this rough warehouse district.

Cicero barked twice, then plunged down a narrow side street. Rosalind immediately turned to follow him, efficiently lifting her elegant demi-train away from the mud.

William shot Hal a long look, then pulled the buggy over and headed the reins to a willing urchin. Both he and Viola jumped down, Sharps carbines in hand.

Rosalind's carriage parked neatly behind the buggy, and the driver leaned out to watch, his face alive with interest. The crowd gathered in the street beyond, goggling at the strange goings-on.

Hal drew his gun and entered the alley, well aware of Rosalind ahead and William and Viola close behind. The three most important people in the world, and the dog who'd stayed with him when none other ever had, were with him now, no matter what happened.

Cicero began to bark rapidly, jumping up and down before a squalid warehouse, whose door boasted a broken lock. The hair on the back of Hal's neck lifted. He could think of no good reason for his parents to be here.

"Did you find him, Cicero? Is Captain Lindsay in there?" he asked.

The terrier launched into a frenzy of barking and scratching at the warehouse door. A putrid scent, of neither mud nor river mist, seeped through the door's cracks.

"What the devil could he have found?" Rosalind asked.

"Stand aside, Miss Schuyler, and let us through."

She looked up into his face and swallowed. Then she moved back against the opposite building, yielding the lead to him.

Cicero's barks were so loud now that Hal could barely hear himself. Evans swiftly scanned the roofline with his drawn gun. He nodded the all-clear and took up watch. The last notes of the *Spartan*'s calliope faded as she rounded the first bend downriver.

William stood at Hal's shoulder. They shared a single glance, each knowing what they would find.

Dear God, not both of them, Hal begged the Almighty.

He hadn't prayed for his father since the war. He gently touched the door, and it swung backward. The reek was stronger now. Blood and death but not yet putrefaction.

Early morning's tentative light slipped into the dark little room beyond. A few pieces of furniture—notably a desk, chair and cot—loomed. A darker lump lay across the floor just inside the door, too large for a single person.

"Lord have mercy," Rosalind murmured.

Cicero dashed into the room and started nudging the unmoving heap. Hal followed and lit the lantern by the door.

Two people lay on the floor. A woman, wearing his mother's favorite black jacket with a triple strand of pearls, was on top. A neat hole was centered in her forehead.

Mother. She'd been shot to death in this hovel.

Hal's throat closed.

A man lay underneath her, his body half obscured by her skirts. Blood pooled around him, speaking of ebbing life.

Dear God, don't let the Old Man be dead.

For a moment, Hal let himself remember all the good times with his father. The trip down the river to Louisville when he'd first steered a boat. The reunion at Vicksburg when two fleets had cheered themselves hoarse . . .

The man stirred then settled.

"Father?" Viola whispered. "Is he dead?"

Hal pulled his mother's body off the floor and onto the cot. A quick twist wrapped its thin blanket around her.

Then his father lay before him, his face so bloody as to be almost unrecognizable. But he still breathed, his lungs barely moving.

"He's still alive, thank God. But just barely."

Viola shoved past her husband and knelt beside her father. Her face was white, but her hands were very steady as she checked her father's pulse. "He needs a doctor," she announced without looking up. "William, rip some bandages. Rosalind, we'll use your carriage."

"Please have Ezra fetch a wagon for my mother's body, Rosalind," Hal added. She nodded and turned to go.

"Daughter." The sound was weak, but it stopped them all.

"I'm here, Father. Just be quiet and save your strength." A tear slid down Viola's face.

"No." The wounded man gasped for breath before he spoke again. "Hal?"

"Here, sir." He squatted down and took his father's hand in his for the first time in decades. "Steady there, Old Man. We've got you safe now."

"Lennox. Shot. Her." The words were broken and compelling.

"Son of a bitch," Hal cursed. He didn't see the glance Viola shot at her husband, of sudden and complete comprehension.

His father stared at Hal through the only eye not totally caked and matted by blood. "You must . . . give her . . . justice," he demanded. His hand turned and gripped his only son.

"Of course. We'll see him finished."

"Sorry I beat you. Sorry I disinherited you, Viola." His voice was fainter now. "Forgive me."

"Of course." Hal and Viola spoke as one. His heart was shredded by grief, but he managed to speak, using the same phrase he'd used so many times before on his gunboat. "Now you stay alive, you hear?"

The old naval captain smiled at him. "I'll see . . . the bastard . . . in hell first."

Chapter Eighteen

Rosalind's heart ached as she watched Hal, Donovan, and Evans carry Captain Lindsay's still body up the stage, under Viola Donovan's supervision, and onto the *Cherokee Belle*'s main deck. The tears that she'd shed barely four months ago, when she followed her father's casket to the cemetery, again burned behind her eyes. She prayed that Hal would hear his father's characteristic bark again.

She followed the cortège aboard, Cicero at her side as if understanding the need for decorum. The sun was shining brightly now, and the earlier fog remained only as scattered fragments. The river and its dangers were unimportant now, compared to Captain Lindsay's well-being. She could almost wish for a return of the enveloping mists, simply to provide privacy for Hal and Viola's grief.

On the deck, the roustabouts were unusually silent as they rushed to clear a passage for the stretcher. O'Brien, after one horrified look when they'd arrived at the levee, had rallied immediately and now chivvied the roustabouts into the fastest possible movement. Sampson had broken off his conversation with some passengers and now led the way. Bellecourt and McKenzie watched from the hurricane deck, hats over their hearts.

Shocked and whispering passengers leaned over the promenade's rail to observe. Clerks and casual laborers stared avidly from the levee. Even the railroad workers studied the strange happenings from the bridge, some using spyglasses.

O'Neill, the clerk, had seized upon Rosalind's trunk as if it were a life raft on a sinking ship. He'd quickly signed for it, labeled it, and now carried it aboard without saying a word.

Under her feet, the *Cherokee Belle* quivered slightly as her boilers built steam. Beyond the stalwart craft, the Missouri River rushed towards the ocean in a flurry of brown water and sundered trees, as if eager to find the treacherous Lennox. Rosalind smiled at the raging torrent in perfect understanding and continued on.

The men deposited Captain Lindsay carefully on his bed. Evans backed out of the stateroom immediately, but Donovan rested his hand on his wife's shoulder. She put hers over his for a moment and flashed a smile up at him, then returned her attention to the unconscious man. Sarah, her maid, stepped forward with a tray full of small boxes and jars, such as a traveling pharmacy might offer.

In contrast to the loving attention paid Captain Lindsay, Mrs. Lindsay's corpse would be buried in Omaha, under the supervision of her freed slaves and Donovan's local factor. She'd be interred at the edge of civilization, with the only kindness coming from her servants and her despised Irish son-in-law's hired help. It would be an ironic end for a woman famous for her enjoyment of society's adulation.

Rosalind hated to imagine what Hal was thinking. His face was graven in stone as he stood beside his father, as if torn by grief and shock too strong to be shown.

Then Roland Jones, the steward, rushed in with an armful of clean linen and a huge pitcher of steaming water. His expression was an interesting mixture of shock and concern, although his hands were so steady that he never spilled a drop.

"Excellent, Roland," Viola praised. "Put that down on the dresser and I'll start washing my father. May I have some hot tea, too?"

Hal nudged Donovan and glanced toward the door. Donovan eased himself out, to stand beside Rosalind in the grand saloon.

"It's ready now, ma'am," Roland answered Viola. "I also took the liberty of asking the chef for some beef tea. And Captain Sampson has sent for a good doctor."

Hal kissed his father's forehead and left the stateroom. He shut the door firmly on Viola's activities and looked at Sampson, his face harsh. "I need to speak to the officers immediately. In your quarters, if you please."

"Of course, sir."

Hal silently offered his arm to Rosalind and took her upstairs to Sampson's large cabin, where he seated her on a chair and stood at her side, as the other men filed in. Sampson, O'Brien, Black Jack Norton, Bellecourt, McKenzie, and O'Neill entered, Sampson and Bellecourt taking seats while the others stood. Even O'Neill's mud clerk and Norton's assistant engineer managed to squeeze into the cabin. Cicero paced restlessly between their feet before plopping himself down next to Hal.

O'Neill's mud clerk tried to close the door but couldn't, given the crowd. Hal gestured for him to stop. "Leave the door open. The men will learn soon enough what's about."

He glanced around the circle of faces. Strong men all, masters of their professions. Every one looked back at him, their trust and eagerness as clear as if written in golden letters.

"First, gentlemen, let me introduce you to Miss Rosalind

Schuyler, my fiancée. I'll make you known to her as individuals later."

"Good day, gentlemen," Rosalind said calmly.

Sampson bowed to her slightly. "Ma'am." There was a general murmur of welcome but no sign of recognition, not that such matters were important now.

Hal's voice deepened, announcing the start of the conclave's true business. Emotion seemed to burn within him like the boilers two decks below, hot and bright under the steady exterior. He must have looked like this during the war, when he told his men they would sail under the massive rebel batteries at Vicksburg.

"Gentlemen, last night Nicholas Lennox, a passenger on the *Spartan*, shot and killed my mother. When Captain Lindsay attempted to defend his wife, Lennox wounded him nigh unto death."

The men growled, raising the hair on the back of Rosalind's neck. She would not have chosen to be Lennox at that moment.

Donovan held his right wrist against his left as if testing a dirk hidden against his forearm, while his eyes glowed incandescent as a blacksmith's forge. It was the stance, and the look, of an experienced knife fighter ready to kill quickly and without compunction.

"Now the blackguard has sailed downstream on the *Spartan*," Hal continued.

"Sacre bleu," Bellecourt spat. "There's nothing between here and the Kansas River that can catch him. And once he reaches Kansas City, he will disappear like the *cafard* he is."

"What about the telegraph?" Donovan asked.

The rivermen shook their heads unanimously and Hal spoke for them. "You can send a cable, but the sheriff would still have to stop the *Spartan*."

"Won't they have to stop for fueling?"

"She can run on wood, as we can," Sampson answered. "Give her a quiet patch of trees, under a bluff or behind an island, and no lawman will catch her."

"She can travel a long ways between stops," Hal added. "Current's running hard and fast now; six, maybe eight knots. When you add the *Spartan*'s ten or twelve knots onto that, she can cover a great many miles before she'll have to wood up."

He glanced around the crowded room, which made Rosalind think of how Farragut's council of war must have looked before New Orleans. The watching faces were as angry as Hal's now, as they hung upon his every word. Evans restlessly fondled his Colt's hilt as he leaned against the door frame.

"What if a telegram reached the *Spartan,* demanding that she stop and turn over Lennox? Would Hatcher obey?" Evans's tone insinuated he hoped Hatcher wouldn't comply.

Norton shook his head. "Hatcher's opinion of the law is profane and well known. He has a habit of breaking policemen's heads whenever possible. And if Lennox has greased his palms well, he'll never stop." The other officers nodded agreement.

"So we can hope that Hatcher acts as a law-abiding citizen, but we can't depend on it," Hal summarized. "It is therefore up to the *Cherokee Belle,* as the fastest boat on the Missouri, to catch him and bring him to justice."

"Hear, hear!"

"We will put ashore all the passengers and their luggage. The *Cherokee Star* will pick them up, when she arrives in three days, or they may take passage on whatever ship or train they choose. In either case, Lindsay & Company will pay for their passage and their accommodations. Understood?"

"Yes, sir," O'Neill assured him.

"I'll make the announcement personally, O'Neill."

"Thank you, sir."

"We'll put ashore all freight, except that required to trim the *Belle* for speed. Bellecourt and I will work with you there, Sampson."

The man nodded, his thin, intelligent face alive with calculation.

"Donovan & Sons will help with the arrangements, both for passengers and freight," Donovan inserted quietly. "Morgan will stay to look after them."

Evans jerked upright with an appalled look, then slowly relaxed. A stray thought crossed his face, and he began to smile, not generously. It was the same expression he'd worn when he sighted the lady in the carriage.

"Thank you, William," Hal said sincerely.

Rosalind was very pleased not to be the target of Evans's interest. O'Brien's question, uttered in his surprisingly melodious voice, brought her back to the present.

"What about the cabin crew and the deckhands? We won't need as many for this trip."

Hal's mouth tightened, but his gaze never wavered. "The *Belle* will travel wherever she must to catch the *Spartan*—whether it's through floodwaters, a heavy dew, or into a drowned forest. She may finish in worse shape than the *Fannie Harris,* when she fetched an artillery battery down the flooded Minnesota."

Rosalind blinked and tried to recall what she'd heard of the *Fannie Harris*. It had obviously been a harrowing passage but just how dreadful?

Hal's audience nodded their agreement, which O'Brien voiced. "Aye, sir, you'll need every hand for that sort of travel."

"If any man wishes to go ashore, he may. I'll not hold it against him," Hal added.

"I'll let them know, sir, but you know they love you. Many of them are contraband that you rescued during the war. They wouldn't leave you now, not if Moses came down and parted the river in front of them."

Hal flushed, clearly embarrassed, and turned the conversation to purely physical matters. "Norton, the *Belle* needs to make her best speed. Do you have enough fuel?"

"Wouldn't hurt to have more coal, if we're readjusting freight," Norton said thoughtfully. "But I took on a sizable amount of those pine knots, to make the fires hotter, at the old mountain man's woodyard. She's a crack boat, sir, and she'll fly even faster today."

"Excellent. Have the carpenter start making spare buckets for the paddlewheel, to replace the ones we may lose to floating debris."

"Yes, sir," O'Brien agreed. In the small room, his voice was quiet and assured—and much more genteel than on an open deck. "And we'll strengthen the bow, lest we encounter anything bigger than branches."

"Thank you. Bellecourt, you'll take the first watch in the pilothouse, with McKenzie. I'll take the second with Donovan, who was a helmsman in Ireland."

Bellecourt lifted an eyebrow. "*Certainement, mon capitaine.* The second man will be most helpful when the river is this strong-minded. But would you not prefer to take the first watch yourself?"

Hal shook his head firmly. "The second watch will see us past sunset. I've the best night sight aboard so I'll handle her then."

Shock blazed through the room. Jaws dropped, and Norton's swarthy skin turned pale. O'Neill crossed himself. A lead weight seemed to wrap itself around Rosalind's lungs.

"If storms come up and pour more water into the Missouri, we could reach the Devil's Rake before dawn, *mon ami,*" Bellecourt said gently. He alone hadn't flinched at Hal's announcement.

Rosalind shuddered. The *Belle* could sink in minutes if she hit an unseen snag in the dark, let alone a whole forest of dead trees. She swallowed hard and forced herself to relax.

She had no one in the world except Hal. If he believed he could sail the Missouri by night, then she'd follow him wherever he led.

"Agreed. But we must take the chance." Hal spoke gently but more urgently. "We must run as long as possible. The *Spartan* has an hour's lead on us now and will gain more before we can depart."

"We're accustomed to running on dark nights, thanks to those Mardi Gras excursions down the Mississippi," McKenzie confirmed. "But Hatcher will probably tie up after moonset."

"It's worth the risk, gentlemen. And remember, right is on our side," Hal insisted. "Lennox attacked Miss Schuyler when she refused to marry him. She escaped and was chased by every policeman, Pinkerton detective, and money-hungry fool for the past four months." He looked at every man in turn. "She's lucky and she did it by trusting the river."

Rosalind managed not to blink. She'd always thought she was relying on poker's river, the seventh card. But Hal was correct too: She had turned to the great Mississippi and Missouri rivers for protection, and they'd kept her safe.

"She brings luck, and the river's blessing, with her," Hal emphasized, slapping the desk. The officers nodded, hard determination stamped on their features.

"A good boat is like a good woman: She won't stomach the taste of evil." Sampson expressed their mood clearly. "The *Cherokee Belle* will fight that brute, as we do. With Almighty God on our side, we'll capture that swine!"

"Amen!" the others agreed, surging up in a wave of enthusiasm. They began to slam their fists against their hands and stamp their feet. Even Rosalind stomped on the deck.

"Every man to his duty, gentlemen," Sampson exhorted. "Time's a-wasting and we've a murderer to catch." Everyone filed out, talking eagerly about what needed to be done before Lennox roasted in hell.

Rosalind rose and turned to face Hal, who must need more weapons in his arsenal. "Will you marry me now, Hal?"

He stared at her in surprise. "Why? Don't you want a fancy church wedding?"

Rosalind shook her head, as she looked into his beloved blue eyes. "Not compared to helping you. Lennox believes you and Donovan murdered his brother. If he slips through your fingers, he must be stopped before he can rebuild his arsenal. If you marry me now, you can demand aid from powerful men."

"The Lindsay family—"

"Can't stop trains from running along the Missouri. Commodore Vanderbilt or Fisk or Huntington or others could. They'd never listen to me, a mere woman, but they'd listen to my husband, who'd be the second largest stockholder in the New York Central."

"I'm not marrying you for your money," Hal snapped.

Rosalind smiled at him. "Darling, I know that but they don't. They'll treat you as one of them, with fear and respect."

"A riverman being treated with fear and respect by railroad barons?" His eyes gleamed with wicked comprehension, and a slow smile dawned on his face. He started to chuckle. "Darling Rosalind, I believe I'd marry you just to see that happen."

He kissed her hands, still rumbling predatory laughter.

Two hours later, Hal and Rosalind stood hand in hand next to Donovan, on the *Cherokee Belle*'s hurricane deck, and waved good-bye to Evans. Her hat's soft black veiling whispered against her cheek as if it, too, were bidding farewell. A frisson danced over her skin, but she ignored it, in favor of savoring Hal's closeness.

Then Bellecourt blew the whistle for departure and backed

the *Belle* into deep water. The Missouri's swift current caught
her, turned her, and launched her downriver as if encouraging the pursuit. The last line was cast loose from the shore as
the paddlewheel bit into the frothing waters. The engines
beat steadily, in the same rhythm felt so often on the journey
upriver. Then they speeded up like a racehorse shifting into a
gallop.

The *Belle* surged forward eagerly, her graceful bow cutting the water like a swan. Billows of black smoke, laced
with brilliant sparks, flew from her tall chimneys. The move
into deep water made the taut hog chains hum softly overhead, where they ran from stem to stern beside the texas.

The crowds on the levee and the great bridge yelled approval. The calliope launched into an enthusiastic rendition
of "Camptown Races" under the warm blue sky.

The race to catch the *Spartan* had begun.

In the west, a line of dark clouds swept toward the river.
Chickens cackled placidly from their coop atop the texas,
the only relaxed travelers aboard.

The roustabouts, softly singing along with the calliope,
were still adjusting crates and barrels on the main deck under
O'Brien's rigorous eye. Loud hammering came from the forge
as Black Jack Norton labored to make spare parts for the engines before taking a nap, since he'd promised to stand watch
with Hal on the night run. The carpenter's hammer beat steadily
as he created spare buckets for the paddlewheel. The two
laundresses had emptied every clothesline so that their station, at the very end of the texas, showed only smoothly painted
wood, instead of the usual billows of white sheets and shirts.

The trio stood before the pilothouse for a long time,
silently enjoying the breeze racing over their faces and through
their clothes. It would have whipped the men's coats open
and displayed their guns, if they hadn't discreetly buttoned
their coats. It swept Rosalind's elegant skirts into a rippling
cascade behind her.

It seemed only a moment before the *Belle* hurtled past the first bend and Omaha dropped out of sight.

"Ready, my dear?" Hal asked.

"Oh, yes." She smiled up at him, unashamedly letting her joy and confidence show in her eyes.

The grand saloon was surprisingly quiet, with neither diners, drinkers, nor gamblers present. The skylights' colors played brilliantly over the empty tables, making the heavily polished wood come alive with brilliant sparks and blazes of light. The magnificent Brussels carpet glowed, while the carved and gilded wood shone like the gates of heaven. The waiters were gathered around a big table, apparently packing the best china and crystal into crates as they sang a sentimental Stephen Foster air. The bartender was handing down every bottle from the ornate bar to the mud clerk, while O'Neill was in his office with the door open, ferociously updating his account books.

Rosalind and her companions found Sampson waiting for them, Bible in hand, outside Captain Lindsay's cabin. "Ready?"

"Completely," Hal answered and patted Rosalind's hand, where it rested on his arm.

Sampson permitted the hint of a smile to soften his face. "I've conducted many a wedding on the river but, I admit, this one brings me special joy. Mrs. Donovan has warned me to keep the affair brief, as Captain Lindsay is very weak. But is there anything that you'd particularly like to see in the ceremony? A special verse, perhaps, or a psalm?"

Rosalind shook her head. "I want to be married as quickly as possible."

"I see. Lindsay?"

"She speaks for both of us."

"Very well."

Donovan chuckled softly and opened the stateroom door. "Viola and I will throw you a grand party later, when there's more time for planning and recovering from it."

The narrow stateroom was immaculately clean, showing no sign that a blood-soaked man had been carried in a few hours ago. The quilted coverlet, sheets, and blankets, once stained crimson—all had been replaced with linens as white as driven snow. A heavy Oriental carpet and a vase of fresh primroses added warmth. The shutters allowed bars of light to pass through the lace curtains, casting a gentle radiance over the scene.

Captain Lindsay was propped up in bed, his countenance slightly feverish. His head was swathed in white bandages, hiding one eye, but the other looked forth like an eagle. Viola Donovan stood beside him, her hand resting on his sheets, with no sign of her previous constraint around her father. Rosalind happily realized that father and daughter had settled their differences.

Hal and Rosalind stood across from the bed, where Captain Lindsay could see them clearly, and Donovan joined his wife. Cicero sat down firmly next to Hal, as if daring anyone to remove him from the role of principal supporter. Sampson took up station in front of the door to the grand saloon, commanding everyone's attention.

Beyond him, the waiters and bartender ceased their labors and the muffled thuds of china and crystal stopped. Now the only sound in the cabin was the steady pounding of the paddle-wheel and the river rushing past.

The crystal pendants on the lampshade fluttered, sending a dance of tiny lights around the small room. Rosalind closed her eyes as she felt a beloved presence touch her cheek. She knew, although she'd never speak of it, that her parents and brothers were here and heartily approved of her choice.

The service was short and simple, as Sampson had promised, but heartfelt on Hal and Rosalind's part. Tears welled up in her eyes when Hal promised to love her for better or for worse. Her voice was husky but clear as she promised to obey him.

His eyes danced at that particular promise. She bit her lip, trying desperately not to laugh, and a surge of pure happiness overcame her. This was Hal, who loved her for her brain as much as her body, who was more interested in teaching her to pilot his boat than playing with her money. She almost shouted the last words of her vows, so that everyone could know her delight.

Hal immediately pounced upon her—before Sampson had given his permission—and kissed her breathless. Rosalind returned his embrace with equal enthusiasm, laughing with pure joy when he eventually freed her. Sampson tut-tutted at their hijinks with mock severity, but his eyes danced. Viola and Donovan, both chuckling, hugged and congratulated them.

Finally Rosalind and Hal came to Captain Lindsay's bedside, as Abraham, Donovan's manservant, handed out glasses of champagne. Rosalind leaned down to kiss his cheek, confident of her welcome as she'd always been around her own father.

"Congratulations, my dear." Captain Lindsay's voice was soft and a bit ragged, but quite clear. He kissed her forehead, then gazed at her intently from his one good eye, as if willing her to understand. "You'll make a fine wife for my son. Just don't be afraid to disagree with him."

Rosalind blushed and wondered whether to tell the Lindsay patriarch that she wasn't the least bit afraid of his heir. Hal's chuckle saved her.

"Rosalind's quite a tiger, sir. She'll say whatever's needed, no matter what I think. And she'll make sure I understand her, too." He dropped a light, awkward kiss on his father's head.

The old man closed his good eye, but a single tear leaked out. His eye was suspiciously bright when he opened it again, but no one mentioned that.

Donovan raised his glass—of lemonade, a proper drink for

a teetotaler. "To Mr. and Mrs. Henry A. Lindsay. Long may they sail together in love and harmony!"

"Mr. and Mrs. Lindsay," echoed Sampson and Viola. All three drank the toast with relish, while Rosalind tried not to grin too idiotically as Hal hugged her. She was so happy that she barely remembered that she was aboard a boat on a flooding river.

Sampson excused himself shortly thereafter and left, as did Abraham. Captain Lindsay, who'd had his one good eye shut for a few minutes, opened it now and watched her narrowly.

"What do you want for a wedding present, m'dear? A fancy trifle bought in Paris or China perhaps?"

Rosalind shrugged and tried to think of something polite to say. She'd always been more interested in men's diversions such as stocks or gambling, than feminine trifles.

"Got all you want of those, eh?"

"Yes, sir," Rosalind said gratefully.

"What about something else? Can I remove an obstacle, or an old enemy, for you?"

Rosalind frowned. "I'm not sure I quite follow your meaning, sir."

"Dunleavy, your guardian. Was he part of Lennox's scheme to marry you? Is he why you had to run away?"

She wondered what he was leading up to. "Yes, sir. He planned to split my money with Nicholas Lennox."

Hal stirred beside her, then went still, but she could almost see the waves of angry protectiveness rolling off him.

"Optimistic fool, if he thought that louse would hand over gold to anyone else." The old captain's voice cracked.

Viola checked his brow and relaxed. But she substituted a glass of water for his champagne before returning to her station behind him.

"You are undoubtedly correct, sir," Rosalind agreed calmly.

The heat of Hal's big body next to her warmed her to her bones—and caused a deep, rich heaviness to grow in her breasts. Dear heavens, soon she'd be alone again with Hal . . . She managed another polite remark for Hal's father, who lay waiting. "I've thought the same myself, on many occasions."

Captain Lindsay snorted and drank some water. His tone was stronger when he spoke again. "I'll remove him for you. Give him a taste of his own medicine."

"Thank you, sir, but—"

Hal rubbed the small of her back lightly. Hunger shimmered through her spine before sinking into her breasts and loins. She wondered distractedly if anyone would notice if she rubbed her legs together to stop the dew from beading on her intimate folds. She caressed Hal's hip, enjoying the solid muscle and the way he quivered lightly under her hand.

"Don't worry about me, missy. I'll have a grand time crushing him into dust," the old captain retorted. "The only difficulty will be keeping my brothers from assisting me."

"Or your nephews." Hal seemed to be watching a scene that she couldn't imagine, but his father recognized it immediately. Then Rosalind remembered how Hal's uncles and cousins had crowded into that town house's foyer, all more than ready to do battle for him against Lennox. She began to smile.

The old man cackled at the vision. "Oh yes, those lads. They would enjoy this, wouldn't they?" He sipped his water, grinning like a lion waiting to pounce on a gazelle. His son wore the same predatory grin. The family likeness was strong.

Then her wicked husband fondled her hip, where it was hidden from sight. Rosalind barely bit back a moan and gulped her champagne in a silent toast to the reunited father and son. Moments later, she was still wondering whether to snatch Hal's hand away or attack him. Her own attentions, necessarily subtle because of their audience, seemed to incite him to more blatant caresses and pats.

Finally Captain Lindsay fell asleep, and Viola silently shooed Hal and Rosalind out.

Hal set their glasses down on a nearby table and slipped his arm around her waist. "I can kiss you in public now," he remarked, blue eyes dancing.

"Henry Lindsay!" Rosalind gasped, as the rich lassitude deepened still further in her loins. She shuddered slightly as dew glided softly down her thigh.

Why, oh why, had she thought that respectability would tame her river devil? And why on earth would she have wanted it to? Still, the entire cabin crew was watching. "We're in a public room. Maybe later," she hissed, "when we're in our own room."

"Madame, your wish is my command." He swung her up in his arms, and Rosalind squeaked, grabbing for his shoulders. Then he strode past a stateroom and opened the door of the Wisconsin, the last stateroom aft on the port side. An instant later, he dropped her on the big brass bed. The same big brass bed she'd known and loved on the voyage upriver. Ezra and the cabin crew must have brought it in here, one of the few beds large enough to hold Hal comfortably, when they moved Hal and Rosalind's belongings.

Cicero had barely enough time to trot in before Hal kicked the door shut.

This close to the stern, the noise and vibration of the big paddlewheel were almost overwhelming. Beneath the floor, the big pitman must be racing back and forth as it transferred power from the engines to the big wheel.

Rosalind bounced up, ruffles flying as her wig slid sideways. Her heart was pounding as hard and fast as the paddlewheel. She gratefully noticed that the shutters were drawn against any prying eyes, and she tried to think of something poetic to say.

Then Hal pounced on her. Dear Hal, who believed in actions more than pretty words. Their mouths met and melded in a frenzy as he pushed her back, his knee thrusting boldly between her legs. All the skirts and petticoats and drawers in Missouri couldn't have stopped her innards from clenching in agonizing hunger. Had it been only a little more than a day since she'd last touched him? It seemed like forever since she'd last tasted his mouth or threaded her fingers through his thick, soft hair. She'd almost lost him back there in Omaha. . . .

He nuzzled her throat, shuddering. Then he licked and kissed and suckled on that most sensitive spot just behind her ear. She groaned and arched up against him, in a desperate plea for more.

He rubbed his leg against hers, setting her fine cambric drawers to rub her inflamed feminine flesh in agonizing mimicry.

"Good God Almighty, Hal!"

He nipped her. She shrieked and climaxed.

Afterwards, she lay sprawled across the big bed and gasped for breath. Hal stripped her clothes off with all the finesse of a gambler raking in an unexpected pot. Buttons popped. Laces snapped. Something ripped, but she didn't care. She trembled as her breasts tightened again.

Two big hands fumbled across her head, and one plucked out her hatpin. The hat sailed across the room, and Cicero yelped in surprise.

"I mean to hear you scream," Hal remarked conversationally, as he tossed her wig onto the bureau.

"What?" she squeaked in a very undignified manner. Her eyes flew open to question him, but any logic immediately vanished at the sight of him. He was magnificently naked, his jutting cock standing as unashamed witness to his eagerness.

"Loudly, of course. Very, very loudly." He pulled her ruined polonaise from her shoulders. "We're married now and I want the whole damn world to know."

"Loudly," Rosalind repeated, dazzled by the simplicity of his goal. Her nipples hardened into agonizing buds, obviously in full agreement with him.

He pulled his knife from its neck sheath and Rosalind closed her eyes against a surge of dew between her legs. Lord have mercy, shouldn't she have a sensible objection to such high-handed behavior, something emphasizing the decorum appropriate to the marriage bed? But all she could think of was how his big strong hands would touch her again, how his goatee would feel against the soft flesh of her inner thighs, how deliciously his tongue would probe her feminine secrets. . . .

She moaned when he cut her corset lacings, and again when he ripped her ridiculously expensive chemise from her. Dew glided down her leg in anticipation, achieving a speed that rivaled the Missouri's.

"Damn but you're beautiful," he muttered. "It's full daylight and I can see every inch. My dear, we're going to have an excellent ride this afternoon."

He dropped to his knees before her, pulled her legs over his shoulders, and kissed the inside of her knee.

"For heavens sake, Hal, not there!" Rosalind protested. She'd lost her wits more than once from caresses which started—but didn't stop—there.

"Really?" He licked the spot and his tongue caught the first trace of dew.

Rosalind groaned. Her core clenched. She writhed.

"Or would you prefer here, instead?" His voice was muffled but his target was very clear. He slurped noisily at her folds.

Rosalind groaned again.

"Remember, you must be very loud," the devil remarked as his fingers toyed with her.

"I've never done that," she protested. "Never! Besides, it wouldn't be ladylike."

"The hell with ladylike, or gentlemanly, for that matter. You're mine and the world's going to know it. Now do better this time or I won't let you climax." He slipped two fingers into her channel and wiggled them experimentally.

She arched abruptly as her hips came off the bed in response. Her head fell back, and she gasped at the agonizing stab of sensation that raced into her breasts.

"Louder now," he exhorted and put his mouth to her. His fingers wiggled again, then stretched her shamelessly just as he blew on her clit.

Rosalind shrieked. She cried out when he pumped three fingers in and out of her, while simultaneously gliding his teeth over her clit. She keened her desire as she wrapped her legs around his head and thrust her hips at him, as he rode her hard with four fingers while stripping her dew with his tongue.

She begged. She cursed him with every phrase she'd learned from Mississippi dockhands when he moved away.

He stopped her mouth with his. She grabbed his head with both hands and kissed him back, bruising her lips as she fought to taste more of him. His big hands lifted her hips with punishing strength and his massive, blazing hot cock slid home inside her.

He fit perfectly. She was made for him and only him.

He tore his mouth away. His chest rose and fell rapidly. His crisp chest hairs brushed her inflamed breasts into further agony. Below, she could feel the soft prickle of their intimate hairs twining together. She arched against him and ground her hips against him in a shameless plea for more.

He slipped his arms under her shoulders and pulled her closer still, until they seemed one flesh. Then he rode her, grunting loudly as he thrust as hard and fast as the *Belle*'s engines drove the big wheel. She wailed her delight in this man. And she howled as the agony grew greater, the pleasure brighter and closer, the pulsations in her core harder and faster.

Until finally, she screamed at the top of her lungs when he shuddered and released himself inside her. Climax blasted through her, pinwheels of light spinning through her like the big paddlewheel just beyond the wall. It was too much for flesh and blood to absorb, and she lost consciousness.

When she came to, she was lying on top of Hal, their flesh still sweaty and clinging to each other. In the far corner, Cicero snored.

Rosalind giggled weakly. She was obviously home now with the ones she loved. She couldn't even regret that Hal had used a condom.

"What is it?" he rumbled, his big hand gently smoothing her short hair.

"I enjoy listening to Cicero sleep. It reminds me that we're together and safe."

"For the moment, yes, we are," he agreed and kissed the top of her head.

She closed her eyes against the reminder of Lennox, then kissed Hal's chest. He pulled her closer and tightened his arms around her.

"Rosalind, I wish I could give you more."

"Do you love me?"

"Yes, with all my heart."

"That's more than enough."

His next words were a deep bass counterpoint to the paddle-wheel's beat. "Rosalind, even for you, I can't live in New York."

She tilted her head back against his arm to see his face. "Then we'll live in Kansas City, Hal."

He bit his lip. "Riverboat traffic is dying, Rosalind."

Riverboats gone? Oh, my poor darling, to lose what you love so much.

"Soon, the only true moneymakers in Kansas City will be

railroads, grain, and steers, none of which excite me. Also, Kansas City likes its women strong but focused on feminine pursuits, like charities."

Rosalind winced. *Charity work.* She'd had enough difficulty attending those functions when her mother was alive and she'd only had to stomach them for an hour or two. They'd have to find an alternative. "There are many frontiers to conquer. We'll simply find a new one."

Hal was silent at that. There was a long pause before he spoke again. "Do you want children?"

Rosalind opened her mouth to utter a strong affirmative then stopped. He was watching her warily, a look in his eyes like a man holding a pair of deuces and staring at a straight flush across the table.

"Rosalind, I love you more than life," he said quietly. "But I cannot bring children into my home, when I know at least three generations of my forefathers beat their sons. I'd repeat the pattern, because it's in the blood. I will make every attempt not to breed."

Lord have mercy, he was asking her to choose between him or children. Expressed like that and with him in her arms, it was no choice at all. Especially with Lennox somewhere ahead, ready and eager to kill Hal. She'd take what she could get, for as long as she could have it.

"I'd rather have you, with or without children, wherever we live." A gambler's move, betting everything on the chance that the cards would continue to favor her.

Hal searched her face. She looked back at him, all pretense gone before his beautiful eyes. Then he tightened his arms around her. They clung together, shaking.

"What about Chicago?" Hal murmured a long time later.

"Chicago? It's a good railroad town," Rosalind answered, a little sleepily.

His voice was a dark purr against the mechanical noise

around them. "I can build a shipping line there, carrying passengers and freight to Canada."

"Excellent." She traced the line of his jaw possessively, lingering on the old knife scar, and yawned.

"I bought property there, after the fire when it could be had cheap," her husband continued. "I have a seat on the Board of Trade, which you could occupy."

Rosalind blinked. A legalized form of gambling, with risks greater than those at a poker table? She could be happy at the Board of Trade for years. Then she frowned. "They'd never let a woman in."

"If they have a problem with how I operate my seat, then they can speak to me." He bared his teeth, and she almost pitied any fat burgher who challenged him. "But if you'd prefer, we can preserve the fiction that you are simply acting under my orders." He grinned wickedly.

Rosalind laughed back at him. "As a good wife, it is my duty to obey my lord and master, no matter how remarkable the request."

"Precisely." Hal kissed her and she savored every gliding touch, reacquainting herself with his taste and sweet strength.

All too soon, he lifted his head, his face steady in a warrior's mask. "But first we need to sleep and gather our strength. It will be a long watch tonight, as we hunt for the *Spartan*."

Rosalind smiled, not sweetly, as she tucked herself comfortably against her husband. She'd happily dance on Lennox's grave.

Chapter Nineteen

"The sheriff's telegram demands that I return you to Omaha," Hatcher announced calmly. "Says you murdered a woman."

"Impossible," Nick shot back. Damn, he hadn't expected Desdemona's body to be found so soon. "Besides, I paid you for passage to Kansas City. You can let me deal with the law there."

"The *Cherokee Belle* is following us at full speed. She'll probably catch us when we tie up for the night."

Nick bit back a curse. "So keep going. Mississippi boats do that all the time."

Hatcher shook his head, his small pig's eyes surveying Nick coldly. "Too dangerous, even with a full moon. The Mississippi doesn't change course every few months, like the Missouri. Its pilots can memorize it and drive the boat safely, day or night. No, we'll have to tie up."

Nick ground his teeth. Money was always the answer. "How much to keep going?" he demanded.

Hatcher smiled, and Nick realized that he'd walked into a trap. *Damn.* "Fifty thousand dollars."

"You could buy a new boat for that," Nick protested, feeling the ground fall out from under his feet.

Hatcher shrugged. "Maybe. I could also hand you over to the law."

"I'll give you a check," Nick said sullenly.

Hatcher shook his head. "Heard you played a big poker game and lost. No, it's gold or nothing."

What could he offer? The New York tenements? No, they wouldn't appeal to a Missouri man. Paul's house? Even half finished, it was worth more than fifty thousand, but it was also the last vestige of Paul's dreams. *Damn, damn, damn.* "I have a house on the Hudson, next to the Roosevelt estate. I'll give you the deed for that."

Hatcher's eyes gleamed. "On the river?"

"Yes."

"Done. The *Spartan* will run day and night, until we reach Kansas City." Hatcher smirked.

Hal paused on the hurricane deck to finish his ham sandwich and assess the *Cherokee Belle*'s current situation. The late afternoon sky was black with clouds, building to deadly thunderstorm heights as they flew before the north wind. Not a bird was in sight, hinting at their need to take shelter from the coming storm.

Far to the west, lightning cracked as sheets of rain fell, whose waters would soon feed the Missouri River. The river was running strong, in a torrent of ash brown water, at perhaps six, or even seven knots. Fast, damn fast. There'd be some new channels, probably even a chute or two, sliced open tonight. Bellecourt and McKenzie must have their hands full, holding the *Belle* to a steady course against this current.

Cicero whined and leaned against Hal's leg. Hal rubbed his ears with a quiet, "Easy now, boy. Don't much like storms, do you?"

Cicero whined his agreement and moved even closer.

Overhead, gray smoke, well mixed with sparks and cinders, poured from the tall chimneys. It wasn't black smoke, so Norton must not yet have the boilers fired as hot as possible. Still, Hal was glad he'd long ago insulated the *Belle*'s chimneys from contact with her fragile woodwork.

Every steamboat was easy to burn; such was the nature of their business. They were built of lightweight soft woods, so they'd travel quickly in shallow waters. The resulting structure was soaked with oil and turpentine from paint, then dried by years of sun and wind. Add a combustible cargo and wood, or coal, stored near the bow—well, it was a wonder more steamers didn't burn, no matter how strongly the government and insurers regulated and inspected them. A riverboat could burn to the waterline in less than five minutes.

As he'd done so many times during the war, Hal double-checked his boat's precautions. The tin roof on the pilothouse, texas, and hurricane deck provided the *Belle* with the latest in protection. All the buckets and barrels placed around her roofs and decks were full of water, ready to fight fires.

Hatcher had sanded the *Spartan*'s roofs instead of buying a metal roof, considering tin as a drag on his boat's speed. It was the typical strategy and tended to work well, unless the sand blew or washed away.

Hal dusted the sandwich's crumbs off as he gave the river another long look. Viola and William Donovan came up beside him silently, unabashedly holding hands.

"Ready?"

"Of course," the big Irishman returned calmly.

They entered the pilothouse quietly to find a sweating Bellecourt and McKenzie straining at the wheel. Both pairs of hands gripped the spokes desperately, muscles standing out on their necks and shoulders beneath their shirts. Their coats were tossed over the rocking chair and a mug of coffee sat cold on the small table.

The glass windows on three sides had been closed and the

big opening in front, never glassed, had been partially covered by boards in the typical foul weather practice, leaving a narrow strip for the pilots to see through.

"Evening, gentlemen. Ready to be relieved?" Hal asked.

"*Mais non, mon brave,* we could continue in this fashion for days," Bellecourt joked. His white hair was plastered to his face and neck. He and McKenzie grunted as they urged the *Belle* to round a hairpin corner.

The boat had settled into the new, straight course before Hal spoke again.

"Alas, I must insist that you permit us to share the delight," Hal said gently and laid a hand on the wheel next to Bellecourt's. William did the same beside McKenzie.

The river's raging power surged up through Hal's hands, along his arms, and into his shoulders. He balanced it against the *Belle*'s strength as his legs braced to support him. Hell and damnation, the current was even stronger than he'd expected.

Bellecourt loosened his grip. Hal tightened his then relaxed slightly as the wheel steadied under his command.

A similar shift took place beside him as William took over from McKenzie. The big teamster was a bit clumsy, but he quickly adapted to following Hal's lead, working well enough not to be replaced by Sampson. Since they'd be traveling by night on a flooded river, Hal wanted every possible hand on the main deck, ready to clear debris or make emergency repairs.

The *Cherokee Belle* didn't waver once.

Bellecourt and McKenzie stepped away, then sank into the rocking chairs, as if their legs would hold them no longer.

"Good afternoon, gentlemen. Norton here," sang a familiar voice through the speaking tube.

"Glad to hear your voice, Black Jack," Hal responded warmly.

Roland Jones slipped into the pilothouse with a carafe of coffee, redolent of whiskey, and sandwiches. The two pilots accepted the coffee gratefully, while Viola requested tea from where she sat on the tall stool.

"We've made up perhaps thirty minutes, *mes amis,* according to the latest telegram," Bellecourt announced. "Hatcher refused to stop, *naturellement.*"

Hal whistled in amazement. "Congratulations, Bellecourt. You've managed to add to your fame as a lightning pilot."

William added his own praise, making for a brief flurry of delighted conversation before they had to pay attention to the next turn.

Hal's back strained as they fought to keep the *Belle* in the center of the channel. The Missouri wanted to cut through the inner corner, using its roaring water and everything they carried. But the *Belle* was too wide to sail so close to the shore.

Lightning cracked less than two miles away, striking a tall elm tree. The rain was closer now, rushing in with the inevitability of the seventh card in one of Rosalind's poker games.

"Missouri's running high, maybe two feet higher than when we came up," Bellecourt commented. "It may finally open that new chute by Spring Creek."

"Which would cut off twenty or thirty river miles, and make up an hour or more on the *Spartan.*" Hal's mind raced as he assessed the possibilities.

"If a pilot is daring and lucky enough to travel a narrow and unknown channel in the dark of the night," Bellecourt warned, "and pass through an oak forest at the end."

"True," Hal agreed and set the *Belle* up for another turn as lightning slashed the skies again. More than one riverboat had met her end while traveling a chute for the first time, even in broad daylight. He hoped Rosalind would sleep through the night so that she wouldn't be disturbed by the dangerous voyage.

There was a long silence before Bellecourt spoke again. "We'll be back in six hours, *mon ami,* unless you mean to tie up before then."

"I plan to stop before the Devil's Rake. The flood's probably shifted it so daylight would be best for traversing it."

McKenzie sighed in relief, but quickly covered his reaction by noisily slurping at his coffee.

Hal's mouth twitched. He might be a close fit pilot, capable of taking his boat successfully through the narrowest channels. But even he balked at sailing through the Devil's Rake by night.

"Eh, *bien,*" Bellecourt said comfortably. "We will see you at the change of watch in six hours. *Bonne chance, mes amis.*" He left with McKenzie, both of them running down the stairs like boys as they dashed for shelter.

Lightning snapped from cloud to cloud, then a thunderbolt hit a tree a boat's length behind the *Belle.* With a loud crack, it slowly toppled over until it barely clung to the muddy bluff.

After a quick glance to see which tree had been hit, Hal ignored the fallen giant in favor of studying the river ahead. With less than an hour before sunset, there wasn't a great deal of light except for that coming from the lightning.

Sampson's voice rose from the main deck, and O'Brien rang the bell. An instant later, deckhands and cabin crew swarmed over the *Cherokee Belle,* locking the shutters over every window and placing canvas covers over every pipe and vent. With a great show of ceremony, O'Brien tamped out his pipe, marking the start of night running for the *Belle.* Now the pilots' vision would see only the river and the land beyond, and not be blinded by any small brightness from the boat.

Another bolt of lightning shot across the clouds, to be

quickly answered by a second and a third that made the skies sizzle and crack. It bid fair to be one of the most spectacular electrical storms Hal had ever seen.

He continued to steer the *Belle*, eyes alert for every change in the river—the standing wave that could signal a drowned snag, the ruffled waters that indicated a shoal, the slightly higher water that meant the inside curve of a change in the channel. William echoed his every move, matching him so well now that they seemed like a single hand on the wheel.

"Do you generally tie up during thunderstorms?" William asked. His tone evinced only the mildest curiosity.

"No," Hal and Viola said in unison. They chuckled, and she went on. "Very few riverboats are struck by lightning. The wind is a greater danger since it can blow a boat over."

"That's more true on the Ohio or Mississippi, where there are longer stretches of straight water." Hal added. "We'll stop quickly if we must but it's not likely."

Hal and William brought the *Belle* safely through another turn, their route now well lit by almost continuous flashes of light and the sizzle of ozone.

Thinking it best to ask the questions now, while they were alone—and still alive, Hal covered the speaking tube to the engine room before he spoke. "Viola, do you know if Nicholas Lennox was Mother's paramour?"

She hesitated. A lightning bolt split a tree a few hundred yards away.

"Viola." Hal's voice was very gentle. "Let me know the truth now, while we're still alive. I dislike going into battle ignorant of what charges my enemy might hurl at me."

"He was her paramour ten years ago," she said reluctantly.

"Was there anything else between them than physical intimacy?"

She was silent.

"Viola, I'm not an utter fool. Mother lectured me many times about my duty to go south and fight for the Confederacy. I suspect she took action herself, as well as spouting exhortations. Spying, maybe, or sending arms south." Sweat trickled down his back between his shoulder blades.

"Yes." His sister's voice was barely audible. "How did you know?"

Hell and tarnation. He'd hoped to be proven wrong. Pain stabbed his heart. If his father learned that he had a treasonous wife, it would have torn his guts out.

A few heavy drops of rain beat on the pilothouse roof. Hal's voice was uncomfortably harsh when he spoke. "There was a great deal of gossip during the war about her unladylike interest in the Cincinnati dockyards and the army headquarters. And her flirtations with prominent men."

"All true. I believe Nicholas Lennox helped her with some of her treason, especially sending guns to the rebels." Viola leaned her forehead against her husband's back, and he murmured something soothing in Irish.

Hal put the rest of the tale together. "Ross must have found out and blackmailed you into marriage. Damn, I wish I'd thrown his rascally body into the Ohio so you wouldn't have had to suffer."

"But if I hadn't married—and buried—Ross, I wouldn't have met William," Viola pointed out, speaking louder to be heard over the rain drumming on the tin roof.

William said something very smug in Irish, and Viola chuckled.

Just then, lightning sparked again, flashing an eerie green fire across the sky. Rosalind burst in through the door and slammed it shut. "Good evening," she managed. Her simple walking dress was plastered to her skin, revealing every detail of her French corset and feminine curves.

"Hello, my love," Hal answered. He should have known that his little gambler would never miss a risky journey like this. Best to keep her mind occupied, now that she'd arrived. He opened the speaking tube again, so Norton could hear every word.

"Rosalind, do you remember that trio of dead oak trees atop the bluff, near Spring Creek?"

"An isolated stand of trees and the bluff eaten away to the south?"

"Precisely. Now keep your eyes peeled and sing out when you see them. You can see more through the side windows than we can between these planks. We should be coming up on those trees very soon."

"Yes, Hal." She took up station at the window closest to where Spring Creek would appear. She spoke again, a few minutes later.

"There it is, Hal, ten points off the starboard bow, maybe a mile ahead."

Hal looked where she indicated, squinting against the water blowing in between the planks. A flash of lightning abruptly lit the shores and the stand of trees. Rosalind was correct, although they'd arrived sooner than he'd expected, thanks to the raging waters.

"Norton?"

"Aye, skipper?"

He shouted to be heard over the rain, now drumming as loudly as any regimental band. "Fire up the engines and rig for collision. We're taking that new chute by Spring Creek."

God willing, they wouldn't strike anything so hard that the boilers would come off their mounts.

"Aye aye, skipper. I'll pass the word to Mr. Sampson."

"Thanks. Ladies, when I tell you, brace yourselves. This will be a bumpy ride."

He prayed they'd be safe, and not thrown about if the *Belle* hit a snag, or ripped her bottom out, or lost her pilot-house to a low-hanging tree branch. But he had to take this route, if he was to catch up with Lennox.

All too soon, the three ancient trees loomed up next to the *Belle*'s bow. The channel should turn to the left here, as the Missouri had run less than a week ago. But now the water didn't bow upwards, marking a curve like a sleigh skidding on ice. Instead, it continued to rush straight ahead.

The Missouri River was cutting a new chute, straightening out a massive oxbow bend and cutting at least twenty river miles off the journey to Kansas City. But had it ripped out the oaks at the foot of the bend yet? Or would those ancient trees smash the *Cherokee Belle* into kindling?

Hal didn't hesitate, but rang down for full speed ahead. "Ramming speed, Norton!" he roared. "Brace yourself, ladies!"

Then he steered his beloved *Belle* into uncharted waters, lit only by lightning. She leapt forward, as the engines roared and cinders shot through the skies overhead. Sheets of water blew into the pilothouse, through the gap in the boards, and half blinded him. Cicero barked encouragement.

A line of willows appeared directly in front, marking the edge of what had been an island. But there was an opening between them, where the Missouri foamed and frothed like a Titan intent on destroying the land.

Crack! A willow swayed and fell into the torrent and disappeared downriver. Hal set his course straight for where the tree had vanished. The *Belle* bucked when she reached the former riverbank, where the land was still closer to the surface than elsewhere. But the engines surged, as strongly as when his old gunboat had charged the rebel rams at Memphis, and threw the *Belle* up and over the obstacle.

Now they were in the chute. The current here was faster than in the main channel, since the Missouri's path was narrower. The river pushed the boat ahead as if eager to see her safe in the old channel. Lightning blazed overhead, providing occasional glimpses of the route ahead.

The *Cherokee Belle* bounced hard and often, feeling every bump in the new channel but surviving somehow. Willows bent before her and under her, then sprang up again in her wake.

A tree limb loomed up, reaching over the hurricane deck towards the pilothouse. Suddenly the current twisted and snatched the *Belle* into a turn.

Her stern swung fast and wide. A loud crash sounded and Rosalind squeaked. The superstructure trembled. Then the gallant boat steadied and raced on, silently telling Hal that all her key elements were intact, especially the chimneys and stabilizing hog chains.

"What the hell was that?" shouted Donovan.

"We just shortened the texas by breaking off the laundry room's roof," Hal shouted back. "The rest of the *Belle*'s fine." And he hoped there'd be a hot bath waiting when he finished this shift, given the way he was sweating to hold the *Belle* in the new channel.

Long minutes later after more thunderbolts blasted the sky, Rosalind sang out, her voice steady. "Oak trees ahead, Hal. It's the grove marking the old riverbed."

God willing, the Missouri had already cut the chute enough to take out enough of those oaks. Otherwise, the *Belle* would be either smashed into kindling when she roared against them, or stranded in a backwater for days.

Lightning flashed, showing Hal a narrow passage just ahead. The Missouri had cut a few oaks neatly away. Others leaned against the raging waters. Would the opening be wide enough for the *Belle*?

"Ready again, Black Jack?"

"Aye, skipper!"

"Then pour it on and may the devil take the hindmost!"

"Give it to her, boys!" roared Norton.

The *Belle* slammed into the gap, intent on forcing her way between two giants. One mighty oak cracked and broke, falling away from its assailant. The other held, stopping the boat.

Hal and William fought to concentrate all of the *Belle*'s strength on one spot. The great engines strained under his feet. The paddlewheel's beat increased until she seemed to be pounding the water into granting assistance. The frustrated water surged under her hull, frothing around the oaks as if intent on carrying them away. Cicero barked and howled, as if begging for help.

Slowly, slowly, moaning like a reluctant god, the stubborn oak fell away. Freed, the *Belle* leaped through, although squeaks and groans told of obstructions pushed aside. She tore into the old channel with a last bounce and flip of her stern.

Hal cursed vehemently and spun the wheel, desperate to turn his boat before she embedded herself in the opposite bank. William added his strength, and together they coaxed the crack packet into obedience. The *Cherokee Belle* abruptly settled into the proper channel and raced on, as smugly as a maiden going to church.

Another lightning bolt lit the skies. Against the brilliant pale green light, a shower of sparks showed where the *Spartan* sailed. She'd clearly been warned, as Hal had expected, and was racing hard and fast. But she was only a few miles ahead now, thanks to the chute.

Rosalind voiced what was likely in everyone's mind. "Do you think we can catch her before the Devil's Rake, Hal?"

"I know we'll catch her. But before the Devil's Rake?" Hal shrugged.

"Then we'll pray," Viola said fiercely. "Lennox must answer for his crimes."

And the rain beat down, as if echoing her plea.

The storm lasted for nearly an hour, as Hal and William fell into a rhythm of steering the *Cherokee Belle* down the wild river. Hal steered closer into the corners than he normally would have, with scraped paint and battered wood as witnesses. Sampson's men efficiently cleared the debris and made any repairs necessary. Norton's engines settled into a steady rhythm, driving the *Belle* faster than she'd ever run before.

A barge, escorted by a small tug, hovered outside the old mountain man's woodyard. The roustabouts quickly threw her a line, reeled her in, and offloaded her precious cargo, then shoved her off again—without the *Belle* once slowing down.

Grinning, Hal blew the *Belle*'s whistle in thanks. Wooding up while underway was far more common on the Mississippi than the Missouri, so the old mountain man must have made special arrangements to be of assistance.

Ezra and Abraham appeared with food and drinks, which Hal and William snatched as they could. All the while, the roustabouts sang stirring plantation melodies about chariots and riding to heaven.

And slowly, with every fiber straining and wreathed in clouds of black smoke and cinders, the *Cherokee Belle* gained on the *Spartan*.

Finally, the rain stopped and the clouds blew past. The Missouri lay before them, every ripple evident in the full moon's silvery light. The water was deeper here than it had been a few days ago, and it was rising fast, as the nearby rivers and streams brought rainwater to the Big Muddy.

Two of Sampson's deckhands removed the planks from the forward window, so Hal could see clearly. Clumps of people occasionally appeared on the bluffs, cheering as the *Belle* sailed by.

Debris bobbed and spun in the foaming waters. Everything from branches to entire trees came to menace the *Belle,* only to be dodged or pushed off by Sampson's men's poles.

They sighted an embarras ahead, its tightly woven rampart of dead trees apparently sneering at their hopes of safe passage. Only men with saws could force passage for a boat through those impenetrable walls. Thankfully, the raging flood had pushed the ten-foot-high thicket against a bluff, and the *Belle* passed by unharmed.

A cold wind raced out of the northwest, carrying the memory of mountain snows and winter frosts. Viola shivered and disappeared. She and Abraham returned with coats and fresh coffee for all.

A puff of cinders from the *Spartan* landed on the *Belle*'s bow. Sampson shouted immediately, and roustabouts sprang forward with buckets. An instant later, it was gone.

Hal bared his teeth in a predator's smile. The *Spartan* was now within a mile.

Norton somehow coaxed more speed from the *Belle*'s engines. Hal found a tighter course through a series of deep bends, ignoring the scrapes as trees tore at the boat's cabin.

And suddenly, the *Cherokee Belle* burst out of a turn and found the *Spartan* less than three lengths ahead of her.

"Ahoy there, *Spartan*!" Sampson shouted through a speaking trumpet. "You have a murderer aboard. Heave to and we'll take him back to Omaha."

"Never!" answered Hatcher. "There are no killers on my boat. I won't stop until I reach Kansas City!"

"Just as I expected," Hal muttered. Steering carefully through the narrow channel, he brought the *Belle* into line behind the *Spartan* as Bellecourt and McKenzie slipped silently into the pilothouse. Almost six hours had passed since they'd gone off duty.

Seen from this close, it was obvious that the *Spartan* had encountered as many or more trees than the *Belle*. Her paint was badly chipped and one of her stacks was awry.

Men ran frantically back and forth in her engine room, causing Hal to raise a speculative eyebrow. Could Hatcher's parsimonious ways have finally created havoc for the *Spar-*

tan's engines or boilers? Or perhaps she hadn't cleared mud from her boilers, causing her lines to clog. Or perhaps an engine or boiler was thinking of blowing a rivet. Or . . .

Truly, there were too many possibilities to consider, and none of them mattered, as long as the *Spartan* was still running fast and free down the Missouri.

Hal carved every fraction he could from the *Belle*'s course, using every trick he'd learned in a lifetime on the unruly river. She crept closer and closer until she was within two lengths of her opponent.

She was also approaching the Devil's Rake. If Hatcher was foolhardy enough to enter that maze of snags and embarrases at night, he could gain a sizable lead on a more cautious *Cherokee Belle*. It would be like threading a two-hundred-foot long needle through the thorn hedge around Sleeping Beauty's castle, instead of a single man on horseback. Hal gritted his teeth.

"Triangle bluff coming up, Hal," Rosalind warned. Her voice was calm, too calm. That bluff marked the start of the two sharp bends that led to the Devil's Rake. A small bonfire burned atop it, and a handful of spectators cast flickering shadows.

The *Spartan* cut the first turn very close. The *Belle* followed her exactly, ignoring the resulting nudge against the riverbank.

The second bend loomed barely three boat-lengths later. The *Spartan* started her turn late, still intent on the fastest possible route. But Hatcher had misjudged the current and the riverbed. The *Spartan*'s stern bounced off the bluff, sending her spinning across the river.

"All-back full!" Hal shouted and simultaneously rang down to the engine room. Norton's answer came before the last note sounded.

Boom! The *Spartan* ricocheted against the opposite shore. Birds burst out of the trees, screeching their alarm.

Metal screeched and cracked with a sound like the souls of the damned descending into hell. Men yelled orders along the *Spartan*'s main deck.

The Missouri snatched the *Spartan* off the shore and brought her back into the channel. A loud crash sounded from her main deck. A man shrieked in terror.

The *Cherokee Belle*'s paddlewheel hesitated, then reversed, throwing up water like a geyser as she fought to stay safe.

A flash of scarlet light showed from the *Spartan*'s main deck. Smoke curled upwards to the starry skies. Her paddlewheel thrashed.

"Lord have mercy, a boiler's fallen over," Viola whispered.

Fire burst out between the *Spartan*'s stationaries, the struts along the main deck which held up her promenade.

"They'll lose the boat within minutes," Rosalind's voice was choked with tears.

"Aye, fifteen minutes at the most but more likely, five. With luck, Hatcher can reach shore before the tiller ropes burn through," Hal added to comfort his wife.

The *Spartan* swept down the Missouri and past the turn. Smoke billowed up beyond the bluff, casting a pall over the full moon.

"All-ahead half," Hal ordered the engine room. Norton answered, the bells crisp and clear, and the *Belle* moved on.

An instant later, she rounded the turn.

The *Spartan* was headed straight for an embarras. "*Mon dieu*, he's lost the tiller ropes already," Bellecourt muttered.

Fire glowed from within her promenade and flickered from her skylights. Screaming men jumped into the rushing waters. The onlookers pointed and shouted from their vantage point. A few climbed down the bluff, ready to pick up survivors.

The smell of burning wood was stronger now, as the *Belle*

came closer. William muttered something in Latin, which Bellecourt echoed. The two men, and Viola, crossed themselves.

Suddenly, flames burst out of the *Spartan*'s texas and leaped onto the pilothouse. It spread rapidly, consuming the flimsy superstructure.

"Lower the boats and pick up survivors," Hal shouted down to the main deck. He began to bring the *Cherokee Belle* to a safe stop.

Just beyond the *Spartan,* the first snags of the Devil's Rake clawed the moonlit sky like an invitation to hell. The broom mounted atop her pilothouse caught fire, sending smoke and sparks flying into the heavens, as the *Spartan* forever relinquished her claim as the fastest packet on the Lower Missouri.

Chapter Twenty

From behind a stack of barrels, Nick kept an eye out for any unwary roustabout roaming the *Cherokee Belle*'s main deck alone. He'd managed to reach her last night and climb aboard the port side, while everyone else was pulling survivors from the starboard side. *Cocky fools.*

Now he had to find a roustabout and steal some dry clothing. The Missouri River had stripped his gun and boots away as neatly as any valet. Every gun aboard this ridiculously tidy boat was apparently either locked up in her powder magazine or riding on a man's belt. This time, he'd do the job himself with his own knives, rather than relying on others' feeble efforts.

Rosalind stirred resentfully when the draft of cold air caught her, immediately noticing the loss of her big, warm bedmate. "Whazzat?" she mumbled sleepily.

"Go back to sleep, my dear. I have to go on duty." Hal kissed the top of her head.

Rosalind yawned and threw off the covers. If Hal was going on duty, she would accompany him. "Can't Bellecourt or McKenzie take the first watch?"

"They handled the wheel, while William and I helped

pick up survivors," Hal reminded her. He took a tray with coffee and shaving supplies from Ezra, then closed the door.

Rosalind stretched and began to dress quickly. "Was Lennox's body ever recovered?"

"No." Hal began to shave. "So we'll continue downstream for another day or so and hunt for him. As well as any survivors we can find. Or corpses."

Rosalind shuddered. "I hope we find all of them soon."

The early morning air was crisp and cold but very clear, as Hal, Rosalind, and Cicero climbed to the pilothouse. Below them, the Missouri was still running fast, but a little lower than the night before. The Devil's Rake's snags and embarrases were plain to see, their branches reaching out like Satan's minions eager to drag an unwary soul down to hell. Egrets and a great blue heron stalked along the water, hunting for breakfast. An osprey dived out of the sky and plucked a fat bass out of the Missouri, exactly where the *Spartan* had sunk.

Rosalind smiled, glad to see the birds' untamed beauty. The *Spartan*'s hulk, the only portion remaining after the fire, might never be found, but life went on for others.

Viola had been very sanguine about her father's recovery. The *Cherokee Belle* had rescued dozens of survivors who now slept on the main deck and the grand saloon's floor, almost piteously grateful for their salvation.

Few of the stokers had been saved; they had probably died when the *Spartan*'s boiler wrenched itself free of its mounts and set her on fire. Hatcher had been found badly burned and unconscious, with a huge gash across his head, probably from a fallen beam. Viola didn't think he'd live to see another night.

Lennox, on the other hand, had vanished without a trace. A few of the *Spartan*'s cabin crew spoke of seeing him in the pilothouse, screaming imprecations as the *Belle* approached.

But no one had seen him after the *Spartan* struck and caught fire.

The pilothouse was neat as a pin, with no sign of last night's exertions. Beneath Rosalind's feet, the engines rumbled at quarter-speed, ready to start downriver at a moment's notice.

"Morning, Norton," Hal called down to the engineer through the speaking tube, as he calmly chewed a bit of clean straw from the empty livestock stall. He always walked through the hold and main deck before coming on duty, in order to gain a feel for the *Belle*'s weight distribution. This morning, Rosalind had sensed a watcher there, but nothing untoward had happened. Now she opened the windows for better visibility, as Hal preferred, despite the chilly morning.

"Ready to get underway?" Hal called into the speaking tube.

"Whenever you are, sir," Norton answered promptly. "We've a full head of steam and the engines are turning."

"Very well then." Hal grasped the wheel and briskly sounded the whistle to signal departure. A roustabout cast off the last line tying the *Belle* to shore, then leaped back aboard.

Both hands on the wheel, Hal calmly backed the *Belle* into the main channel and let the Missouri's tumultuous waters turn her around. She sailed downstream at half speed, strong enough to remain under control despite the fast current, but still slow enough to stop if a survivor or body was found.

Few sounds other than wanton snoring emerged from the texas's cabins, now stuffed with exhausted officers and cabin crew sleeping off the night's exertions. Two roustabouts had just started to hose down the main deck. Breakfast's first rustlings came from the kitchens but the boat was still remarkably peaceful. No freight was being rearranged while O'Brien shouted and cursed. No querulous passengers shouted, demanding coffee and fried bacon.

Rosalind purred. She would be happy to stand at Hal's side like this, forever.

Hal changed course slightly so the *Belle* could dodge a drowned tree. Suddenly a dirk flashed through the open door in the rear and embedded itself in the great wheel, less than an inch from Hal's thumb. He spun around, his hand still gripping a spoke.

What on earth?

A filthy Lennox, barefoot and dressed in ill-fitting roustabout's garb, leaped in and attacked Hal with a bowie knife. Cursing harshly, Hal kicked Lennox in the leg and forced his attacker back a step.

The *Belle* took advantage of his inattention and yawed, slipping sideways toward a large snag. Rosalind jumped for the wheel. Cicero let loose a volley of barking.

"I've got her, Hal!" she shouted.

Hal released the wheel, just as Rosalind grabbed it with both hands. The current yanked at the *Belle,* mocking her attempt to take control.

Hal drew his Arkansas toothpick and crouched, his back against Rosalind. He trusted her with his beloved *Cherokee Belle,* even in the middle of the Devil's Rake.

Rosalind took a deep breath and vowed to be worthy.

"Finally ready to die?" Hal snarled at Lennox.

"Are you? You'll look better dead, just as your slut of a mother did," Lennox retorted. He seemed to be edging back and forth in front of Hal, probably looking for an opening. The pilothouse had seemed spacious before. Now Rosalind couldn't imagine how the two men would have room to fight.

"Lindsay, what's going on up there?" Norton demanded through the speaking tube.

"Black Jack, Lennox is here!" Rosalind shouted. Cicero barked lustily and lunged at Lennox.

"Damn you, Lindsay!" Lennox cursed. "You'll be dead before noon. And Donovan too."

Steel clanged and slid against steel in the confined space, but Rosalind couldn't turn to look. Her every faculty was fixed on the crooked waters before her, its shores lined with life-threatening snags and embarrases.

Shouts came from the main deck, but would help arrive in time? A snag loomed up on the starboard bow. Planting her feet for better leverage, Rosalind strained to turn the *Belle* against the raging current.

Hal growled, his back against Rosalind. He was ice cold and deadly calm with the need to protect her. He couldn't fight here, not when the slightest misstep would risk her life. He had to take this fight into the open, even though that would give the advantage to Lennox's quickness.

He charged straight at Lennox. He slammed his shoulder into the villain's chest and drove him backward. Fire burned along his ribs, long and deep. Lennox had landed a nasty cut.

They broke through the pilothouse's back wall, shattering the wood and glass. Both men rolled as they dropped a yard down and onto the texas's roof. They came to their feet immediately, just as Cicero sailed out of the pilothouse. He leaped between Hal's legs and bit Lennox's ankle.

"Damn your mangy mutt!" Lennox shook off Cicero and Hal charged again. His knife nicked the other's shoulder before Lennox blocked him.

They circled each other on the texas's narrow roof, their knives glinting with crimson in the dawn's light. A few feet away, chickens squawked in surprise from within their coop. Beyond that lay the laundresses' station, once a tidy mimic of a sunporch, but now an assembly of torn walls and broken poles.

The *Cherokee Belle* was weaving a bit, not surprising with a cub at the wheel. But Rosalind was keeping her to a remarkably steady course. She'd do. Now Hal just had to subdue or kill Lennox, so she could stay alive.

The texas's roof was tin, lightly covered with frost on this spring morning and edged only with knee-high gingerbread. The ornamental wood wouldn't have stopped Cicero from falling off, let alone a man. Below that was the hurricane deck, also topped by frosty tin and edged by flimsy gingerbread. It held other obstacles to fancy footwork, such as steps to the different texas cabins, the roof bell, and the taut hog chains.

From far below, Hal could hear Sampson ordering his men to intervene. He would have laughed at Sampson's startling use of foul language if he hadn't had other things on his mind.

But Sampson's roustabouts wouldn't arrive in time. And Lennox was the most dangerous opponent Hal had ever faced, as he'd learned in New York.

Lennox charged Hal, his bowie knife flashing in a nasty backhanded stab. Hal blocked it instinctively. For a moment, they strained together, their heads less than a foot away.

Lennox's face was contorted with hatred and determination. "I'm going to gut you," he snarled, "and your filthy mick brother-in-law. And when I finally get my hands on that bitch, I'll teach her who's master."

Hal snarled and pushed down harder on Lennox's arm. The force was too much for the other's balance, and he slipped on the frosty tin, breaking loose of Hal's hold. The villain stepped back, looking for a chance to break through Hal's guard.

Hal studied him warily, knife cocked and ready to strike. He'd like to see this cur on the gallows, the one audience he wouldn't be able to cozen. He had to keep his enemy close and away from the stairs down to the hurricane deck, lest he escape yet again.

He attacked, using his size and a dozen brutal moves learned on hundreds of riverfront docks to herd Lennox. Their knives clashed and rang.

Once, old memory warned Hal, and he ducked. Lennox's knife cut his cheek, not his throat, just above his old scar. He used his momentum to stamp on Lennox's bare foot and nicked his arm. Lennox broke free, cursing, then ran for the shelter of the big chicken coop.

Cicero growled and charged after Lennox. Hal ran down the chicken coop's other side, as chickens squalled their anger. He crouched at the end and listened for his enemy.

A quick glance confirmed that Lennox, snarling at Cicero, now stood in the small open space behind the chicken coop. Less than a yard behind him gaped a ragged hole, where the laundry room's roof had been. Beyond that, a few barrels of water, scape pipes, and the verge staff marked the edge of the hurricane deck, which sloped gently down to the spinning paddlewheel. They were so close to the stern now, the paddlewheel's vibrations ran through Hal like another heartbeat.

Below his feet, doors slammed as his friends began to leave their cabins to help him. And the hog chains glinted briefly in a flash of morning sun, on either side of the texas.

Cicero charged at Lennox, barking like a horde of demons.

Lennox instinctively stepped backward. One foot, then the other, dropped into the laundry room. He grabbed for the edge, but the broken wood broke away in his hands. His voice broke on an obscenity as he disappeared.

If he could catch Lennox while the blackguard was disoriented from the fall . . .

Hal jumped down onto the hurricane deck, using the gingerbread to steady himself. Moving a little stiffly, Lennox emerged from the laundry room. Cicero barked ferociously overhead.

Suddenly Rosalind cursed, and the *Belle* yawed to port, probably dodging a snag. Then Rosalind overcorrected her and jerked her back to starboard.

Lennox staggered and his knifepoint dropped. Just a little—but enough to provide an opening.

Hal bit down on his knife blade, leaped up, and grabbed the hog chain with both hands. It hummed quietly in his grip, as if the *Belle* were lending him her strength. He swung himself across the *Belle* and into Lennox's chest.

Lennox flew backward and off the deck, shouting a single loud profanity. It rose to an inhuman and chilling note, then fell silent.

The *Cherokee Belle*'s paddlewheel staggered, and the entire boat vibrated. Gradually it recovered its composure, and the packet sailed serenely on, catching a blaze of sunlight. On a damn straight course, too, worthy of Hal himself and remarkable for Rosalind's inexperience. Footsteps announced the arrival of the *Belle*'s officers and crew.

Hal looked over the stern, knife at the ready. A red mist rose through the water and curled to follow the current. But where was Lennox?

Beside him, his friends looked for their common enemy. Cicero barked loudly, as if daring Lennox to show his face. Hal scanned the river downstream, where a big embarras rose like a biblical warning.

It rocked as a wave passed through it, and its points dipped toward the river. When it steadied, two legs appeared, caught on a tangle of sharp branches just above the water and clad in sodden, cheap woolen trousers. A torso hung below the surface, sending off a steady crimson flow.

Lennox, or rather, his body. The Missouri had pronounced judgment on the murderous blackmailer.

Bellecourt crossed himself.

"A good boat will never tolerate the presence of evil," Sampson remarked and holstered his Colt.

"Now Rosalind can sleep at night," Hal said slowly and took a long deep breath. Now he could have a life with her.

Almost a year later, Hal sat in the library of his New York home with his father and William. The big town house had been Rosalind's family's Manhattan home and was now Hal and Rosalind's New York base. It was a remarkably comfortable house, filled with art, and furniture that begged for use rather than posing for a critic's approval.

The library was an immense room, two stories of leather-bound books and statues of great thinkers. A huge fireplace stood at one end, and a smaller one at the other, both framed by informally arranged leather chairs and century-old mahogany tables. Soft Persian carpets covered the oak parquet floor, gleaming in the light from alabaster lamps.

Across the room, Cicero let out a soft yip and rolled over on his monogrammed bed in front of the fire. His paws beat the air as he chased something exciting in his dreams. Pausing to smile at Cicero's contentment, Viola and Rosalind talked together eagerly. Probably about Viola's pregnancy, given their hushed tones.

Rosalind always tried not to let him know how very excited she became when talking about a coming baby, or cooing over a new arrival. Why, she'd even welcomed his scapegrace niece, Portia Townsend, into this house on more than one occasion.

His beautiful, loving wife who was a strong helpmeet in public and as fiery as the *Cherokee Belle*'s boilers in the bedroom. He was the luckiest man in the world to have her at his side. But she never spoke to him about children, and she always glossed over, with a gambler's smooth manners, friends' inquiries as to when they'd start a family.

"How's business, William?" the Old Man asked.

"Couldn't be better, especially the army contracts. And thank you for the advice from Pierpont Morgan, about the chances of a business panic later this year. I've been consolidating my holdings, as he suggested, to reduce the risk of being caught with worthless stocks and bonds."

"As have I," Hal contributed. "I've been selling off stock in poorly managed railroads and concentrating on the well-run firms. Who'd have thought that all that gossip about which railroad a riverman least wanted to face would be so handy?"

The men chuckled together at the situation's irony.

"Has the *Cherokee Belle* started upriver from Kansas City yet?" William asked.

"This morning," Hal answered. "She wintered on the lower Mississippi in the cotton trade. Sampson also tried her as an excursion boat, with a trip to Mardi Gras in New Orleans and several wedding charters."

"She's a very elegant packet. I'd think she'd be very successful," the Old Man approved.

"Extremely profitable. In fact, we were able to keep the full crew on for the entire winter, rather than laying them off for four months."

"Excellent. Between your Missouri River boats and your new Chicago fleet, you'll soon rival the Vanderbilts. Speaking of which, how was Commodore Vanderbilt when you had breakfast with him, son?" his father asked.

Son. The acceptance implied in that simple word warmed his heart.

"Very polite."

William whistled softly. "Amazing."

Hal shrugged. "Rosalind's grandmother was very good friends with the Commodore's mother, who stood godmother to Rosalind's mother."

"Ah, the one person that arrogant man has ever respected," the Old Man said with a sigh of understanding. He sipped his tea, obviously considering the implications. Deep lines had formed in his face, and weight had melted off him after his wife's death. But the color had slowly returned to his countenance, and he now occasionally played with his grandchildren. He'd even smiled when he learned of Viola's pregnancy. "I presume he's joining us tonight. Even he wouldn't miss a chance to dine with the President and General Sherman."

"Yes, the Commodore will be at the Pericles Club for our initiation."

"As will Belknap," William added. "He is a member, after all. Apparently your discussion with him about Etheridge's ledger book, sir, had quite an effect."

The Old Man lifted an eyebrow. "Really?"

"He took great pains to assure me that he holds me in the highest regard and trusts Donovan & Sons will continue to provide excellent service to the U.S. Army for many years to come," William quoted, his California drawl changing to a nearly exact mimicry of Belknap's unctuous tones. "Despite the fact that I'll be the first Irish papist to enter the hallowed halls of the Pericles Club, something he didn't bother to mention."

Hal and his father broke out into simultaneous laughter, which William quickly joined. The two women glanced up and smiled approvingly. A warm glow suffused Hal at the display of family unity.

The Old Man calmed down first, wiping tears of mirth from his eyes. "Dear heavens, how I did enjoy compelling those stuffy old fools to admit you, William. They simply could not counter my argument that a Lindsay's son-in-law had the right to join, as stated in the club's original charter."

"I am very grateful to you, sir." William reached out and gripped his father-in-law's hand. The Old Man turned his to return the salute, and they stayed locked like that for a minute.

The Old Man had definitely become a different fellow. He was no longer a man who wouldn't speak to a disobedient daughter or her Irish husband. He was now someone who had forced society to accept that Irishman as a true son of his house. Hal would never have thought so much change was possible.

The two released their grips and took up their coffee cups, as if jointly backing away from too much emotion. "What

are you giving Rosalind for her twenty-fifth birthday, Hal?"
William asked softly.

"Diamonds." Hal kept his answer equally secretive. "She's
done so well as a trader that I wanted to give something
spectacular. I plan to give them to her tonight, not tomorrow,
so she can wear them at the banquet."

"Magnificent present. She should be very pleased," the
Old Man commented.

A shiver passed down Hal's spine. Would Rosalind be
pleased? Was it truly the best gift he could give her?

"Why, your mother . . ." The Old Man's voice trailed off.
By unspoken agreement, neither he, Hal, nor Viola spoke of
her in private. Publicly, they'd utter pious platitudes that hid
the vicious betrayals she'd visited on them all.

"I gave Viola an amethyst and diamond necklace last
Christmas." William's melodious voice filled the awkward
silence, but Hal wasn't listening.

Were his mother's tastes an accurate prediction of what
Rosalind would like? His mother had cared only about her
beauty and her climb to the top. Even her children had been
simply a means to improving her life, rather than beings to
be loved and protected. She'd even turned her back when her
husband had beaten her son.

It was impossible to imagine Rosalind doing the same
thing. She'd fight like a tigress to protect her child, as she'd
fought to bring the *Cherokee Belle* safely through the Devil's
Rake. She wanted children, and he could give them to her.
But did he have the courage to do so? Generations of Lindsays
had beaten their sons, supposedly to improve them. The thought
of seeing his own child broken and bleeding hit him like a
blow to the stomach. Could he break that pattern?

The answer came suddenly. He wouldn't be alone. Rosalind would help him fight his inheritance so that their children would be safe. Hal's eyes narrowed as he watched her.

Could he take the chance? More importantly, could he continue to deny the woman he loved more than life?

He drummed his fingers on the big armchair as he considered his choices.

That evening, Rosalind desperately held on to the bedpost of her mahogany Chippendale bed as Nellie O'Hara, dear Bridget's younger sister, tightened her corset. Even after almost a year, her body still preferred to remember its shape in men's clothing and obstinately objected to adopting fashionable feminine curves.

Mary pulled hard on the laces without a word. Like her late sister, she was a marvelous maidservant. But unlike Bridget, she preferred to remain silent whenever possible.

Rosalind leaned her forehead against the tall post at the foot of the bed and closed her eyes. She was fully dressed, except for her gloves and the crowning glory of her Paris gown. Her hair was pinned up with glossy curls added, her chemise and petticoats' silk swirled around her legs, and her mother's diamonds shone in her hair.

She had to look her best at tonight's banquet, her first as Mrs. Henry Lindsay at the Schuyler town house in Manhattan. Mrs. Grant would be there, and Mrs. Sherman as well. All the doyennes of Knickerbocker society had enthusiastically accepted Rosalind's invitation. Mercifully, Viola would also be present.

All of this was to celebrate the initiation of Hal and Donovan into the Pericles Club, New York's most ancient and prestigious private men's club. It was traditional that the new members' wives fêted the other members' wives, while the men formally initiated their new fellows. And since President Grant and General Sherman would preside over the ceremonies, their wives would attend the ladies' banquet, making this one of the most important social events of the year.

Her laces abruptly relaxed. "What on earth are you doing, Nellie?" Rosalind looked over her shoulder.

Her husband cocked an eyebrow at her as Cicero leaped on to the settee, under a Reynolds portrait of a velvet and feather-clad belle. "I'm not Nellie—and you can't breathe when you're laced that tightly. I prefer you to be gentler, with soft curves to fill my hand."

He was dressed in all the glory of his full-dress naval uniform—pristine white shirt, crisp blue wool trousers, polished boots. He lacked only his uniform coat, with its gold braid, but his magnificent body, with all those delicious muscles, showed very clearly through his shirt and trousers.

Rosalind sighed in appreciation and lust, stronger now after a year of marriage. Her breasts firmed, rubbing uncomfortably, and excitingly, against the cage of her corset.

Then she turned her face to the bed and closed her eyes. She had to be downstairs in a few minutes. Captain Lindsay was undoubtedly pacing the entrance hall, waiting for Hal. William and Viola had probably already joined him. The guests would start arriving any time now, building to the First Lady's entrance.

"Hal," she protested reluctantly, "it's time to finish dressing. You need to leave with the Captain and William before the ladies arrive."

His eyes twinkled. "Truly?"

He slipped his arms around her and kissed her cheek.

"Hal, please . . ." Her words sounded remarkably like a plea for more. She strengthened her voice. "You mustn't disturb my clothes."

That sounded more convincing, if unexciting.

He kissed her neck in that marvelous place he'd mapped so well. Rosalind gasped as fire danced down to her toes. Her hips wriggled.

"That's my lady." He licked her neck, and then set his teeth gently against the spot.

Rosalind shot up onto her toes as her core clenched. Her nipples were definitely trying to break through the corset now. His hands cupped her breasts and rubbed them through the corset's fine silk. Rosalind quivered.

He played with her, circling and tugging on her nipples until she thought she'd go mad. She leaned her forehead against the cool mahogany and tried to think of something else. Anything else. The price of coal. The startling amount of champagne ordered for tonight's banquet. Hal's firm derrière . . .

He lifted her breasts out of their silk and steel prison. "Beautiful. Priceless. A man would die to hold such treasures." He pulled them gently, each nipple entrapped between his fingers.

"Hal, I love you but . . ." Rosalind moaned. Her hips pulsed. Dew beaded between her legs.

He rubbed himself against her hip. His cock pulsed through her petticoats' silk like the *Cherokee Belle*'s paddle-wheel vibrating her decks.

Rosalind moaned again, and dew slipped down her thighs. She lifted her leg and tried to wrap it over his. He growled something and moved closer, sliding his leg between hers. His rough wool trousers rubbed her heated feminine folds through the fragile barrier of her petticoat. It wasn't enough.

"Hal, please finish me," Rosalind begged, uncaring whether her maid was within earshot.

He chuckled hoarsely and tossed up her petticoats.

Rosalind arched and spread her legs shamelessly as he entered her slowly, so slowly. His cock was a brand, stamping her from the inside out as his, only his. Fiery hot and slick, she could feel every elegant detail, from the fat beauty of his cockhead to the endearing ruffle his foreskin made when he was fully erect to . . .

Every detail? Something about that was significant. But she couldn't manage to think clearly, not with him so deep and thick inside her.

A wave of love washed through her, so deep and strong it felt like the Missouri at full flood.

Rosalind arched her back and ground herself down onto his magnificent cock. "I love you, you big sailor."

Hal laughed hoarsely. His hips surged forward, driving him deeper inside her. Her core pulsed eagerly.

He threw his head back and moaned, then began to propel himself in and out of her, steady and strong, like the pitman driving the *Belle*'s wheel around and around.

She gripped the bedpost and swayed against it as he took her urgently, harshly, desperately. Sparkles mounted through her veins and into her bones. She clenched around him with every stroke as her body grew hotter and hotter. Her skin was tight, almost too tight to hold the sensations and the heat building inside her.

And she sobbed his name, over and over, the only words that mattered in the world.

He howled. His seed erupted out of his cock and filled her. He jetted again and again, flooding every hidden crevice and fold with his heat and love. The deep pulses were too much for her to resist.

Rosalind screamed in pleasure and satisfaction as she flew apart. Ecstasy blazed through every bone and sinew, up her spine and into her toes. She shuddered with a pleasure too great to be borne as rapture's great waves stormed her.

Afterward, she tried dazedly to recover her footing. Cream was flowing down her legs under her silk petticoats. She'd have to wash there before she went downstairs.

She really was remarkably wet, far more so than she'd ever been after a single ecstatic joining with Hal. Deep inside, she was also full of something moving around in her, as if it had its own currents to follow. Something different from what her own dew provided.

She spun around and stared at her husband. "I'm dripping!"

Hal glanced up and his mouth quirked. "I imagine so," he answered mildly. He was standing by the washbasin, wiping down his cock with a fine linen hand towel. His very wet cock.

"Happy birthday, Rosalind," he added as he began to button up his trousers.

Her jaw dropped open. "You tried to make me pregnant." The implications were dazzling and totally unexpected. She managed to stammer a bit of logic. "But I thought you didn't want children."

"I realized I want to see you happy, more than I fear continuing the old pattern of heavy-handed paternity. I know we can raise happy children together, because you won't turn your back if I try to beat them."

She snorted. "You wouldn't do that." She limped over to him, stiffening her knees against the tremors still rocking them after his lovemaking.

He met her halfway and kissed her hands. "Perhaps. But you give me courage to try." His great chest rose and fell. His hands trembled.

She reached up and kissed him gently, a pledge and a promise of happy times to come. "Promise me," she whispered.

"Anything, my love."

"You'll do that again."

"You have my word."

Author's Note

The *Cherokee Belle*, *Spartan*, *Cherokee Star*, U.S.S. *St. Paul* (City-class gunboat), and U.S.S. *Anacostia* (frigate) are entirely fictional, although based as closely as possible on real riverboats and Civil War-era gunboats. The Devil's Rake existed as described, although I have changed its location slightly.

All characters, except President Grant, General Sherman, Commodore Vanderbilt, and William Worth Belknap, are also fictional creations. William Belknap, Secretary of War from 1869 to 1876, was impeached by the House of Representatives for accepting bribes, although he had already resigned under threat of impeachment. He was tried in the Senate but found not guilty because some senators felt they lacked jurisdiction, since he was no longer in office. The corruption described in this book is based on the evidence presented during his Senate trial.

Dan Allen's establishment in Omaha existed, although I have described it and its staff to suit this story's needs.

Many thanks to the staff of the Steamboat Arabia Museum in Kansas City, Missouri, the Kansas City Public Library, and the Douglas County Historical Society in Omaha, Nebraska for their willingness to share their towns' histories. Special thanks to Bob, an education specialist at the Discovery Center, Kansas City's Urban Conservation Campus, for vividly describing the Missouri River's birds and fish as they were in 1872. And an extra big thank you to MSgt. Ani Stubbs, USAF, for describing the weather in 1872 Omaha.

My deepest thanks go to the passengers and crew of the *Delta Queen,* an historic paddlewheel steamer currently sailing America's rivers. Whatever professionalism and pleasure portrayed onboard the *Cherokee Belle* is but a fraction of the warmth found at the *Delta Queen*.

All errors are strictly my doing. For a detailed description of my sources, please visit my website:

www.dianewhiteside.com

If you loved this Diane Whiteside book,
don't miss her other books,
available from Brava!
Devilish temptation is just around the corner . . .

IRISH DEVIL

He was her only chance for survival . . .

Born to wealth and privilege, but now widowed and betrayed on the unforgiving Arizona frontier, Viola Ross must choose between starvation and marriage—to her husband's killer. Or take a scandalous risk and turn her back on polite society by becoming the mistress of William Donovan. With his reputation for ruthlessness and a piercing stare that can stop any man—or melt any woman—Donovan seems fully capable of defending her with his bullwhip and bowie knives. Not to mention what else he can do with those big, callused hands . . .

As desire flares between Donovan and Viola, a killer's lust for Viola turns to deadly vengeance. For his allies are the very men who once destroyed Donovan's family, and this time, they'll let no Irish Devil stand in their way . . .

"**W**hat can I do for you, Mrs. Ross?" He kept his voice gentle, his California drawl soft against the muffled noises from outside.

She took a deep breath, drew herself up straight and tall, and launched into speech. "May I become your mistress, Mr. Donovan?"

"What?! What the devil are you talking about?" he choked, too stunned to watch his language. He knew his mouth was hanging open. "Are you making a joke, Mrs. Ross?"

"Hardly, Mr. Donovan." She met his eyes directly, pulse pounding in her throat. "You may not have heard, but my business partner sold everything to Mr. Lennox."

He nodded curtly. He must have been right before: she needed money. "I met Mr. and Mrs. Jones on their way out of town. I won't be doing business with them again," he added harshly.

"Quite so. But my only choices now are to marry Mr. Lennox or find another man to protect me. I'd rather be yours than an Apache's."

"Jesus, Mary, and Joseph," William muttered as he stood and began to pace. *Think, boyo, think. She deserves better than being your woman.* Heat lanced from his heart down his spine at the thought of her in his arms every night. Marriage? No, she'd never agree to a Catholic ceremony. "There are other men, men who'd marry you," he pointed out hoarsely.

"I will not remarry. Besides, Mr. Lennox blocked all offers other than his."

"Son of a bitch." The bastard should be shot. "What about your family?"

"They disinherited me when I married Edward. Both families refused my letters informing them of his death."

How the devil could a parent abandon a child, no matter what the quarrel? His father had given everything to protect his children.

William's gut tightened at the thought. Condoms were helpful but not a guarantee. If she stayed in his bed long enough, the odds were good . . .

"You could become pregnant," he warned, his eyes returning to her face. Blessed Virgin, what he wouldn't do to see Viola proud and happy, holding his babe in her arms.

"I can't have children."

"The fault could be in the stallion, not the mare," William suggested, his drawl more pronounced. And this stallion would dearly love to prove his potency where another had failed, his cock caroled.

Breathe deep, boyo, let the lust fade, his brain warned. *You were trained by the best and you'll not leap upon a woman.*

Viola stared at him and firmly shook her head. "All of Edward's siblings have at least three children. No, the difficulty is entirely mine."

He considered her slender body thoughtfully as he remembered other fragile women who'd rarely, if ever, conceived. Viola could be correct about her infertility.

More to the point, she was stubborn enough to continue insisting on this madness of becoming his mistress, no matter what arguments he mustered. Perhaps if he took her, he could sate his hunger before her inevitable departure. His cock eagerly agreed with this reasoning.

He moved to the window before speaking again, trying desperately to think. She needed to be warned about what to expect if she stayed with him.

"I have strong demands and unique tastes." His voice was darker now. If she came to his bed, he'd play the games he loved, no doubt about it. But he'd never mastered a woman who hadn't consented and he never would.

"And I understand you pay Mrs. Smith's girls very well to satisfy them. I should think you would be glad to have a woman constantly available to you." A hot flush lit her cheekbones and her pulse pounded in her throat as she licked her lips.

Blessed Virgin, she was aroused by this conversation, but did she know what he was talking about? His fist hit the rough wall. "Mother of God, Mrs. Ross, do you have any idea of what I might do with you?"

She ignored his profanity. "No, but I'm willing to learn."

THE SOUTHERN DEVIL

Even a perfect gentleman has a little devil in him.

Once an orphaned and starving Confederate war veteran, Morgan Evans is now a wealthy man respected for both his business acumen and chivalrous Southern manners. He would be the perfect catch for any woman, but only one holds his constant attention. Jessamyn Tyler Evans has been his obsession since the time she derailed one of his spy missions by holding him hostage in her bed for days. her innocent explorations awakened a fierce hunger inside the young Morgan, and the passion and intimacy they shared frightened them both. Jessamyn spurned Morgan for his cousin, and Morgan vowed that someday he would drive her as wild with desire as she had driven him. Now Jessamyn has returned. The payback has begun . . .

Jessamyn has an obsession of her own: hunting for a legendary family treasure in the hills of Colorado. To do so, the spirited widow needs a husband, and Morgan Evans is only too happy to join her masquerade for a price: She must submit to being his, body and soul, surrendering herself to whatever he demands. It's a devil's bargain to be sure.

Their union is as treacherous as it is passionate—and the only thing they can trust. Searching for a treasure that my not exist—a treasure others would kill for—two lovers are moving deeper into unmarked territory, where no threat is more perilous than everything they feel . . .

He trailed his fingers slowly down her cheek, leaving tendrils of heat behind. How could he have this effect on her with just his voice and a teasing touch?

He smiled down at her, all hot eyes and white teeth. "I told you the next time we were alone, after the War, that I would do what I wanted to do with you. That you would be the one crying out in hunger and ecstasy. Correct?"

Jessamyn nodded slowly. "You did say that."

He tucked a strand of hair behind her ear. She shivered, eyes fixed on his.

He kissed her forehead and nuzzled her cheek. His voice hardened subtly as he whispered in her ear. "That you'd be the one promising anything, in exchange for another touch, not me. True?"

Jessamyn swallowed hard but told the truth. "Yes."

He lifted her chin with a single finger, his other hand lightly clasping her waist, and let her clearly see his determination. "You're mine now. I've spent years studying, practicing ways to drive you insane with lust."

Jessamyn closed her eyes, shaking, and strongly wished she knew someone else who could take her into those mountains.

He touched his tongue to her lips, teased them open.

Breathed lightly into her mouth until she sighed and relaxed slightly. Sucked gently on her lips until her whole mouth was open and yearning for him. Then his tongue entered her, swirling over her teeth, teasing her tongue, twining and dancing with it.

She moaned softly and stretched up to meet his kiss, utterly absorbed. He kissed as if they had all the time in the world, as if days and weeks and months could go by while he learned the taste and shape and feel of her mouth.

THE NORTHERN DEVIL

Every woman needs a devil by her side.

Rachel Davis would rather risk death than remain a prisoner of the ruthless man intent on gaining her inheritance. Trapped on a private train with the villain, she makes a desperate bid for escape and runs into the arms of an unlikely savior. Aristocratic, arrogant, and deeply cynical about love, Lucas Grainger is her last choice for a husband—even a husband of convenience. But desperate times call for desperate measures. Taking Lucas to bed and submitting to his tender, hungry desires may be her only hope . . .

Lucas Grainger has sworn never to take a wife, but he's not about to let anyone else marry Rachel. He has his own reasons for marrying the gentle, quick-witted widow, reasons she need not know. But holding Rachel night after night awakens deeper hungers than he has ever known, and a calculated marriage soon yields to a blissful, blinding—and dangerous—passion. For if Rachel knew who Lucas really was—of the dark secrets that haunt him—she'd never choose him as her protector . . .

Theirs is a union both erotic and enduring, and any man who tries to part Lucas from the woman he loves will have the devil to pay . . .

He whispered against her ear, his warm breath fanning her cheek. "It's time for our private feast. Oysters? Cheese? Chocolate?"

He caressed her again, the barest movement of his fingertips against her jaw, his hooded gaze scorching. "Or another taste of my wife?"

She blinked and ran her tongue over her lips, even as her brain tried to come back to life. They'd never discussed what he liked to do in the bedroom. "Lucas, perhaps we could talk a little—"

He raised a disbelieving eyebrow. "Talk? Now? When we can do this instead?"

His lips claimed hers again. Unable to disagree with his logic, Rachel moaned and arched against him, her mouth opening farther, her tongue twining with his. His kisses' rhythm swirled through her, washing away all consciousness of anything else. Her pulse began to throb softly, regularly to the same beat. Deep within her core, a soft, rich fire shimmered into life, magically linked to his lips and her breasts.

He left her mouth, to her groaned disappointment, and

tasted her face, kissing her cheeks, nuzzling her forehead, delicately nibbling her nose. "You're a passionate woman, Mrs. Grainger, and a very sweet one. I need to taste every inch of you."

And turn the page
for a sneak peek at Diane's next book,

KISSES LIKE THE DEVIL

Coming in February 2009. . . .

Doors slammed below and the train's first passengers began to spill into the square, gaily bargaining for a ride to the town's more upscale districts.

Morro woofed deep in his throat and rose, wending his way between the two humans to look over the balcony.

A single man stepped out of the station, isolated by a swirl of travelers. He was tall and broad-shouldered, clad entirely in black. His broad-brimmed hat readily identified him as an American, a rarity here in Eisengau despite its famous summer music festival and military maneuvers. His clothes were well-made yet neither dandified nor a uniform. Straight black hair brushed his collar and his skin was tanned golden brown from the sun, something seldom seen amid these stone walls. His blade-sharp nose, high cheekbones, and stubborn jaw could have been carved by a master sculptor.

He paused on the top of the steps to look around, graceful as a hawk scanning a meadow, yet utterly unselfconscious. His brilliant blue eyes flashed over the crowd like light passing through the finest stained glass—and lingered briefly on the old pension, where Meredith stood. Her breath caught in her throat. How many newspaper articles about American adventurers had she devoured? How many cheap novels about men like him had she bartered for? And to finally see one in the flesh . . .

Morro thrust his muzzle between the banisters and took a long, considering sniff.

Despite any claim to logic, Meredith opened her mouth to hail the American.